Lynsay Sands

Always

AVONBOOKS

An Imprint of HarperCollinsPublishers

This is a work of fiction. Names, characters, places, and incidents are products of the author's imagination or are used fictitiously and are not to be construed as real. Any resemblance to actual events, locales, organizations, or persons, living or dead, is entirely coincidental.

AVON BOOKS
An Imprint of HarperCollins*Publishers*
195 Broadway
New York, New York 10007

Copyright © 2000 by Lynsay Sands
Excerpt from *About a Vampire* copyright © 2015 by Lynsay Sands
ISBN 978-0-06-201956-1
www.avonromance.com

First Avon Books mass market printing: December 2015

Avon Trademark Reg. U.S. Pat. Off. and in Other Countries, Marca Registrada, Hecho en U.S.A.
HarperCollins® is a registered trademark of HarperCollins Publishers.

Printed in the U.S.A.

10 9 8 7 6 5 4 3 2 1

For a dear friend, Helen Owens

Prologue

England
June 18, 1189

"WOMEN are the spawn of the devil!"

"Come, my friend, surely not?" Robert of Shambley murmured chidingly. "You are just disillusioned at present by Delia's actions."

"Name me one female as courageous or faithful as a knight," Aric challenged, grabbing his mug and swigging half his ale in one gulp. He had arrived at Shambley this morning, and had been working very hard at drinking himself into oblivion for most of the afternoon and well into the night. Robert, good friend that he was, was keeping him company.

"My brain is too ale-soaked to rise to such a challenge," his friend admitted wryly. "I could, however, name a knight or two—or even a king's son or two—who are not so faithful or courageous as they should be."

"Aye." Aric sighed as he thought momentarily of the king's sons and how they rebelled against Henry, seeking to steal his crown at every turn. Then he rallied. "That just proves my point! It is *good* Queen Eleanor who eggs her rotten spawn on in these endeavors. *Women*. They are a curse upon the earth."

"Hmm," Robert murmured, glancing over his shoulder as the door to the kitchens opened and a buxom young serving wench hurried out with two fresh pitchers of ale. He tugged playfully at her skirt as she set the pitchers on the table, then, ignoring the baleful look Aric was giving him, he winked at her as well.

Smiling knowingly, the blond wench whirled away, skirts flying, and she sashayed back through the door, her hips rolling provocatively.

"Mayhap they are, my friend," Robert murmured as the door closed behind her. "But they do have their uses, too."

"Aye. In bed." Aric muttered, then added bitterly, "And some of them are too eager to be useful to all. Delia certainly seemed quite enthusiastic in Lord Glanville's stables when I caught them there together."

"I would not judge all women by your ex-betrothed, Aric. She is—"

"A faithless, cheap whore who apparently spread her legs for everyone," he suggested dryly, then gulped more ale. Slamming his mug down, he said, "I vow I shall *never* marry. I have learned my lesson. There shall be no faithless wife for me. Being cuckolded by my betrothed was enough. I shall *never marry*. Not for land or estates. Not for all the wealth in the kingdom. Not even under threat of torture!"

"What about under threat of death?" asked an amused voice, and both men turned wide eyes to the shape that now filled the open door that led out into the bailey. The man who addressed them was tall, and he wore a black cloak with the hood drawn up to cover his head, casting his face in shadow. The new arrival's features, however, were not nearly as troubling a matter to the two men he had surprised as how he had managed to make his way into the keep unannounced. Frowning, both Aric and Robert were on their feet in an instant, grimly reaching for their swords.

A second man entered Shambley Hall. Upon recognizing the thin little man who now stepped into the keep, Aric relaxed. He saw Robert's hand loosen on his own sword.

"Bishop Shrewsbury," Robert called out in greeting. "My apologies, my lord. My father's men should have heralded your arrival."

"They were ordered not to," the first guest announced, flicking back the cowl of his cloak as he strode forward. His features were strong and his hair, once red, had faded to a gray that matched his piercing eyes.

There was a brief moment of silence as Aric and Robert gaped; then Robert pulled himself together enough to offer a deep bow. "My liege. Had I been warned of your coming I could have prepared—"

"I did not realize myself that I would be coming. 'Sides, I wanted no one to know." Shrugging out of his cloak, King Henry II handed it to Shrewsbury as the smaller man rushed forward to take it. Henry then turned his attention to removing the heavy mail gloves he wore. Slapping them down on the table, he grabbed Aric's empty mug, poured fresh ale into it, and downed a good quantity of the stuff. He turned to eye the two younger men consideringly.

"You must be hungry after your travels, my liege," Robert murmured, obviously shaken by this unexpected and exalted visit. "I shall order a meal prepared."

"Nay!" The king caught Shambley by the shoulder and shook his head. "I ate at Burkhart. Sit. Both of you."

Aric and Robert exchanged a startled glance at the mention of Aric's family home, but neither man said anything as they dropped onto the bench at their king's order. Their backs to the table, they watched silently as Henry poured himself another drink, quaffed it, then paced a few short steps toward the silent Bishop Shrewsbury. He turned sharply.

"So." His eyes bored into Aric. "You will not marry?"

Aric shifted uncomfortably under his king's steely gray gaze, his own eyes sliding first to Robert, then to the bishop's enigmatic expression. His ale-soaked brain whirled in confusion. "Ah . . . well—" Aric finally began reluctantly, only to be interrupted.

"Not for land or titles? Not for all the wealth in the kingdom? Not even under threat of torture, I believe you said," the king quoted grimly. Aric squirmed where he sat, unsure how exactly he had displeased his sovereign, but knowing that somehow his words had done so.

"I have no desire—" he said at last, only to be interrupted again.

"What if I, your king, were to order it?"

That took Aric aback. He hesitated, his mouth opening and closing; then he began to shake his head in bewilderment. Why would the king care if he married? The question sloshed around inside his head, but he could see no ready answer. Aric was a second son. Not heir to any vast estates. He had no duty to produce an heir.

Apparently taking his head-shaking as a refusal, the king's infamous temper rose to the surface. His eyes blazing, he was suddenly in front of Aric, leaning forward and forcing the young knight to lean back until the table was digging uncomfortably into his back.

"What if I threatened to have you killed if you did not consent to marriage?" Henry snapped. He paused and, apparently thinking that specifics were necessary to convince him, added, "Drawn and quartered. With a dull blade. Your head placed on a pike and your four parts displayed in all four corners of my kingdom. What then?"

"Marriage sounds pleasant," Aric managed to get out, embarrassed to hear the sudden rise in pitch his voice had taken under his liege's threats. He sensed rather than heard Robert's relief beside him, and wished wholeheartedly that he could feel that relief, too, but with the king still glaring at him, his face a bare few inches away, fire spitting from his eyes, and his breath warm on his face, Aric wasn't feeling any yet. Though he did suddenly feel quite sober. It was a desperately uncomfortable sensation.

A satisfied smile curving his lips, the king straightened abruptly as if he had not just been threatening the younger knight. "I am glad to hear it. I would rather have you for a son-in-law than decorate Westminster with your head."

"Son-in-law?" Aric said blankly, then glanced sharply at Robert, confused. The king had three daughters, Matilda, Eleanor, and Joan. But all three women were already married. Robert looked as befuddled as Aric felt, but his friend did nudge him and nod toward Henry, seeming to suggest he ask what they were both wondering. Sighing, Aric turned to the King and began, "I do not understand, Your Majesty. Your—"

The king was no longer standing before them, though. He had snatched back his cloak from the bishop and was wrapping it around his massive shoulders even as he strode back toward the door. Shrewsbury was hard on his heels. It seemed now that they had garnered Aric's promise, both men were leaving.

Aric glanced uncertainly toward Robert. His own instincts, the ones that had saved him time and again from death while in battle, were urging him to either remain where he was, or flee up the stairs to his room. Of course, his instincts were a bit muddled right now. They were probably wrong. The fact that Robert was suddenly on his feet, grabbing his arm and urging him to follow King Henry and the bishop unfortunately seemed to indicate his error.

Sighing, Aric grabbed up the king's chain-mail gloves—he had left them on the table—and hurried after the two nobles, aware that Robert was following.

"But, Your Majesty," he called out as he caught up to them. "Your daughters are all married."

"Not Rosamunde," the king answered promptly. Pausing at the door, he glanced back at Aric, opened his mouth to speak, then blinked at the sight of the gloves that Aric held out. "Oh. Thank you," he muttered, taking the gloves and tugging one onto first the right hand, then the left. He opened and closed his fingers into fists a few times to assure the gloves were on properly, then flipped the hood of his cloak back over his head.

"Get your cloaks. 'Tis wet tonight," he ordered, then strode out of the keep. The bishop followed.

Robert and Aric exchanged a grimace, then hurried to do his bidding. It wasn't until they had fetched cloaks and headed out of the castle to chase the two dark figures striding toward the stables that Robert murmured what Aric had been thinking. "Was not the fair Rosamunde the king's mistress? The one he installed at court and loved openly?"

"Aye," Aric muttered. He had met her on a visit to court with his parents when he was ten. Hers had been a beauty unsurpassed. Skin like white silk with just a hint of blush to it. Hair as fine as gossamer thread, that shone brighter than gold. Eyes the color of the sea on a clear day. Her laugh had tinkled like a bell, and she had been kindness itself.

There had been rumors at the time that the king planned to set Queen Eleanor aside in favor of his lovely paramour, but Rosamunde had died the following year. Which had spawned new rumors. Had the queen killed her out of fear of losing her place and title? But the question had remained unanswered and the story became just a tale told by the fire at night. Few believed it anymore. After all, the queen had been imprisoned for inciting her sons' rebellions long ere the fair Rosamunde's arrival—what had she to fear from a king's mistress?

"Your Majesty?" Aric said as soon as he and Robert were within speaking distance of the man in the billowing black cape. "You did say Rosamunde?"

"Aye. My daughter, Rosamunde. Born to me by her mother, that fair beauty of the same name. A lovelier creature never lived," he told them grimly as they reached the stables. Pausing outside the doors, the king let the bishop rush inside and order fresh horses prepared. He himself turned to Aric and announced, "Our daughter is nearly as lovely. It is she you will marry."

"But—"

"Do not 'but' me, Burkhart!" Henry snapped. Stepping forward, he poked him in the chest to emphasize every word. "You can live in wedlock or die a bachelor. You *will* marry her!"

"Aye, my liege, but why?" Aric asked quickly. Henry straightened, a blank look on his face.

"What do you mean, why? Because I like you. Because I think you will make her a good husband. Because I *say* so."

Aric grimaced, and didn't point out that threats to have him drawn and quartered were not the actions of someone who liked him. Instead, he said, "I meant, why *now*, Your Majesty?"

Henry scowled, then sighed. "Well, I have been searching for the perfect husband for her for quite some time, but none seemed good enough. I have always thought you a likely candidate. Not perfect, mind you, but promising. But you were already betrothed. Now you are not."

"I became unbetrothed only today," Aric pointed out dryly.

"Aye. I was on my way to Rosshuen to offer him her hand. We stopped at Burkhart Castle to switch horses. We were there when the messenger arrived with the news for your father: the betrothal was off and you were here drowning your sorrows. It seemed providential. I have always liked you and your family. You are honorable. And Rosamunde—my sweet love—spoke well of you. I think you impressed her, or as much as a boy of ten could. . . ."

The king's eyes had a faraway look, then he returned. "Shambley was a day's travel closer, and time is of the essence. I . . ." Pausing as he recalled his rush, Henry turned to bellow a sharp order into the stables, then turned back. "So *you* are the lucky bridegroom."

"How fortunate for me." Aric sighed, then flashed an apologetic grimace as the king glared at him sharply through the drizzling rain. "But why now, my liege? You are supposed to be in Chinon. Your son Richard and the king of France—"

"And John," Henry inserted harshly. "He has joined them."

Aric and Robert exchanged a grim glance at that. It seemed the rumors were true then. The king's favorite son had joined the rebellion. That news must have been a blow for the old monarch. The appearance of

Shrewsbury with two of Shambley's best horses in tow drew their attention, and King Henry impatiently moved to meet the man.

"Good, good," he said with approval, looking the beasts over quickly. "Nice horseflesh, Shambley. Give your father my compliments when next you see him. How is he, by the way?"

"Oh. Better, my liege. Improving daily," Robert assured him. The king took the reins of one of the beasts and proceeded to mount him. Robert's surprise that the king was even aware of his father's illness was obvious, and Aric supposed it *was* a bit startling, when the king was plagued with so many of his own troubles.

"Good." Settling in the saddle, he scowled down at them. "Well, what are you waiting for? Mount up!"

Following his gesture, Aric and Robert blinked at the two horses the stablemaster was now leading out, then quickly moved forward to do as they were bid.

"As far as everyone knows, I am still in Chinon," Henry announced. "I am presently believed to be sequestered, nursing my heartache at loss of Le Mans."

"Le Mans?" Robert asked with dismay.

"Aye." The king turned his steed toward the gates and urged him forward. Shrewsbury was immediately at his right, keeping pace. Aric had to spur his horse forward to keep close enough to Henry's left side to hear him as he went on. "Richard attacked Le Mans. I ordered the suburbs outside the gate set afire to hold him off, but the wind turned. Le Mans is ashes."

Aric winced at this news. The king had been born there. His father, the Count of Anjou, had been buried there. The loss of his birthplace would have been hard to bear. And that assured Aric that there was more to this story that he needed to know.

"What was that?" Robert asked, from Aric's left side. "Did he say Le Mans burned?"

Waving the question away, Aric addressed the king instead. "And yet you slipped away to see to your daughter's wedding? Why not wait until after all is settled?"

Henry looked displeased at the question, but after a glare at Aric for his impertinence, he snapped, "To ensure her safety should things not go my way."

"Safety from what?" Aric pressed. If he was expected to keep her safe, he had to know where the threat might lie.

The king was silent so long, Aric had begun to think he would not answer; then he suddenly announced, "There are rumors that Eleanor had Rosamunde's mother killed. I believe them."

"But Queen Eleanor was locked up at the time of her death," Robert pointed out, crowding Aric's mount with his own as he tried to keep abreast of the conversation.

"Aye, but she has servants, those who are faithful to her and are willing to do her bidding."

"But would she have wished Rosamunde dead, enough to murder her?" Aric asked, frowning at Robert and tightening his hold on his own mount's reins, trying to keep him from crowding the king's horse as they neared the gate.

"As you'll recall, my wife is eleven years my senior. I was nineteen when we married and she thirty. And she was newly divorced from Louis VII, the King of France. She lost her title as queen of France, married me, and became queen of England when I acceded to the title. Think you she would risk being set aside again? Another annulment? Lose another crown?" He shook his head grimly. "Nay."

Leaning forward to peer around Aric, Robert asked, "Why did you not—"

"Punish her? Have her killed for the deed? I wanted to. But I made a promise to Rosamunde. She made me swear never to unseat Eleanor. She did not want to be queen, just mine. Sweet, naive girl. She said it would accomplish no good and merely cause more political upheaval for me. 'Sides, she feared for our child. She was terrified that Eleanor might see the child dead for revenge."

There was silence for a moment; then Aric murmured, "I did not know that there had been a child."

"No one knew. Her mother wished it so."

All was silent but for the clip-clop of the horses' hooves as they crossed the bridge over Shambley's moat; then the king announced grimly, "The hounds are nipping at my heels, lads. My sons wish to bring me down. Ere that happens, I will ensure my daughter's future."

"So we are heading to collect your daughter and see her and Aric married?"

Aric glared at his friend. Robert sounded too damn cheerful. But then, he was not the one about to be forced into marriage to the bastard daughter of the king of England. Dear God, just the thought of it made him cringe. Now Aric's whole life would be spent with a spoiled little—

"Aye," the king interrupted his thoughts. "She has spent her life at Godstow Abbey. We shall go there and see to the marriage; then Shrewsbury and I shall head back to Chinon. You, Shambley, can help Aric get her back to your keep to collect his men. Between the two of you, you should be able to keep her safe." He glanced at his soon-to-be son-in-law. "I would have preferred your men accompany us, Aric, to supply a proper escort afterward, but that would have slowed us down. One thing I do not have is time."

When Aric nodded silently at that, Henry apparently decided all was settled. The king urged his mount to a gallop. All Aric could think, as he urged his horse to follow, was *I am to be married*.

Chapter 1

*L*ADY Adela, abbess of Godstow, frowned down the length of the table at the nuns all seated for the nooning meal. Sister Clarice, Sister Eustice, and Lady Rosamunde were missing. It was not unusual for Sister Clarice to be late. The woman was late for everything. Most likely she had forgotten to fetch the incense for the mass that would take place after the meal, and had gone to retrieve it. Sister Clarice always forgot the incense.

As for Sister Eustice and Lady Rosamunde, however, the two were always punctual, as a rule. However, they had not been at the morning meal either. Come to that, they had not been at matins, lauds, or prime. At Godstow, it took an emergency to keep a nun from mass, and this would be no exception. Sister Eustice and Lady Rosamunde had been in the stables through the night and well into the morning, working over a mare who was having difficulty birthing her foal.

But surely they were not still at that! she fretted, then glanced sharply toward Sister Beatrice, who had stumbled over the passage she was reading. Seeing that Beatrice along with all the other women were peering up the table at her, Lady Adela arched an eyebrow questioningly. Sister Margaret, the nun seated on her right, made a motion with her hands. Margaret held one hand up, the fingers fisted but for the baby finger, which hung down like the udder of a cow. With her other hand, she imitated the motion of milking.

Adela blinked, then realized that she had picked up the pitcher of milk and held on to it, thoughtlessly, as she worried about the missing women.

Passing the pitcher to Sister Margaret, the abbess gestured to the others to continue with their meal, then rose and moved to the door. She had barely stepped into the hall when she spotted Sister Clarice hurrying down the corridor, a slightly guilty flush on her face. Unable to speak during mealtime, Lady Adela once again arched an eyebrow, demanding an explanation of the woman's tardiness.

Sighing, Clarice raised her hand and propped two fingers upward until they were inserted in her nostrils, somehow managing an apologetic look as she did so.

The action was a pantomime to announce that she had forgotten to provide incense for mass—as Adela had suspected. Shaking her head, the abbess gestured for Clarice to continue on to her meal; then she made her way out to the stables.

The building was silent but for the faint rustle of hay as various animals shifted and glanced curiously toward her as Adela entered. Gathering the hem of her skirt close to avoid trailing it through anything unpleasant, she made her way down the rows of stalls until she reached the last one. There, Sister Eustice and Lady Rosamunde were kneeling by a panting mare. She stood for a moment, peering affectionately at their bent backs as they toiled over the laboring beast; then her mouth dropped with dismay as Sis Eustice shifted and she could see exactly *how* Lady Rosamunde was toiling.

"What in God's name are you doing?"

Rosamunde stiffened at that horrified exclamation from behind, her head whipping briefly around to see the abbess gaping at her with dismay. Then she swiftly whirled back to soothe the mare as the animal whinnied, its muscles shifting around her hands.

Leaping to her feet, Eustice ushered the horrified Adela a few steps away, babbling explanations as they moved. "The mare was having difficulty. She labored for hours before we realized that the foal was backward. Lady Rosamunde is trying to help."

"She has her hands *inside* the mare!" Adela pointed out with horror.

"She is trying to turn the foal," Eustice explained quickly.

"But—"

"Is it not the nooning hour?" Rosamunde whispered with exasperation, removing the hand she had been holding the foal's feet with to pat the mare's rump soothingly. The animal was becoming distressed by the tone of voice the abbess was using.

"This is an emergency. God will forgive our breaking silence during mealtime if 'tis an emergency," Adela responded promptly.

"Aye, well, let us hope our mare does," Rosamunde muttered, shifting swiftly out of the way as the horse began kicking its legs in a panicked attempt to regain its feet.

Sister Eustice moved at once, hurrying to the horse's head and grabbing it to hold the mare still. She murmured soothing coos at the frightened animal.

Worry almost overcame her, but Adela managed to contain herself as Rosamunde dropped back on to her knees at the rear of the reclining horse. Unlike Sister Eustice, who was garbed in the plain habit of a nun, the girl was decked out in a stable boy's pants and overlarge top, its billowing sleeves rolled back to leave her arms bare. It was the costume the girl usually wore when working in the stables. Rosamunde felt it much more appropriate than a gown, and Adela, despite her better judgment, had done little to sway her from wearing the scandalous garb. She had always been fond of the girl, and there was no one of import around to disapprove anyway. However, she had already explained to the child that she would have to shed the stable-boy clothes for good—along with many other things—once she took the veil and became a nun.

Adela's thoughts fled, her face twisting into a half grimace, half wince as Rosamunde once again eased her hands into the horse, reaching to grasp its foal and try to ease its way into the world.

"Thank the good Lord's graces that your father, the king, is not here to see this," Adela murmured, remembering to keep her voice calm. She did not wish to frighten the horse again.

"To see what?"

All three women stiffened at that deep baritone. Eustice's eyes widened in horror as she peered past the abbess toward the entrance to the stables. Her expression was enough to tell Adela that she had correctly recognized that voice. The Lord, it seemed, was not feeling particularly gracious today. The king *had* come to see what his daughter had gotten up to under her care.

Straightening her shoulders, Adela turned resignedly toward Henry, hardly noticing the men with him as she forced a smile of greeting to her face. "King Henry. Welcome."

The monarch nodded at the abbess, but his attention was on his daughter. She glanced over her shoulder at him, a bright smile replacing the anxiety on her face.

"Papa!"

Henry started to smile, but ceased as he took in the sight of her. "What the devil are you doing in the stables, girl? And all dressed up like a boy, too." He glared at Adela. "Do I not pay you people enough to hire a stable boy? Do you spite me by putting my daughter to work with the animals?"

"Oh, Papa." Rosamunde laughed, unconcerned by his apparent temper. "You know that it is my choice. We must all work at something—and I prefer the stables to scrubbing the convent floors." The last of her statement was a distracted mutter. She turned back to what she was doing.

Henry's curiosity drew him forward. "What *are* you doing?"

Rosamunde glanced up, a scowl of anxiety on her face. "This mare has been in labor for more than a day now. She is losing strength. I fear she shall die if we do not help her along, but I cannot get the foal out."

His brows drawn together, Henry peered at where her arms disappeared into the mare at the elbows. Horror covered his face. "Why, you—What—You—"

Sighing at his dismayed stammer, Rosamunde calmly explained. "The foal is backward. I am trying to turn it, but I cannot find its head."

Henry's brows rose at that. "Will it not hurt the mare having you dig about inside her like that?"

"I do not know," she said pragmatically, reaching farther into the animal. "But both mother and foal shall surely die if *something* is not done."

"Aye . . . well . . ." Frowning at her back, Henry said, "Leave that for . . . er . . ." He peered toward the nun now moving back toward Rosamunde and the horse.

"Sister Eustice," Lady Adela supplied helpfully.

"Aye. Sister Eustice. Leave it for the sister to deal with, daughter. I do not have long here and—"

"Oh, I could not do that, Papa. It would ruin the sleeves of Sister Eustice's gown. This will not take long, I am sure, and then—"

"I do not give a damn about the sister's sleeves," Henry snapped, starting forward to drag her away bodily if need be, but a pleading glance from his daughter made him halt. She did so look like her mother. Henry had found it impossible to refuse the mother anything. Why should their daughter be different?

Sighing, he removed his cloak and handed it to Eustice, then shrugged out of his short surcoat and handed that over as well.

"Who taught you to do this?" he asked gruffly, bending to kneel beside her in the straw.

"No one," she admitted, flashing him a smile that warmed his heart. It immediately made him let go of his impatience and anger. "It just seemed to be the thing to do when I saw the problem. She will die otherwise."

Nodding, he shifted as close to her as he could get and reached his hands inside the mare to help. "It is the head you cannot find?"

Rosamunde nodded. "I have the rear legs, but I cannot—"

"Aha! I have it. It is caught on something." He paused. "There we go."

Rosamunde felt the back legs slip from her grip and shift away. She just managed to tug her hands free of the mare as her father turned the animal within its mother until its head was at the right angle.

"The mare is too weak. You will have to—" even as the words left her mouth, her father tugged on the foal's head and front legs. Seconds later it slid out onto the straw.

"Oh," Rosamunde breathed, peering at the spindly-legged creature as it wriggled on the straw. "Is it not adorable?"

"Aye," Henry agreed gruffly; then he cleared his throat, grabbed her arm, and urged her to her feet. "Come. Time is short. 'Sides, 'tis not fitting for a girl of your position to be participating in such things."

"Oh, Papa." Laughing, Rosamunde turned and threw herself into his arms as she had when she was a child. Henry quickly closed his arms around her and gave up the reprimand as she knew he would.

"So that is the king's daughter."

Aric shifted on his feet, his gaze leaving the girl the king was embracing to glance at his friend. "It would seem so."

"She is lovely."

"Quite," Aric agreed quietly. "Unless my memory fails me, she appears a copy of the fair Rosamunde."

"Your memory fails you not. She is an exact likeness of her mother," Shrewsbury agreed. "Except for the hair. That is wholly her father's. Let us hope she did not inherit his quick temper along with it."

"She has been raised right, my lord Bishop. With all discipline and goodness, and the disobedience worked out of her," the abbess announced staunchly, glaring at Shrewsbury for the very suggestion that the girl might not have been. Then, seeming to regain herself, she forced a smile and in a much more pious tone murmured, "It is most gratifying that His Majesty received my message. We feared, when we heard that he was in Normandy, that he might not receive the news in time to make it back for the ceremony."

Aric exchanged a glance with Robert, then asked carefully, "What ceremony?"

"What ceremony?" Adela echoed with amazement. "Why, Lady Rosamunde takes the veil tomorrow."

There was silence for a moment after that announcement; then Robert murmured, "The king will no doubt be a bit surprised by that."

"*What!*" Henry's roar drew their attention.

"I believe he just learned," Aric muttered. Turning, he found Henry a sight to see. The king's face bore a furious scowl and was so red as to seem almost purple. Even his hair seemed to have picked up some of the fire of his temper and shone more red than gray. He stormed angrily toward them, hands and teeth clenched.

His daughter was hard on his heels, a startled and somewhat bewildered expression on her face. "I thought you knew, Papa. I thought you had received my message and come to witness—" Her words came to an abrupt halt when her father paused in his stride and turned on her in a fury.

"It shall not happen! Do you hear me? You are not, I repeat, *not* going to be a nun."

"But—"

"Your mother—God rest her soul—insisted on the same thing ere she died, and I could do naught about it. But I can and *will* do something now. I am your father, and I will not allow you to throw your life away by becoming a nun."

Rosamunde looked briefly stunned at those words; then, seeing the stiff expression on the abbess's face at the insult in her father's words, she allowed her temper free rein. "It is not throwing my life away! 'Tis perfectly acceptable to become a bride of God! I—"

"Will God see you blessed with children?" Henry snarled, interrupting her curt words.

She looked taken aback briefly at that, then regained

herself to snap, "Mayhap. He saw Mary blessed with Jesus."

"*Jesus?*" For a moment it looked as though he might explode, or drop dead. His face was purple with rage.

It was the bishop who intervened, drawing the king's attention with the gentle words, "Your majesty, it is a great honor to become a bride of God. If Rosamunde truly has a calling, it is not well done to force her to—"

"*You!*" Henry turned on the man. "I will not hear your religious drivel. Thanks to your dillydallying, we nearly did not arrive here in time. If I hadn't chanced to hear of Aric's broken betrothal and saved a day's riding by choosing him as groom instead of Rosshuen, we would have been too late!" Whirling on the abbess, he roared, "Why was I not informed of these plans?"

The abbess blinked at him, taken aback. "We . . . I thought you knew, my liege. It was Rosamunde's mother's wish that she follow in her footsteps and become a nun. She said so on her deathbed. As you had not arranged a betrothal, I thought you agreed."

"I do not agree," he snapped, then added, "And I have been making arrangements. But what I meant was, why was I not informed of the imminent ceremony?"

"Well . . . I do not know, Your Majesty. I did send word. Some time ago, in fact. It should have reached you in plenty of time for you to attend. We hoped you might."

The king turned on Shrewsbury again at that news, eyes narrowed and accusing, but the bishop flushed helplessly and murmured, "We have been moving around quite a bit, my liege. Le Mans, then Chinon . . . Mayhap it arrived after we left. I shall, of course, look into it the moment we return."

Henry glared at him briefly, then turned on his daughter. "You are not taking the veil. You will marry. You are the only child of mine who has not turned against me. I will see grandchildren from you."

"John has never turned against you."

"He has joined with my enemies."

"That is just gossip," she argued with disdain.

"And if 'tis true?"

Rosamunde's mouth thinned at the possibility. Truly, no man in history had suffered so from betrayal as her father. Every one of his legitimate sons, her half brothers, had come to turn on him under the influence of their mother, Queen Eleanor. "There are still William and Geoffrey," she whispered, mentioning Henry's other two bastard children.

His expression turned solemn at that, and he reached out to clasp her by the shoulders. "But they were not born of my fair Rosamunde. The love of my life. I am a selfish old man, child. I would see the fruit of our love grow and bloom and cast its seeds across the land, not be stifled and die here in this convent. I would see you marry."

Rosamunde sighed at that, her shoulders slumping in defeat. "And so I shall. Who is to be my groom?"

Aric stiffened as the king suddenly turned toward him.

"Burkhart." The king gestured for him to step forward, and Aric unconsciously straightened his shoulders as he did so. "My daughter, Rosamunde. Daughter, your husband, Aric of Burkhart"

"How do you do, my lord?" she murmured politely, extending her hand. Then, grimacing apologetically as she saw its less than pristine condition—it was stained with residue from her recent work with the foaling—she retracted it and dropped into a quick curtsy instead. "I regret my apparel, but we were not expecting company today."

Before Aric could even murmur a polite response, the king announced, "You should change."

Her head whipped around. "Change?"

"Aye. You will not wish to be wed looking so."

"The wedding is to take place *now?*" Dismay was the only word to describe her reaction, and Aric could actually sympathize. It was all a bit dismaying to him as well.

"As soon as you are changed. I must return to Chinon."

"But—"

"See her properly dressed," the king ordered Sister Eustice, then snatched up Adela's arm and urged her out of the building. "I would have a word with the abbess."

Rosamunde gaped after them, then glanced at Eustice with a start when the sister took her arm and urged her to follow. "I am to be married."

"Aye." Eustice glanced worriedly at the girl as they stepped out of the stables. The child was unnaturally pale.

"I thought I was going to be a nun like you."

"Everything will be fine," Eustice murmured reassuringly, directing her through the convent doors and down the hallway to the left. King Henry and Adela were already out of sight.

"Aye," Rosamunde agreed, drawing herself up slightly. "All will be well." Then her shoulders slumped, and she whispered bewilderedly, "But I was to be a nun."

"It would seem you were never truly meant to take the veil."

"Oh, but I was," Rosamunde assured her. "My mother wished it so. She told the abbess. And my father never arranged a betrothal. I was born to be a nun."

"It would seem not," Eustice corrected gently.

"But what if the Lord wants me to take the veil? What if he is angered that I am not to be one?"

" 'Tis more likely the good Lord has his own plans for you, Rosamunde. Else He would have stopped your father from arriving until after it was done. Would He not?"

Frowning, Rosamunde tilted her head to consider that. Sister Eustice continued, "It seems to me that it must have been God Himself who led your father here in time to prevent the ceremony. Were your father even a day later in arriving, the ceremony would have been done by now."

"Aye," Rosamunde murmured uncertainly. "But why would God wish me to marry when there is so much good I might do as a nun?"

"Mayhap He has something more important for you to do as a wife."

"Mayhap," she murmured, but it was obvious by her tone that she was having trouble fathoming that possibility.

Sighing to herself, Eustice urged her into moving along the hall again, managing to get her to the small cell that had been Rosamunde's room since childhood. Ushering the bemused girl inside, Eustice urged her to sit on the side of her tiny, hard bed, then turned to search through the girl's small clothes chest for the dress Rosamunde had made to wear while taking the veil the next day. Coming up empty-handed, she whirled to frown at Rosamunde. "Where is your white gown?"

Rosamunde glanced up distractedly. "White gown? Oh, Sister Margaret offered to hang it for me, to let out any wrinkles."

"Ah." Nodding, Eustice turned toward the door. "Wait here. I shall return directly."

Rosamunde watched the door close behind her friend

and mentor, then sank back on the bed with a sigh. She was having difficulty absorbing what was happening. Just that morning, her life had been fixed, her path a comfortable, secure one. Now events had careened out of control, changing the course of her life, and she was not sure it was in a direction in which she wished to go. It looked as though she had little choice, however. Her father's decisions were final.

So she would be married, to a man she had never met before, a man she had gotten only a fleeting glimpse of moments ago when her father had introduced them. She should have looked at him longer, but had found herself suddenly shy. It was a new sensation for her. But then she had had very little occasion to be in the presence of men during her life. The only men she had ever even met were her father; his servant and constant companion, Bishop Shrewsbury; and Father Abernott, the priest who ministered the Sunday mass at the abbey. The reverend mother said mass the rest of the week.

She had known a stable boy, several years before. But he had not been around long. A week, perhaps; then he had cornered her in a stall, and pressed his lips against hers. Too startled to react at first, Rosamunde had just stood there. By the time she had gotten over her surprise, curiosity and the beginnings of a sort of shivery pleasure had kept her from protesting. Much to her shame, she hadn't even stopped him when he had covered one of her budding breasts with his hand.

Rosamunde had considered stopping him, knowing that anything that felt so wickedly interesting had to be a sin; everything fun did seem to be sinful, according to the sisters. But she did not know if she would have stopped him on her own, for Eustice had come upon them. One minute she had been wrapped in the lad's enthusiastic embrace, and the next he'd been dragged away and was having his ears boxed. Eustice had then dragged Rosamunde off to lecture her: she must never let a man kiss and touch her so again. It was evil. Lips were for speaking, and breasts for milking—and that was that.

The abbess had sent the stable boy away that very day.

"She did not look pleased at the news of her upcoming marriage," Robert murmured.

Shifting on the bench seat where the nuns had seated the men to eat while they waited, Aric turned his gaze from the food he was unable to choke down—despite how delicious it looked—and peered at his friend. "Nay," he agreed dismally.

"Well, mayhap 'tis just a result of surprise."

Aric grunted with little conviction.

"She is quite lovely."

Aric grunted again. He looked far from cheered by the news, and Robert sighed.

"Surely you do not fear *she* will be unfaithful? This girl was raised in a convent, man. She could not have learned the lying, cheating ways of a woman raised at court."

Aric was silent for a moment, then shifted his position at the table and murmured, "Do you recall my cousin, Clothilde?"

"Clothilde?" He thought briefly, then laughed. "Oh, aye. The girl whose mother would not allow her sweets, lest she grow in size, or lose all her teeth ere she married."

Aric grimaced. "Not a single sweet passed her lips ere her marriage, but they had a great tray of them at her wedding feast."

"Aye." Robert laughed again as he recalled the event.

"She quite liked sweets once she tried them. As I recall, she nearly ate the whole tray all on her own."

"She still likes them. Perhaps more so because she was deprived of them for so long. In the two years since her marriage, she has grown to six times her original size. She has lost three teeth at last count."

Robert winced. "Do not tell me you fear your wife will grow overlarge and lose her teeth?"

Aric rolled his eyes, then sighed. "What is missing in a convent?"

"Well, I realize they can be strict in these places, but I am sure they have an occasional sweet or—"

"Forget the blasted sweets!" Aric snapped. "*Men*. Men are missing in convents."

"Aye, well, but that is the very reason behind their existence and—Oh!" A chagrined look on his face, he shook his head. "I think I see. You fear that having been deprived of the company of men all these years, your wife soon will find herself overly fond of their company."

Aric muttered under his breath and turned away with mild disgust at the length of time it had taken to get his point across. Surely his friend had not always been so dense?

"Aric. Friend. Do not allow Delia's behavior to color your views. She was raised by her uncle, Lord Stratham, the most notorious reprobate in the land."

"Yet my mother was not."

"Ah." Robert sighed.

"She was raised most strictly."

"Yes, but—"

"And *she* could not contain her passions."

Robert shook his head. "I can see you will not be easily reassured, but 'tis not as bad as all that. If you fear she will become overfond of the company of men, you merely have to keep her away from court. Keep her in the country, where the only men she may meet are peasants and serfs. Surely she was brought up with enough sense not to dally with one of *them*." He clapped his friend on the back encouragingly.

"Oh, aye. The king would most likely be very pleased should he never see his daughter again," Aric muttered. Robert frowned.

"Oh, there is that. He will most likely wish her at court on occasion."

"Most likely," Aric agreed dryly.

"He appears to hold great affection for her." Robert's frown deepened as he thought on that. "That could be a problem, could it not? Jesu! A king for a father-in-law," he marveled in horror as he realized the full significance of it. "Should you not make her happy, he might have you drawn and quartered. What a spot to be in!"

"Robert."

"Aye?"

"Stop trying to make me feel better."

Rosamunde's fretting ended abruptly at the opening of the door. Sighing, she pushed herself to a sitting position as Sister Eustice reentered with the gown she had fetched lying carefully over her arm.

"The creases are all gone, fortunately enough," the nun informed her and started to push the cell door closed, but paused when the abbess's voice sounded in the hallway. By the time Adela arrived at the door, both Rosamunde and Eustice were waiting curiously. Adela took one look at Rosamunde's expression and hurried forward.

"Oh, my dear child," she murmured soothingly, seating herself on the cot beside the girl. She embraced her briefly. "All will be well. You will see. God has a special path for you to follow and you must trust in him."

"Aye, 'tis what Sister Eustice said," Rosamunde whispered as tears welled in her eyes. Oddly enough, the small droplets of liquid had not threatened until the very moment that the abbess offered comfort. It had always been that way. While both Eustice and the abbess had taken the place of her mother on that beautiful woman's death, it was the abbess to whom Rosamunde had turned to bandage her banged-up knees and soothe her hurts. And it never failed that Rosamunde could stand absolutely anything with a stiff upper lip and grim smile until the abbess came around; at the first sight of Adela's kind face, though, she always broke down.

"Oh, now. Shh, my child. Do not cry. You must have faith in the Lord. He chose this path for you. Surely there is a reason."

"I am not crying out of fear of what is to come. Well . . ." she corrected honestly, "mostly I am not. Mostly I am crying for what is ending."

Bewildered, the abbess shook her head slightly. "What is ending?"

"I will have to leave you all, the only family I have ever known. Aside from my father," she added loyally.

Eustice and Adela shared a dismayed look, their own eyes filling with tears at the realization. They had been too distracted to consider that truth.

"Well . . ." Sister Eustice glanced desperately around, everywhere but at the young woman who had been her student in the stables since being a small child—young Rosamunde had latched onto Eustice's voluminous skirts and trailed after her the moment she had gained her feet and been able to walk. The nun had taught her everything she knew, and the look on Eustice's face conveyed her misery at their separation.

"Aye," Adela murmured unhappily, her own watery gaze on the floor. She had been taken with Rosamunde from her birth. The baby's red curls and sweet smile had melted her heart as nothing else ever had. Contrary to tradition, she herself had overseen the girl's lessons in the schoolroom. She had spent hour after hour feeding the child's expanding mind, encouraging patience, and curbing the temper that seemed always to come with redheads. The rewards for her effort had been great. Rosamunde was everything she had ever wanted in a daughter. With a grimace of pain, the abbess rose to her feet.

"Every bird must leave the nest one day," she said practically. She moved to the door, only to pause and glance back uncertainly. "I never thought you would leave us, Rosamunde. I was not warned." Adela sighed unhappily. "Thinking you would not need the knowledge, there was much I neglected to teach you about marriage and the marital bed."

"The marital bed?" Rosamunde frowned worriedly as she noted the sudden stain of embarrassment on the older woman's cheeks.

The abbess stared at her, at a loss for a moment, then turned abruptly away. "Sister Eustice shall enlighten you," she said abruptly. She started to slip out of the room, then paused to add, "But quickly, sister. The king is most impatient to have this business done."

The door closed, leaving Eustice staring at it in stupefaction.

Chapter 2

"THE marital bed."

Rosamunde turned her gaze from the closed door to Eustice at the other woman's firm words. The sister had drawn up her shoulders, her expression full of purpose, Before she could continue, though, Rosamunde asked, "Shall I dress while you explain?"

Eustice blinked at the interruption, then sighed and nodded. "Aye. Your father appears to be in something of a hurry. Mayhap that would be for the best."

Slipping off the bed, Rosamunde quickly removed the breeches she had been wearing to work in the stables. Eustice immediately took them from her and began to fold them neatly as she began again. "The marital bed may be unpleasant, but it is your sacred duty as a wife."

"Unpleasant?" Rosamunde paused in undoing the laces of her tunic. She eyed the other woman with dismay. "How unpleasant?"

Eustice made a face. "Quite, from what I gather. My mother used to stay abed at least half a day after my father exerted his husbandly rights," she confided.

Rosamunde's eyes grew round at this news. "It must be very draining, then."

"Oh, aye," Eustice agreed with a firm nod. "And noisy."

"Noisy?" Rosamunde sank to sit on the bed again.

"You are supposed to be changing," the nun reminded her. Rosamunde stood again and began to fuss with the laces of her top. Sister Eustice admitted. "When I was a child, my sister and I listened outside our parents' bedchamber one night." She flushed at Rosamunde's arched eyebrows, and shrugged. "I was a naughty child, forever getting into mischief. Not unlike someone else I know," she added pointedly, making Rosamunde grin. "Anyway, we listened and . . ."

"And?" Rosamunde prompted.

Eustice scowled at her. "Continue to change," she instructed. She was silent until Rosamunde began to drag her tunic up over her head, then she continued. "And they made all sorts of racket. The bed ropes were squeaking, and my parents were moaning, groaning, and screaming."

Dragging her top off over her head, Rosamunde gaped at her. "Screaming?"

"Aye." Eustice grimaced.

"Are you sure it was the bedding? Mayhap they were doing something else."

Eustice considered that briefly, then shook her head. "Nay. I told you, the bed ropes were squeaking."

Rosamunde began to crumple the shirt she held distractedly as she pondered her friend's words. She took some water from a basin in the corner of the room and gave herself a quick wash.

"Here." Eustice lifted and held out the white gown.

Rosamunde traded the top for the gown, which she immediately began to pull over her head. Pushing her hands into its sleeves, she tugged the gown down over her hips and tugged until it lay straight. She set to work at the laces.

Glancing up from folding Rosamunde's top, Eustice frowned at the sight of her and set it aside to grab a brush. Moving behind Rosamunde, she brushed the girl's hair into a glossy cloud that lay somewhat tamely about her shoulders. Then she set the brush aside and urged the girl toward the door. "We had better hurry. Your father was nearly foaming at the mouth with impatience."

"But you haven't told me—"

"I will on the way," Eustice assured her as she dragged the door open. Ushering her out into the hall, she pulled the door closed, then heaved a sigh and escorted her down the hall. "As I told you, marital relations are unpleasant, but they are your duty now. But there are times when it is not allowed. For instance, while a woman is—" Pausing abruptly, she turned wide eyes on Rosamunde. "It is not your woman's time, is it?"

"Nay," Rosamunde murmured, unable to contain a blush. Such things were never discussed.

"Good." Eustice smiled her relief. "That would be a fly in the king's ointment. Consummation would be forbidden if you were."

"Ah," Rosamunde murmured with a solemn nod, a little baffled, but anxious to have the sister get off that subject and move on.

"It is also forbidden while pregnant or nursing, of course."

"Of course," Rosamunde murmured, gamely.

"Also during Lent, Advent, Whitsuntide, and Easter week."

"Mm-hmm." Rosamunde nodded.

"Also on feast days, fast days, Sundays, Wednesdays, Fridays, and Saturdays."

"So, 'tis allowed only on Mondays, Tuesdays, and Thursdays?" Rosamunde asked with a frown.

"Aye. Thank goodness today is Tuesday."

"Yes, thank goodness," Rosamunde said with a grimace.

If Eustice heard the sarcasm, she chose to ignore it, merely continuing with her list. "It is forbidden during daylight, while unclothed, or in a church, of course."

"Of course," Rosamunde agreed quietly. That would surely be sacrilege!

"It is only to be performed in an effort to gain a child, and then it is to be performed only once. You should not enjoy it. You must wash afterward. And you should not partake of any fondling, lewd kisses, or—"

"What exactly is *that*?" Rosamunde interrupted, and Eustice glanced at her impatiently, her footsteps slowing.

"You know very well what kissing is, Rosamunde! I caught you at it with the stable boy when you—"

"I meant the fondling," Rosamunde interrupted, annoyed to find herself flushing guiltily at the memory of the incident with the stable boy.

"Oh, well." Eustice scowled. "It is touching . . . anything. *Including* breasts. Lips are for speaking and breasts for milking—and that is that," the nun said firmly. She sighed, her eyes shifting upward. "Now, what else . . . ? Oh, aye, you must refrain from any of the *unnatural* acts."

"Unnatural acts?" Rosamunde asked uncertainly.

Eustice grimaced. "Simply do not put your mouth on any part of him, or let him put his mouth on any part of you. Especially parts covered by your clothes."

Rosamunde's eyes widened, and Eustice made a knowing face.

"It is not proper."

"I see," Rosamunde murmured, then raised her eyebrows. "But why must I *not let* him do so? I mean, if men are morally superior—as Father Abernott is constantly reminding us—surely he already will know all this?"

Eustice nodded at that. "True. No doubt he does know all this. I am telling you so that you do not make mistakes. Now, here we are," she pointed out, drawing to a halt at the doors to the chapel. She turned to Rosamunde. "Do you have any questions?"

"Aye."

"Oh." The sister didn't bother to hide her unease, but raised her eyebrows in question. "What is it?"

"Well . . ." Rosamunde swallowed. "All you have told me are things I must not do. I am still not quite clear on what exactly *does* occur."

"Oh, of course." Eustice paused and considered the easiest way to explain it, then shrugged. "You have seen the animals from the stables when they are in season."

It was not a question, but Rosamunde nodded anyway.

"Well, 'tis the same thing."

"It is the same?" Rosamunde asked with distaste. Her mind flooded with various pictures of different beasts mating. Cats, dogs, goats, sheep, cows, and horses suddenly filled her mind, a veritable orgy of stable animals.

"Aye. Now you see why it is so distasteful to ladies," Eustice said heavily.

Rosamunde nodded in wide-eyed agreement, then asked, "Will he bite the back of my neck?"

Eustice blinked. "Bite?"

"Aye. Well, when I spied the cats behind the barn, the male cat was biting the female on the back of the neck as he covered her."

"Oh, nay. That is only to keep the female in place. You, being a dutiful wife, will not need such action taken."

"Nay, of course not," Rosamunde agreed. Eustice turned to open the door to the chapel a crack and peer curiously inside.

"Will he wish to sniff my behind?"

Eustice shrieked, then slammed the chapel door closed and whirled to gape at her.

"Well, you said 'twas the same as animals," Rosamunde said innocently. "And they sniff—"

"Lord love us!" Eustice interrupted fervently. She opened her mouth to speak, but paused at the mischievous twinkle in the girl's eye. Her gaze narrowed. "You are being naughty again," she accused. Rosamunde managed a solemn expression.

"Oh, nay, sister."

"Hmmm. Then shall we—"

"What does the covering consist of exactly?" Rosamunde interrupted.

"Covering?" Eustice echoed, her confusion obvious.

"Mating. For instance, when Angus the bull approaches one of the cows and mounts her. What is he doing, exactly?"

Making a face, Eustice considered her question briefly, then explained. "Angus has a thing. . . ."

"A thing?"

"Aye. It is about . . . oh . . . yea long." She held her hands about a foot or so apart. "And round. Well, not round, but—it is shaped rather like a cucumber."

"A cucumber?" Rosamunde tried to picture the man in the stables sporting a foot-long cucumber between his legs.

"Aye." Eustice seemed to be gaining strength—and speed—as she continued. "Angus inserts his cucumber into Maude, stirs it about a bit, spills his seed, and 'tis done."

"Well," Rosamunde murmured now, trying to be

optimistic. "I suppose it could not possibly be worse than scrubbing the stone floors in the winter." A body usually came away with chapped knees and an aching back. Spending hours kneeling on the damp stones in the drafty old convent was her least favorite task.

"Hmm. Except for the pain, I doubt it is."

"Pain?" Rosamunde eyed her sharply.

Eustice nodded reluctantly. "I have heard there is pain, Rosamunde, and I gather there is even blood. At least, the first time."

Rosamunde paled. "Blood?"

"Aye. They say that it proves the bride's innocence."

"But—"

" 'Tis the price we pay for Eve's sin."

"Eve's sin," Rosamunde muttered resentfully. How often had Father Abernott spit that phrase at them? He had hammered it into them to the point that those words were practically branded on her soul. "I thought Jesus died for our sins? Or was that only for men's sins?" she asked dryly.

Eustice was saved from dealing with that question. The door beside them opened and a somewhat frantic abbess slid out. "Whatever is taking you so long? The king is quite wroth at this delay."

"Rosamunde had some last-minute questions," Eustice explained dryly.

"What sort of questions, dear?" the abbess asked kindly.

"Did not Jesus die for our sins?" Rosamunde asked.

"Aye. Of course he did," the abbess assured her quickly, but was obviously confused by the comment.

"Then why do we suffer pain in the consummation and bleed?"

Adela's shoulders sagged, blowing her breath out in dismay. With a look that was somewhere between consternation and fond regret, the abbess merely said, "We really do not have time for such complicated theological discussions now, child. Mayhap you should ask Father Abernott that after the ceremony. Come now. Your father really is eager to have this done."

Father Abernott was a stuffy little priest, normally puffed up with self-importance. Performing the marriage of the king's daughter, illegitimate or not, at the king's request, and in his very own exalted presence, had the man inflated beyond endurance. Haughtiness was oozing off him as he presided over the ceremony. The congregation was made up of the king, Shrewsbury, the groom, a second man who appeared to be the groom's friend, and every single nun who resided within the convent—the others having begged the abbess to allow them to attend. Most of them had been at the abbey since Rosamunde's arrival and had watched her grow to womanhood with interest and affection. They were like family to Rosamunde. Which was why the abbess had given in to their pleas and allowed them to witness the ceremony. Their presence seemed merely to add to the priest's pretentious behavior, however.

Barely able to stand the man's self-satisfied expression, Rosamunde ignored his words and turned her gaze to his bald pate instead. The sight of his shiny scalp made her lips begin to tremble with wicked amusement. Every single one of the unflattering names she and some of the younger nuns had come up with to describe the man when they were annoyed with him were rolling through her mind one after the other, and threatening her with inappropriate laughter.

She quickly lowered her gaze to the skirt of her gown. It was the best she had. Made of the softest linen, it fit her upper frame snugly, then flared slightly at the waist. Hours had been spent crafting this gown, for Rosamunde had wanted it to be just right. But she had created it for taking the veil, not taking a husband. Not an earthly one, at any rate.

Stifling a small sigh, she glanced curiously at the man beside her. He seemed rather big to her, and Rosamunde was five-foot-nine herself. She had been told that her mother was more petite, but her father was over six feet tall. She could only assume that God had split the difference with her.

She had always felt tall. Most of the women here in the convent were at least two or three inches shorter than her. Rosamunde had always felt a bit gawky and overlarge around them. Next to this man, however, she felt almost petite. He was as tall and powerful-looking as her father. She had noticed that about him before, though it was really all she had noticed at the time. Now she took a more thorough inventory of the man she was suddenly to wed.

He had a broad chest. Thick, strong arms. Thighs that bulged with strength from years on horseback. Nicely shaped calves and ankles. Hair like bright sunlight. Eyes the deep green of a grassy glen. Rugged features that hinted at battles fought and most likely won. Skin weathered by years spent vulnerable to the elements.

He certainly looked healthy enough, she supposed. Handsome as well. The laugh lines on his face were a good sign, she thought optimistically, then sighed as she tried to recall his name. Her father had said it on introducing them, she was sure. What had it been? Issac? Erin?

Aric, she recalled suddenly. *Aye, Aric*. Her husband. *Aric*.

Aric who? she wondered briefly, then shrugged. The second name was beyond her recollection.

"My lady."

Rosamunde turned swiftly forward at that imperious demand, flushing brightly at being caught staring. She realized she had missed something. Most likely something important, too, she decided when the priest shook his head with disapproval. "My lady, should I repeat your vows?"

Aric peered at the girl beside him as she whispered her vows. He had been uncomfortably aware of her eyes on him as the priest had performed the first part of the ceremony. She had been examining him so intently he had begun to feel uneasy. Now he subjected her to a similar perusal, hoping she was too distracted to notice.

She had nearly taken his breath away when she had entered the chapel. The transformation from hoyden to lovely damsel was quite thorough. For a moment, he had not realized that it was she, and he had the brief mad thought that Henry's fair Rosamunde walked again—a ghost here to witness her daughter's wedding. But then he had realized that the locks that framed her lovely face were not the golden halo that had graced the mother, but the fiery red her father's hair had been in his youth.

That realization had barely told him that this was his bride, when his attention had been turned by Robert's amazed gasp. Then the girl was at his side and the priest had begun. Now Aric took the time to look her over. Her face was a perfect oval. Her skin was purest ivory with the faintest dusting of freckles. Her features were flawless. She had full lips. A small, straight nose. Keen gray eyes like her father's dominated her face. Those eyes sparkled with intelligence and intensity, and Aric had actually felt the energy rolling off of her as she had entered the room. It had seemed to strike out at him like a physical blow. She had inherited that from her father, too. Henry had that sort of presence. Or once had. Lately a great deal of that energy seemed to be drained from the great man. He seemed worn down by his cares. His sons, Aric suspected, were at the heart of that.

"My lord."

Eyebrows rising, Aric turned to the sanctimonious little priest, grimacing as he realized he had been caught out just as his bride had moments before. Feeling Robert's amusement, Aric nudged his dark-haired friend irritably with an elbow as the priest huffily repeated his words.

Despite his feelings on the marriage, when Aric spoke the vows back, his voice was strong and firm. The king wished Aric to marry his daughter. He would marry her. And he would keep her safe and well—as a husband should. But he had learned his lesson well from Delia. He would not risk his heart. Even the king could not force him to do that.

Rosamunde blinked as the priest pronounced them wed. Was that it? A few words in Latin? Making a promise or two? And you were bound for life? A firm hold on her arm drew her bemused gaze to her father. He turned her away from the priest and ushered her out of the chapel.

"All will be well."

Rosamunde's eyebrows rose at the anxiety belying her father's assurance as he led her down the dim hall. "Of course it will," she agreed, trying to soothe him even though she wasn't at all sure what she was referring to. Frowning slightly, she glanced over her shoulder to see that the bishop, her new husband, and his friend were following. They were trailed by the abbess, Sister

Eustice, Father Abernott, and every single one of the nuns.

Rosamunde peered back at her father, surprised to see the concern on his face as he urged her down the corridor that led to the private cells. He appeared hardly aware of her presence, despite the firm hold he had on her arm. Also, it seemed to her that he was trying to reassure himself more than her.

"I always preferred Burkhart. I weeded out dozens of men, hundreds of them over the years, and he was always the best option for you. He is strong, wealthy, and honorable. He will be able to protect you, yet treat you with the care you deserve. I am sure he will. All will be well."

"Of course it will," Rosamunde repeated, trying to ease his obviously troubled mind. Lord knew her father had enough to worry about without concerning himself with her welfare.

Seeming almost startled by her voice, he stopped suddenly and glanced at her anxiously. "You are not too angry with me over spoiling your plans to take the veil, are you? You—"

"Of course not, Father," Rosamunde interrupted quickly, her heart aching at his uncertainty. She had never seem him thus. He had always been strong and commanding. "I could never hate you."

"Nay. Of course not," he said, and found a smile. "I am sorry about this, daughter."

"Sorry?" Rosamunde frowned. "About what?"

"I wish there were more time. You deserve more time. You deserve all the care and consideration in the world, and I would pay my entire treasury if it would give you that time, but—" Shaking his head when he noticed her confused expression, he kissed her quickly on the forehead, opened the door they stood beside, and urged her through it. "I promise he shall be as gentle as time will allow. . . . Else I shall have him drawn and quartered." He said the last rather loudly, to ensure that her husband heard, she suspected.

It was terribly confusing, but not nearly as much as the fact that she now found herself back in her cell, the small chamber that had been her bedroom since she was a child. Confusion plain on her face, she turned quickly back, forestalling her father when he would have closed her door. "What are we doing here?"

Much to Rosamunde's amazement, her father, His Royal Highness, the king of England, actually blushed. He mumbled a response that was wholly incoherent except for one word that seemed to leap out at her like a snake from beneath a rock.

"Bedding!" she cried out in shock. "Now?"

Her father actually reddened further, looking about as embarrassed as she was shocked. "Aye."

"But, 'tis still daylight! Sister Eustice's list said 'twas a sin to"—she paused briefly, then whispered the word *fornicate* before continuing in her normal voice—"while 'tis light out."

Her father straightened abruptly, his embarrassment fleeing before his irritation. "Aye? Well Sister Eustice be damned! I will see this marriage consummated ere I leave. I'll not risk an annulment or some other such thing once I am out of the way. I want you protected should I die, and so you shall be."

"Aye, but could we not at least wait until dark and—"

"Nay. I do not have time for that. I must return to Chinon as soon as possible. So . . ." He gestured vaguely toward the bed, some of his embarrassment returning. "Get you ready. I shall have a word with your husband."

On that note, he pulled the door closed, leaving her alone.

Aric watched the king close the door on his daughter. He straightened his shoulders manfully and waited for the monarch's attention to turn to him. He, Shambley, the bishop, the priest, the abbess, and all the nuns had stood silently listening as the king had made his apologies and threats. The man was definitely upset. Aric supposed it was hard for any father to accept the idea of his sweet and innocent young daughter being bedded, but this was the king's idea, after all. Aric certainly didn't appreciate the constant threat of being drawn and quartered being tossed at him repeatedly.

Sighing inwardly, Aric had to wonder how he always managed to get himself into these things. Would he survive the wedding night, and if he did, just how long would it be before some inadvertent future misstep saw him drawn and quartered anyway? Just now Delia was looking like an extremely attractive alternative to this. Even with her thighs wrapped around old Glanville. He ought to save himself all the trouble and anxiety and commit suicide right now. Aric sighed. He wasn't the suicidal sort.

Several moments of silence passed before the king finally turned from the closed door to scowl at him. The expression on the man's face hardly supported his earlier avowals of liking Aric and thinking him the best option to husband his daughter.

"Well," he said finally, some of his apparent dislike fading. He propped his hands on Aric's shoulders and clasped him firmly. "Rosamunde is my greatest treasure. The fruit of my love. I entrust her to you. I trust you will treat her gently, and handle her with the utmost care."

"Of course, Your Majesty," Aric murmured dutifully.

Nodding, the king turned to Bishop Shrewsbury and held out one hand. The man immediately handed over two candles. Taking them, Henry lit them both off a torch in a holder fastened to the wall, then turned to Aric and held them up side by side. "Do you see the mark I made on both of them?"

Aric nodded as he saw the notches made in the wax. Both were at the exact same spot, less than a thumb's width down the candle.

"Well, that is how long you have to get this done," he announced. He handed over one of the candles.

Aric's hand closed automatically around the candle, but his eyes were wide with horror. He measured the notch again. It wasn't much more than a quarter of an inch from the now-lit wick. By his guess that was—

"Why, that's not even ten minutes!"

Henry nodded unhappily. "In truth, 'tis closer to five. . . . And the candle is lit and already burning your time away. You had best get to it."

Aric gaped at him in horror, already seeing his head on a pike. "But—"

"Do not 'but' me, Burkhart. Had I more time, do you not think I would give it to you? She is my daughter, man. She deserves a feast with great revelry and celebration for her wedding. Mayhap someday we can give her that. But not today." Turning, he handed the second candle back to Shrewsbury, then took Aric's arm in one hand. He reached out with the other to push open the door to Rosamunde's room. "Today we must do the best we can. And that means that you will be gentle, caring, and"—Henry pushed Aric, holding his candle, through the door—"quick. We shall be waiting out here."

The door slammed closed on the king's last word, and Aric was distracted by the need to shelter the flame of his lit candle from the breeze that was created. Once the risk of its being blown out had passed, a rustling sound drew his gaze to the girl who now stood by the head of a small bed.

His bride. She faced him, still in her white gown—not looking fearful or nervous, as he had expected, but oddly resigned. Grim, even. Aric was pondering that when a drop of wax slid from the candle he held, splashing onto the flesh of his hand. That reminded him of the time constraints on this situation.

Sighing inwardly, he glanced around the spare room, looking for a spot to set the candle. There wasn't much choice in the matter. All that the room contained was a bed and a chest, both of which were lined up against one wall, leaving barely a footwide length of space to walk in. Aric set the candle carefully on the chest, noted that he had already used up much of his time, then straightened and turned grimly to the girl. "You have not undressed."

Her eyes widened slightly. "That is not necessary, is it?"

Aric grimaced. She had been raised in a convent, so of course she knew that the Church considered it a sin to carry out marital relations while naked. The Church did like to take the fun out of the deed. He did not have the time now, but he promised himself that he would try later to soften her views on such things, else the task of getting her with child would be a terrible burden. He did want a son. In the meantime, he had to disrobe, at least partially; she would hardly appreciate the cool metal of his armor against her flesh.

He removed his tabard, set it across the chest by the candle, and straightened to begin work on his hauberk when she, apparently taking it as some sort of cue, suddenly scrambled to the bed and crawled onto it. Aric continued with the removal of his hauberk, tugging the heavy mail shirt off over his head, only to pause with it in hand when he saw that she appeared frozen on all fours on the bed. She was situated in the middle of the hard little cot, on her hands and knees, her white-clad derriere poking into the sky. What was she doing? He stared at her behind silently for a moment, but when she stayed like that, he shifted uncertainly, then cleared his throat. "Ah . . . is there something amiss, my lady?"

She turned to peer along her back at him questioningly. "Amiss, my lord?"

"Well . . ." He gave a small, nervous laugh and gestured to her posture. "Your pose," he clarified. "What are you doing?"

"Awaiting your pleasure, my lord," she answered calmly.

Aric's gaze narrowed slightly at that. "My pleasure?" he asked carefully.

"Aye. Sister Eustice explained the matter to me," she assured him, then turned her head away and waited, still on her hands and knees.

Sister Eustice explained the matter to me. Aric frowned over the words, then set his hauberk on the chest and straightened. He propped his hands on his hips as he considered her. After a moment he cleared his throat, drawing her gaze back around. "What exactly did this Sister Eustice explain, my lady?"

Her eyebrows rose slightly. "She explained about the bedding. About how 'twas like Angus and Maude."

"Angus and Maude?" His ears perked up at the male name. "Who the devil is Angus?"

"Our bull."

"Your bull," he echoed blankly. "And Maude would be—"

"The abbey cow."

"Of course," he said faintly, understanding dawning

on him. Horror followed. "And this Sister Eustice told you that—"

" 'Tis the same thing," she filled in calmly, then added, "You will mount me, insert your cucumber—"

"Cucumber?" His voice cracked on the word, and she flushed with embarrassment.

"Well, your bull-thing then," she improvised quickly, biting her lip when he suddenly dropped to sit on the edge of the small bed and lowered his head into his hands in defeat.

"I am dead," she thought she heard him mutter through his hands. "My head shall decorate Westminster for sure."

Frowning at his misery, Rosamunde dropped to her haunches and eyed him uncertainly. "My lord?" she murmured.

"I should have married Delia," he continued. "Cuckolded I may have been, but better cuckolded than drawn and quartered."

"Who is Delia?" Rosamunde asked, annoyed.

"My betrothed, and the reason I am surely going to die," he answered matter-of-factly, then almost conversationally added, "If she had been faithful, I would not be in this fix. Hell, if she had at least been smarter about her infidelity I would not be leaving here with my head on a pike."

"You are betrothed?" Rosamunde asked with confusion.

"Aye. Well, I was, but then I caught her in the stables with Glanville and I broke the betrothal, sent a messenger to inform my father, and rode to Shambley to get drunk, which is of course a day closer to Burkhart Castle than Rosshuen's home. You see now if Shambley's father had built his damn castle a little farther away, it would be Rosshuen in this fix instead of me!"

"I see," Rosamunde said carefully, wondering if her father had married her to a madman.

"There is an awful lot of talking going on in there!" Rosamunde and Aric both gave a start at the words shouted through the door, listening with amazement as the king added, "I want action! I will have the proof that this marriage was consummated!"

"They are waiting outside the door?" Rosamunde hissed in disbelief. Aric couldn't help himself; he began to laugh. There was an edge of hysteria to his laughter. Could the situation get any more difficult?

"Burkhart!"

The angry warning in that voice got through Aric's moment of madness. He stood abruptly to tug his tunic off over his head, then tossed it atop his hauberk. Reaching for his breeches, he considered the best way to approach the situation. He was fretting over it so much that he didn't notice the approval on his bride's face as she took in his wide, muscular chest and flat stomach. He *did* notice the way her face suddenly fell in disappointment, however, when he finished removing his mail stockings and brais.

"What?" he asked with dismay, pausing, brais still in hand.

"Well." She hesitated, then admitted in a near whisper, "I am just surprised, is all. Your cucumber is not nearly as large as Angus's."

Aric stiffened at that, annoyance rising up within him despite knowing that no man's "cucumber" could possibly be as large as a bull's. He straightened abruptly and snapped, " 'Tis large enough for the job at hand."

"Aye, I am sure 'tis," Rosamunde soothed quickly.

"And 'tis not called a *cucumber*," he added irritably, his pride stung enough that he did not care if those waiting outside the door heard. "Or a bull-thing."

"What is it called then?"

"Various things," he muttered, considering several of the names used before choosing the one he liked best. "Some call it a cock."

"Nay." Peering at the appendage in question, she shook her head firmly.

"Nay?" He frowned.

"A cock is a male chicken, my lord. That looks nothing like a male chicken."

His mouth moved briefly, nothing coming out of it as his face went from a lovely shade of chartreuse to a rather violent maroon. Then he snapped, "Manhood, then. You may call it my manhood."

Rosamunde's gaze dropped to it doubtfully once more. It seemed far too small and shriveled for anyone to want it to be representative of his manhood, but he did seem to be sensitive about it, so she felt it best to keep that opinion to herself. Still, it was much smaller than what Eustice had described, and she did have worries that he might not be able to perform adequately with such a handicap. On the other hand, it would be much less painful than she had expected. It was hardly the size of a baby's fat little leg. Brightening at that thought, Rosamunde flashed him a smile and quickly returned to her hands and knees, poking up her behind in preparation for his attentions.

"All right. I am prepared. You may insert your cu– Er . . . *manhood* and stir it about now."

"Stir it about?"

"What are you two doing in there? Exchanging recipes?" King Henry snapped, the door shuddering under a blow. "I will have an end to this talk of stirring and such. Let us have some action!"

Rolling her eyes at her father's impatience, Rosamunde glanced at her new husband and grimaced.

"Well, that is what Sister Eustice called it," she explained in an impatient hiss, then added, "Though it looked more to me as if Angus was just plowing in and out."

Aric gaped at her and dropped onto the side of the bed with dismay. Good Lord, what had he gotten himself into? Never had he considered that bedding his bride might be such a trying experience. *God's truth*! He did not think he could accomplish the feat. She was a lovely woman, but her mind seemed full of the oddest damn things. Insert it and stir it about, indeed!

Considering his distraught countenance, she sighed. "Is aught amiss, my lord?"

"Aye," he answered heavily. "You seem to have the wrong idea about all of this."

Eyebrows rising, she sat back again to face him and firmly shook her head. "Nay, my lord, Eustice was most plain about it."

"Aye, well. Eustice was wrong. Men do it differently than bulls."

"Nay."

"Nay?"

"You are wrong, my lord. I have seen many animals having at it and—"

"Having at it?"

"Aye. And they all seem to do it the same way— whether they are cats, pigs, horses, or bulls. You may trust me on this, my lord."

Aric merely stared at her bleakly. With all of this animal husbandry as her source of knowledge, it seemed to him that persuading her otherwise without simply showing her was impossible. On that thought, he shifted closer, grasped her by the arms, and pulled her into an embrace.

Rosamunde gasped in surprise, then stiffened as his mouth covered hers. She began to struggle at once, opening her mouth to protest, then found herself with a mouthful of tongue, which she promptly tried to spit back out. Turning away, she finally managed to free herself from him and said with a gasp, "Nay! 'Tis a sin. 'Sides, you cannot pass your seed like that, my lord. You know what must be done."

So saying, she turned away to kneel on her hands and knees before him on the bed, her derriere directly before his face.

Grimacing, Aric opened his mouth to speak, but whatever he would have said slid abruptly from his mind when she suddenly reached back, caught the hem of her gown, and dragged it up over her hips, leaving her lovely behind bare to the world. Or, more specifically, to his wide eyes.

Good Lord! His gaze dropped briefly away from the image of her buttocks to his manhood, and he grimaced at the vagaries of the male body. His manhood had shown absolutely no interest in this ordeal since 'his' bride's mention of cucumbers, bull-things, or stirring things about. Even the kiss had done little for that problem. She had remained so still and unresponsive under his attentions that all he had felt was a sort of desperate panic. Now, however, she flashed her round, pink cheeks at him and his manhood deigned to awake. In fact, it was even now urging him simply to mount the woman, and slide himself into her moist heat, as she was requesting. That would not do at all, of course. There would be no moist heat if he did not see to producing some in her, but it was damnably difficult to figure out how, should she not even wish him to kiss her. He was at a loss.

"My lord." Rosamunde glanced over her shoulder with irritation at his delay, then paused as her gaze fell on his man-thing. Much to her surprise, it seemed to have grown since she had last seen it. Impossible, she told herself, but there was the proof of it. He *was* larger than when she had last looked. Impressive. Amazing, really. Though, of course, it was still not as large as the cucumber Eustice had described. Shrugging such considerations away for now, she glanced at his face to see the irritation there and sighed. "Is there something amiss, my lord? Can you not simply get this business done? My father is waiting on us."

"Time is almost up," came the king's voice through the door. Aric grimaced as he glanced to the chest to see that, indeed, as he had been suffering the tortures of the damned, the candle had burned away three-quarters of his allotted time. Cursing, he mounted the bed behind her and grasped her hips, then paused. The situation aside, the king aside, and even her unfavorable comparison of him to her damn bull aside, he could not simply plow into her and cause her the pain he knew such behavior would inflict.

Sighing, he considered her back and shoulders briefly, then leaned forward slightly and slid his hands up her waist until he was cupping her breast beneath the chaste cloth of her gown.

Rosamunde stiffened, confusion running through her, as she felt his large, rough hands close over her breasts. She had no idea what he thought he was about, and Eustice's words were pounding in her head: *Lips are for speaking and breasts for milking—and that is that.* Did he think to milk her like a cow? Good Lord, her new husband was proving himself incredibly slow in doing what needed doing.

She felt something bump about between her thighs like a curious dog sniffing; then his mouth pressed against the base of her neck. She decided to get this ordeal over with. Bracing her hands on the top of the hard cot, Rosamunde thrust backward into him, impaling herself with one determined thrust. Then she promptly commenced a howling that had the king pounding at the door.

"What the devil is going on in there? Burkhart! What have you done to my daughter? Burkhart!"

Aric sighed as he heard those angry words over his new bride's howls. Marriage to the king's daughter, as he had feared, was turning out to be quite a trial.

"Burkhart!"

"Just a minute," Aric shouted impatiently toward the door, then grasped Rosamunde's hips when she started to pull away from him. "You, too. Just stay still for a minute." He felt her stiffen again and sighed. "Wait until the pain passes, else you will just hurt yourself more."

He saw her head bob in a brief nod and he grimaced to himself, grateful at least that she had stopped her wailing. After another moment, during which he felt himself shrink within her, he cleared his throat and glanced at the back of her head. "I am going to withdraw now."

She hesitated, then peered back uncertainly. "Are you not going to stir it about and plow in and out?"

Aric felt sympathy tug at him as he took in her tear-filled eyes and flushed face. As hard as this had been on him, for her it had been worse. Yet here she was, ready to allow him to continue if necessary. "I think 'twould be better if we just saved that for next time."

"Thank you." She sniffled, and he rolled his eyes, wondering if there would ever be a next time. She would probably never let him near her again. She certainly had made this about as hard on herself as she possibly could have. *Good Lord!* It hadn't exactly been a joy for him, either. Muttering under his breath, he drew himself away from her. The moment he was clear of her body, she went limp, collapsing on the bed in a heap as if he had taken her backbone with him.

Shaking his head, Aric shifted off the bed, turned, and offered her a hand, helping her to her feet when she accepted it. Once she was standing, he tore the top linen from the bed, used it to quickly clean himself of the traces of blood their merging had caused, then handed it to her and moved to the end of the bed to quickly don his clothes. He dressed with his back to her, giving her privacy to tend to her own needs, then blew out the candle, took the linen from her, held his arm out for her to place her hand on, and opened the door. They exited the room together, husband and wife, two strangers who had done what needed to be done.

Chapter 3

I'T's about damned time! What the hell did you do to my baby?"

Aric paused, drawing Rosamunde to a halt as the king suddenly blocked their path out of the room. He wasn't at all surprised by the man's ferocious scowl. He was a bit startled, however, when his young bride suddenly stepped in front of him protectively.

"Nothing, Papa," she said, then she flushed and stammered, "W-well, I mean, h-he d-did—" Turning suddenly, she grabbed the linen from Aric and shoved it at her father, saying, "He did what he was supposed to do."

King Henry's frown faded somewhat, and his face colored with slight embarrassment as the linen fell open, revealing the small stains. "Aye, well . . . Of course he did." Nodding, he handed the linen over to Bishop Shrewsbury. "There's the proof. There will be no annulment. The boy did it. For king and country, eh, lad?" he joked lamely, then cleared his throat. He took Rosamunde's arm and started abruptly up the hall, dragging her along with him and leaving the others to follow again.

He remained silent as he rushed her through the

corridors and out into the courtyard, then gestured for the others to wait there as he urged her into the stables.

"You are all right, are you not?" he asked, drawing her to a halt inside the stable doors and turning an anxious look down on her.

"Aye, of course," Rosamunde said, flushing slightly. She would die before admitting to the tenderness she was sporting between her legs.

"I am sorry it had to be so rushed. I am sorry for a lot of things," he added with a grimace. "I should have spent more time with you over the years. Visited you more often. But there was so much to do, so many problems, and time passes so quickly."

" 'Tis all right, Father. I understand," Rosamunde assured him, even managing a quirky smile. "You had a country to run."

"Aye, but you . . . Your mother . . ." Reaching out, he caressed her cheek, his eyes filling with a combination of nostalgia and grief. "You look so like her, child. At times it pains my heart to look on you." Sighing, he let his hand drop. "Had she lived . . ."

"Things would have been different," Rosamunde whispered, her throat suddenly tight.

"Very different." A single tear slipped from one of his gray eyes, and he turned abruptly away, moving into the first stall to begin to saddle the horse that waited there.

Glancing around, Rosamunde spied Bishop Shrewsbury's saddle and quickly moved to collect it. She began saddling the horse in the second stall. Leading his own horse out of its stall a moment later, Henry glanced to where she was tightening the last strap on Shrewsbury's mount and shook his head.

"You should have left that for me. You have ruined your gown."

Leading the horse into the aisle, Rosamunde glanced

down at her dress, then quickly dusted the dirt away as she paused before him. "Nay. 'Tis just in need of a cleaning."

He smiled slightly. "Would that all problems could be washed away as easily."

Eyes sharpening, Rosamunde peered worriedly at his grim face. "Things are not so bad, are they? Surely 'tis just rumor that John has joined Richard?"

"All will be well," her father assured her firmly, then caught both reins in one hand and her hand in the other. "Come, I would speak to your husband ere I go."

Aric was leaning against the convent gates, away from the others, when his wife and her father came out of the stables. He watched the king leave the horses with Shrewsbury, who waited by their bags; then he gave his daughter a gentle push toward the waiting nuns, and made straight for Aric. His sovereign came straight to the point.

"I know there was no discussion of dower, and you must fear I would deposit my daughter on you without one, but that is not the case. I value her much too highly for that. Shrews—" he began, glancing around, then paused as the other man hurried forward. "Give me the—Thank you."

Turning back to Aric with the parchment the man held out, he presented it to him. "This gives you title to Goodhall in northern England—so long as you are married to Rosamunde. Should she be widowed, the estate goes with her. And—" He turned back to the bishop again and gestured.

The cleric immediately returned to four large sacks he had been standing near. Lifting two of them, he carried them forward, handed them to King Henry, then turned away to hurry back for the other two. All four were set on the ground before Aric.

"These are listed as part of that estate. Four sacks of gold. Use them as you will, but be sure to purchase her some fine clothing. Her mother looked lovely in silver. Make sure she has a silver gown." He paused and frowned at Aric's dubious expression. "I shall not be an interfering father. I trust you will treat her fairly and well."

"Of course, my lord."

"Of course. Despite my words, I did not pick you lightly, Aric. I have considered this a long time. And I have long thought you would suit my Rosamunde. As I have always respected your father, I did not wish to break the contract he arranged for you as a child. However, I was not sorry to hear it was broken. It was fortuitous for me—and for you, too, I think."

He turned to gaze at the girl surrounded by weeping nuns, missing the expression that flashed across Aric's face. "Care well for her, Burkhart. She is my real treasure. The only thing of value I leave behind." His gaze returned to Aric. "You will come to love her quickly. She is like her mother. No man could resist her pure and gentle heart and spirit. She is all things good. She will be devoted to you. Treat her gently . . . Or else."

Spinning abruptly on his heel, the king moved back toward where he had left his daughter, leaving Aric to wonder what the "or else" entailed. It wasn't hard for him to figure out. Being drawn and quartered. Suffering the rack. Beheading. The options were endless. Dear God, Aric thought wearily. What had he gotten himself into?

King Henry scowled as he approached the flock of women surrounding his daughter. His look was enough to send most of them scurrying away. Ignoring the abbess and Sister Eustice, who refused to be frightened from her side, Henry caught Rosamunde up in a quick, fierce hug, then set her away and smiled sadly. "You grow more like your mother every time I see you. Except for your hair. That is mine." He reached out to fondle a fiery tress briefly; then his gaze sharpened on her. "Do not take the temper that goes with it out on your husband. Try always to think before you speak or act. There is much my temper has done that I would have undone. Often, once words are spoken . . ." He let the tress drop and shrugged.

"Father?" she murmured uncertainly.

Forcing a smile, Henry hugged her again. "All will be well, little one. I have picked a fine man to husband you. He will be patient and kind and caring. Be a good wife for him in return, hmm?"

"Aye, Papa."

"There's my good girl." Patting her awkwardly, he nodded, then turned to walk away. Rosamunde had the oddest feeling that it was the last time she would see him. Spurred by that sudden fear, she chased after him, hugging him from behind before he mounted his horse.

"I love you, Papa," she whispered.

Henry paused and turned in her embrace, hugging her close as well. "I love you, too, child. And so shall your husband, but you must promise me to obey him. Always. Promise?"

When he pulled back to look at her, Rosamunde nodded solemnly. "I promise, Papa."

Nodding, the king set her aside again and mounted his horse. Rosamunde watched as he rode away through the gates with Bishop Shrewsbury. He looked straight ahead as he went, never looking back. Or at least, she didn't think he did, but her vision was rather blurred with tears as she watched.

When the two horsemen finally disappeared from view over a rolling hill, she turned back to the convent yard to find only Sister Eustice and the abbess still present. The other nuns had returned to their duties, having already said their good-byes. As for the two men, she learned where they had gone the moment she paused before the abbess.

"Your husband and Lord Shambley have gone to prepare the horses to leave."

"Leave?" Rosamunde exclaimed with dismay.

"Aye. I extended an invitation to them to spend the night here, but they refused."

When Rosamunde merely stared at her with a lost expression, Adela reached out to hand her a small cloth sack. "These are your things. Eustice packed them for you. I had her put some cheese, fruit, and bread in there for the journey as well." Then she patted her hand gently. "'Twill be all right. You are frightened right now, I know, and that is to be expected, considering this abrupt change in your life, but all will be well."

The clip-clop of horses' hooves drew their attention then as her husband and Lord Robert led three horses out of the stables. Rosamunde blinked in surprise at the sight of the third horse all saddled and ready to go.

"Marigold is yours now," Sister Eustice murmured, noting her startled expression as she gazed at the horse. "A wedding gift from us. So you will not go off totally alone and friendless."

Tears filling her eyes, Rosamunde swung around and hugged first one woman, then the other. "I will miss you," she said with a gasp, then whirled away and rushed blindly toward the men and waiting horses.

Her husband quickly helped her to mount, then

turned to get onto his own horse. Taking her reins in hand with his own, he nodded at the abbess and Sister Eustice, then urged his horse into a trot that took them quickly through the convent gate.

Tears rolling down her cheeks, Rosamunde stared staunchly forward, unable to look back. She was leaving the only home she had ever known.

The abbess and Sister Eustice watched them leave with tear-filled eyes. It was Adela who finally closed the convent gate on their departing figures and urged Eustice away from the door.

"'Tis frightening sometimes, is it not?" she commented. They moved slowly back up the path.

"What?" Sister Eustice asked, brushing her tears unhappily away.

"Life," she answered solemnly. "This morning she was ours, and to be with us forever. Tonight she is gone."

Eustice paused, her expression horrified. "Surely she will visit?"

The abbess took her arm to get her walking again. "Mayhap, but she will not be our little Rosamunde now. She will be Lady Burkhart of Goodhall."

"Goodhall." Eustice tried the name out, then smiled slightly. "'Tis a fitting place for our Rosamunde."

"Aye. 'Tis fitting."

"Mayhap this was God's plan for her, after all."

"Of course it was. Everything comes about through God's plan," the abbess murmured quietly.

"Your bride does not appear to be much of a rider."

Eyebrows rising slightly, Aric peered over his shoulder at the woman trailing them. They had started out on either side of the young woman's horse. His mind awhirl with thoughts and worries about the marital state that had suddenly been thrust on him, Aric had quickly lost track of her. As soon as they had hit the trees, in fact, they had had to switch to riding single file and he had taken the lead, leaving Robert to take up the back behind his bride.

The trees had thinned out somewhat, however, and Robert had just now moved up beside Aric to murmur his comment. To say she was not much of a rider, he saw now, could in no way be interpreted as an exaggeration. If anything, it was an understatement. The woman was bouncing around upon the back of her mare like a lumpy sack, going up as the horse was down, her bottom slamming down again as the horse's back came up. It seemed that, while she might have worked daily in the stables with the animals, exercising the horses by riding them had not been a part of her duties. He would bet Goodhall Castle that she had never before even been on horseback. And while he pitied the horse she rode, it was her he was more worried about. Or, to be more specific, her bottom. If it were not sore yet, it surely would be soon, and Aric could hardly make her ride while in pain.

Noting the discomfort on her face, he frowned. He had set a mild pace at first, but had every intention of picking up the speed as soon as the trees thinned out a bit more. That was the fastest way for them to travel, since they did not yet have the benefit of his men accompanying them.

Aric supposed that the three of them could have rested the night at the convent rather than setting out at once, but he had not missed Robert's discomfort there. He himself had not felt quite at home, either. There was nothing like an abbey full of holy brides of God to make a man feel an interloping sinner. Besides, he knew Robert was worried about his father. The man had been at death's door not long ago. He had seemed to improve just before the king's arrival, but had not yet been out of the woods long enough to make them comfortable. He knew his friend would prefer to return as promptly as possible.

Of course, the distraction of traveling also helped Aric ignore the fact that his entire life had just taken a decided turn. For better or worse, he was not yet sure, and until he was, he was more than happy to delay having to face the fact. So he had decided upon an immediate return. Unfortunately, it was not to be a comfortable ride. Without their men, they had to depend on speed to make the trip safe. The roads were full of bandits and thieves who were more than happy to prey on the weak. Two men and a woman traveling alone would be attractive prey, especially nobles.

He had intended to ride hard and fast, trading back at the stables for the horses they had exchanged on the way out and traveling through the night to reach Shambley the following morn. That was when he had assumed that his wife had been trained properly in all things. Now he realized that he had assumed too much. The girl had obviously not been taught to ride. He wondered briefly what other training had been neglected, then shrugged such worries away. Her lack of skills would matter little if he did not get her home unscathed, which he might not do at this pace. Unfortunately, it was becoming obvious he could not force her to a faster gait. She would bounce right off her mount.

But this would not do.

Muttering under his breath, Aric reined his horse in and turned him back toward his wife. She hid her pain at once and sat up straighter in the saddle, doing her best to appear a proficient rider. Impossible, the way she was jostling about, Aric thought, but he merely nodded at her politely as he reached her side.

Without a word, he reached out, hooked her around the waist, and scooped her off her mare with one hand, while taking the reins of her mount from her suddenly slack grip with the other. Urging his horse forward, he tossed the reins of the now riderless mare to Robert, then set off at a gallop. Rosamunde, emitting a surprised gasp, said nothing, much to his relief. He had no desire to make explanations or to argue. He was tired and likely to be much more so ere he reached Shambley.

Rosamunde swallowed and shifted carefully within her husband's arms until she was comfortable. Part of her wanted to protest riding with him, wished to retain her mount, and with it her independence. The other part, mostly her bottom, was grateful. Her husband's horse seemed to have a much smoother gait. It seemed Marigold was a very poor mount. On top of that, the jostling just seemed to irritate the residual tenderness she was feeling between her legs.

Recalling the promise to obey that she had made to her father, she decided that this was an instance where she should and relaxed, her back easing unconsciously against her new husband's chest. It was not yet the supper hour, yet she was already terribly drained. She was tired enough to sleep as they rode, she realized with surprise, then recalled that she had been up through the night midwifing a mare. That explained her exhaustion. She could only hope that they would stop soon for the night, else she very much feared that she might fall asleep where she sat.

Aric slowed his horse at Robert's whistle and waited for him to catch up. The trio had been riding for many hours now, and it was well past the supper hour. The sun was setting, night creeping in. His wife had been asleep since shortly after he had taken her onto his horse. She lay nestled in his arms, her head resting beneath his chin, her hands tangling themselves in his cloak. The dying rays of daylight were dancing in her fiery tresses, casting shadows on her ivory skin. She felt warm, like sunshine in his arms, though, and smelled faintly of roses.

"She did not last long."

Robert's words drew Aric's gaze to his friend. Weariness rimmed the man's eyes and had brought a pallor to his face. Still, he smiled slightly as he commented, "If possible, she seems more exhausted than we are."

"So it would seem," Aric agreed, glancing down at Rosamunde's slumbering face. Even their voices were not making her stir. She was as still as death. If it were not for the fact that he could feel the heat of her, he might have feared for her life. "It would seem that she has not inherited her father's energetic fortitude."

"Mayhap," Robert murmured, then added, "But as I recall, she did tell our king that the mare had been in labor for two days and a night. Mayhap she was up through the night in attendance."

Aric nodded thoughtfully. That was quite possible, and would explain both her weariness and the costume she'd been wearing when first he'd seen her.

"Think you we should stop for the night?"

Aric glanced at his friend sharply, startled by the question. He had expected to ride out the night. His bride could sleep in his arms the entire way, if necessary. He knew Robert wished to return as swiftly as possible.

"I, too, am tired," his friend explained wryly. "Too many nights spent by my father's sickbed, or worrying the twilight hours away pacing below stairs, combined with the two-day ride to the abbey, are beginning to wear on me. I am ready to drop off in my saddle as well, and I know I am not as alert as I should be to guard against attack."

Aric glanced down at his bride once more. Truth be told, he, too, was exhausted, and he supposed that he was not very alert either. A night of rest might be better than risking being attacked while they were both in such a depleted state. Glancing back at his friend, he nodded. "We shall stop at the first spot that looks a likely haven."

Smiling wearily, Robert urged his horse out in front and took over the lead, his eyes eagerly scanning the land they crossed. A little more than an hour later they had reached a good site, a clearing on the edge of the river.

Rosamunde did not awake. Not when Aric drew his mount to a halt; not when he passed her gently down into Robert's waiting arms so that he himself could dismount; nor when he took her back and laid her gently on the cloak Robert hurriedly whipped off and spread on the ground.

The two knights did not bother with food. After tending the horses, they took the time only to get a small fire going, working together to accomplish the deed. Then, with silent, but mutual consent, they moved to lie down, one on either side of Rosamunde. Both were asleep almost at once.

It was a terrible storm. Rosamunde could tell that before she even opened her eyes. The thunder was rumbling, snorting, and grunting with deafening loudness. She had never heard it so, and was amazed when she opened her eyes and it was not already raining. She herself was as dry as dust where she lay. Where was she?

Not in her bed.

Not in the convent.

On the ground.

With a roof of trees overhead, their leaves and branches black against the slightly lighter sky.

A rustle from somewhere to her right drew her suddenly wary gaze, and she peered past the body beside her into the darkness beyond. Nothing moved that she could tell, but then no matter how she strained her eyes in an effort to see, she could not make out much, only still black shapes that may have been bushes and trees.

The resounding roll of thunder came again, and Rosamunde gave a start where she lay, her attention drawn to the source of the sound: the body on her right. Her *husband*! Or was it his friend? She could not be sure in this light. The body was just a great hulk of blackness in the night as he snuffled and snorted and shifted restlessly in sleep.

She hoped it was her husband's friend, for if it was her husband, she could foresee a future of restless nights. Used to having her own bed—not to mention her own room, no matter how small it had been—Rosamunde did not think she could tolerate such raucous noise in her marriage bed.

Snnrrr-kgle!

She nearly jumped out of her skin when those first thunderous snores from her right were echoed, this time from her left. Her head swiveling on the ground, she peered wide-eyed with horror at the body lying there, another hulk of darkness. It was almost indistinguishable from the first. She had noticed at the convent that the two friends were of a similar size. She sighed. It seemed they also had a similar inclination to snuffle in their sleep like pigs nosing in the dirt for food.

Sighing, Rosamunde closed her eyes and begged the

good Lord for patience. Her inclination, as the men again began their thunderous snores, was to sit up and sock them both. But she tempered that instinct. Such was not the way of a nun. And while she had not taken the veil, she would be as good, patient, and pious as if she had. Was that not what a man wished for in a bride? According to Father Abernott, it was the kind of bride God preferred, and surely what was good enough for God was good enough for her snorting husband. Whichever one he was.

She had just come to that conclusion when the man on her right suddenly shifted about in his deep sleep and tossed one heavy leg over her. It was followed by an arm snaking out to catch her at the waist and cuddle her closer. Its owner muttered something that ended with "lovey."

For a moment she did not even breathe. She was almost afraid to. She had no idea which of the two men was presently mauling her, but she hoped to God it was her husband, for whoever it was had his hand firmly closed over one of her breasts. His face was nestled against the other.

This would not do. This would not do at all.

Discomfort in her chest made her realize that she was well on the way to suffocating herself, and Rosamunde forced herself to release the breath she had been holding and suck in fresh air.

Oh, dear, oh, dear, oh, dear. What to do?

If she were sure it was her husband, she supposed she would not have to do anything except to continue to lie here, uncomfortably still, and wait for him to remove himself. Even if he was doing what Sister Eustice had warned her against. However, she was not sure it *was* her husband, and there was no way for her to be sure in the darkness that enveloped them.

How would it look if it were Robert and her husband

awoke to discover them in such a state? *Nay.* This would not do at all. Biting her lip, she peered over at the dark shape that was his face. He was nuzzling her breast through her gown in a distressingly familiar fashion. It was terribly discomforting for her.

Easing her arm out from where he lay upon it, she raised it awkwardly around his back and tickled with a feathery touch at what she guessed to be the back of his neck.

The man stirred slightly, releasing her breast to brush irritably at his neck.

Rosamunde was able to remove her hand in time to avoid the swat, but repeated the action as soon as he returned his hand to her chest. He immediately swatted at his neck again, but this time followed by rolling away from her.

Rosamunde heaved a sigh, but quickly realized that her relief may have been premature. He was off of her chest, which was grand, but he was now lying flat-backed across her arm, covering it from just below her shoulder to her fingertips. She was trapped.

Muttering one of Sister Eustice's favorite expletives, she turned onto her side and slowly, gently, carefully eased her arm out from beneath, managing to do so without waking the man.

Another round of snores erupted on either side of her, and Rosamunde sat up abruptly before she could be rolled up on again. Moving carefully to avoid accidentally waking either man, she got to her feet and eased cautiously out from between them.

This time when she heaved a sigh of relief, it came from her very toes.

Aric shifted where he lay, his nose twitching, a smile gracing his lips. He could swear that the scent of meat grilling over an open fire was teasing his nose. But it could not be. He must be dreaming. It was very hot where he lay, and the night had been cool.

Blinking his eyes open, he stared at the bright sunlit sky above, then jerked to an upright position with a curse. It was full daylight. The sun was already a quarter of the way across the sky. He had overslept. Impossible. Why had his friend not awakened him?

A glance to the side answered that question: Robert was asleep. But he also saw that the redhead he had married the day before was not.

A frantic survey of the clearing showed that a bonfire raged several feet away. That was why he'd been so hot! And the scent of roasting meat had not been a dream; the meat was rabbit, and it had been killed, cleaned, and impaled on a branch that was presently suspended between two Y-shaped branches over the fire. His wife, however, was nowhere in sight.

Reaching out, he shook Shambley. "Robert, wake up. Damn!"

Aric was on his feet, sword in hand. Robert rolled sleepily over to peer up at him. "What is—" He blinked. "It's full morning!"

"Aye," Aric agreed grimly, turning slowly, scanning the surrounding trees.

"Jesu! How did we oversleep so?"

"We were overtired."

"Aye, but—what are you looking for?"

"My wife."

Robert's eyes widened at Aric's terse words, his gaze dropping to the bare ground beside him. "Where did she go?"

"That is what I am trying to discover," Aric snapped impatiently, stilling at the sound of someone thrashing their way toward them through the brush.

Robert was on his feet and at his side in a trice. Swords at the ready, back to back, the knights prepared to confront whatever approached. They both sagged with relief as Rosamunde stepped out of the woods.

She had changed into brais and a loose tunic, and pulled her hair back from her face, securing it in a ponytail at the base of her neck. Her face was dirt-and soot-smudged, her hands scratched and filthy, and her arms, where her sleeves were rolled up, were streaked with dirt. She was carrying a huge stack of wood, made up mostly of small-and medium-sized branches she had gathered. She beamed on seeing them awake and about.

"Good morn, my lords," she called out with disgusting good cheer. "Did you sleep well?"

Robert smiled sheepishly at the question, but Aric's lips tightened grimly as he took her in. "What have you done?"

Rosamunde's sure steps faltered near the fire, confusion covering her face. "My lord?"

Aric gestured toward the roaring blaze at the center of the clearing, and Rosamunde's eyebrows rose.

"The fire you built last night died," she explained uncertainly. "So I—"

"Created an inferno?"

Rosamunde swallowed at his cold voice. He sounded furious. "I—"

"I am surprised that this forest fire you made has not drawn every bandit and thief in Anglia to us. Certainly the smoke billowing above the trees is enough to get their attention and lead them here. Why did you not simply climb up a tree and shout, 'Here we are! Come kill and rob us!' "

Rosamunde paled at his words. Letting the wood she held drop to the ground, she moved quickly to kick dirt onto the fire, doing her best to kill the flames. "I am sorry, my lord. I did not think. I was sitting about waiting for you to awaken and I got the idea to catch and cook something to take with us for our lunch and—"

"That is another thing," Aric interrupted grumpily. "Getting us killed by bandits was not enough. You then decided to lure every wild dog and wolf for miles with the smell of cooking meat."

"Aric!" Robert placed a restraining hand on his friend's arm.

"What?" Aric snapped impatiently.

In contrast, Robert nearly whispered his own words. "Surely there is no need to be so harsh?"

"Am I wrong?"

"Nay. There is truth to your accusations," he admitted quietly. "But Lady Rosemunde obviously was not aware of it. Would you speak so to a new squire should he make a like error?"

Aric frowned at that reasoning, then let his shoulders relax. He sighed. Shambley was right, of course. Rosamunde could not have known these things. How could she? It was doubtful she had ever even left the abbey ere this, let alone camped outside and learned the dangers that lurked beyond the convent's walls. Yet he had attacked her as if she had deliberately set out to get them killed. He would never have been so sharp and impatient with a new squire.

It did not take much soul-searching to recognize the real source of his anger. He was embarrassed at his own carelessness. Not only had he overslept, but he had slept through the racket she must have caused by finishing all those tasks in the clearing that morning.

She had chased, caught, killed skinned, and cleaned a rabbit, then built a roaring fire to cook it over, and fashioned a makeshift spit. She had even moved the horses to another spot with fresher grass. Yet even the jangling of the horses' harnesses had not stirred him. He was a warrior. Such sounds should have awakened him.

Good Lord! Had she been one of those bandits he had been snarling at her about only moments before, they would all be dead. So much for his sworn oath to the king, her father, to protect her!

It did not salve his conscience that Robert, too, had slept through her activities. He was not the one who had sworn an oath to the king. Worse, Aric was angry with himself, and he had taken it out on her.

Sighing, he nodded at last at Robert to reassure him that not only had he heard his words, he heeded them. He turned to apologize to the woman who was now his wife, but instead squawked her name in dismay. "Rosamunde!"

She was on her knees beside the fire, her back to them, her bottom—snug in tight brais—in the air and pointed in their direction. It had been bobbing gently up and down as she worked at something he could not see, but she had shifted slightly just before he shrieked. Now her behind was still, her whole body gone stiff.

Glaring at Robert—a grin had suddenly covered his friend's face at the vision Rosamunde was thoughtlessly presenting them—Aric hurried over to block his friend's view of her derriere. Pausing, he took a moment to attempt to rein his reawakened temper in, then leaned over her slightly to peer down at what occupied her. "What are you doing?" he tried to ask calmly.

Rosamunde winced at the harshness of his voice. Aric was intimidating enough when he was bellowing and roaring at her from across the clearing, but now he was looming over her like murder, his body a dark cloud that cast her in shadow as he scowled down at her. She supposed she deserved his ire, though. It *had* been foolish of her to build such a huge fire. Cooking the rabbit was another mistake. As soon as she had understood that, she had moved to correct her error. Grabbing the stick the meat was impaled on, she had dropped to her knees beside the fire, set the rabbit on the ground, and quickly dug a small hole. She had laid the rabbit in the hole, and was in the process of burying it when her husband's voice had interrupted her.

Quickly raising a hand, she wiped furiously at the tears leaking from her eyes. It was foolish to cry. Tears solved nothing. Knowing that, Rosamunde rarely ever did, but just now she was unable to help herself. It seemed she could do nothing right. First the fire, then the meal . . . Burying the rabbit to stop the smell was probably wrong, too. The way her luck was working that morning, she had probably set the horses to graze in a field of nightshade and they would be dead by noon.

"I am burying the rabbit to hide its scent, my lord," she explained herself quietly.

"Nay. Do not do that," her husband protested, kneeling beside her and quickly catching at her hands as she would have thrown more dirt on the meat. When she stilled, but refused to raise her face to look at him, he sighed and made his tone gentler. "Forgive me. I am as grumpy as a bear when I wake up. I should not have yelled so. I should have realized you could not have known about the dangers out here, and been more patient. Instead I was over harsh and am sorry for that. Forgive me?"

Her tension easing, Rosamunde nodded, but still would not look at him.

Aric released her hands and tugged the rabbit out of its would-be grave. "Let us see if we cannot rescue this."

"But what about the dogs and wolves?" she glanced up in surprise.

Aric took in the drying tears on her face with self-disgust. He had caused those. He was not doing very well as a husband so far. He had protected her as poorly as a shield made of stale bread, and treated her with less kindness than he would a new squire. This was most likely not what the king had intended when giving her into Aric's care.

Forcing a smile, he shrugged slightly. "Aye, well, 'tis not just the four-legged variety of beast its scent would tempt, but the two-legged as well, and I am one of those. It smelled delicious and nearly finished. Is it?"

"Aye," she admitted with a sigh.

"So with the fire out, the scent will no longer carry on the wind. There is no sense in letting this excellent fare be wasted." Even as he spoke, he began to brush the dirt from the rapidly cooling meat. "How long have you been awake?"

Watching dubiously as he brushed at the rabbit, she shrugged distractedly. "I am not sure. A couple of hours or more, I should think. It was still dark when I awoke."

"You are an early riser."

"Everyone rose early at the abbey."

"Hmm." Standing, he went to the river's edge and submerged the meat in the clear water, giving it a quick swish back and forth to remove the worst of the dirt. Dangling it from one hand, he turned it this way and that for a quick inspection, then nodded in satisfaction. "Good as new."

Rosamunde eyed first the meat, then her husband doubtfully, but said little as he returned to the fire and dangled the mistreated meal over the few glowing embers that remained of her once glorious fire. He turned it about over them briefly, then turned to her with a grin, holding the meat out as if making a grand offering.

"Cleaned and dried, madam, and perfect for our consumption."

After a brief hesitation, Rosamunde accepted the meat. She peered at it closely as Aric moved off to have a word with his friend. Amazing, she thought, and shook her head. The wild herbs and spices she had found, shredded, and cooked onto the meat had all been rubbed or washed away, but most of the dirt seemed still to cling to it. She had no idea how he had managed that. Still, mayhap that was how he liked it.

Smiling in mild disgust, she moved to pack the meat away until the nooning meal, deciding as she did that she would stick with the fresh fruits and bread that Sister Eustice had thoughtfully packed away for them to take. If they wished it, the men could eat the rabbit.

Chapter 4

"DELICIOUS!"

"Aye, the best I have ever tasted."

"I am delighted you are pleased, my lords," Rosamunde murmured, biting the inside of her lips to prevent her amusement from bubbling out. It was difficult to take their praise of the rabbit she had cooked seriously when they kept pausing to spit out bits of stone and dirt. The men were just trying to be kind. They had been nauseatingly nice ever since setting out that morning.

Rosamunde had ridden on Aric's mount with him again. As had happened the day before, he did not ask or invite; he merely mounted, took his reins in one hand, and leaned over to scoop her up with the other. And as she had the day before, Rosamunde had held her tongue. But it had been harder this time. Her tenderness from the day before was gone now, and she was not used to being coddled. There was very little coddling in a convent. Rosamunde had learned to be self-reliant at a young age, and while she disliked the discomfort of riding her own mount, she did appreciate the independence. Still, she had kept her silence, attempting to maintain her vow to her father to obey her husband.

She had not said a word all morning as they had

ridden. Mostly she had spent the time dividing her gaze between the passing scenery and watching Robert's horse. She had thought when they had first set out that the horse was favoring one of its legs, but after watching him for a moment, she had decided that she must have been mistaken. Still, she had glanced over at the beast every once in a while to be sure. Other than that there had been little to distract her attention, and she had been about to burst with boredom by the time Aric had called a halt to their journey and announced it time to stop for some of the "fine rabbit" she had cooked for their lunch.

Now they sat, companionably eating. Neither man seemed to notice that she had forgone the rabbit and stuck with the provisions Eustice had packed. She supposed they were too busy digging dirt out of their own meals.

Grimacing and spitting out another small stone, Robert chewed and swallowed the meat that remained in his mouth, then raised an eyebrow at Aric. "As I recall, 'tis only another hour or so ere we reach the next village."

"Aye. I thought to trade the horses there."

Rosamunde stilled suddenly. She had not really been listening to the conversation, but those words caught her attention. "Trade the horses?"

"Aye," Aric answered as he brushed a clod of dirt off the meat into which he had been about to bite. It seemed he had not cleaned the hare as thoroughly as he had thought that morning. He had not managed one bite of the meal without at least half of it tasting of grit. It served him right, he supposed. He had behaved in a beastly fashion that morning. Mayhap it was justice that he eat a lunch fit for nothing but swine.

"Nay!"

Aric stilled at his wife's dismayed cry, turning away

from his meal to peer at her. She went on: "Nay, my lord. You cannot trade my Marigold. She was a gift from the abbess. You cannot trade away a gift."

Aric blinked at her ferocious expression in surprise, but it was Robert who asked gently, "Marigold?"

"My horse. Her name is Marigold." She stood impatiently. "I named her. In fact I saw her into this world. 'Tis why the abbess wished to give her to me. We have a special bond. You cannot trade her in, my lords."

Robert glanced at his friend, frowning slightly at Aric's, blank expression as he eyed his wife, then explained gently, "We must travel quickly, my lady. 'Tis too hard on the horses to travel night and day without rest. We must trade them."

"But Marigold was a *gift*. She is mine. 'Sides," she added, realizing that an emotional appeal might have little effect. "They rested last night while we slept."

The two men exchanged a glance; then Robert murmured, "We did rest quite a while."

"Aye, but we have also ridden them hard all morn."

"Only a couple of hours, really," he argued. "We slept late if you will recall."

"Aye." Frowning, Aric thought it over briefly, then acquiesced. "All right. We will trade only our horses. You may keep Marigold for now. She has been riderless most of the way, anyway."

"Thank you, my lord," Rosamunde whispered, real gratitude in her eyes. She beamed at him before getting quickly to her feet and hurrying over to offer her precious horse the apple she had been about to eat.

"Marigold," Robert murmured the name with amusement. "Only a woman would name a horse after a flower."

"Aye." Aric watched his wife as she held the fruit out for the horse to take a bite, then heaved a sigh. "We shall have to trade her in eventually. Even riderless 'twould be cruel to force the beast to travel night and day till we reach Shambley. I am afraid we have merely delayed her upset."

Robert was silent for a moment; then he murmured, "We could always stop for the night again tonight. Allow her horse to rest."

Aric glanced at him sharply. "I thought you wished to travel as quickly as possible to get back and ensure that your father is still on the mend?"

Robert avoided his eyes and shrugged. "No doubt he is up and about by now. He always was a quick healer."

Aric watched him narrowly. Something was up. He could tell. What was his friend keeping from him?

After a moment of withstanding his suspicious gaze, Robert sighed and admitted, "I am not all that eager to return."

"Oh?"

"Aye. Just ere he fell ill, my father was beginning to take on about my fulfilling my own betrothal contract."

"Ah." Aric grinned. "And you fear that when you return he will bring it up again."

"Bring it up?" Robert gave a short laugh. "After an illness that almost took his life before he could see those blasted grandchildren he is always carping about, and upon seeing your new bride, he will harp on me endlessly." He sighed. "A delay of a day or two will not be a trial for me."

"Hmm." Aric peered back at his wife. The horse had finished the apple. Chattering cheerfully to the animal, Rosamunde petted its mane soothingly. Mayhap they could risk another night out in the open. The horse *had* been a gift, after all, he thought. His bride now turned her attention to Robert's mount, apparently to give it some attention, too.

* * *

Rosamunde shifted to a more comfortable position and sighed. It was several hours since they had stopped for the nooning meal. It seemed like forever that they had been traveling. Rosamunde had never been so bored in her life. It had been interesting at first, she supposed. The excitement of new experience, the beauty of the scenery and so on . . . but it had not enthralled her for long. Besides, Rosamunde was not used to being silent for such an extended period. The only time silence had been required at the abbey was during meals, and then there had been amusing little hand gestures that they had used to communicate.

Sighing, she glanced surreptitiously up at her husband's face from beneath her eyelashes. He sat stiff and straight-shouldered in the saddle, his eyes alert and flying over the terrain they passed, his face grim and serious. Neither he nor his friend, Robert, had exchanged a word since setting out upon this journey, except for their brief conversation when they had stopped to eat. And Rosamunde, too, had been equally silent. Mostly because, should she try to speak, she was likely to bite her own tongue off at this pace they were riding. Probably that was why the men were so silent as well. At least she hoped that was why. She did not wish to believe her husband was always so taciturn.

Husband. She marveled at the title that now belonged to the stranger in whose arms she rode. A stranger who had many rights and privileges over her. Her *husband.* She had never thought to have one. Never even considered the possibility. *Dear Lord.* Her life had certainly taken a different path than she had expected. She pondered that rather dazedly and was still doing so when they stopped for the night some time later. It kept her quiet as she was lowered to the ground so that her husband could dismount.

Without waiting to see what he would do, Rosamunde immediately moved to attend to her horse, automatically going through the grooming functions that were necessary even as the men began to tend to their own beasts. She had removed the mare's saddle and begun brushing her horse down when she noticed how skittish Robert's horse was.

Appearing distracted, the man continued to wipe down the beast, then left it to graze, moving off to begin gathering wood for a fire. Aric finished with his own mount and went to help in making the preparations for the night ahead. But Rosamunde was working much more slowly, her attention divided between her task and Robert's horse. The steed was not eating, though he should have been hungry.

Recalling her concern that the horse might have been favoring a leg earlier, Rosamunde finished with Marigold and moved to the other horse's side, soothing the creature with gentle words as she began to examine him.

"Is something amiss, my lady?"

Rosamunde paused at that curious question from Robert as he approached. He had stacked the firewood in the center of the spot they had chosen, but had not set it afire yet. There were still a few last dying rays of light left, and, as she had learned that morning, it was not safe to have a fire until darkness arrived. That helped hide the smoke it gave off.

"Aye," Rosamunde murmured grimly, straightening from examining the horse's hind legs. "This horse is ill. He has the lockjaw, I think."

Frowning, Robert peered at the animal, then raised a hand toward the beast's snout, his eyebrows rising when the horse immediately shook its head nervously and took a step back. Rosamunde tugged gently on the reins she held and murmured soothingly, caressing its powerful shoulders. She had been prepared for that reaction. It was the same one she had received on examining him.

"I think you may be right," he agreed with amazement as he peered at the horse's tightly closed mouth. "Aric!" he called, as the second man returned to the clearing with more branches. "Come here. My horse is ailing."

Setting the branches down by the others, Aric moved to join them. "What is it?"

"Rosamunde thinks 'tis the lockjaw."

His eyebrows rising, Aric performed the same action Robert had, and the animal pulled his head up and back at once. "It could be. What makes you think—?"

"He shied away every time Robert got too close to his head while preparing him for the night, then would not eat or drink with your horse, though he must be starved."

Aric peered at the horse consideringly. "Still, it could be—"

"There is also a festering scratch on his hindquarters. And look at his eyes."

Sighing, Aric grimaced. "The lockjaw."

"Aye," Robert agreed unhappily. "I shall see to it."

Taking the reins, he led the horse silently into the forest. Rosamunde watched them go silently, then turned to Marigold, giving her a soothing pat. Whether it was meant to soothe Marigold or herself, she was not sure. Robert was going to kill the horse. He had no choice. The lockjaw would kill the animal, but in its own good time, and not until after subjecting the poor beast to horrendously painful muscle spasms and starvation. It was cruel to do anything but put the animal down. She knew that. Still, it was hard to accept.

"It looks as if Marigold will have a rider on the morrow."

"Aye," Rosamunde murmured solemnly.

Aric shifted slightly; he could see that she was upset about Robert's mount but knew not how to comfort her. " 'Twill be for only a little ways."

She glanced at him curiously, and he explained, "We are little more than half an hour from the village we first traded our mounts at. They are keeping them for us to collect on the way back. He will most likely ride his own mount from there."

"I see."

Nodding, Aric glanced away, then turned irritably toward the fire. "Come. I will build a fire; 'tis dark enough now and there is a chill in the air this night."

Sighing, Rosamunde followed him back to the camp. Seating herself on a handy log, she reached automatically for the small sack that contained the last of the rabbit meat, bread, cheese, and fruit they had. Her ears straining to hear any telltale sounds from the woods around them, she began to unpack the meal as her husband started the promised fire.

It was quite a while before Robert returned. His expression was grim when he did. Rosamunde felt a twinge of sympathy. The task he had performed would not have been an easy one. She remained silent as they began to eat, but once finished, she began to get fidgety. The men were both silent, staring into the fire with similarly thoughtful expressions, but Rosamunde was ready to go insane from the lack of activity. First she'd bobbed quietly about on a horse's back all day, now this. It was drawing on her nerves.

"What is the matter?"

Rosamunde stiffened, her nervous shifting coming to a halt at her husband's rather annoyed question. Sneaking a quick peek at his face, she grimaced, then cleared her throat. "Not a thing, my lord. What would make you think that there was anything wrong?"

"You keep sighing."

"Do I?" Frowning slightly, she shifted and started to sigh again, then caught herself. "Where are we headed, my lord?" she blurted, almost desperate for conversation.

"To Shambley."

Rosamunde accepted those words with interest. "Why?"

"To collect my men."

"Oh," she murmured. "Then where shall we go?"

"To Goodhall."

"Is that where you live?"

"'Tis where *we* shall live," he corrected. "It is your dower land."

"It is?"

"Aye."

The silence closed in around them again and Rosamunde sighed. Her husband *was* the taciturn sort, it seemed. *Wonderful.* Glancing to the river that ran along the side of the clearing, she searched her mind for something to discuss. "Where is it you are from, my lord?"

"Kinsley."

"Where is that?"

"Northern England."

"Is that where your family lives?"

"Aye."

Rosamunde frowned at the answer. He wasn't very forthcoming with information. "Do your parents still live?"

"My father does."

Rosamunde waited for him to expound on that. When he remained silent, she asked, "Have you any brothers or sisters?"

"One brother. Two sisters."

"Older or younger?"

"Older brother. Younger sisters."

Rosamunde waited again, then decided to give up. His closemouthed behavior was very trying. Perhaps his brusqueness was because he was tired. Traveling was a bit wearying. It was *annoying* to her, at any rate. All that dust kicking up at her. And after this second day of travel she felt as if she had rolled on the ground. Dirt and grit seemed melted into her very skin.

Her gaze moved toward the river, this time with a touch of longing. All that water. It would have been nice to have a bath. Of course, that was impossible out in the open. There was no tub to fill, or even pails with which to fill one.

Aric raised his eyebrows questioningly when Robert nudged him. When the other man gestured, he glanced toward his wife to see her staring at the river with yearning. His gaze took in the slow-moving water. He debated within himself briefly, then decided. "Would you like to bathe?"

Rosamunde sat up straight at that question, her eyes widening. "Could I?"

Aric shrugged. "I do not see why not."

Her mouth widened into a glorious smile. She fairly beamed at him. "That would be lovely."

Aric blinked and nearly smiled back, then caught himself and stood abruptly. "Come along then."

Standing eagerly, Rosamunde followed him to the river's edge, then along it for a distance until they were out of sight of the camp they had made. When he stopped suddenly, she stopped as well. She peered at him questioningly.

"Go ahead," Aric murmured, crossing his arms over

his chest and leaning back against the nearest tree to wait patiently.

"Go ahead and what?" she asked slowly.

"Go ahead and bathe."

Rosamunde turned, surveying the area. "Where?" she asked with bewilderment.

Aric frowned at her obtuse behavior. "In the river."

"Outside? In the open?"

His eyebrows lifted at her horrified expression; then he recalled that she had just come from an abbey full of nuns. Women had raised her, and he doubted very much if the good sisters were much into skinny-dipping. Proper baths were probably the only kind they had.

Sighing, he straightened. "I would supply a tub if I could. Unfortunately, while traveling, one has to make do with what is available. The water will be colder than you are most likely used to, and you will have to use my cape for a towel, but there is no one to see, and you will be able to wash the dust away."

Rosamunde simply stood where she was, silent. She had never bathed in a river. She had never bathed outside the abbey at all. Once a month all the nuns took their turn in the tub the abbess had placed permanently in an empty cell. The rest of the time they made do with standing washes—unless they fell into the mud or a pile of dung, or somehow managed to make a mess of themselves. Usually, though, only Rosamunde and Eustice did that. They tended to end up having a bath once or twice a week due to one calamity or another. Still, she had never bathed out in the open before. The abbess would not think it was proper. It would be lovely to clean off all of the dust and dirt from their travels, though.

When his wife continued simply to stand silent and

still, contemplating the water, Aric shifted impatiently and turned back the way they had come. "Well, if you are not going to bathe, we may as well return to—"

"Oh, no, wait. Please." Rosamunde grabbed his arm to stop him, then released it and stepped back shyly as he turned to face her. "I should like a bath."

He was silent for a moment, then nodded and returned to the tree he had leaned against before. "Hurry up, then," he ordered gruffly, recrossing his arms.

Rosamunde glanced from him to the water, then back. "Did you intend to watch, my lord?" she asked at last.

"Of course. 'Tis my job to watch over you."

"Aye, but—Well . . . You . . ."

He arched one eyebrow, amusement tugging at his lips. "Shy?"

Much to his fascination her whole face was transformed with the fire of sudden temper; then she turned her face away briefly. When she turned back, her expression was flat again. "Proper," she corrected him grimly. "I was raised properly, my lord. Proper does not include stripping down to bathe before strangers."

"I am your husband."

She stilled at that solemn and quiet reminder. He *was* her husband. He had every right to watch her bathe. He had a right to a lot more than that. Bathing suddenly seemed a lot less attractive. Perhaps she was not so dusty after all. "I will wait," she decided meekly.

Shrugging, Aric turned back toward camp and led the way.

Rosamunde cast one last longing look at the river, then followed him.

Robert's eyebrows rose in surprise as they returned to camp. "What? Did you not take a bath after all?"

Flushing, Rosamunde dropped onto the log she had occupied earlier. "I decided I was too tired to be bothered," she lied, too embarrassed to explain her own reticence. Realizing that Aric had not reclaimed his spot by the fire, Rosamunde glanced over her shoulder to see him spreading his cape out on the ground. Once it was spread to his satisfaction, he lay on the far edge of it and relaxed.

"What are you doing?" she asked curiously.

"Going to sleep."

Rosamunde gaped at him. "Already?" she asked in dismay, too distressed to remember that she had just claimed to be too exhausted to bathe.

Aric noticed and started to smile, but caught it back, keeping his expression solemn and his eyes closed as he answered. "We are setting out at dawn on the morrow."

Her eyebrows rose at that. "Why so early?"

Aric scowled. Wives were not to question husbands. Did she not know that? It would seem not, he decided when she repeated the question a little louder, as if he might not have heard her the first time. He supposed, should he not answer her, she would shout her words a third time.

Opening his eyes, he lifted his head to give her a look. The expression was to inform her that he really need not explain himself, but was humoring her. He said, "Because."

"Because why?" she persisted.

Scowling, he closed his eyes and let his head drop back to the ground. "Because I just said so."

Scowling, Rosamunde glanced toward Robert as he stood, stretched, then moved to lay out his own cape beside Aric's. "Are you going to sleep, too?" she asked with dismay.

"Dawn comes early," he said with an apologetic smile.

Rosamunde frowned at that, then glanced toward her husband as he spoke again.

"Come to bed."

She scowled at the order. The abbess was the only person who got away with such peremptory behavior. And her father, of course. "No, thank you. I am not yet tired."

"Rosamunde."

"Aye?"

"It was not a request."

She glared at him briefly, considering refusing to obey what had obviously been an order, but then sighed. He was her husband. And she had promised her father to try to obey him. Unfortunately.

Muttering under her breath, she stood and made her way resentfully to where the two men lay. Robert had overlapped Aric's cloak with his own and settled himself on the opposite edge of the two garments. He left the center space for her, she supposed. It was a very small space. They must think her tiny.

Grimacing, she managed to wedge herself between the two knights. It helped when both of them shifted onto their sides, facing each other across her body, to give her more room. Stretching out as much as she could on her back, she stared up at the stars above.

Aric felt the arm next to his own moving gently and frowned, his eyes opening to see that Robert, too, had noticed it. His eyes were open as well, and their gazes met across his wife's gently bobbing body, then they both glanced downward to see her right foot wagging away.

They glanced at each other again, eyebrows arching,

then to her scrunched-up face. She was squinting up at the sky with displeasure.

Clearing his throat, Aric waited until Rosamunde glanced at him, then asked, "What *are* you doing?"

"Looking at the stars."

"No. With your foot. What are you doing with your foot?" he clarified.

Rosamunde blinked, then glanced blankly down at her foot.

"It was wagging," her husband explained dryly, aware that it had stopped as soon as she had turned to peer at him.

"Oh." Rosamunde smiled at him meekly. "Sometimes it does that before I go to sleep," she murmured. It was something she did not even notice anymore. It was a habit she had seemed always to have had. The action tended to soothe her to sleep when she was not really tired. Like now. Despite having risen ere the dawn and ridden all day, she was not tired. Rosamunde tended to need little sleep. It was a trait she had inherited from her father. Four or five hours was all she needed a night.

"Well, do not do it tonight," Aric ordered, then closed his eyes.

Rosamunde made a face at him and stuck her tongue out. A movement from her other side made her glance toward Robert to see amusement on his face. He had obviously witnessed her childish actions. Feeling herself blush in the darkness, she quickly turned her face upward and peered once again at the sky. She was still staring at it several minutes later when the first snores disturbed the peaceful night.

The first one to snore was her husband, the sound a loud, ominous rumble that made her stiffen where she lay. It seemed louder even than it had been that morning, but that might be because he was now lying on his side, facing her, his mouth only inches away, his breath tickling her ear with each exhalation. He followed the first snore with half a dozen or so more before Robert suddenly erupted into an answering rumble from her other side.

Sighing, Rosamunde closed her eyes and tried to pretend she was deaf.

Chapter 5

Is that Shambley?"

Aric glanced irritably at the top of Rosamunde's head as she sat before him. Everything about her seemed to annoy him today. It had started that morning. Despite having awakened ere the dawn, as he had intended, his wife had already been up and gone.

After rousing Robert, he had gotten to his feet and quickly reclaimed the sword that had lain at his side through the night, then had turned to survey the surrounding trees, trying to determine in which direction to look first. Before he could make up his mind, though, his wife had come sauntering into the clearing. Her face had been clean and glowed with good health. Her hair had still been damp from the bath she had obviously just taken. Her skirt had been raised slightly and held forward to make a temporary basket for some berries she had collected. Again, as on the last day, she had smiled at them with disgustingly good cheer and wished them good morn.

Aric could not have said which annoyed him more: her good mood that early in the morning, the fact that she had awakened before him once more, or that she had taken a bath without him around to protect her.

Recalling the way he had snarled and growled at her the morning before, and not wishing to repeat the activity, Aric kept the irate words that had trembled on the tip of his tongue to himself. He'd simply stomped off into the woods to attend to personal necessities, leaving her alone in the clearing.

His mood had not improved much by the time he returned, nor had it since then. In contrast, she had been as cheerful as sin all morning, chattering happily away about what a lovely day it was as they had partaken of the berries she had picked, humming merry tunes under her breath as they had ridden along. She had greeted his horse and Robert's as if they were old friends when they had reclaimed them from the stable where they had been left, and chatted knowledgeably—and, in his eyes, in a far too friendly manner—with the owner of the stables. Aye, she was in rare form, and it was driving him crazy.

"Aye. That is Shambley," his friend answered.

" 'Tis nice," she said and Robert and Aric exchanged a glance.

Describing Shambley as *nice* was like calling a bear slightly furry. Shambley was amazing. Built of silver-gray stone, it was flanked by forest, and seemed almost to float on the crystalline water of its moat. No matter what direction you approached from, or from which angle you saw it, the castle was magnificent.

Shaking his head, Aric urged his horse onward, moving at a slower pace to allow Robert to take the lead. Moments later they had ridden through the gates and arrived at the keep steps.

"Aric! Robert!"

Both men brought their horses to a stop, smiling indulgently at the young girl racing down the stairs to greet them.

"Lissa." Robert dismounted quickly, throwing his reins over his horse as he caught the child up in a hug. "Hello, moppet. Miss me?"

"Nay." The girl laughed at the way his mouth drooped, then chided, "You have only been gone a week. 'Sides, 'twould have been impossible to miss you; the keep has been full of people since you left."

Robert arched an eyebrow as he set the child down, and she made a face. "Aunt Esther and Aunt Hortense descended on us the day after you left," she explained. Her expression showed quite clearly her opinion of the houseguests.

"Hoping to see Father die, no doubt," Robert muttered as Aric set Rosamunde on the ground and quickly followed her off the horse.

"Aye." The girl grimaced. "They were most distressed to find him recovering. Though they did try to hide that once they got over their surprise. I think they had hoped that with Father out of the way they could nest here, sponging off Mother for the rest of their days."

Robert wore an expression of displeasure not dissimilar to the girl's. He muttered something uncomplimentary about vultures under his breath, then smiled wryly at Aric as his friend led Rosamunde forward. "It would seem we should have traveled at our own leisure on the way back. We have returned to a full house."

Aric started to nod, then glanced down as Lissa suddenly launched herself at his chest, hugging him as fiercely as she had her brother. "Hello, little one," he said. Rosamunde's eyes widened as Aric smiled affectionately at the child and hugged her back. It was the first sign of any soft emotion she had seen from the man she had married, and startling because of that.

"I missed you, Aric. You left without saying goodbye."

Rosamunde's gaze dropped to the girl at those words, not terribly surprised to see that she was staring up at Aric with a starstruck look of devotion.

"Oh, ho! You did not miss me, but you missed Aric!" Robert waggled his eyebrows in mock horror, eliciting a disgusted look from the girl.

"You are my brother," she pointed out with the weary disdain of someone much older than her years. "I have been saddled with your presence all of my life. Aric is my beau."

Rosamunde's eyebrows rose at that, nearly disappearing into her hairline when she saw the blush that suddenly rode on Aric's cheeks. Giving her a pained smile, Aric cleared his throat. "Lissa is Robert's little sister," he explained unnecessarily.

"And she very generously offered herself as his paramour—to aid in mending his heart after Delia broke it," Robert explained. Wicked amusement danced in his eyes at his friend's discomfort.

"Delia?" Rosamunde murmured curiously, but before anyone would explain, Lissa turned to eye her suspiciously.

"Who is she?" the girl asked belligerently, her arms still wrapped around Aric.

Robert's grin deepened. "Lissa, meet Rosamunde, Lady Burkhart."

"How do you do?" Rosamunde murmured politely, extending a hand in greeting.

Staring at the hand as if it were a dead fish, Lissa asked ominously, "Lady Burkhart?"

"Aric's wife," Robert explained with amusement. "That is why we left in the middle of the night without warning. Aric was off to be married."

Lissa did not look pleased by this news. The child paled miserably, her small arms dropping from Aric, tears filling her eyes. Turning swiftly toward the stairs, she started up them. "I shall tell Mother you are here."

Aric watched her go with a sigh, then gave Robert a remonstrating look.

Managing to look somewhat chagrined, his friend shrugged. "She had to hear the news sometime."

Aric did not look convinced. Rolling his eyes, he shook his head and took Rosamunde's arm to lead her up the stairs behind Robert.

The great hall they entered was in a state of chaos. They had arrived a bit earlier than they had expected. It was not quite the nooning hour, yet the room was crowded with people, some running this way, some the other. And causing it all were two women yelling orders and roaring commands.

"Ah," Robert murmured. "Aunt Hortense and Aunt Esther."

Rosamunde glanced at him curiously, but remained silent as the women bellowed orders.

"Fetch me my embroidery, girl. This mead will not do. 'Tis too sweet; bring me another. Why is it so cold in here? Can no one here build a proper fire?" Each of these demands, from a slender, horse-faced, older woman seated by the fire, sent a servant hurrying off as if bitten. One fetched the required embroidery, another took the cup of mead and flew off for the kitchens, and a third hurried to build up the fire.

Not to be outdone, a rotund woman with a florid face who sat in a second chair by the fire immediately began expelling her own orders. "My, 'tis hot in here. What? Are you trying to boil us all to death with that blaze, girl? Throw some water on it. Here, take my shawl back to my room. And someone fetch me a sweet treat to tide me over until the nooning meal."

More servants went scurrying, and Robert glanced at

Rosamunde with amusement. "My aunts. They never married and live off a yearly allowance in London. When they come here, they like to play lady of the manor."

"I see," Rosamunde murmured. Her gaze slid to the stairs and, to the woman who was descending them. She was of an average size, but that was all that was average about her. Her hair was a stunning blond so pale as to be white, and her features were magnificent, though at the moment they were full of weariness. The woman seemed almost to be dragging herself down each step as if too weary to lift her feet. Her shoulders were slumped, and her expression a picture of exhaustion. This was Robert's mother, Rosamunde decided. She looked very much like a woman who had spent days worrying and fretting over a husband, only to have relatives such as the two aunts descend on her the moment he showed signs of recovering.

Espying Robert now, the woman proved Rosamunde's guess correct.

"Son!" she cried, and her entire attitude changed. Her weariness dropped away like an old shawl as she flew down the rest of the stairs to greet them.

Lady Shambley seemed a wonderful woman. She was much like Rosamunde had always imagined her own mother would have been. Obviously relieved and overjoyed to see her son, she hugged him tightly, then welcomed Aric and Rosamunde just as warmly.

Ushering them to the trestle tables, she sent for ale and mead and updated them on Lord Shambley's health. He was recovering nicely, slowly regaining his strength. He was even sitting up for several hours of the day now, and Lady Shambley soon expected him to be demanding to be allowed below stairs.

Much to Rosamunde's surprise, she did not question

them much on how Aric had come to be married so suddenly. But then, Rosamunde supposed that Lady Shambley was aware that Bishop Shrewsbury had arrived the night they had left so precipitously. Everyone knew that Shrewsbury went nowhere without the king and vice versa, so it had probably taken very little guesswork to figure out how the marriage had come about.

Once they had finished the beverages she ordered for them, Lady Shambley suggested her son go above stairs to see his father. After he left, she then offered to take Aric and Rosamunde on a tour of her gardens. Aric declined the offer, excusing himself to go and speak with his men, who had been waiting comfortably at Shambley while he raced about the countryside. That left Rosamunde and Lady Shambley alone for their tour.

They had just reached the gardens when Lissa found them and told Lady Shambley that her husband wished to see her.

Nodding, Lady Shambley asked her daughter to start the tour for her, and promising to return as soon as she could, she hurried off. Rosamunde watched her go, then glanced sympathetically at the rebellious-looking Lissa. She was just wondering how to start a conversation with the girl when the scamp started it for her.

"I do not care if you are the king's bastard or not; if you hurt him like Delia did, I shall . . . I will"—she frowned, apparently not having considered what threat to use, then finished grimly with—"pull all your nasty red hair out by the roots and choke you with it."

Rosamunde's eyebrows rose at that. "Bloodthirsty little thing, are you not?" She laughed wryly, then asked, "And how did this Delia hurt him?"

When Lissa merely glared at her, her mouth a stubborn line, she added, "Well, if you will not tell me, how can I be sure not to repeat her mistake?"

"By staying in your husband's bed, and not straying into other men's brais."

"Ah." Rosamunde felt herself blush at the deliberately crude words. "I see."

"I am sure you do," Lissa said dryly, and whirled away to stomp back into the castle.

"Meow," Rosamunde murmured as the door slammed behind the girl. Sighing, she gathered her skirts and followed.

Lunch was a lively affair, with the aunts Hortense and Esther struggling to be heard above each other and win the most attention. Lissa spent the mealtime glaring at Rosamunde down the length of the table. It was almost a relief when the meal was over and Aric took her arm to urge her to her feet. But it was not until she heard Lady Shambley's words that Rosamunde realized they were leaving. Their hostess had risen, too.

"It was such a pleasure meeting you, my dear. You must make Aric bring you again so that we can have a longer visit. Anytime after Aunt Hortense and Aunt Esther leave would be grand," she added with a pained smile.

Confusion taking over her expression, Rosamunde glanced from the woman to her husband uncertainly. "What?" No one had bothered to mention that they would be departing immediately.

"We are leaving," Aric said, steering her toward the door. "The men are mounting up even as we speak."

"Oh." She could not help the slight disappointment she felt. Despite the glaring Lissa, the horrid aunts, and the fact that there was no bedchamber available for her, Rosamunde had been rather looking forward to a night indoors again. The great hall floor would have been preferable to dirt, and a real bath instead of the ice-cold dip she had in the river the other morning would have been welcome. Most of all however, she would have been grateful for the respite from riding. Obviously she was not going to get one, however. With a sigh, she glanced over her shoulder to offer a smile of gratitude to Lady Shambley as Aric ushered her out of the keep. "Thank you for the chance to rest and eat. It was lovely."

"You are more than welcome," she was assured graciously, as they reached the mounted men waiting at the bottom of the steps. Aric mounted immediately, then reached down to pull her up before him.

"You were not planning to leave without saying good-bye now, were you?"

Rosamunde glanced around to smile at Robert as he quickly descended the steps toward them. He had not attended the nooning meal. Lady Shambley had said he was taking his meal with his father.

"Would I do that?" Aric responded. He smiled, then added, "'Sides, why would I say good-bye? I thought that surely, from what you said on the way here, that you would be traveling on with us."

"Do not tempt me," Robert muttered dryly, then sighed and shook his head. "If I could come up with a plausible excuse, I would accompany you. Can you think of one?"

Aric laughed. "You are on your own there, friend."

"I feared it would be so," he said wryly, then held out a hand that Aric clasped firmly. "Godspeed and safe journey. I will see you when I see you."

"Aye. And to you as well."

Nodding, the man stepped back, watching forlornly as Aric turned his mount toward the gates and led the way out.

They rode through the rest of the day. The sun was setting when Aric finally called a halt to their travels.

Stopping the horse in a clearing, he eased Rosamunde to the ground. Not wishing to embarrass her, he pretended not to notice when she staggered on legs long unused and grasped at his leg to maintain her balance. Dismounting, he staunchly ignored the pain that accompanied the sudden rush of blood through his own legs and led his horse to one of his men.

"Take care of the horses, Smithy," he ordered calmly, then began to shout orders to the others, sending some to collect wood for a fire, others to hunt up some game for supper, and told the remainder to begin setting up camp. He then turned and made his way into the woods. He was gone before Rosamunde could ask what it was exactly she was expected to do.

Deciding it was up to her to find something with which to occupy herself, she made her way through the woods, intent on capturing a rabbit to go with whatever the men brought back for supper. She had barely taken one step out of the clearing when Garvey, her husband's first in command, stepped before her, blocking her path.

Eyes widening, Rosamunde came to a halt, then murmured an apology and went to step around him. He was immediately in her path again. "Excuse me," she snapped, a bit impatiently.

"I realize that it has been a long ride, my lady, but it would be better if you awaited my lord's return to attend to personal needs. I am sure he will not be long, and shall be happy to accompany you then."

Rosamunde blinked at him rather blankly. It took her a moment to realize that he thought she had to relieve herself and was suggesting she wait to do so until Aric could accompany her. Flushing slightly, she shook her head. "I assure you, sir, 'tis nothing personal I intended on doing."

One bushy brown eyebrow rose at that, but

otherwise his firm expression did not change. "Then if you would tell me what it is you require, I will be happy to send one of the men to attend to it."

Rosamunde frowned, then sighed and offered a sweet smile. " 'Tis quite all right, good sir. I need no assistance; I merely thought that since my husband has shown a preference for my broasted rabbit, I would snare one for his supper."

A strained smile tugged briefly at the corners of the man's mouth, then was gone. "Never fear, my lady. One of the men will surely bring back a rabbit."

Rosamunde hesitated. She had not meant to suggest that the men could not manage to hunt on their own, but realized how her words must have sounded to this man. Smiling wryly, she shook her head. "Of course, you are right. No doubt they shall bring back several." The man relaxed enough to offer a smile and nod, but stiffened up all over again when she again went to step around him, saying, "I shall just help collect some wood, then."

He was back in front of her at once, his expression firm as he shook his head. "The men shall collect wood for the fire, my lady. Why do you not return to the clearing and rest? It has been a long day for you, and tomorrow will be longer."

Rosamunde glared at him, feeling her temper rise, then whirled on her heel and flounced back into the clearing. She was all aquiver with impatience and the need to be useful. She had sat silent and still on that damnable horse for days now, and it was driving her mad. She had to do something. Anything.

Spying the stack of wood growing in the center of the clearing, she sighed and hurried forward. Here was something for her to do: she could build a fire.

She had barely begun to build one when she found

herself gently but firmly ushered away from the wood by another man. "Why don't you go rest, lass?" the man said as he deposited her back where she'd begun.

They are trying to be kind, she assured herself grimly. *You should not lose your temper over this: they are only trying to be kind.* Still, she found herself glaring at the back of the man building the fire as he clumsily set about his chore. She could have built a far better fire—and more quickly—if she had been given half a chance.

She was still fuming over that when the first of the hunters returned with his catch. Aric must have chosen a spot near the river again, for the man carried half a dozen fish he had managed to spear. Pinning a determined smile on her face, she hurried forward to meet the man as he neared the fire. "Oh, my, what lovely fish. Well done, sir," she praised brightly. "Shall I help you to clean them?"

Despite preening at her compliments, still the man refused her help, assuring her he would do well enough, that she should rest. Rosamunde was about to insist when she spied another man returning carrying a couple of rabbits. Deciding that he looked a more likely sort, she turned away from the man with the fish and hurried to the newcomer's side.

When Aric returned from his dip in the river some time later, it was to find his wife seated despondently beside the fire, her unhappiness apparent in her posture. Sighing, he strode quickly toward her.

He had not forgotten her when he had stalked off to have his dip. In fact, he had rather been thinking of her. Riding behind her all the day, the soft curves of her body against his own, her sweet hair flying in his face . . . well, it had made it hard for him to concentrate on anything but the thought of planting himself deep within her again.

And do some of that stirring and plowing she had talked about.

He had thought that opportunity would come once they reached Shambley, but they had arrived to find there was no bed available. Aric would not take his bride on a great hall floor for all to see, nor would he take her in camp surrounded by his men. Unfortunately, he had not bothered bringing a tent on this trip when he had hied off to his friend's home. He had been upset at the time, having just caught his betrothed in another man's arms, and had actually not bothered to take the time to collect much of anything. Thus he now found himself without the necessities that made travel bearable. His wife would be far from comfortable until they reached Goodhall. He himself would not fare much better. Having to camp out in the open every night, with his wife mere inches away and his men only a few feet farther.

That being the case, he thought it best to hurry them all home to Goodhall. There he would finally be able to show his wife that the marriage bed was not a barn, nor was it supposed to be a torture rack. He just had to restrain himself until then. Which was why he had neglected to tend to his wife's personal needs until he had cooled off his desire somewhat with a cold dip in the river. It seemed, however, that his wife was now in a state of misery. He supposed she was in dire need of relieving herself. That was the only reason he could think of for her appearing so wretched.

"Come," he said quietly, taking her arm and urging her to her feet as soon as he reached her side. He quickly hustled her out into the surrounding woods, pausing only when he found a spot for her to use without being seen by any of the men. "Here you are."

Rosamunde stared rather blankly at his back when

he turned it to her, then down and around at her sur-
roundings. His soldier's suggestion about personal needs
still fresh on her mind, it did not take her long to realize
what Aric expected her to do. Still, while Rosamunde
supposed she really could benefit from relieving herself,
she was a bit confused by her husband's abrupt manner.

Sighing, she shrugged, then tended to her needs. She
found herself embarrassed despite the fact that his back
was turned, since she knew he could hear her every
move. Deciding once again that camping out really was
not for her, Rosamunde finished with her business, and
approached him with a sigh.

"You must teach me to ride, my lord."

Aric whirled around, obviously surprised by her demand. But Rosamunde hardly noticed. Her mind was
caught up in her own thoughts. She had determined that
the reason Aric's men would not allow her to help was
because they thought her helpless. And since they did
not know her, the only reason she could think of for
their mistaken assumption was because she could not
ride and had to be taken up before their lord on his
horse like a child. Oh, she had realized by now that it
was not truly Marigold's fault that she bounced about
so. Robert had ridden her well enough after he'd had to
put his own mount down, and that had proven that the
problem had been Rosamunde's own. She had ridden
against the horse rather than with it. Now she thought
that if only her husband would teach her to ride, she
would show these men that she was not helpless; then
they would allow her to do her share.

"I must, must I?"

"Oh, aye. 'Tis a valuable skill, my lord, and surely it
would be easier on your horse to carry only you?"

Aric nodded solemnly at that, then turned and led the
way silently back to the camp. It was not until they

reached the fire that he answered. "I shall teach you tomorrow at first light."

"Nay! Not like that! Oh, damn!" Pulling on the reins he had yet to let go of, Aric drew Marigold to a halt, then leaned his head wearily on the horse's side, trying to regain his temper. When he had agreed to this asinine idea of teaching his wife to ride, he had thought it would take only a few minutes. Half an hour at the most. Unfortunately, his wife was turning out to be a turnip. She certainly rode a horse about as well as one, bouncing around in an ungainly fashion on the beast's back, no matter how many times he tried to instruct her differently. They had now been at their lessons for most of the morning and his men were looking on with dubious expressions that stated quite clearly what they thought of their new lady's ability.

"My lord," Rosamunde got out through gritted teeth. "Mayhap if you did not yell so much—"

Some of the men began to nod their heads slightly at her words, but Aric bellowed, "I am *not* yelling!" That brought a doubtful look to all of their faces. The soldiers watched with interest as their new lady narrowed her eyes. She was looking at their lord as if he were a bug that had just crawled up her skirt, and they were not at all surprised when she said in a hiss, "Very well. If you would stop 'not yelling,' then mayhap—"

"Do not even say it!" Aric exploded, interrupting her and sending her horse skittering a nervous step to the side. Rosamunde looked over at his men, most of whom had dry looks on their faces, as if they had just sucked a lemon. It was obvious to them as well that their lord was just making both his wife and the horse nervous and jittery with his impatience. But then, this had been a folly from the beginning, and every man knew it. It seemed a proven fact as their usually patient lord roared, "If you are about to suggest that your lack of skill is my fault—"

"Nay, of course not. But every time you yell, you make Marigold more nervous, and then I get more nervous, and our performance worsens." The men were all nodding again, and that bolstered her resolve. "If you would stop yelling, perhaps we could—"

"You *are* saying it is my fault!" he roared, incensed, and the men all sighed and shook their heads. Marigold skittered another step away, growing even more tense. Aric seemed too infuriated to notice. "Well, to hell with that! Teach yourself how to ride, then!" Tossing the reins up into her face impatiently, he turned and started to stomp away.

"Very well, I will!" she snapped back, slapping the reins angrily. Marigold bolted, more than happy to get as far away from the bellowing man as possible, she charged off into the woods, carrying her mistress with her. The sudden furor that erupted behind them—as the men all began yelling and scrambling for their horses to give chase—seemed only to spur the animal on.

His back to his stubborn, incompetent wife, Aric was the last to realize what she was about. At first he was completely flummoxed when his men began yelling and suddenly clambered onto their horses, but when they went charging past him, he glanced over his shoulder to see the tail end of his wife's mount disappearing into the trees. With a curse, he headed for his own horse.

Plastering herself to the mare's neck, Rosamunde prayed and held on for dear life. As Marigold weaved and bobbed through the woods, branches scratched at Rosamunde's face, slapping at her legs and back. She was at first too intent on keeping her seat to recall any of her husband's instructions. But as several minutes passed, she realized that she was no longer bouncing about on the horse's back; she was finally riding *with* the beast. Elation made her relax and grin. She was riding! *Well!* That would show her blowhard husband.

Taking a deep breath as the woods thinned out somewhat and Marigold found a trail to follow, Rosamunde eased back into a sitting position. She let her breath out in a relieved sigh; she was still able to keep pace with the animal and did not suddenly start bouncing about again. She had learned to ride. And not at that sedate little trot Aric had been forced to maintain with the two of them on his horse. *This* was true riding. The wind was whipping through her hair. The trail was flashing by underfoot. They were nearly flying, they were going so fast. This was grand! She had never felt so alive before. Why had the abbess never taught her to ride?

A series of shouts from behind her finally drew her attention, and Rosamunde peered over her shoulder. The men giving chase were a sight to see. Their hair plastered to their heads by the wind, their bodies hunched over the horses, the men were truly giving it their all. But they were losing the race. Marigold was faster than their warhorses, Rosamunde realized with some surprise and no little bit of pride. Since she had raised the horse herself, she felt this ability somehow reflected on her.

Laughing suddenly, she pulled gently on the reins, inordinately pleased when Marigold, having run off the worst of her fear and nervousness, immediately began to slow. She was still laughing as the men reigned in their own mounts around her. "I did it!" she cried. "I was really riding her! It was fantastic," she continued enthusiastically. The anxiety immediately began to fade from her pursuers' faces, slowly replaced by smiles.

* * *

Aric closed his eyes and sighed. He had spotted his wife's flame-colored hair amid the men circling her. The last few minutes had been hell for him; he had envisioned her broken body lying on the ground, and any injury to her would have been his fault. He had been positive that she would be hurt in this mad run, so the sight of her sitting calmly amid his men was a relief. But then he heard her chattering happily away and laughing, and his own men chuckling in response. She looked and sounded far too comfortable and happy surrounded by his warriors. Worse yet, every single one of them wore an enchanted grin as they listened to whatever she was expounding on.

Riding, he realized as he drew near enough to catch her words. It appeared that while the rest of them had been terrified for her safety, she had been exhilarated. She now considered herself an excellent rider. *Women,* he thought with disgust. They were the most inconstant of creatures and the most nonsensical. Only a woman would—after a moment before being the worst rider Aric had ever seen—survive one wild ride and consider herself an expert.

"Husband," she cried suddenly, spotting him. "Did you see? Was it not grand? We were nearly flying. I vow Marigold is the fastest horse here. And I rode *with* her. Did you see?"

"Aye," he said quietly, urging his horse through the other mounts to reach her side. Pausing there, he took her reins from her and turned back the way he had come, drawing her horse behind him.

"Husband?" she murmured uncertainly as her husband's men fell into line behind them. "You are not angry, are you? I mean, think of it. With that little run, we probably made up scads of the time that we wasted on my lessons. Is that not true?"

"It would be . . . if we were headed back to Shambley. However, we are *not* headed back to Shambley, so all that this little jaunt managed to do was slow us down some more and tire out the horses."

"Oh," Rosamunde sighed unhappily, her shoulders slumping. Marigold had run the wrong way, taking them back the way they had come. If she had realized that, she would have turned the beast in the right direction, or in the very least have stopped sooner. Instead, she had let the mare have her head and again delayed their arrival home. It seemed she could do nothing right.

Chapter 6

ROSAMUNDE dismounted on her own, pride the only thing keeping her from bursting into tears as she did. She could not believe the pain she was in. While it had been uncomfortable riding in front of her husband, it was agony after a day of riding on her own. Her muscles ached in places she had not even realized that she had them. It was horrible agony. But she was damned if she was going to admit it. Curse her husband; she suspected it would please the insufferable man to know the pain she was in. He had not spoken a word to her since informing her that she had added time to their trip.

They had ridden nonstop since then, not even pausing for a midday meal, and for most of that time Rosamunde had been in pain. She was too proud to admit it and beg for mercy, though. She would not be coddled. If the men could handle it, so could she. Her muscles would grow used to the saddle, and she would win their respect. She was determined. And determination was the only thing that kept her from accepting one of the men's kind offers to see to her horse for the night.

Glimpsing the sympathy in the man's eyes, Rosamunde shook her head, thanking him kindly for the offer, but refused firmly. She set about the task herself. She listened to her husband give the same orders he had the day before; then he disappeared into the woods.

Sighing, she finished with her horse, murmured a good-night in the animal's ear, then moved determinedly to the pile of wood already being stacked in the center of the clearing. But when she attempted to offer her assistance, she once again found herself gently brushed aside and directed to a fallen log upon which to seat herself. As she had the night before, she then tried to assist in cleaning and cooking the wild game the men brought back, but she once again found her efforts and offers brushed aside. Sit and rest, they said, sit and rest.

Rosamunde sighed impatiently and glared around. Weary as she was after her first day in the saddle, the last thing on earth she desired was to sit on her poor, abused behind. Why would the men not let her help? Had she not earned at least a modicum of respect today? Why did they treat her like a helpless creature who needed coddling? She did not understand it. In the abbey, where there were only women, the sisters had performed all the necessary tasks. Here they would not allow her to do a thing.

Then she suddenly had a thought. What if it was because her husband had not given her orders ere leaving? *Of course!* He had bawled out orders to the rest of them, but he had left without instructing her. Mayhap they believed that meant Aric did not wish her to do anything. Of course, they could not know that for the three-day journey from Godstow Abbey to Shambley, her husband had not had to shout orders. She had known what to do and done it without direction.

Aric just happened to return as that thought occurred to her. Rosamunde hurried forward, presenting herself before him with a pleased smile, thinking she was about to resolve the confusion. "Hello, my lord," she greeted with forced good cheer, glancing surreptitiously about to see if anyone was listening. No one appeared to be, but there were several men close enough to hear. That was good.

Aric peered at his wife suspiciously, knowing instinctively by the way her eyes darted around the clearing as she addressed him that she was up to something. "Hello, wife."

When she merely raised an eyebrow inquiringly, he arched one of his own in return. Frowning slightly, she leaned forward a bit. "You have not given me my orders."

Aric's other eyebrow rose as she whispered those words, then smiled at him encouragingly. "Orders?"

"Aye, my lord. The men will not allow me to help because you have not given me any orders. You must give me my orders—and loudly enough that they will hear and know what I am to do."

"I see," he murmured, though truly he did not. "Fine, then. Wife, sit you over there and rest," he ordered loudly.

"Nay!" Rosamunde gasped in dismay.

Aric's eyes narrowed at her denial. "Nay?"

"Nay," she repeated. "You are not supposed to order me to sit. You are supposed to order me to do something."

"I *am* ordering you to do something. I am ordering you to sit and rest."

Rosamunde glared at him rebelliously, then sighed as she recalled her vow to obey him. "Fine," she snapped ungraciously. "I shall *sit*."

Turning on her heel, she stomped over to a log by the fire and dropped to squat upon it, wincing as her tender behind connected with the makeshift bench.

Noting her wince, Aric hesitated, then sighed. He moved to her side at once. "Come." His behavior seemed familiar, and Rosamunde sighed as she was dragged off into the bushes. As he had the night before, he led her to a secluded spot for her to attend to her personal needs. But, rather than return her to the clearing afterward, he led her to a spot by the river. It appeared secluded and private.

"Go ahead. Bathe."

Rosamunde peered from the water to her husband. Recalling his insistence that he would watch her bathe when he had taken her to the river on the way to Shambley, she sighed. "I do not wish to."

"It will soothe your muscles. Bathe."

His words were not unkind, but, "I—"

" 'Tis an order."

Rosamunde's mouth snapped closed and an expression of resignation covered her face. She could not deny a direct order, could she? He looked speculative.

Her mouth a grim line, Rosamunde fiddled with the clasp of the belt that hung loosely around her waist. Unclasping it, she started to set it on the ground.

"What is that?"

Pausing, she raised her eyebrows at her husband. Aric was peering at the small sheathe attached to her belt.

"Hand me your belt," he ordered.

Rosamunde handed it over silently and shifted her feet as he slid her dagger out of its holder. He examined the intricately carved hilt with interest.

"It was a gift from Eustice," she told him to break the silence. "It comes in very handy when working in the stables."

"I imagine it does. It's beautiful." He slid the dagger back into its sheath, then arched an eyebrow at her. "You are not undressing."

Sighing, she raised a hand to toy with the lacings of her gown, her gaze moving around the clearing. They seemed to be alone. No one would see her. Except Aric. She eyed him unhappily. "Will you not at least turn your back?"

"How shall I know if you run into difficulty? I am uncertain of the strength of the current here. It may be strong enough to drag you under. If I am not watching, how shall I know?" he asked simply.

Rosamunde frowned at that, then smiled brightly. "So that you know all is well, I shall talk continuously."

"No doubt."

Rosamunde stiffened. "What does *that* mean?"

He gave an amused shrug. "I have noticed that you like to talk."

"And you seem not to like to talk at all! Mayhap if you spoke more, I would speak less."

"I talk when I have something to say, not simply to hear my own voice."

She glared at him briefly, then propped her hands on her hips. "Turn your back."

"I do not have time for this. A dip in the river will ease your aches. Otherwise you will not be able to ride tomorrow. Take your clothes off and get in the water," he said in a growl. She paled, then flushed bright red at the direct order. Reluctantly she raised her hands to begin tugging at her lacings.

She was slow as a turtle on shifting sand. By the time Rosamunde had her gown undone and began to shrug it off her shoulders, Aric was ready to burst. It was the most erotic thing he had ever seen in his life, as inch after inch of pale perfect flesh was revealed to him: the base of her neck, the curve of her shoulders, then her arms and the linen shift she wore beneath the dress as it dropped to her waist. Now, partially revealed to him, she quickly pushed the gown over her hips, stepped out of it, and whirled toward the water.

Aric was quicker. Catching her by the arm, he drew her to a halt before she had a chance to immerse herself. "Nay. You will remove your shift."

Even he could hear the husky note of desire in his voice, and he frowned at it.

"The abbess said only loose women run about in the nude. Good women wear their shifts, for propriety's sake. Especially in the bath, so that they do not catch a chill," she murmured, her head down.

"Do you have another shift?"

After a hesitation, she shook her head.

"Then you will have to wear it when you again don your gown. If it is wet, it will give you a chill. Remove the shift."

The expression she raised to him was agonized. It was clear his bride was painfully shy. He was beginning to get the impression that no one had ever seen her nude. Except for him, of course—but that had been only her bare behind and the backs of her legs. Feeling like an ogre, he glanced away, then sighed and turned his back. "Talk."

Sighing in relief, Rosamunde hesitated only briefly, then shrugged out of her shift. The abbess would understand, certainly. This was not a nice cozy bath indoors, where she could rest by the fire to dry her hair and don fresh clothes. When camping out-of-doors, some proprieties had to be sacrificed.

"You are not talking."

"I am not in the water yet," Rosamunde explained as she dropped her shift and moved the last couple of steps to the water. "Oh, 'tis cold." She gasped as the liquid lapped over the foot she set carefully into it.

" 'Twill feel warmer quickly."

"Will it?" she asked curiously, then admitted, "I have never bathed in a river before. Actually, I have never bathed anywhere but the abbey's old wooden tub. And the water then was always warm and sweet. Well, not *always,*" she added reluctantly.

Made curious by her tone of voice, Aric murmured, "When was it not warm and sweet?"

He could actually hear the embarrassed grimace in her voice as she admitted, "Once or twice when I was a child . . ."

"Why?"

She hesitated, and when she finally spoke, her answer was obviously reluctant. "If I was naughty, I was sometimes made to bathe in cool or cold water."

"They made you take cold baths if you were bad?" he asked incredulously. He'd never heard of such a practice.

"And eat cold meals . . . Or badtasting ones," she added wryly.

"Badtasting?" he repeated with amusement.

"Burnt to a cinder, or with so much spice it was disgusting, or no spice at all so that 'twas bland."

"It sounds more like torture than a reprimand," he muttered, frowning.

"It was." She sighed dramatically, then added, "And that was not even the worst of it. Once I was old enough, punishment became scrubbing the abbey floors on my hands and knees, or whitewashing the walls, or cleaning the fireplace."

Aric tried to picture her scrubbing the floors, or covered with soot as she washed out the fireplace. He shook his head. "I did not notice any children scrubbing floors or fireplaces while we were there. Did the abbess hide them because the king was there?"

"Oh, nay. No one else ever got such punishments."

"What?" He actually glanced over his shoulder at that. She was as yet only knee-deep in the water, giving him his second view of her lovely derriere, this time covered in goose bumps. She had a nice bum. Each cheek looked perfect and round and still not much more than a handful. Swallowing as that thought struck him, Aric turned away again.

"No one else had to perform such punishments."

Aric frowned at her words, confused for a moment. What was she was talking about? Oh, aye, he thought, clearing his throat. Naughtiness and punishment. The kind the abbess had meted out, apparently only to her. That made no sense to him. Why had she not been punished like the other children? Why, if he had been the abbess, he would have taken her across his lap, pulled her skirt up over her behind, and applied the palm of his hand to her sweet, pink-cheeked buttocks. He imagined it now. Well, maybe it would have been a problem. Even now, in his mind's eye, when he should have been spanking her, his hand was running over her curves in a most unpunishing way.

Shaking his head, he forced himself back to the conversation. "Why were you punished differently from the other children?"

Rosamunde glanced curiously over her shoulder at his gruff voice, but could tell nothing about what had caused it. His back was stiff, and firmly turned to her as it had been when she had taken off her shift. "The other children got the switch as punishment. The abbess was not allowed to touch me."

"Ah," Aric murmured with sudden understanding. "Your father."

"Aye," she answered, then gasped as she finally moved deeper into the water.

Aric waited until she had stopped muttering about

the temperature of the water, then asked curiously, "Were you often naughty?"

"Only every chance I got."

Aric grinned at the pert answer, but asked, "What is there to do to be naughty in an abbey?"

"Oh, hundreds of things," she said airily. "I was the naughtiest child there. Always in trouble. I was a chatterbug, forever forgetting and talking during mealtimes, which were supposed to be silent. That got me the horrid meals. A sister or the abbess would take my plate away and return with something thoroughly unpleasant—to help me remember."

"And the cold baths?"

"When I would not sit still during mass. Adela claimed I was too excited and needed cooling down."

"Thus the cold bath," he muttered wryly.

"Aye. Also if I muddied my gown. That meant extra work for Hester, so to make up for that and ease her burden, the abbess told her not to bother with heating water for my bath. Instead, she made me cart cold water for myself."

"Ah," Aric murmured, but he was thinking that her naughtiness seemed hardly naughty, but simply excessive energy. Something she had inherited from her father, no doubt. That man never sat still for a moment. Just like Rosamunde. She was even shifting restlessly about as he drifted off to sleep each night. In fact, the only time he had seen her actually sleep was the first day of their travels, when she had fallen asleep in his arms. And that had been after she'd been up through the night with the mare. He suspected that seeing her sleep or even sit still for any length of time would be a rare occurrence.

"How many children were there at the abbey with you?" he asked suddenly.

"There were five in my earliest memories," she answered slowly. "But one died when I was still quite young. Two were quite a bit older and left when I was about six, then two others when I was eight."

"Did no other children come to the abbey?"

"Nay. The abbess had been taking children in only because she needed money to run the convent. But Father paid her well enough that it was no longer necessary."

"Did you miss the others when they were gone?"

"Nay. I did not see them much. I was younger, and they—" She cut herself off abruptly, stirring Aric's curiosity.

"They . . . what?"

"They did not seem to like me much," she explained painfully, making Aric frown. Older children rarely liked to hang around with the younger ones. Still, he got the feeling that there was more to it than that.

"Why do you think they did not like you?" he asked carefully.

There was a silence filled only by the night sounds around them; then she sighed. "Sister Eustice said it was because I never got beatings. I never complained at how awful the meals were when they replaced my dinners, and none of the others knew about the cold baths or cleaning. They thought I got special treatment and resented it." There was a splash of water; then she said with a defiant tone, "I was rather glad when the last two left. That was when I got to start working in the stables with Sister Eustice."

Aric frowned. It sounded as if she had known quite a lonely life.

Another spate of mutters and gasps told him that she had sunk further into the water, and he could not resist a glance over his shoulder to see how far she had gotten.

She was in up to her neck now, and all he could see was the back of her head. Suddenly she ducked that under the water, too. She came up gasping a moment later and whirled toward him, mouth open. It snapped closed as she glared at him. "You are looking, my lord."

"You stopped talking," he murmured mildly. He again turned his back.

After a moment of irritated silence, she asked, "How long is it till we reach Goodhall?"

"A week, give or take a day."

"A week."

He heard a slight sigh between the splashes of water as she moved about. "Have you seen it? Do you know what it is like?"

"Nay."

"I am sure it is lovely. Father would not banish us to a hovel . . . Would he?"

He was surprised at the uncertainty in her voice. Was she unsure of the man's love for her? Something that had seemed obvious to him appeared not so obvious to her. "Nay. I am sure it is lovely."

She was silent for a moment, then asked, "What was your childhood like? You said you had a brother and two sisters. What are they like?"

Rosamunde peered at him curiously as she asked the question, and saw the way his back suddenly went ram-rod straight, his shoulders seeming almost to grow a good inch out of his body. His voice when he spoke was as chilly as the water had seemed when she first stepped into it.

"Hurry up and get out of there. We should return to camp."

She continued to stare at him curiously for a moment, then moved thoughtfully out of the river. She began to pull her clothes on again. Here was a mystery.

Her husband hadn't at all liked her question about his childhood. Had it been bad, or did he simply not wish to share it with her?

She would learn in time, she decided grimly.

Rosamunde shifted on her mount and glanced at her husband's back hopefully, but as far as she could tell, there was no sign that he intended to stop for the night anytime soon. It was unfortunate, really, because she had to relieve herself.

Shifting, she glanced at the scenery around them and sighed. After a week of travel, everything was starting to look identical. She saw the same trees, the same grass, the same river, the same clearings. She could almost believe they had been traveling in circles. Painful circles. After nearly a week on horseback, her behind seemed to have blisters on top of more blisters. And while it had seemed a grand adventure at first, Rosamunde had decided she preferred doctoring horses to riding them.

She also preferred living in the abbey to roughing it with her husband and his soldiers. While there had been a lot of rules regarding behavior in the abbey, it seemed to her that life was even worse out in the real world. Silence may have been demanded in the abbey during meals and mass, but silence was all she got from these men. Not that they did not talk. They did. To each other. But the only things said to her seemed to be "Nay" or "Rest yourself." Oh, yes, and "Come." Her husband greeted her with that ere dragging her off to allow her to perform personal tasks.

She had not had an actual conversation with anyone since her bath in the river. She had bathed once since then, but then it had been in the morning while everyone else was still sleeping.

She had tried starting conversations that first night

after her bath. While sitting around the fire eating the food the men had prepared, she had chattered away, asking questions and trying to find some topic of interest. But her husband had only grunted in response, then had suggested she go to bed. When she had protested that she was not tired, he had ordered her to sleep. She had lain down, but she had not slept.

The next morning Rosamunde had risen before the others, tended to her personal needs, collected what berries she could find, and returned to the clearing to find the men stirring. Once again, throughout the morning she had tried to get her husband to talk. She had chatted merrily away in an effort to bring about a return of the temporary rapport they had shared by the river. It had not worked. He had sat silent and unresponsive, perhaps even unlistening, through her litany of childhood memories. Finally, she had given up. They had traveled in a depressing silence since then, long days on horseback that did not end until the sun set.

The only change Rosamunde had effected since that time was that she now had a chore to perform when they finally stopped each night. She had taken to tending to the horses. Not that her husband knew. And if the others knew, they ignored it. Actually, she did her best to hide it from them. She pretended to be attending to her own horse, moving quickly to Marigold's side whenever any of the men came near the spot where the fellow in charge of the horses worked.

She liked Smithy, for unlike the other men, he did not seem to mind if she assisted him. He had tried to shoo her away the first time, but in the presence of a wounded or ailing animal, Rosamunde could not be shooed, and Smithy had been working with a horse with an injury. The beast tended to catch up one of his hind legs every now and then while trotting. Rosamunde had recognized the animal's condition, and as soon as she had diagnosed it as stringhalt, Smithy had relented. Now after a week, he even seemed grateful for her assistance.

It was her first success since leaving the abbey, if such could be called a success. At least the man allowed her to work with him. Sighing, she glanced toward her husband's back, surprised to see that he had actually stopped. Reining her horse in beside his, she glanced down into the valley below, taking in the green everywhere: a verdant valley with a river running through it, and a lush forest that moved up a smaller incline directly in its center. Leaves obscured the spires and turrets of the keep that rose below, like a magical castle.

"Goodhall." She murmured the name with a certainty that surprised her. She had never seen the place, had not even been given a description, and yet she knew exactly what she was looking at. It was perfect. It was quaint. It was beautiful, and it was the home her father had chosen for them. She felt tears of gratitude well in her eyes and blinked them quickly away. Somehow, his gift of this keep to her said more of the king's feelings than all the times that he had told her he loved her. Suddenly she knew he had meant it.

This was a castle fit for a princess in a fairy tale. It proved that her father saw her as special. Rosamunde's gaze flickered to her husband as he suddenly urged his horse forward. She spurred her own to follow.

Though Goodhall was a dream come true from a distance, it was a little less so once they had entered the bailey. The potential was there, and it was still a lovely castle, but it had been let go a bit. It was obvious from the bailey that the chatelaine had been lax. The damage was not enough to be too upsetting, only enough to make Rosamunde realize that there was work to be done. And that she had no idea how to do it.

She was just starting to fret over that when her gaze automatically sought out and found the stable. Her breath caught in her throat in a combination of dismay and rage. If the castle was a bit run-down, the stables were a ruin. The walls boasted holes big enough for the horses to stick their heads through. Without thinking, merely reacting to the sight, she turned Marigold toward the building, urging her into a trot.

Rosamunde had not gone far when Aric's barking of her name made her rein her mount in and turn to take in his thin-lipped expression. "I thought to check on the stables, my lord. They—"

"Here." He pointed at the ground beside his mount.

Rosamunde hesitated, then sighed and rode back to his side.

Apparently satisfied with her obedience, Aric turned and continued on to the keep steps, assuming that she would follow. Seeing little choice in the matter, she did. They had barely paused before the stairs to the keep and begun to dismount when the main doors opened and a man began to hobble out on the arm of a servant.

He was old, as ancient a man as she had ever seen. And he had not aged well. His hair, what was left of it, stood out from the sides of his head like tufts of white grass. One side of his wrinkled old face was lifted in a smile of greeting, but the other side seemed to be making a good effort at sliding off of his old bones. The mouth drooped downward; the eye was closed. His whole left side seemed to be sagging. His left shoulder was slumped, the arm hung limp at his side, and his left leg dragged behind as he hop-limped determinedly out the door.

Rosamunde stared at the man with brief amazement.

Despite the shriveled, dilapidated state of the man's body, he was obviously the chatelaine here. Which explained the state of affairs. A man in such shape could hardly be expected to keep on top of things. Her only question was why her father had not replaced the man and allowed him to retire. He was as battle-scarred and careworn as anyone she had ever met. If anyone deserved a rest, it was this man.

She had just come to that conclusion when Aric took her arm and urged her forward.

"My Lord Burkhart. Welcome to Goodhall," the man rasped as soon as they paused before him. The greeting was given with a drawing up of one shoulder, like a soldier before inspection, the attitude so dignified that one could almost ignore the fact that due to the slack side of his face, the words came out as "Ma Or Burhar. Wahom hoo ooha."

"Thank you." Aric murmured with a warm smile that carried over into his voice. "I take it you received word of our imminent arrival?"

"Aye. We received a message from the king several days ago." If they paid close attention they were able to decipher his slurred speech. "I have had the servants working to prepare everything. I hope it meets with your approval."

The words were a question of sorts, a concern that all was well. Suddenly the way he stared blankly through them with his one milky eye explained why. As well as being paralyzed along the left side of his body, the man was blind in the one eye that would open. That explained the question in his voice: he could give the orders, but could not see if they were carried out. Once again she found herself wondering why this man had been left in charge. Was he an old friend of her father's? And was her father simply loyal to his friend, or had he neglected the proper reassignment of Goodhall for too long?

"Everything looks wonderful," Rosamunde answered quickly. Aric glanced at her with a combination of amusement and annoyance, then shook his head slightly. She apparently thought so little of him that she believed he might have reprimanded the man for something so obviously beyond his control.

Not that she noticed his look, though, for her gaze was fixed on the old chatelaine. His face broke out in a smile. "You must be Lady Rosamunde."

"Aye, my lord," she murmured warmly, clasping the hand he extended toward her.

"Lord Spencer, at your service, my lady. Long and faithful servant of your father's—until time and fate made me useless."

"Not useless, my lord, surely," she chided gently. "Just look at how you keep this place." She tried not to let her dismay at its condition show in her voice. It was not this old man's fault.

"You are very gracious, my lady. Your father said as much to me. He told me also that you were as lovely as your mother inside and out, so I can actually picture you in my head."

Rosamunde smiled anxiously at the words. "You knew my mother?"

"Oh, aye. A fairer lady never walked this earth than the fair Rosamunde." A gentle smile of reminiscence covered his face. "Even Eleanor, in her day, could not have outshone her." He nodded as if to verify the statement, then frowned slightly. "But I am being rude by keeping you standing out here. You have traveled far and must be tired and thirsty. Come, I ordered food and drink to be prepared."

Holding tightly to the arm of his silent aide, he turned

back toward the door, and started to make his slow, agonizing way back up the stairs.

Taking her arm, Aric followed just as slowly. Rosamunde frowned over her shoulder toward the stables as she went. She would rather have checked the building out first, but knew her husband would not allow it. She would check on it later, she assured herself silently, the first chance she got.

The first chance she had was not until after supper was finished. Aric was busy chatting with Lord Spencer and not paying her the least attention. Standing, she moved slowly around the great hall, peering first at the Goodhall seal and crest, then at the swords on the wall. She was aware that her husband had noticed her leaving the table, but after seeing her wander aimlessly about briefly, he'd turned his full attention to the older gentleman who was telling tales of battle and his life.

Lord Spencer had explained during the meal how the king had chosen Goodhall for them. It was one of Henry's many holdings that had no heir.

The castle had been the Spencer family home for as long as anyone could recall. When he was young, Spencer himself had married and brought his bride here to live. They had been happy, and his wife had given birth to several children. Six, actually, but only two had survived infancy. Then, when his son was sixteen and his daughter fourteen tragedy had struck: the woolsorter's complaint, a deadly disease that had struck their sheep. It had spread quickly to his people, too, before they had realized what it was they were dealing with and could take the necessary precautions. Half the village died, along with half the inhabitants of the keep. His lady wife had been one of the first to go, then his daughter, then his son. They were dead and gone long before he had even returned to hear the news.

After he'd discovered his loss, Spencer had returned to his king's side to devote his life to battle—hoping to die and be reunited with his wife. But fate had played a cruel trick, and he had been blinded during an attack. That had kept him from battle, his only hope of dying without taking his life, and he would never do that. Suicide was a sin. Thus, he was cursed to live out his life until God saw fit to end it. God, he pointed out wryly, was taking his own sweet time.

Rosamunde had been touched by the tale. Lord Spencer's love for his wife and children was obvious in his voice as he spoke, his grief still raw these many years later. She had wondered briefly what it might be like to be so loved, with so much passion and gentleness that two decades later the very name of one's wife could bring a tear to a man's blind eye.

A woman who was so loved was a very lucky woman indeed, Rosamunde decided as she slid out the front door and hurried down the stairs of the keep. She would just check the stables and look in on Marigold. Most likely it would be as the castle had been: from the outside it looked neglected and uncared for, but inside it was spotless and well tended. Surely the stables were like that too, she assured herself. She crossed her arms and frowned at the chill night. This was the last day of June, but now that the sun had set, the air was cold. The breeze was also heavy with threatening rain, and a fine mist had settled over the bailey, carried by a northerly wind.

A storm started as she reached the stables. A flash of light in the distance made her pause and glance toward the north, but there was nothing to see. A moment later the roll of far-off thunder rumbled through the air.

Rosamunde felt the first large, wet drops of rain, then hurried into the stables. She paused instinctively just inside the door to allow her eyes to adjust to the sudden darkness.

But there was no darkness to adjust to. The great gaping holes she had seen when they had arrived assured that the interior was just as well lit by the night sky and lightning as the bailey had been. The holes also made it just as windy and wet inside as it had been outside. She realized this with a frown, her gaze moving over the rows of stalls as the horses began to shift nervously about. Frightened by the storm and unhappy at being partially exposed to the elements, they were neighing and whinnying in displeasure.

"Ah, stick it up yer arses and quit yer complaining. Ye're inside, aren't ye? Yer bellies' full and yer feet're dry."

Rosamunde stiffened at that surly voice, her head cocking as her gaze shot toward the back of the stables from whence it had come. It was not until the clouds shifted again, and the moon popped out once more, that she spotted the man lounging on a stack of hay at the back of the stables. He was half slouched, his head lolling forward and from side to side as he contemplated a pitcher he held in his hand.

The stablemaster? she wondered, then grimaced slightly. Who else could it be? Shifting impatiently, she moved toward the man until she stood before him.

He was drunk. Rosamunde could smell the liquor from where she stood. It was amazing that she could, considering the overpowering stench of animal refuse in the air. It didn't take much thought to figure out where that was coming from. She could feel it under her feet. She had walked through and now stood in a puddle of the mess. As she had noticed on first entering the bailey, the stables had been foolishly situated in a slight depression. Either that, or over the years the land had settled and taken the stables with it. The very center of the stables had a sort of trough running through it that acted as a drain or gutter down the center of the stables. Its watery contents were really rather disgusting, but from what she could see of the place, it was the only way any of the refuse was removed. It certainly did not look as if the gentleman presently singing a bawdy tune to himself as he clutched his pitcher did any actual work. Certainly not mucking out the stalls and stables. This was disgusting, a true sty. And unsanitary to boot. If some sort of plague had not already struck, it was likely to soon.

Rage overwhelming her, Rosamunde opened her mouth to berate him but was interrupted.

"What are you doing out here?"

Rosamunde blinked at those grim words, then whirled about as she realized that they had come from behind her. It seemed that her exit from the keep had not gone unnoticed after all. Her husband stood in the entrance to the stables, glaring at her as if *she* were the one who had done something wrong.

Gathering her wits quickly, she tried for a smile. It quickly turned into a frown as she explained herself. "I thought to check on the stables, and to see that the horses were well tended. Marigold—"

"Return to the keep," he cut her off abruptly.

"But just look at the stables, husband. And the stablemaster." She stepped aside, glancing behind her as she did to see that the man was now unconscious. "It is a disgrace. He should be replaced at once. Your man Smithy could do a far better job. And the stables should be rebuilt as well. On higher ground, and—"

"Return to the keep."

Rosamunde hesitated at his firm words. He did not

sound as though he would appreciate being disobeyed. *Disobeyed.* There was that word again. Obey Aric? Why had she repeated that vow, then made the promise to her father on top of it? Because, she admitted, she had been too stunned at suddenly finding herself having to get married to consider the words she was saying at the time. If she had been thinking properly, she would have refused. Or at least modified them somewhat. For instance, she might have said "obey to the best of my abilities," or "obey when I agree to," or something. It was most inconvenient to have made a promise to obey, and now have to try to do so.

Sighing, she let her shoulders drop slightly and walked forward. He took her arm as she made to move past, spearing her with his eyes as he did. "I will not have you racing about the bailey willy-nilly. The stables are not a place for a lady. You shall confine yourself to tending to the keep—as a proper wife should."

Her eyes widened in horror at that, and his hand tightened slightly on her arm.

"Do as I say, Rosamunde."

Swallowing, she nodded silently, her mind and body suddenly having gone numb. This was inconceivable. Never to be allowed into the stables? *Impossible!* It was what she did. It was what she had always done. It was her job!

Unaware of her thoughts, Aric released her arm and gestured toward the keep, satisfied when she stumbled out of the stables and headed toward the building.

His gaze slid around the stalls then before turning unhappily to the stable master. Aric grimaced with distaste. He turned and followed his wife. While he did not care for being told how to do his job as lord of the manor, his wife was right. The stables were a shambles. The stablemaster would have to be replaced, and a new building erected. Still, in the shape the man was in there was no sense in berating the stablemaster now, and it was not possible to see to the animals in the meantime.

While his wife had also been right in stating that his man Smithy was an excellent replacement, the soldier, like most of the others, had taken to his ale with enthusiasm after their week-long travels. He would not be of much use just now. The horses would have to make do for the night. He would deal with the situation on the morrow. He would assign Smithy to the stables, as well as a couple of other men to help him with the immediate task of mucking them out, and boarding up the worst of the holes. Then new stables could be built.

Sighing, Aric shook his head. It was only one of many things he suspected would need doing. But this would all have to wait till the morrow. He was weary after their travels and wished only to find his bed. But first he had to arrange for quarters for his men.

Chapter 7

ROSAMUNDE dropped onto the chair by the fire and sighed miserably. It had been two weeks since their arrival at Goodhall. Two long, slow, boring weeks that had passed like years. She had never been so miserable in her life, had never felt so useless. Not even during those first few days of the journey here from Shambley, when the men had refused to allow her to do anything, had she felt so hopelessly unneeded. At least then her days had been filled with the distraction of her various aches and pains, and the necessity of staying in the saddle. But these last fourteen days she had had nothing to distract her. Nothing. She was restricted to the castle and had not been allowed to step out of it since the night of their arrival. Her husband insisted she was to stay in the keep and tend to it, but there was nothing that needed her attention. The castle staff had been running themselves quite nicely for decades without her, and her input was hardly needed now.

Oh, she had tried. That first day after arriving, she had made a tour of the interior of the castle, looking for something—*anything*—to do. But everything was chugging along just fine without her interference. If anything, she seemed merely to get in the way of one servant or another as they went about their chores. She had wandered aimlessly about for a while, then finally moved to sit before the fire.

But simply sitting immediately begun to chafe at her. Rosamunde was not used to being inactive. With her body forced to stay still, her mind had promptly begun running in circles. She worried about the state of the stables and whether her husband intended to do anything about them. She considered the stables back at the abbey, and wondered how the mare and new colt were doing. Had the prolonged and unusual labor weakened the mare's constitution? Was she still well? Or had she fallen prey to some infection or lung complaint? That was always a threat for a horse after such a dangerous and sapping experience. Was the colt all right? Was it feeding? How were Eustice, Clarice, Margaret, and the abbess? These things became a tangle in her mind.

And so had gone her time. Sitting before the fire, fretting, and growing more depressed by the day while her husband got to wander all over the estate. He was familiarizing himself with his new holdings, and Lord Spencer and his man accompanied him everywhere as he did. Aric had assured the man he need not bother, but Spencer had insisted. He was the previous owner, he'd said, and it was his responsibility. The two men rode out in a cart early each morning, the disabled man's servant driving, and did not return until after Rosamunde had gone to bed.

Aric had spoken very little to her in that time, and he certainly had not bothered her about his husbandly rights. Not that she would have enjoyed them, but at least if he had, she would have felt she was accomplishing something. Instead she sat remembering her days at the abbey, and thinking of the women and animals she had left behind. She missed them all. She was even beginning to miss Father Abernott. That, more than anything, told her how desperate her situation had become.

The sound of the great hall door opening and closing caught her ear. Rosamunde straightened slightly to glance around the back of her chair to see who had entered. At first she didn't recognize the slumped figure shuffling wearily toward the trestle table, but then she did, and promptly leaped to her feet.

"My lord Bishop!" Filled with pleasure, she rushed forward to greet him. "What are you doing here? Are you and my father come for a visit?" Her gaze shifted to the door. "Is Father still out with the horses? I should—"

"Nay." Shrewsbury caught her arm, drawing her to a halt as she would have rushed past him. "Nay, child. He did not accompany me. The king is not here."

"Not here?" The words came out as an exhalation of breath. Her expression showed her shock. The bishop was the most faithful of servants. She had never seen the man travel without her father. Nor had she ever seen her father without Shrewsbury in attendance. "What? Why?" she stammered in confusion. He patted her arm, sadness washing over his face. He shook his head.

Rosamunde felt nausea roll up within her as she took in his expression. "He's not—"

"Aye. He is dead."

"He . . . But—it cannot be!" she managed to cry at last.

"I fear it is. He fell ill on our return journey to Chinon. He tried to fight it, but what with the business with Richard and the king of France . . ." He shook his head. "He had been able to get no rest. They kept at him like hounds on a fox."

"Damn them," Rosamunde whispered. Tears pooled in her eyes and spilled down her cheeks.

"Aye. Then, when he actually received proof that John had gone over to Richard's side, he seemed to lose the will to live."

"Oh, *no*," Rosamunde cried out. Her heart was breaking for the pain that such a betrayal must have given her proud father.

"He died July sixth at Chinon. I stayed only long enough to see him borne to Fontevraud to be buried, then came to you. He wished it so. 'Twas the last order he gave me, to come to you. To be sure that all was well with your marriage. He wished you to know of his deep love and pride in you. And he bade me to tell you not to be sad. He was tired and desirous of rest. He also said— though I confess I did not understand at the time, and still do not—he said to say to you 'Always.' He said you would understand."

"Always?" she repeated brokenly, then recalled their parting and the last words he had said to her. *I love you, too, child. And so shall your husband, but you must promise me to obey him. Always.* Her heart seemed to split in half as his words echoed in her head. She was so desolate with sorrow at that moment that when she heard the pained keening that drifted past her ears, she did not at first realize it was her own. It was when Bishop Shrewsbury's lined face came close and he put out a hand to touch her that she recognized that the high, soft wailing came from deep within her own throat.

Gasping in a shuddering breath, Rosamunde pulled away from his touch. She could not bear to be comforted just then. She could not be comforted. She had lost her king and her father, a man she had assumed would always be there for her.

Spinning on her heel, she fled the castle, heading automatically for the one place she could find comfort—the

one familiar place in this new life of hers, her only link
with the women and the place that had safeguarded her
all of her young life. She ran to the stables, stumbling into
the drafty building and staggering immediately to the
stall that housed Marigold. Hurrying inside, she threw
herself at the mare. Her arms wrapping around the animal's thick neck, she buried her face in her mane and
sobbed. Marigold whinnied once, then drew her head
slightly to the side and back, pressing her snout briefly
against Rosamunde's crown as if to offer comfort.

Bishop Shrewsbury found her several moments later.
Joining her in the stall, he touched her shoulder gently.
" 'Tis all right, child. All will be well."

"Nay. It will not. How could he leave me? Now I
have no one." She sobbed miserably.

"Hush." Pulling her away from her mare, Shrewsbury enclosed her in his withered arms and rocked her
gently. "You have your husband, still. Burkhart is a
good man."

"Aye," she murmured, sniffling. "He is a good man."

The bishop stilled at her toneless agreement and
pulled back to peer at her with a frown. "Is everything
not well with your marriage, child? Are you not happy?"

Wiping her tears away with the backs of her hands,
Rosamunde pulled away with a shrug that only made
Shrewsbury's frown deeper.

"He does not abuse you?"

"Nay. Of course not," Rosamunde assured him
quickly, then sighed when the old man continued to look
suspicious. "It is just . . . I do not think that I was meant
for marriage, my lord. I cannot seem to do anything right.
I was not trained in the more refined arts expected of a
wife. I cannot do needlepoint. I do not know how to run
an estate. I feel so useless here, and . . ."

"And?" he prompted gently.

Rosamunde flushed with embarrassment, but admitted with shame, "I know we are not supposed to enjoy the marriage bed, but I did not just not enjoy it. I found it painful and humiliating!" She grimaced. "Truly, I do not know why Father Abernott insisted on lecturing on adultery so often. I cannot imagine anyone willingly performing the activity."

"Ah." The bishop flushed bright pink and turned away slightly before asking carefully, "Have you—Has your husband . . . er . . . approached you since your wedding day?"

"Nay. And I am glad for that. But it also makes me feel guilty, for it just seems to be something else that I am no good at," she admitted miserably.

"My poor child." Shrewsbury shook his head sadly. "If your father had realized how miserable you would be, I am sure that he would not have insisted on this marriage."

"I wish he had not," she admitted bitterly. "I wish he had just left me at the abbey, or had arrived too late to stop my taking the veil, or—"

Her voice died as the stable doors opened and men's voices filled the drafty building. Her husband entered, followed by Lord Spencer, his servant, Joseph, and a couple of men-at-arms.

Rosamunde pulled abruptly out of the bishop's comforting arms and faced her husband, guilt at her disloyalty weighing her down. She had admitted that she wished she had not been forced to marry him.

Aric spotted the embracing couple the moment that he entered the stables, but it was not until the woman stepped out of the man's arms and moved out of the shadowed stall to face him guiltily that he recognized her as his wife. For a moment, he was overwhelmed by a sense of déjà vu, and he was cast back to the day he had caught Delia and Glanville in the stables. But then he noticed the tears in Rosamunde's eyes, and the man stepped up behind her, the light suddenly revealing to him that it was Bishop Shrewsbury.

It didn't take Aric's mind but a moment to switch from one concern to another. He went from fear that his wife was yet another faithless wench, to a sudden panic that the king had returned to check on his little girl and her happiness; the king was never without the bishop. His mind immediately began racing. Had the king already talked to the girl? Had she told him . . . what had she told him? Was she miserable?

Drawn and quartered, drawn and quartered. The words sang through his head merrily, and Aric swallowed as sweat broke out on his forehead. He had been rather stern with his young bride about what she could and could not do. He also had not spent any time trying to please her. He had not even troubled himself to talk to her or have a game of chess. And, dear Lord, he had not bedded her since the wedding. Had she told the king that?

"I know I am not supposed to be in the stables, my lord. I apologize for disobeying you so."

His wife's soft, sorrowful words drew Aric's thoughts, and irritation drove the anxiety out of him. She *had* disobeyed him. The wench had disobeyed a direct order from her own husband. Well, that would hardly look impressive to the king, would it? She had flouted a direct order. He had been flouted! Well, he was deviled if he would put up with that. The king be damned. A man could not allow himself to be flouted that way. Drawing himself up, he glared at her sternly. "Being sorry is not good enough. Get back to the castle at once. You will go to our room and stay there."

She hesitated briefly, just long enough for him to suspect she would rebel; then her shoulders seemed to sag, and she shrugged indifferently. "As you wish."

Slipping past Aric, she wove her way through the men and horses and out of the stables. Then she broke into a run, heading blindly for the castle. Tears were streaming down her face again as she pushed through the keep doors and rushed up the stairs to their bedchamber. Once there, she threw herself across the bed and began to sob in earnest—for the loss of her father, for the misery of her life now, for herself.

She was still weeping silently into a crumpled-up portion of the bed's top linen several moments later when a scratching at the door caught her attention. Sniffling, she raised her head to peer at the door blankly, then sat up and stood to walk over to it. The sound came again. Opening the door, she glanced out into the empty hallway, a frown tugging at her lips. No one was there. Closing the door silently, she turned away, only to pause in surprise as she saw a small black ball of fur leap onto the lighter-colored furs that covered the bed.

Wiping the last of her tears away, she moved toward the bed after the creature, realizing that this must have been the source of the scratching. She should have looked down. No doubt the animal had scooted into the room as she had opened the door.

Rosamunde recognized it at once as one of the kittens from the kitchen. She had seen four of them on an old pile of straw stacked in a corner of the kitchen that first day when she had toured the castle. Their mother had been absent at the time. Hunting up a mouse or two somewhere for her own meal, no doubt. Rosamunde had managed to trip up a lad carrying a tray of steaming bread as she had knelt to pet the tiny creatures. That had been when she had decided to give up bothering the servants and had relegated herself to sitting silently by the fire, where she could cause no more harm.

Seating herself on the edge of the bed now, she scooped the kitten into her arms and began to stroke it. This one was a male. She had noticed that morning. It had been all over her at the time, eager for any attention and affection she was offering. Now it mewled a complaint and tried to avoid her hand. Frowning as she realized that it only shrank away from her when she petted near its tiny head, she examined it carefully, murmuring comfortingly despite her concern. There were burns and melted hair on one ear. It had gone too near to Cook's fire, that was obvious, and she was not at all surprised. In the few moments she had spent with the kittens that morning, she had noticed that the black one, the only one that did not have its mother's gray coloring, was also the most curious and adventuresome.

Setting the kitten back on the bed, Rosamunde rose quickly and moved to collect the sack that held all her worldly belongings. Digging through it quickly, she came up with the smaller sack inside that held the medicinal herbs Eustice had packed away for her. With a sense of purpose, she moved back to the bed to tend the kitten's injuries.

Aric watched his wife hurry from the stables, then turned to face Shrewsbury. A frown tugged at his mouth and cut deep furrows into his forehead. He noted the displeasure on the older man's face. It was obvious the king's man did not approve of how he had dealt with his wife. Aric felt a moment's discomfort at that look as he realized that the exchange would most likely be reported back to Henry, but then he shrugged that brief worry aside and straightened his shoulders. Rosamunde was his wife. And she had disobeyed him. He would even have been within his rights to beat her for such an offense. Not that he would. He had dealt with her most mildly, he assured himself.

"What news?" he snapped at last, irritated by the other man's silent censure.

"Is this the care you show the king's daughter?"

Aric stiffened at the accusatory tone. "My *wife*,"—he stressed her title and place in his life—"disobeyed an order. As a leader, his majesty will know that such actions cannot be tolerated. If one of my men disobeyed, it could mean death for us all."

"Lady Rosamunde is not a warrior."

"Still, she disobeyed an order," he persisted grimly. "She was told not to spend time in the stables anymore. 'Tis not a fitting place for a lady."

"I see."

Aric swallowed at the silky hiss of those words, suspecting he might have made an error. As the king's most trusted and valued man, Bishop Shrewsbury was nearly as intimidating as the monarch himself. His position gave him much sway with the man. Certainly more sway than a new son-in-law, Aric thought unhappily. As Shrewsbury's next words were issued with gentle firmness, he was positive he would need a better explanation than the one he had offered.

"So you are suggesting that while assisting in the stables was fitting for the daughter of a king, 'tis not fitting for your bride?"

"Nay!" Aric shifted impatiently, cursing his own foolish tongue. "Stables are not the safest of places for a lady, my lord Bishop. She is much safer in the keep."

"I do not recall her safety being in question at the abbey," the man murmured, then cocked his head slightly. "And they had everything there that they do here: horses, hay, saddles. Of course, they did not have men. Are you, mayhap, suggesting that one of your own men might do her harm?"

Aric gave a start at those words. Shrewsbury had always been a shrewd fellow. It was why he was so valuable to the king. Still, it startled Aric that he had picked up on the one thing that made a difference to Aric. Even if he had put the wrong spin on it.

"Nay, of course not," he said at last. "My men are sworn to protect their lady. But—"

"She has grown up in the stables," the bishop interrupted quietly. "Spent the majority of her life in them. 'Tis the task she was given at the abbey. She has a special way with injured creatures, 'tis the gift God gave her. The abbess recognized that and put her under Sister Eustice's care to nurture her special ability. One should always use the gifts God has given." He paused, then murmured, "If you will not allow her to do the work God set out for her to do, mayhap you should have the marriage annulled. Return her to the abbey to become a bride of God—as she had planned."

Aric stiffened with anger at the very suggestion. Shrewsbury added, "'Tis what she wishes."

Aric blanched at that, and the older man went on. "She has told me so. She is miserable here. Lady Rosamunde was not raised—or trained—to run a household. She was raised to take the veil. Return her to the abbey," he urged.

Aric struggled with his temper, then, said, "The king—"

"Is dead," Shrewsbury finished.

Every man present went still.

"Dead?" Aric echoed in disbelief. The older man nodded solemnly, weariness and grief encompassing his face. Aric turned to peer rather blankly at the other men, numbly noting their expressions. Not one of them could have looked more shocked or pained had they just been told that their own fathers had left this world. Down to a man, they had all gone so pale as to appear gray, their faces blanched and sickly-looking. There was even a touch of fear on each face. What upheaval could follow such an event? Their king was dead—a king whose sons had struggled and fought, backbiting and betraying their own father in an effort to wrest away the throne. Would the sons now fight among themselves for that same title, causing civil war and strife? Pitting baron against baron with their greed? It was a likely possibility. Neither man—the older son, Richard, nor the young favorite, John—had shown even a thimbleful of loyalty to their father. There was little reason to expect that either man would now extend any loyalty to each other.

"Does Lady Rosamunde know?" Lord Spencer asked with concern. Aric turned back to Shrewsbury in time to see him nod again.

"Aye. I told her soon as I arrived. 'Tis why she was in the stables—seeking comfort from the animals she cares for."

Aric winced at those words, knowing he deserved their sting. He had not even noticed her distress let alone consoled her, and she must be sorely distressed by this news. He had merely chastised her and sent her away. It seemed that he was destined to make mistake after mistake with his wife, damn his own stupid hide. Sighing, he rubbed the back of his neck wearily. "When did he die?"

"July sixth at Chinon."

"Do his sons know yet?"

"Of course. Richard was informed at once." Shrewsbury grimaced. "When he paid his respects, blood began to pour from the king's nose."

"Murder," Lord Spencer's man muttered with dismay. "The dead bleed only when their murderer is present."

Aric frowned. That was an old wives' tale. Still . . . "Was it murder?"

Shrewsbury shrugged, looking wearier than seemed previously possible. "It depends on what you consider murder, I suppose. He fell ill shortly before arriving back at Chinon. He was weak and suffering. He wished to rest, but those sons of his gave him no peace. He could not rally—the world was against him, or he felt it was. He died alone but for Geoffrey, myself, and a handful of servants. We saw him buried at Fontevraud Abbey the next day. Then I came directly here, for he asked me to with his dying breath. He wished me to check on Rosamunde, to keep an eye on her. Make sure she was happy. He wished me to give her a message as well."

"What was the message?"

"I gave it to her," the bishop replied evenly.

Aric shifted in irritation, but tried to hide his annoyance just as quickly. "When will Richard's coronation be?"

"I do not know. It will be soon, I am sure. Richard will hardly waste any time on grieving."

Aric nodded grimly at those bitter words. That much was true, but Aric was less concerned with Richard's feelings over his father's death than he was over the man's feelings on the subject of his half sister. Did he even know she existed? And if so, would he be concerned with her welfare, or would he see her as a possible rival for the throne? That was doubtful. A woman had yet to rule England—and a bastard surely had less claim than a legitimate son. Still, Henry had wished Rosamunde married to protect her from danger, and Aric now had to wonder if Richard could be a problem.

" 'Tis obvious the king made a mistake."

The bishop's words dragged Aric's attention away from his thoughts. A frown curved his face in irritation. "What mean you?"

"I mean 'tis obvious that this marriage was a mistake. I beseech you, my lord, set her free. Let her return to the abbey and become a bride of God. 'Tis what she was raised to be. She was not trained to run a household. She knows not how to be a proper wife. She is miserable trying."

"She will learn soon enough. 'Sides, the king wished this marriage."

"The king wished his daughter safe and happy. He would not wish her to be so miserable."

Aric stiffened. "She is *not* miserable. She just misses her old life. It will pass."

Shrewsbury clucked in disgust. "Her unhappiness is obvious, my lord. Surely even you see it. She has been taken away from all that she knows and loves and given nothing in return."

"She has been given a husband and a new home in return. She shall come to be comfortable here. She will be happy after a time."

"How can she? She—"

"The king wished this marriage," Aric interrupted grimly. "It shall stand."

They glared at each other briefly; then the bishop gave a short bow. "Forgive me, I had not realized you were so enamored of Rosamunde. I thought you just as reluctant a groom as she was a bride. I thought only to save you both some misery. But it is obvious from your reaction that you are pleased with this marriage."

Aric blinked at those words, his mind in an uproar as he realized what he had just done. Good Lord, the bishop had just given him a chance at freedom from this unwanted marriage—and he had refused even to consider it. Worse yet, he had been angered by the very suggestion. Did he really want to keep Rosamunde to wife? His answer to that question came rather promptly. *Yes*. He wanted her. But before he could ask himself why, Bishop Shrewsbury spoke up again.

"I trust I might rest here awhile, my lord?" he asked quietly. Aric sighed at the question. He could hardly refuse the man his hospitality, though right then he would have liked to.

"Aye," he said grimly, then glanced toward Joseph and Lord Spencer. "Will you see to his comfort? I would check on my wife."

"Of course, my lord."

Nodding, Aric made his way wearily out of the stables, his head almost spinning with all he had learned. His mind seemed resistant to absorbing the demise of a man he had thought would outlive them all. King Henry II. Strong, agile, energetic Henry. He had never seemed to stand still, never seemed to rest. And he was dead. Incredible. Horrible. So terribly sad.

God, if he was struck by this so dreadfully, how much worse must it be for Rosamunde? She was the man's daughter, he thought with dismay.

And he had yelled at her for seeking comfort from a horse! What the devil was the matter with him? He knew what the matter was, of course. For one brief moment—until he had recognized that the man with his wife in the dim stables was Shrewsbury—he had feared history was repeating itself. Jealousy and fear made fools out of men, and he had behaved like a fool. It was no wonder she wished to return to the convent. He had hardly given her a reason to wish to stay. The bedding, for instance; he had not exactly given a stellar performance on their wedding day. If he had had more time . . . But he had not!

His shoulders slumped wearily. It was terribly disheartening to learn that his wife was so unhappy. The king had entrusted him with the care, safety, and happiness of his most beloved child, and he was flubbing it horribly. He had not even allowed her to try to explain her presence in the stables, he had simply exploded. Of course she would run to the stables for comfort upon hearing of her father's death. She loved that horse. Mayhap she had even heard that Shrewsbury had arrived and, thinking her father would be with him, had rushed out to greet the man. Whatever the case, he should not have been so harsh with her.

Well, he would make up for that. He would offer her the comfort she needed now. And when he did eventually attempt to bed her again, he would ensure it was a good experience for her.

Aric grimaced. He had thought of little else but getting her into bed again for the last two weeks, but not necessarily with eagerness. After the fiasco of their first time, attempting it again wasn't very appealing. In fact, it gave him the shudders just to think of it, he admitted to himself with some shame. How humiliating that was to admit, even to himself, which he had finally done last night when he realized that he was finding excuse after excuse to avoid their bedchamber—all in an effort to avoid his husbandly duties. Not that his wife was likely to demand he perform them.

But it was a task he would have to see to eventually if he wished for legitimate heirs. He would just have to face it. Perhaps he could ply her with wine first to make her relax; then he would take his time. He would not let the king down again. He was only grateful that Henry had not learned of his failure ere his death. Not that Aric feared repercussions now, but he would be sorry to have disappointed him.

That thought making him grimace, he hurried up the steps and into the keep, then rushed through the great hall, straight up the stairs to their chamber. Pausing at the door to their room, he straightened his shoulders, preparing himself like a man girding himself for battle, then opened the door and stepped inside. There he paused. The tears, weeping, and wailing that he had expected were absent. The room was silent. His wife was fully clothed and fast asleep on the bed, her body curled protectively around a furry ball atop the bed linens. It seemed that, once again, she had turned to an animal for comfort.

He stared at her silently for a moment, debating what to do; then she sniffled miserably in her sleep. Aric peered more closely at her face. Her nose was red from weeping, her eyelids pink and puffy.

Return her to the abbey. Have the marriage annulled. Her unhappiness is obvious. Bishop Shrewsbury's words echoed in his head, and he frowned at his sleeping wife. He was not going to return her. She was his. They were married.

The possessive thought took Aric slightly by surprise. He had not wanted to marry her—had even resented being forced to and been colder to her for that, he realized now with a bit of insight that shamed him. Aye, he had resented being forced to marry after the debacle of his broken betrothal to Delia. But he had also been helpless to refuse the king, so he had taken out his anger on the slender woman sleeping in the bed. He had not beaten her. Nor treated her truly poorly, at least not in a way for which anyone could take him to task. But he had done very little to make her feel wanted or appreciated. Instead he had done the opposite, letting her know in myriad different ways that he didn't need her, didn't want her. Yet now, at the mention of the possibility of returning her, he felt anger stir within him.

Nay, he would not lose her. But neither would their relationship continue as it had. He would try now to make her happy, and he would start by being there to offer her comfort when she awoke. He eased the door closed before moving toward the bed, removing his sword belt as he walked.

The furry ball was a kitten, he saw as he paused beside the bed and carefully hung his scabbard from the bedpost. And both the cat and his wife were smack-dab in the middle of the bed. He considered shifting her over to the side a bit to make more room for himself, but decided not to disturb her. He deserved the discomfort of sleeping at the edge of the bed. He had not proven himself a very considerate husband; this day's events had pointed that out quite painfully. He had been so caught up in his own worries and fears that he not taken the time to consider how she must be feeling. She had, after all, been all set to take the veil.

A nun.

He could not see this vibrant creature who had frolicked on the riverbank as a woman of the church. He could not imagine those lovely, fiery tresses of hers shorn from her head, a stiff habit its only covering. He could not fathom her perfect body hidden beneath loose, shapeless clothes. The enthusiasm and passion he had spied in her on the way here could never have been subdued by strictures and rules. Nay, she would have felt stifled as a nun, he felt sure.

On the other hand, what the hell did he know? After all, she had spent her life in a convent. She knew better than anyone what taking the veil meant, and yet had been prepared to make the vows. It made him wonder how she saw him. Did she resent his presence in her life?

Did she fear the power he now wielded over her? Hate him because he stood between her and her God?

He did not know. Her behavior since leaving the convent really gave him no clue. She had been quiet around him, following his orders with little more than a nod. Shrewsbury's comments in the stables were the only clues he had as to how she truly felt about this situation. And his words did not bode well.

Sighing, Aric began to undo his surcoat. It would be quite the trick to crawl into bed without awaking her, but he would try, he decided. Shrugging the garment off, he hung it from the bedpost as well, then quickly tugged his tunic off over his head.

Dropping the shirt to the floor, he left his brais on, gently lifted a corner of the top bed linen, and eased onto the edge of the mattress. With her in the center, there was very little room left around the edges. He was going to be hanging out of it. He deserved that, he again supposed, carefully lifting one leg, then most of the other under the linen before reclining on his back.

She hadn't stirred at all, he saw as he tried to settle comfortably on the slice of bed she had unintentionally left him. The kitten had roused, however, and was sitting up slightly in the curve of her arm, glaring at him in a rather offended fashion. It was only then that Aric noticed the bandage fastened over the animal's ear, brought down around his head, and tied off under his neck. It took away somewhat from the haughty attitude the cat was attempting, and Aric grinned slightly.

Apparently further peeved by such misplaced amusement, the kitten twitched its tail, stood, turned its back to him, and settled down once more, nestling against Rosamunde's cotton-covered breasts.

"You win," Aric muttered to himself wryly. When the cat cast a disdainful glance over its shoulder at him, he arched his eyebrows slightly. A smile that did not reach his eyes tugged his lips wide, briefly baring his teeth. "Enjoy it while you can, puss. It will be me nestled there after this night. You can count on that."

The kitten's eyes seemed to narrow in unpleasant understanding at that. Then it turned its head away again and merely nestled closer to Rosamunde.

Sighing, Aric forced himself to relax. He might have a long wait ahead of him until his wife awoke and needed him, but he was determined to be there for her when she did.

Chapter 8

IT was a spitting hiss and several tiny claws digging into his behind that awoke Aric some little time later. Jolted awake, he shifted swiftly and glared at the culprit. It seemed that he had turned onto his side as he drifted off, probably in an effort to fit better upon the bed, then started to roll onto his back, and on top of the tiny cat between him and his wife. The creature was all puffed up now, its back arched, the hair on its back and tail standing on end as it glared at him with its back pressed firmly against his wife's chest. A chest that shifted now as Rosamunde stirred slowly to wakefulness.

Aric watched, entranced, as she blinked sleepily, first at the upset kitten, then at Aric himself. All signs of tears were now gone from her face. Her eyes were sleep-shadowed in the dim light of the dying afternoon. "What is about?" she murmured in confusion; then as the sleep cleared from her mind, she realized who she was looking at. "Oh. My lord."

Wiping the last of the sleep from her eyes with one small hand, she sat up slowly and peered about the darkening room, at him reclining in bed, then down at herself, taking in the fact that she was still dressed. The kitten hissed at Aric again as he, too, started to sit up, drawing her attention to its position, hunched against her with raised hackles, and she soothed it automatically with gentle strokes and soft words. "Hush, little one. 'Tis all right."

"I must have rolled on him," Aric explained, finding his voice at last. When Rosamunde immediately bent a concerned gaze to the animal, he added, "I do not think he was harmed."

"No, I am sure he is fine," she agreed, then raised uncertain eyes to him again. She was silent for a moment, obviously still half-asleep and confused by the fact that she was abed in the middle of the day. Then recollection struck her. Her eyes widened slightly, and tears filled them. Pain swept over her face, blanching all color from her and twisting her expression.

"Wife?" he murmured uncertainly.

"He is dead." The words were flat, expressionless. Disturbed by her silent grief, Aric shifted closer, careful to avoid getting too near the kitten and its tiny, razor-sharp claws; then he slid an arm around her shoulders and tugged her gently against his chest. After the briefest hint of resistance, she collapsed against him, her silent tears becoming loud, wrenching sobs.

Feeling helpless in the face of her pain, Aric closed his eyes and began to smooth a hand gently over her hair. "Shhh. 'Twill be all right. Let it out," he whispered.

"Nay, my lord. 'Twill not be all right." She sobbed, shuddering with the effort to speak past her grief. "Now I have no one."

Aric stiffened at the words, then silently cursed himself for the cold way he had treated her. Truly, he was now all she had. He realized it with a sort of shock. Her mother had died when she was but a child. Her father was dead. She had been ripped from the bosom of the abbey where she had grown up. She had no one but him. Oddly enough, he found himself a little frightened by that thought. Still, he murmured the words, "You have me."

Her short, bitter laugh made him stiffen briefly; then she said, "You do not want me, my lord. There is no need to pretend that you do. My father forced you to marry me as surely as he forced this situation on me."

Aric hesitated over that, unsure what to say, then cleared his throat. "Well, mayhap neither of us wished this marriage, but surely we can make the best of it. Can we not?"

"The best of what?" she asked bitterly. "We have been here two weeks now and all I have learned is how useless I am. I know not how to run an estate. How to direct servants. How to do figures or needlepoint. I am not even any good for bedding."

Aric grimaced. Truly their first time together had been a debacle, but that was hardly her fault. Well, for the most part anyway. While she had been given a poor education indeed in the nuances of the marriage bed, on the bright side, it was better than the vast experience and knowledge Delia apparently had. Besides, everything would have ended differently had he had the time necessary to prepare her properly. The brief and brutal in-and-out he had been forced to perpetrate had been unpleasant for both of them.

"The first time is always unpleasant and awkward," he assured her with quiet authority. "The next time will be different. You shall see."

"Truly?" She pulled away slightly, just enough to take in his features, and he nodded solemnly.

"Truly."

"Then you are not disgusted with the very thought of having to bed me?"

He gave a short, sharp bark of laughter as his gaze swept over her. Disgusted at the thought of having to bed her? Was she truly so ignorant of her beauty? he wondered faintly, raising a hand to caress the side of her face. Nay, he was not disgusted by the thought of her warm and naked beneath him, her flesh glowing pink with desire. He felt himself stir with desire at the picture that formed in his head. He had been married for over three weeks and still had yet to see his bride completely nude. She had insisted on wearing her gown the day they were married, and while he had seen her nude while she was bathing, all he had glimpsed was her naked back. But he could imagine. He *had* imagined it nearly every single time he had looked at her.

"Nay," he said at last. "The thought of bedding you does not disgust me. Far from it. And I shall prove it to you," he said firmly.

His wife's reaction to that was rather prompt. Confusion flashed across her face, followed by uncertainty, then resignation. Then, quick as lightning, she shifted onto her hands and knees on the bed, her derriere once again propped in his face. There was no mistaking it for eagerness. It seemed pretty obvious that while she had certainly not enjoyed the first time—and wasn't looking forward to this time—she simply wished to please him as a wife. And with her derriere in his face as a reminder of what he would have to overcome to claim her, Aric felt some—well, all right, *all*—of his desire slip away like dust in a breeze.

Sighing inwardly, he cleared his throat. "Tonight," he murmured.

Rosamunde peered back over her shoulder at him uncertainly. "Tonight, my lord?"

"Aye, tonight. Now." He sought about for a reason

why now was not possible, then latched onto the obvious. "Is it not time for sup?"

Eyes widening slightly, Rosamunde glanced toward the window to see that the sun was on the last quarter of its downward journey. It was indeed time for sup. She turned back to say as much to her husband, only to find him already out of bed. He was tugging his tunic on even as he strode toward the door.

"Come along. The food will be cold do we not hurry." Slipping through the door, he left her to follow in her own time.

Rosamunde watched the door close behind him, then shook her head. She reached out absently to give the kitten a pet before shifting to get off the bed as well. It had almost seemed to her as if he had been eager to escape. She must have been mistaken, she thought uncertainly. After all, had he not said that the thought of bedding her did not disgust him?

On the other hand, not being disgusted at the idea and actually being eager to do something were not the same thing, some part of her mind pointed out. Rosamunde sighed as she brushed the worst of the wrinkles out of her gown. Well, she supposed it was not all that important. After all, she was not exactly eager to attend to the deed herself.

Sighing again, she moved toward the door, shaking her head over the fact that she now had that humiliating event to look forward to again tonight. She should have kept her mouth shut.

"Well, I am to bed."

Aric gave a start at that announcement from Lord Spencer and peered at him with alarm. "What? So early? Why not have another drink with me first?"

Smiling wryly, the blind old man shook his head. " 'Tis already well past the hour I usually retire. And I fear if I have one more drink, Joseph shall have to carry me to my chamber. I shall see you in the morning, my lord."

Aric grunted his own good night, his eyes moving a bit desperately over the people left at the table. It had been an unusually quiet meal. Lord Spencer had offered his condolences to Rosamunde as soon as she arrived to eat a mere few minutes behind Aric's own arrival. Tears had pooled in her eyes as she had accepted the kind words, but had not slipped down her cheeks. They returned to fill her eyes several times that night, and her mood had seemed representative of the other castle inhabitants. Henry had been loved here. Rosamunde had been quiet through most of the meal, and retired almost directly afterward.

Aric had remained behind to drink with the men, a vague sense of unease building in him as the table slowly emptied. Now he peered gloomily along the nearly empty trestle tables, wondering when everyone had turned into such early birds.

"I suppose I should retire as well."

Those words from Bishop Shrewsbury drew Aric's alarmed gaze. The prelate was the last man at the head trestle table besides himself. "What? Did you not wish to take the opportunity to argue with me some more over returning Rosamunde to the abbey?"

Halfway to his feet, Shrewsbury paused to glance at him sharply. "Are you considering doing so?"

Aric frowned irritably and shifted in his seat. "Nay. But we could argue the fact."

Shaking his head, the bishop continued to his feet. "I am too tired from my journey here to argue in vain. Mayhap tomorrow I can offer an argument you will listen to."

"Mayhap," Aric agreed dryly, thinking that if tonight went as he feared, he might very well concede to the wisdom of returning her.

Startled by his own thoughts, Aric frowned and lifted his ale to his lips, trying not to think too hard. But it was impossible not to. Half of the truth had already leaked out, and the other half was eager to join it. He was sitting here at the table, drinking ale after ale, trying to get up the courage to go to bed.

Good Lord, he was afraid to go above stairs because he knew he had to bed his wife when he got there. He had told her he would. And he wanted to; truly he did! It was not lack of desire that held him back. He wanted her so much that he could taste it; it was sharp and dry, with the promise of sweetness. The week-long journey first to Shambley, then on to Goodhall had been sweet torture for him. If he closed his eyes, he could still feel and smell her in his arms as she had ridden before him on his horse. Her hair had been soft and silky against his cheek. The sweet scent of roses had assailed him when he dipped his head forward to hear her words. Her back had been against his chest, her bottom unintentionally nudging him where she sat between his thighs. The bottoms of her breasts had continuously grazed the tops of his hands as he had sat, arms around her, holding his mount's reins. It had been sweet torture to hold her so. As had been lying next to her each night since arriving at Goodhall.

If feeling and smelling were not enough to spark his desire, he could actually see her as well: her wet body glistening in the moonlight as she stood naked, the river swirling around her as she washed the day's travels from her perfect body.

At least it had appeared perfect to him. Long, coltish legs, slender waist, the curve of one small, firm breast.

Just how he liked a woman: with enough curves to be feminine, but not swollen by them.

Feeling himself tremble with desire under this imagined assault to his senses, he took a shallow breath and forced her from his mind.

Desire isn't the problem, he thought as lust eased its hold on him. *So why do I hesitate to bed my wife?*

The answer came quickly. Fear. He had known this night would come since that debacle on their wedding day. Had anticipated it with equal parts anticipation and anxiety. Part of him was sure this second time would be different. There would be no rush, no need for him to gloss over her education of proper marital relations. Another part of him, however, was still wincing at that consummation of their wedding day and afraid this would end the same. This was his wife. Not some maid or camp follower with whom he could spend a careless night and never worry about. He could not rise afterwards, give her a cheerful farewell, and be about his business. She would be there in the morning—and at night. Every morning and every night. If he muffed this *again*, he would be faced with it every morning for the rest of his life.

Recognizing the reason that held him back was helpful in a way. As Henry had always said, it was always good to know one's enemy. Smiling wryly at his own dramatic thoughts, he decided enough was enough. He was going above stairs to bed his wife, not to slay a dragon. Still, he straightened his shoulders determinedly and took a deep breath ere rising from the table. He managed to take two steps away before pausing to swing back, snatch up his ale, and down the rest of it in one long gulp.

Slamming the mug on the table, he swung away and crossed the great hall to the stairs with determined steps.

That determined stride carried him up the stairs and down the hall to his bedchamber before he lost it. Pausing at the door, he hesitated, grimaced to himself, then leaned his forehead against the door's rough wooden slats. He sighed. This was ridiculous, really. He was acting like a weak-kneed virgin. Aric was far from being a virgin. So far from it that he did not think he could recall what it had really felt like. He had had his first woman before the age of twelve. She'd been a camp follower, one of the many prostitutes who followed warriors from battle to battle, plying their trade between skirmishes to whoever had the coin for it. He had been a squire at the time. It had been his first time out and he had been eager to earn his spurs.

He had earned his spurs all right, he thought now, recalling his enthusiasm that first time. In the end, he had not even had to pay for the experience. She—he could not recall her name anymore—had called it her good deed, "breaking in the boy." At the time he had puffed up like a bantam rooster, completely misunderstanding her words. Only later, after more experience, had he realized that she had most likely given him the free tumble out of pity. There had been no need for foreplay; he had been as hard as a dead chicken before he even opened his brais. He had managed to kiss her once, lift her skirts, and even insert himself inside her, but that had been as far as his excited young body had gotten before releasing itself. Thinking back, he would be surprised if it had taken a full minute.

Shaking his head with the embarrassment of an adult recalling youthful antics, he closed his eyes. He had not performed much better his second time. But his third time, well, that had been a different experience entirely. Whether from the skill of the woman, or the fact that he was so drunk, he could not say, but he had learned a great deal with her. *Molly*. He doubted he would ever forget *her* name. She had made a good start on teaching him all there was to know about the relations between men and women—and enjoyed the teaching. Aric had continued that learning with each new experience over the intervening years. He had found himself popular with women of every kind. And there had been many of them, whores, maids, and ladies.

So he should really stop dallying outside his bedroom door and get to the task at hand. He should also stop thinking of it as a chore. It was *not* going to turn out like the last time. He was not twelve anymore.

Rosamunde sat in the bed, petting a purring Soot—that was the name she had chosen for the injured kitten— and awaiting her husband. Aric had stayed on at the table with the men when she retired, no doubt continuing the discussion of what he had seen so far on his tour of the estate and what needed doing. That had been the discussion through most of the meal. Rosamunde had listened silently. But as the meal and discussion had continued, she had noticed that there was no mention of the stables or stablemaster except to comment in a rather vague way that new stables would eventually have to be built.

Desperate to avoid thinking of her father's death and thereby avoid the possibility of bursting into tears at the table, Rosamunde had latched onto that fact and had allowed the anger it stirred inside of her to grow. That anger had stiffened her back and had helped her to keep her dignity. It had carried her through the meal and seen her safely upstairs. But once alone in the room, with only Soot to distract her, her anger had faded and her thoughts had wandered. They had touched on the loss of her father, but the grief that had seared her heart then had turned her to quickly finding something else to ponder, and there had been two doozies awaiting: what she saw as her miserable failure as a wife, and the fact that her husband would come through that door soon, expecting to perform marital relations with her. With such thoughts for company, it was almost a relief when she heard the door open and saw her husband entering the room.

She was sitting on the bed when he entered, still fully clothed and petting the kitten. Managing a smile, Aric closed the door and moved to the bed. Pausing there, he sat down on the edge of it and glanced absently around the room. A fire was burning low in the fireplace and kept the evening chill at bay. Other than that, the room looked pretty much as it had since their arrival. There was nothing to distract him from the matter at hand.

"Husband?"

Giving a start at her soft voice, he glanced at her questioningly.

"Did you still wish to—"

"Aye," he interrupted her anxious words quickly, then glanced down at the cat she still held on her lap. "I shall just . . . er . . . remove this little fellow," he announced, certainly not looking for a reason to put it off for another moment. Ignoring the claws and teeth that immediately scourged his hands, Aric scooped the spitting little bundle out of her lap and carried it quickly to a chair by the fire. Settling it there, he then turned back to the bed, only to pause. His wife had shifted while he removed the kitten. She now knelt on her hands and knees on the bed, her skirt hiked up over her waist. The ludicrous posture continued to throw him.

Shoulders slumping, he closed his eyes and counted to ten, then forced his eyes open again. He straightened his shoulders and moved determinedly back to the bed.

"Wife—Rosamunde." He corrected himself almost at once and managed to force a smile when she glanced back at him over her shoulder. "Come here." He gestured to the side of the bed where he stood, and her expression clouded with confusion.

"But I thought you wished to commence the—"

"Aye, but first I wish you to come over here," he interrupted.

Rosamunde frowned slightly. His expression was irritated, his voice almost a growl. Obviously she had angered him in some way. Yet again. Sighing inwardly, she straightened and turned on her knees, then crawled across the bed to pause before him, her expression uncertain.

Taking her by the shoulders, he pulled her gently forward, bending at the same time until his lips brushed across hers. Rosamunde pulled back at once in confusion. "What are you doing?"

Closing his eyes, her husband gave a long-suffering sigh. "I am kissing you."

"Oh." Feeling slightly foolish, but still not understanding why he was wasting time with kissing her, Rosamunde allowed him to draw her forward again, remaining still and passive as his lips moved softly over her own—until his tongue slid out to touch her lips. Startled, she tried to pull back again, but he held her in place, persistently nudging with his tongue until her lips opened in response, allowing him entrance. His tongue swept inside then, his mouth tilting more and opening wider over hers as he found her own tongue and said a delicious hello. She withstood the attention for several moments, aware of the odd, tingly, hot sensation building in the center of her, then pulled away, fear giving her the strength to break the embrace.

Eustice had said there should be no lewd kissing. Rosamunde wasn't sure if this kiss would be considered lewd, but was sure anything that made her feel so good was probably bad.

"Do you not think we should get to the bedding part?" she asked anxiously.

Aric smiled slightly. Her lips were swollen and rosy from his kiss, her eyes alive with both budding desire and fear. "This is part of it, wife."

He saw doubt cloud her expression, and, remembering their wedding day, and the things she had said when he had tried to consummate their marriage, he decided to clear up any leftover problems right away. "Wife. The nun, the one who told you about cucumbers and such—"

"Eustice," she supplied helpfully, and he nodded.

"Aye. Well, I want you to forget everything she told you. She was wrong."

"She was?"

"Aye."

Rosamunde nodded solemnly at that. "I did wonder," she admitted quietly, and Aric raised his eyebrows.

"You did?"

"Aye, well." Her gaze dropped down to his lap. "It really does not look much like a cucumber. More like a mushroom, really. I—" His hand over her mouth silenced her at once, and Rosamunde's eyes moved back up to his face to see that his eyes were closed, his face slightly red.

Shaking his head, he opened his eyes, a pained expression on his face. "Let us just agree that she was wrong. That I am your husband, and that I shall be more than pleased to teach you all that you need to know on this matter. Agreed?"

Rosamunde nodded, and Aric removed his hand, but he did not give her the chance to speak again. Covering her mouth with his lips, he concentrated his attention on kissing her as he knew she had never been kissed before. He made love to her mouth with his own until she was trembling in his arms and making squeaky little sounds of pleading and pleasure, her fingers digging into his arms. Then he let his hand slide down her shoulders, along her elbows, to grasp her hands. After giving them a gentle squeeze, he tugged them up to his own shoulders, then behind his neck, placing them there to keep them out of the way before skimming his fingers back along her arms to her shoulders. He then slid them down and around to find and cup her breasts through her gown.

Her body went as taut as a bow, her arms tightening almost painfully around his neck, her mouth sucking almost viciously at his own. Aric paused, merely holding her until she became used to his touch. Her reaction eased, her arms loosening somewhat, her kiss and posture melting.

His wife was very responsive, it would seem. He realized it with a heady sense of power, and smiled against her lips before allowing his mouth to trail its way across her cheek to her ear, to nibble softly there. Rosamunde's reaction was immediate. Shuddering in his arms, she nuzzled into the caress, a low moan sliding smoothly from her lips. Quite pleased with himself, Aric released one breast to clasp her bottom through her gown. He pressed forward, grinding her gently against the proof of his own arousal while gently squeezing and fondling the breast he still held through the material of her gown.

Suddenly she broke away again. Chest heaving, she scooted back on the bed and eyed him with wide eyes, her gaze dropping to the bulging front of his brais, then back to his face.

"I should—" She gasped, then whirled on the bed, taking up her dratted pose on hands and knees again, and Aric sighed inwardly. It seemed he hadn't *quite* made her forget those damned directions that crazy nun had given her. Shaking his head, he quickly stripped off his clothes, then moved around the bed to settle himself on it before her. Frowning slightly, she straightened to sit on her haunches uncertainly. Aric quickly scooted forward.

Satisfied that she had no room to try to take up her position on all fours again, he then lifted a hand to caress one of her breasts. He slid the other down to catch and lift the hem of her gown enough for his hand to snake beneath. Holding her confused gaze with his own knowing one, Aric ran his hand lightly up the outside of one leg, then slid it between her thighs, finding with his fingers that which he sought.

Rosamunde leaped upright off her haunches as if she had been shot with an arrow. Aric immediately removed his hand from her breast. Sliding it around her waist, he applied firm pressure on her back, to press her against his chest and keep her there as he continued to play with her.

"What?" She gasped, her hands reaching back to catch and clench over the hand behind her as she tried to speak. "What are you doing?"

"Touching you," he answered matter-of-factly, bending to nibble at her neck as he slid his hand out from beneath hers and raised it to find her breast again.

"Why?" she managed in a strangled tone.

"Do you not like it?" he asked, then laughed huskily when she immediately shook her head. "Liar," he whispered by her ear before nipping at it. "I can feel that you like it."

That made her stiffen even more than his touch did. "You can?" she said in a squeak.

"Aye, your nipples are hard." He pinched one through the cloth of her gown, wishing he could get the dress off of her and wondering how long that was going to take him. "And you are all wet and welcoming down here." He slid a finger inside her as he spoke, satisfied by the low moan she tried to swallow. She was moving against his hand now, probably not even aware of her actions, and Aric was finding his own excitement increasing with hers. He kissed her, covering her mouth with his and devouring her. Then he nudged the fiery red strands of her hair aside and ran his lips over her throat, sucking, then nipping, pausing briefly at the surprised "Oh" that slipped from her lips.

"Oh, what?" he asked, his words coming out in a growl.

"I—It . . . it does not hurt. When you bite my neck. I felt sure it would." She moaned.

Aric was confused by her words, but wasn't of a mind to discuss their meaning at the moment. He wanted her damned dress off. Now. He wanted her flesh against his. He wanted to close his lips around one sweet breast, then the other, then back. . . . God, at this moment he thought he could die with his face between her breasts and be happy.

Shaking off the hands that clutched his, he distracted her with deep kisses as he began tugging at her lacings, catching her sigh of disappointment with his mouth when he removed his other hand from between her legs to help with the task. Once the lacings were undone, he quickly pushed the gown off her shoulders, then caught her naked breasts in his hands. Rosamunde arched into his touch, gasping something into his mouth, covering his hands with her own as he palmed and caressed her swollen flesh.

That didn't satisfy him for long. He wanted her breast at his mouth. He wanted to roll the pebblelike nipple across his tongue and teeth. Releasing her breasts, he caught her by the waist, lifted her slightly, and caught one of those tempting nipples between his teeth, sucking it deliciously into his mouth.

Rosamunde immediately caught his head on either side and tried to push his lips away with confusion. She said with a gasp, "You will get no milk from me."

"Mayhap not from here just yet, but I will from here." Aric covered the apex of her legs with his palm as he said that against her flesh, then moved his head to her other nipple. Sister Eustice's words whirled in her mind: *Lips are for speaking, breasts are for . . .* Rosamunde lost her train of thought as Aric caught her gown and pushed it down over her hips to pool around her knees. Then he pushed her backward on the bed.

She landed with a soft "Ummph," her eyes wide as she watched him pull the gown off her legs and toss it carelessly aside. Her hands immediately moved to cover her nakedness, but Aric brushed them aside, then lay down beside her.

Leaning over her, he kissed first one breast, then the other, and Rosamunde caught his head in her hands, running her fingers through his dark hair. Then his lips moved away, trailing kisses down her belly, and she closed her eyes as she was assaulted by a quivery sensation pinging its way from her belly outward. She felt his lips brush one hip, then the other, and she shuddered and twisted under the tickly touch of his hand at her thigh. She spread her legs at his urging, drawing them up as she did, until her feet lay flat on the bed, her legs bent, but she was hardly aware of having done so. She concentrated instead on the trail his lips were taking.

He sprinkled kisses down one thigh to her knee, and paused to kiss and lick at the inside of that knee before switching to do the same to the inside of the other. His lips burned a trail up that thigh, then found and stopped at the center of her. Rosamunde arched off the bed, a choked sound slipping from her lips as she snapped her legs closed around his head.

Aric caught her thighs and pressed them open again as he laved her, aware that sweat was beading on and rolling off his forehead. His body was as stiff and hard as a sword, and he was hard-pressed not to simply shift between her legs and thrust himself into her. Her passion was a living thing, her response as free and unrepressed as any man could wish—and she was driving him crazy. Mewls, sighs, gasps, and groans were coming from her lips with little concern for propriety. Her body was thrusting and arching. Her head was thrashing back and forth as if she were in the throes of a seizure. Her nipples were pebbles on her goosefleshed breasts that cried for his attention. Her eyes were squeezed shut. Her hands were clenched frenziedly in the bed linens. And all his body wanted was to drive itself deep into her and find the warm, wet home it ached for. Yet he was determined to make up for that first debacle, that hellish consummation, so he controlled himself.

But she was making it damned hard. Her desire heated his own, and he watched in fascination as she struggled with her body's need. Just when he thought he might explode without ever even entering her, a high, piercing cry suddenly streamed from her lips, her body bucking beneath him as she sobbed out in release.

Aric was on his knees at once. Positioning himself between her thighs and clasping her buttocks, he raised her slightly and slid smoothly into her. He saw her eyes open in surprise as she caught her breath; then her eyes dropped closed again and her tongue came out to lick at her upper lip briefly as she arched into him. Now she was moving with him, shuddering, raising her hips to his, whimpering with passion. His own excitement increased by hers, Aric met her push for push, startled when he felt her hands suddenly at his buttocks, drawing him in, her nails digging into his behind and urging him on. Then she threw her head back and cried out as passion overwhelmed her again, and Aric felt himself explode within her.

Aric lay on the bed on his back, his hands caught beneath his head, his eyes closed, and a smile curving his lips. He was rather proud of himself. He felt rather like a stud bull. He had performed even beyond his hopes. His timing had been impeccable, his rhythm perfect. He knew he had given his wife immeasurable pleasure. He need never fear her disliking the marital bed again. This was a new beginning for them. Aye, he was sure he had wiped their first time completely from her mind.

A muffled sob caught his ear and erased his smile, replacing it with a frown. A second one brought his eyes open and his head around to peer at his wife with alarm. She had rolled away from him and now lay half on her side and half on her stomach, her shoulders trembling with the depth of her emotion as she wept into the linens. Aric gaped at her briefly, totally bewildered at this reaction to what they had just done; then another escaping sob made him draw himself up to a half-sitting position and reach over to rub her back comfortingly.

"Wife?" he murmured uncertainly, frowning when her shoulders merely began to shake all the harder. "Wife?"

Concern drawing at his features, he moved his hand to her shoulder and rolled her onto her back, determined to give her comfort. His head jerked back, however, his eyes widening incredulously when he saw that she hadn't been sobbing at all, but was in a paroxysm of laughter. Scowling as the almost hysterical laughter continued, now unmuffled, he glared at her.

"Just what is so damned amusing?"

"I . . . It . . . Ohhhh." She gasped breathlessly around her laughter, then managed, "I thought I would rather wash the abbey floor in winter." When Aric blinked at her in confusion, her laughter deepened. She rolled a bit on the bed before her laughter slowed enough for her to explain. "Oh, my lord. Truly, Eustice did not have a clue about it."

Aric frowned slightly. "The nun?"

"Aye." Rosamunde giggled, then mimicked the woman, "'Well, you've seen the animals. 'Tis just like that.'" Shaking her head, she laughed so hard that tears came to her eyes. Aric smiled wryly until she said, "You must have thought me the veriest fool! No wonder you have coddled me so. Even I would have refused to allow me out of the keep and near the stables were I in your position."

"Aye, well, regarding the stables," he muttered, then grimaced. He had not really coddled her, though it might seem so to her, but he had been rather harsh about her tending to the animals in the stables. Even Shrewsbury had taken him to task for that. And all because he feared her being unfaithful.

Fear was an awful thing. It could make prisoners out of men. In this case, it seemed his fear had been likely to make a prisoner of his wife. For that was the only way to keep her from all temptation, to lock her alone in a tower of the castle. And he had been well on his way to doing that, he realized with dismay. Oh, certainly, he had only restricted her to the castle as yet, but he had noticed at the table this night that there were an awful lot of men in the hall, and he had worried over his wife's curiosity about them. No doubt, eventually he would have denied her the hall, then the kitchens. . . . They had a male cook after all. Aye, Aric had been headed down a dangerous path. It was time to head down a different one. Tonight was a new beginning after all.

Aye, he would allow her access to the stables, he decided now. Smithy had told him that she had assisted him with the horses on the way here and claimed that she was exceptionally knowledgeable and had a special way with them.

That had not surprised him terribly. She had spent most of her life in the abbey stables, nursing and tending to the beasts. Aye, mayhap he was wrong to deny her that. He would allow her access to the stables—men or no men. He would not have her miserable, as Shrewsbury claimed she was, he thought, then frowned at her next words.

"And to think I wondered why Father Abernott was forever lecturing against adultery. 'Tis no wonder it happens so often if 'tis always as pleasurable as this." Shaking her head in slight wonder, she glanced at him curiously. "What were you saying about the stables, my lord?"

Aric stared at her tight-lipped for a moment, his mind closing like a steel trap. He snapped, "If I ever catch you there again, I'll lock you in this room for a week." Then, flouncing onto his side away from her, he glared at the wall by the door, determinedly ignoring the startled and even slightly injured eyes he knew must be digging into his back.

Chapter 9

ROSAMUNDE ripped her dark bread in half with a sigh, then ripped it in half again, the action accompanied by another sigh. She was tired this morning. It had to do with the fact that she had been awakened repeatedly in the night by her husband. The first time she had awakened from an incredibly erotic dream to find that it wasn't a dream at all; her husband was teaching her some more about the truth of what went on in the marital bed. A small smile pulled at her lips now as she recalled the night, the passion, the many times she had awakened to a new experience. It made her shake her head to realize just how many different ways there were to do "it." Animals really were missing out. And Eustice . . . Well, her lack of experience in the matter was more than obvious.

Rosamunde rolled her eyes slightly at her own naiveté on her wedding day and felt herself blush as she recalled perching on her hands and knees on the bed fully clothed. Good Lord, Aric must have thought her a turnip. That thought was followed by another sigh as her smile faded, because it was becoming perfectly obvious that he still thought her one. Apparently she was good for nothing but sitting about in the keep, twiddling her fingers. It was the only reason she could think of for why he refused to let her go to the stables. He didn't think she was capable of anything worthwhile.

"My, my, my. What long, drawn-out sighs are these from a newly married lady?"

Glancing around with a start, Rosamunde saw Lord Spencer approaching the table. He was leaning heavily on his servant, Joseph, and seemed in a lot of pain. Realizing that his joints must be giving him some trouble, she felt her lips curve with concern, but tried to keep it from her voice as she murmured a good morning.

"And good morning to you, too," he responded, easing onto the trestle table's bench beside her. "But you have not answered my question. What could cause such unhappy sighs from a lovely lady still newly wed?"

Rosamunde started to sigh again, then caught herself and smiled wryly. " 'Tis just—" she began, then cut that off as well, not wishing to betray her husband by complaining. " 'Tis just that I miss the abbess and the other women from Godstow," she muttered finally, for that was part of the truth.

"Ah. I suspect 'tis more than the good ladies of the abbey you are missing," Lord Spencer surprised her by saying. "I suspect that you miss your work in the stables there as well, do you not?"

"How did you know?" she asked with amazement, and he smiled wryly.

"I may be blind, my lady, but I am not deaf—though people often seem to think one goes with the other when speaking around me." He grinned slightly, then reached out to feel about for her hand. He then patted it affectionately, as if to assure her that she was not one of those people of whom he spoke. "Bishop Shrewsbury mentioned it yesterday, first in the stables, then at the table after you left."

"Oh. I see," Rosamunde murmured, beginning to toy with her food again. "Aye, well, the stables are where I spent most of my time at the abbey," she explained uncomfortably after a moment. "I worked with the animals there and . . . aye, I guess I miss it."

"I take it the bishop's words have not swayed young Aric in allowing you to work in them, then?"

"He does not wish me anywhere near the stables," she muttered gloomily.

"Ah." The old man sighed and shook his head. "So I gathered yesterday. Well, perhaps if he will not allow you to go to the stables, we could bring the stables to you," he murmured mysteriously, but before Rosamunde could question him, he turned his head slightly, paused briefly as if listening, then called out, "Good morn to you, my lord. I trust you slept well?"

Turning in her seat, Rosamunde saw Aric descending the stairs. A warm smile of greeting immediately curved her lips as her gaze slid over him. Her memory was presenting her with various images of him from the night before—and he wasn't clothed in a single one.

Aric felt some of the tension that had been gripping him since awakening loosen as he spied his wife at the table. Much to his annoyance, she had been gone ere he awoke again, but her expression now went a long way toward soothing him. Her lips were slightly parted, a warm smile of greeting playing upon them, and her eyes were smoky with secret thoughts he suspected had to do with her activities of the night before. Activities that now filled his mind.

He had been like a starving man presented with a feast last night, gorging himself on the pleasure of her body, never feeling quite sated, never getting quite enough. At least not for long. Even his irritation with her comments about adultery had not ruined his appetite for more than a few moments. Oh, aye, he had rolled away in a snit and stared at the wall until finally dropping off into a fitful doze. But it couldn't have been more than an hour later that he found himself awakening from an erotic dream about the woman lying asleep next to him. He had peered at her sweet face in repose for a moment, silently drinking in her beauty, but had been unable to resist touching her. Touching had led to kissing, and kissing to tasting her sweet, tender flesh, and that in turn had led to . . .

Aric had rested again afterward, only to awaken hungry for her once more a short time later. And so had gone the night: wanting her, taking her, resting. Then wanting her again. This morning, he had awakened wanting her again which was why he had been so annoyed to find her gone. Looking at her now as her tongue crept out to wet her parted lips, Aric knew that if Lord Spencer were not present, he would be hard-pressed not to lift her onto the table and take her right there. *Hell, maybe I should just drag her back upstairs and—*

"My lord?"

Blinking at Lord Spencer's voice, Aric tore his eyes from his wife and glanced toward the old man seated beside her. Only then did he realize that while his mind had wandered, his feet had halted before his wife. He had just spent who knew how long simply gazing down at her like a randy teenager.

"I slept well enough," he answered at last, his tone a bit short as he forced himself away from his wife and toward the lord's chair. It was a high-backed, carved monstrosity that Lord Spencer had insisted he take over. "And you?"

"Very well, thank you," the old man answered, seeming to follow Aric's progress along the table despite his blind eyes. He waited until Aric had seated himself on the other side of Rosamunde and been presented with a beverage and cold cheese and bread before saying, "I had an idea just ere I was drifting off to sleep last night, my lord."

"Oh?" Aric murmured absently as he picked up the cheese. His gaze wandered to his wife's fingers as she absently shredded a hunk of bread. She had long, lovely fingers. He had noticed last night, while kissing each of them individually, then sucking them into his mouth one at a time and rolling his tongue over—

"Aye. I understand you do not wish Lady Rosamunde to attend the stables."

Aric stiffened at Lord Spencer's words, the memory that had been filling his mind—not to mention his brais—dissipating quickly as the man went on.

"But it has occurred to me that perhaps she could still be of some service to your stablemaster. Smithy? Is that not his name?"

Rosamunde gave a start at that, her gaze turning questioningly to Aric for verification that he had replaced the old stablemaster with his own man. He had not bothered to mention it to her.

"Aye, that is his name," Aric allowed carefully, trying to ignore the happiness that filled his chest when Rosamunde suddenly beamed at him as if he had done a grand thing.

"Aye. I thought so. But my memory is not as good as it used to be." Lord Spencer straightened slightly to add, "He mentioned in the stables after you left us yesterday that Lady Burkhart appeared quite knowledgeable about animals during the journey here. She apparently helped him to identify one or two problems he might otherwise have missed. He said that he might appreciate her advice and—"

"I have already made it clear that I do not wish my wife anywhere near the stables," Aric began.

Lord Spencer immediately nodded, but continued. "Oh, aye. And I would not suggest otherwise. However, I thought mayhap Smithy might be allowed to seek her council—here at the keep, I mean—should he come across something he feels she may be able to help with."

Rosamunde held her breath in the silence that followed the man's wonderful words, afraid to look at her husband lest she somehow make him decide against allowing such a thing. It was a long silence—long enough that Rosamunde's lungs began to ache from lack of oxygen before she heard her husband say, "Aye. I do not suppose that would hurt."

Releasing her breath in a noisy gust, Rosamunde leaped to her feet with excitement. "Oh! What a marvelous idea, my lord! Thank you." She squeezed Lord Spencer's hand in gratitude, then whirled and launched herself at her husband where he sat. "And thank you, my lord, for allowing it. Thank you, thank you, thank you," she said between pressing tiny butterfly kisses all over his face as he caught her by the waist. "You are a *wonderful* husband."

"Aye, well," Aric murmured, smiling slightly even as he gently set her away. His gaze moved uncomfortably to Lord Spencer, who was smiling in their general direction. "I shall go out there right now and tell Smithy he may seek your council."

"Oh, but you have not even broken your fast," Rosamunde protested as he rose.

"Aye, I know, but . . . after the news Bishop Shrewsbury brought us yesterday, I quite forgot to mention to Smithy that we would be riding out to continue our tour again today. I must go have him prepare the wagon."

"Oh." Rosamunde sighed.

Smiling slightly, Aric tipped up her face and kissed her quickly on the lips. Her disappointment was obvious, and it warmed his heart that she would apparently miss him. Her exuberance over his agreeing to allow Smithy to ask her council, on the other hand, made him feel slightly guilty. It took so little to please her. She did not ask for furs or jewels; simply being allowed to have some involvement with the animals sent her into ecstasy. He should have thought of this possibility on his own, he berated himself, then glanced toward Lord Spencer as the other man rose from his seat.

"I shall accompany you, my lord," he murmured, then turned a smile in Rosamunde's general direction. "Have a good day, my lady."

"Thank you," Rosamunde said at once, then watched as the men made their way slowly toward the keep doors. Once the door closed behind them, her gaze slid down to the bits of bread littering the table before her. Quickly scooping them up, she wondered distractedly how soon it would be before Smithy visited her for her assistance. While she didn't wish illness on any of the horses, she did look forward to being involved in tending to them again, if only in this minor way. Her thoughts were interrupted by a solemn "Good morn."

Glancing toward the stairs, she saw Bishop Shrewsbury descend the last of them and start toward her.

She greeted him with a smile as she dropped the bread crumbs into her husband's empty mug. "Good morn, my lord Bishop."

"It looks as if I am a late riser this morning. Everyone has eaten and gone, I take it?"

"Nay. I mean, aye." Rolling her eyes, she shook her head. "You are not a late riser, my lord Bishop. Lord Spencer and my husband came down only a moment ago, but they both decided to forgo breaking their fast and head right back out to complete their rounds of the estate."

"Ah. I see. What a shame. I was hoping to have a word with him. Your husband, that is." His gaze slid toward the door briefly, as if he were contemplating whether he might catch up. Then he apparently decided against it and seated himself at the table before glancing at where she still stood. "You were not leaving, too, were you?"

Rosamunde hesitated, then smiled. While she wasn't really hungry, what else did she have to do until Smithy should need her? Taking her seat again, she shook her head. "Nay. I shall keep you company."

"Good, good." Murmuring a thank-you to the servant who set a mug of mead and hunks of cheese and bread before him, he smiled at Rosamunde. "I am glad you can keep me company, for I have a question or two you might be able to answer."

Rosamunde's eyebrows rose slightly. "What kind of questions, my lord?"

"Well, I could not help but notice that there did not appear to be a priest present at the table last night. And, obviously there was no morning mass today."

Rosamunde shifted uncomfortably under his censorious gaze, guilt rising within her like a wraith that wrapped itself around her throat and choked her. After a lifetime spent in a convent where they had held matins, lauds, prime, and tierce throughout the day, Rosamunde had hardly missed the masses since leaving the convent. Of course, they had traveled without benefit of a priest to accompany them here, but once they had arrived, the morning masses had not been reinstated. In fact, the first night of their arrival, Lord Spencer had mentioned that the priest who had served this castle and its people since Lord Spencer's early childhood had recently passed on. He had yet to be replaced.

Rosamunde's guilt was because she had not been at all upset by that news. Truthfully, she had been happy to leave her husband to tend to the problem in his own good time. Of course, that was a terrible sin. She should have been distressed and insisted that he see to the matter at once. She had been raised properly, after all.

"Aye, well, I fear the priest who served here passed on just days before our arrival," she now admitted uncomfortably. "I believe my husband has taken steps to remedy the situation."

"Really? Well, mayhap I could be of some assistance in that area myself in the meantime."

Rosamunde blinked at him in surprise. "Assistance, my lord Bishop?"

"Certainly. I could take up that office while I rest here a while. At least until a new priest is found and settles in. Yes. That is a most satisfactory resolution." He smiled at her a bit wryly. "That way, I shall not feel so much as if I am dependent upon your charity. I shall earn my keep, so to speak."

"Oh, my lord, having you stop here awhile is not charity. Why, you are practically family," she assured him quickly.

"You are such a sweet child," he murmured affectionately, reaching out to squeeze her hand. "And so lovely, like your mother. She was a sweet lamb, too. So gentle, so beautiful. Such a waste, her dying so young," he added. He shook his head and gave her hand a pat before making an obvious effort to force the sad memories away. "Well, I am quite excited at the prospect. This will give me the chance to practice my rusty old skills ere I am given my own church to tend to."

Rosamunde's eyes widened slightly. "Do you intend to go back to ministering then, my lord Bishop?"

"Well." He gave her a self-deprecating laugh. "I doubt young Richard would wish an old man like me for counsel. Especially since I was loyal to his father. Aye, I shall most likely return to doing the work of God, as I was meant to do. And frankly, I'll be quite happy in the doing," he added conspiratorially. "While it was exciting at first to hold such an important position at your father's side, I found it rather wearying in these last years. The quiet life of the church shall suit me just fine." He nodded in satisfaction, then pushed his mead away and rose to his feet. "In fact, I think I shall go have a look at the chapel right now and see what shape it is in. If all is well, we may be able to hold the first mass tomorrow morning. If you will excuse me, my dear?"

"Of course." Rosamunde smiled at his obvious pleasure and watched him leave the keep. She started to rise from the table herself, only to pause and glance toward the doors curiously when they swung open once more. Her eyes widened slightly when she saw Smithy's head pop in. There was no mistaking his relief as he spied her by the table, and he was through the door in a heartbeat and hurrying across the room toward her.

"My lady," he said anxiously as she moved curiously forward to meet him. "I am in charge of the stables now, and—"

"Aye, I know," Rosamunde interrupted, pausing as they met halfway across the great hall. "Congratulations."

"Aye, well . . ." He grimaced slightly and shook his head. "I am not knowledgeable enough to handle the job, really. I'm a soldier."

"You will be fine," she assured him gently. "You have

a natural affinity with animals. I saw it, sir. You will work far better with them than that drunken—" She bit off the rest of what she would have said.

"Aye, but . . . well, I handled the horses well enough, but handling them is all I have ever done. I've wrapped a few sprains, patched a few wounds in a pinch. That sort of thing. But I have never had to tend truly ill or ailing horses. That was always taken care of by the stablemaster of whatever keep we were at."

"Oh. Well, you shall learn in time, sir. In the meantime, my husband has said that I may advise you—"

"Aye. His lordship told me as much ere leaving. That's why I'm here. There is a problem."

"Already?" Her eyes widened in amazement.

"Aye, and it is Black," he said heavily.

Rosamunde blinked at the name. It sounded familiar, but—"Oh, my!" She gasped suddenly. "My husband's horse?"

He nodded grimly. "And His Lordship is quite fond of the beast, too, so you can imagine the state I have been in over it. You will never know how grateful I have been that he has not wished to ride him this last week. Thank God Lord Spencer is blind and must travel by wagon."

"Oh, surely he would not blame you," she assured him quickly.

"Nay," he agreed doubtfully, then added, "But he would be fair upset. He is mighty fond of Black, is Lord Burkhart."

Rosamunde frowned slightly at this news, then shook her husband's possible unhappiness aside. "What is wrong with him?"

"He started sneezing a couple of days after we arrived," Smithy began.

Rosamunde made a sound of disgust. "It's that damn

drafty hovel they call a stable," she said unhappily. Smithy nodded in miserable agreement.

"Aye. I coddled him quite a bit and covered him as best I could to keep him warm, but I don't know what else to do. I was hoping that his being able to rest would help, but he seems worse every day. He is sickening. He's off his feed. Out of sorts. He tires easily. He just is not himself. And . . ." He hesitated, biting his lip miserably.

"And?" Rosamunde prompted.

"And now he has a wheeze in his chest, and he's hot to the touch," the man admitted. He sounded as if it were his fault.

"Oh, dear. That does sound worrisome." Taking his arm, she urged Smithy around and back toward the door. "Come, I shall take a look and see . . ." Her voice trailed away even as her steps slowed. "I cannot go see. My husband has ordered me never to enter the stables again."

The relief on the new stablemaster's face vanished, his expression falling into one of doom. "I am dead. If his horse dies . . ." He shook his head miserably.

Patting his arm soothingly, Rosamunde considered the problem briefly, then came to a decision. "He shall not die. We will mend him."

"But you cannot go to the stables," he cried in despair.

She smiled. "Then you must bring Black to me."

"Bring him here?" Hope and doubt struggled briefly on his face. Not waiting to see which would win, Rosamunde took his arm and walked toward the keep doors, almost dragging him along with her.

"Come, now. Courage. Just go get him and bring him back here. I shall wait on the steps," she murmured as they stepped out into the noisy bailey.

The stablemaster sighed, but nodded and hurried away.

Rosamunde watched as he bobbed and weaved his way toward the stables; then she began to pace impatiently back and forth on the top step. She was still doing so when she finally spied him leading her husband's steed out of the stables. Pausing, Rosamunde eyed the animal as Smithy led him across the yard. It was easy to see that his description was correct. She could not tell about the horse being off his feed, but the beast was definitely tired and out of sorts. The stablemaster had to veritably drag the beast across the yard, and was having to keep a good distance between himself and the horse as he did. Every time he got close, Black tried to bite him.

Worried now, Rosamunde quickly descended the steps and hurried to meet them. They were still a good twenty feet from the keep when she reached them. Murmuring soothingly to the horse, she took his head in her hands, frowning at the discharge about his eyes and nose, then quickly looked the rest of him over, just to be sure there were no other symptoms she should be aware of.

"It is nothing serious, is it?" Smithy asked anxiously. She nodded and muttered to herself.

Moving back to join him at the front of the horse, Rosamunde sighed. " 'Tis a cold."

"A cold?" he asked blankly. "I didn't know horses could get colds."

"Oh, aye," Rosamunde informed him knowledgeably. "Horses are not really much different from men. They can get colds, the melancholy, stomach complaints . . ." Pausing, she reached up to caress the horse's mane. "And he has a cold. Probably from the dampness in that old stable."

Smithy frowned at that, but only asked, "What do I do for him?"

"We must take him inside."

"Inside? Inside where?"

"The keep," Rosamunde explained calmly. "He must be kept warm and dry. You cannot accomplish that in that moldy old wreck of a building."

"Aye, but . . ." Smithy paused, terror covering his face. "Oh, nay. I do not think His Lordship will approve of that."

"Well, then, he should have fixed the stables as I told him to," Rosamunde snapped, taking the horse's reins from him and turning back toward the keep. "Come along," she ordered, leading the horse forward. Once she reached the stairs, she paused to glance back at the stablemaster questioningly. "Are you not coming? You may learn something useful."

"Ah . . . My lady," the man said pleadingly.

He looked completely miserable, Rosamunde realized, and sighed, considering the matter briefly before moving back to explain her thoughts in a manner that sounded more acceptable. "Sir Smithy," she began reasonably, "my husband does not allow me in the stables, but he has allowed that I might help you—and you do need my help with Black. If I am not allowed in the stables, then we must tend to him here, do you not think?"

"Aye," the thin man answered, but he was shaking his head even as he said it. "My lady, His Lordship surely wouldn't wish his horse in the castle."

"Would he wish him dead?"

"Nay." He looked horrified at the very idea.

"And did he not tell you I might help you?"

"He said you might *advise* me."

"And I shall. Inside the keep. 'Tis too cold out here for Black." When the man still looked unhappy at this decision, she sighed impatiently, then turned back to catch up Black's halter. She urged him forward, muttering, "I am only trying to obey my husband's wishes."

Smithy watched wide-eyed as she urged the horse up the stairs, in quite a quandary. He was rather certain that Aric was not going to like coming home to find his steed in the keep. On the other hand, Smithy was fairly certain that he would like it less if he came home to find his horse dead.

"Sirrah! Do hurry!"

Sighing at Rosamunde's impatient call as she and the horse reached the keep doors, he replaced his cap on his head and straightened his shoulders. "In for silver, in for gold," he murmured philosophically, hurrying after them.

"My lord!"

Aric frowned at Smithy's alarmed cry as he entered the stables, then peered at the suddenly pale man suspiciously. "Aye. 'Tis me. What is the matter?"

"Matter?" the thin man said in a squeak, looking slightly trapped. "I . . . well, nothing. I just . . . You . . . I mean, I was not expecting you back so soon. Her Ladyship felt sure you would not return ere the sup."

"And no doubt he would not have had he not run into us," a different voice replied.

Aric glanced around at that cheerful tone to see that his friend Robert Shambley had followed him into the stables. Aric's father, Lord Burkhart, was a bare step behind as he walked forward to join them. Aric, Lord Spencer, and his servant had been about two hours into this last day of their tour when they had come across the travelers. It seemed his father had gotten wind of his troubles with Delia and traveled to Shambley to see how his son fared. There he had learned of the events of the last three weeks.

From what Aric had heard, Gordon Burkhart had spent the night at Shambley Hall, intending to travel on to Goodhall alone the next morning to meet his new daughter-in-law. But a messenger had arrived with the news of the king's death that morning, and Shambley had decided to join his friend's father. The two had been concerned by how this tragedy would affect Aric and his wife; both were aware that the king had arranged this marriage to ensure Lady Rosamunde's protection. Now, with her father dead, if there was something to threaten her, it would rear its head soon.

Both men had been amazed upon hearing that Aric was still touring his new lands. And he had felt shame as Lord Spencer had spoken up, taking the blame. The older man claimed that the necessity to conduct the tour in the wagon was the reason for the extended length of time of the tour, but the truth was that it was Aric's own dillydallying that had prolonged the task. He'd had great long visits with nearly every single one of his new vassals, accepting every invitation to stop for a meal, and chatting long with everyone in an effort to avoid going home to bed his wife. Of course, that had been until last night. He had determined this morning, as he had waited for the wagon to be readied, that he would pick up the pace and try to finish his inspection today.

Instead, upon meeting his father and Robert on their way to Goodhall, he had forsaken the tour altogether. He had made Joseph turn the wagon toward home, to accompany his guests and their men-at-arms back to the castle.

"Hello, Smithy," Robert said now. "I see Aric has delegated you to minding the horses full-time."

"Er . . . Aye, my lord," the man murmured nervously, moving suddenly forward and toward the door of the stables. "Nice to see you again, my lord. And you, too, my lord," he added with a nod toward the senior Lord Burkhart. "I have to . . . er . . ."

He had nearly slipped through the door before Aric brought his escape attempt to a halt. "Get back here. Where do you think you are going?"

Smithy paused and licked his lips nervously. "W-well, I just th-thought to warn—I mean to . . . er . . . inform Her Ladyship that you were b-back."

Aric's gaze narrowed on the obviously anxious man. "Then she is not here? I was beginning to suspect that she had gone against my wishes and come down to work in the stables."

"Oh, nay, my lord," Smithy assured him quickly. "Nay. She would not go against . . . well, she would never come down to the stables after you explicitly ordered her not to. I just thought she might like to know that you are back and—"

"I will inform her of that myself," Aric said grimly. "You have work to do. See to my father's and my friend's horses."

"Aye, my lord," the man said, misery obvious on his face. "As you wish, my lord."

Frowning now, and aware that something was most definitely up, Aric eyed the new stablemaster silently for a moment, then turned and hurried out of the building, heading for the keep at a fast clip.

"What is going on?" Robert asked curiously as he and Aric's father hurried to catch up.

"I do not know, but I intend to find out," Aric muttered grimly.

"What was that about you refusing to allow her to work in the stables?" His father asked curiously. "Surely the girl would not wish to?"

"Aye, she would, if you can imagine," Aric said with obvious displeasure.

"It was her job at the convent," his friend explained now to Gordon Burkhart. "Apparently all of the nuns—and the girls preparing to take the veil," he added quickly when Aric glared at him. "Apparently they each had a task that was their own. Tending to the injured and ailing animals was Lady Rosamunde's chore. She appeared quite skilled at it," he added defensively, mistaking Aric's father's surprise for displeasure. "She caught on to the fact that the horse I was riding on the way back to Shambley had the lockjaw before I even knew aught was amiss. Did she not, Aric?"

"Aye," he agreed unhappily. "And no doubt she is skilled at it, but—"

"Of course she is skilled at it." All three men turned as Shrewsbury approached, his expression severe. "That is because she has spent a lifetime honing the natural talents God gave her." Pausing before them, he turned a harsh expression onto Aric. "But you would allow those skills and talents to go to waste. Instead you insist she fritter her time and life away running *your* keep."

"I do not intend for her to waste anything," Aric said stiffly. The bishop's eyes widened, his expression softening with hope.

"You have decided to let her return to the abbey, then?"

"Nay," Aric snapped, then more calmly said, "She is my wife and shall *stay* my wife. And she shall run my home. But," he emphasized harshly when Shrewsbury looked ready to interrupt, "I shall allow her to assist Smithy with the animals. I have already told them that he may consult her on the more difficult cases."

"You are willing to allow . . ." The bishop could not have looked more surprised. "You seemed so adamant on—"

"She will not be in the stables. Smithy will come and

consult her if he needs her assistance with an animal," Aric said grimly, aware of the solemn expression on his father's face as he listened to all of this information. Turning before anyone could offer further argument, Aric continued on toward the keep, aware that the others followed.

Aric reached the keep doors just as Joseph opened them for Lord Spencer. The older man and his servant had headed directly to the keep upon returning, while Aric and the others had stopped in at the stables. The older man moved at a much slower pace, old age and rheumatism making his journey up the keep stairs a slow and torturous one.

Aric waited patiently for Joseph to usher the old man in, then followed. He had barely stepped inside the door, however, when a wave of heat hit him, making him pause. It was a warm summer day outside, but it was positively stifling inside. Before Aric could glance toward the fireplace, the only source of heat in the great hall, an exclamation from Lord Spencer drew his gaze. The blind man had also paused just inside the door, but his face was raised, his nose working as if sniffing out an unpleasant scent.

"What . . . ?" the older man murmured with bewilderment.

Aric arched an eyebrow curiously, then glanced toward his father, Shambley, and Bishop Shrewsbury. The trio crowded into the keep behind them. "Is there something amiss, my lord?" he asked Lord Spencer.

"That smell." The old nobleman frowned uncertainly.

Aric sniffed the air and began to glance around the empty great hall. "I do not—" His voice came to a choking halt as his gaze reached the fireplace. The great hall was not empty after all, he saw. His eyes widened with horror as they fell upon a horse standing calmly before the fireplace. At least he thought it was a horse. It was hard to tell. The animal was completely covered in clothing. Various gowns and miscellaneous clothing had been wrapped around his legs, head, neck, torso, and even tail. A great cape had been draped over the top. And—to add insult to injury—a feathered cap was perched jauntily on the animal's head.

Chapter 10

"THERE is a horse in my great hall," Aric muttered in disbelief.

"Ah, I knew I smelled something," Lord Spencer murmured with satisfaction, then continued on toward the trestle tables. Joseph followed behind him. The bishop hesitated a moment to peer curiously at the horse, then followed the other two men, meandering away as if there were nothing unusual afoot.

"There is a horse in my great hall," Aric repeated, turning a rather dazed expression to his father.

"Aye, it would seem so," Gordon Burkhart agreed. Crossing the room, he began to walk slowly around the animal, examining what he could see of the horse through the clothing bundled around it. There was not a spare inch of coat showing through the material. Not even enough to tell them the color of the beast. The only thing visible was its face, and that was half-hidden as well.

"There is a horse in my great hall." Aric was starting to sound almost plaintive now as the fact sank in, but nobody paid him any attention. Instead Robert joined Lord Burkhart in examining the beast and murmured, "Do you think it is male or female?"

"Well." Gordon hesitated "One can't tell by the way it's dressed. That appears to be a gown wrapped around one leg. And there is a shift on this one. But those appear to be brais on that leg there. If I am not mistaken, I believe that may be Aric's great cape across its back."

Robert's eyebrows rose as he peered more closely at the cape in question. "I believe you may be right. That *is* his cape."

"My cape?" Aric cried with alarm, moving forward to look at the item in question. Then he said, faintly, "My God! It *is* my cape. There is a horse in my great hall wearing my cape."

"So . . ." Robert bit the inside of his mouth to keep from laughing at his friend's distress. " 'Tis wearing both gowns and brais. That explains one thing to me."

Lord Burkhart raised an eyebrow at that. "That 'tis a gelding?" he suggested dryly.

Robert grinned, but shook his head. "No, and I am not looking to find out."

"Then what does the clothing tell you?"

"That this is Lady Rosamunde's work." When Lord Burkhart raised his eyebrows at that, Robert grinned. "She is the only person I know who wears both brais and gowns."

"Does she? Does she indeed?" Gordon asked with interest.

"There is a horse in my great hall!" Aric roared, drawing both men's attention to his furious face.

"Aye, Aric. We have noticed that," his father pointed out. Something that looked suspiciously like amusement tugged at the older man's distinguished face.

Aric opened his mouth to bellow some more, but the words caught in his throat at a highly suspicious sound that came from the posterior section of the horse. "What was that?" he snapped.

"Ah, well," Lord Burkhart murmured, raising one hand to calmly cover the bottom of his nose. "It sounds and . . . er . . . *smells* rather as if the poor animal has, er . . . flatulent colic."

"Flatulent—"

When his friend peered at him blankly, Robert hid a laugh behind a cough and murmured a less polite, but more common term. "The stomach staggers, Aric."

"Stomach staggers? *Stomach staggers!*" His eyes rounded in horror one second before the smell suddenly hit him. "Oh, God! He's *farting!*" Waving a hand frantically in front of his face, he hurried a safe, distance away, one step behind his father and Robert.

"*That* is no doubt what I smelled when I entered," Lord Spencer called cheerfully from the table, which was a safe distance away. His words drew an appreciative glance from Bishop Shrewsbury.

"You have a very good nose, my lord," the late king's man complimented. "I did not smell anything at all when we entered. Still do not, in fact."

"Ah, well." The blind man shrugged the compliment away. "When you lose your eyesight, your other senses tend to sharpen in an effort to compensate."

"That cap the horse is wearing looks quite familiar to me, Aric," Robert commented, drawing his attention from the conversation at the table. "Is that not the new one you purchased on your last trip to London?"

Aric glanced back toward the horse and went suddenly still, his mouth working, but nothing came out of it. His friend was right. That was his hat perched on the animal's head! His brand-new hat. He was still standing there a moment later when Rosamunde came jogging lightly down the stairs, her attention on the stockings she was slipping off of her hands.

"Here we are, then. These should help keep your feet

warm. Not a hole in the bunch," she sang out cheerfully as she reached the bottom of the steps and crossed the hall toward the bundled animal. "Now, we shall just get these on your feet." Stopping beside the animal, she bent to run her hand over one of the horse's fetlocks. The horse raised his foot at once, apparently willing to cooperate, and that was when Aric found his voice, managing to draw her attention to their presence with a bellow.

"*Wife!*"

Dropping the horse's hoof, Rosamunde straightened abruptly, her eyes wide with horror as she spotted the crowd standing near the trestle table. "Husband! You are returned!" she cried with dismay, then suddenly stepped in front of the horse as if she thought she might be able to hide its great bulk behind her own small frame. "What are you doing here?"

"What am I . . ." Aric began with disbelief, then, "What the devil is *he* doing here?"

"Who?" she asked innocently as he started across the room toward her. As if she thought, for one bloody moment, that they all could not see the horse standing behind her, he thought with amazement.

The animal was now nuzzling her shoulder as if trying to remind her of its presence and pointing out that he was the "who" in question.

"Wife," he began again.

Shoulders slumping at his warning growl, Rosamunde sighed, then stomped the floor impatiently with one dainty foot. "You were not supposed to be back so early. You did not return until sup yestereve, and I thought sure that you would be late again today. I would have had him moved somewhere else by then," she complained, somehow making it sound as if this were all his fault. Then her gaze slid to the two men accompanying him and her eyes widened slightly. "Oh! Lord Shambley.

Hello again. Welcome to Goodhall!" A bright smile on her face, she hurried forward to offer her hand as if nothing were amiss.

Ignoring a fuming Aric, Robert took her hand in his, bowed gallantly, and pressed a kiss to her fingers. "My lady," he greeted, his eyes sparkling with humor. " 'Tis a pleasure to see you again." Then, straightening, he turned slightly to introduce the older man at his side. "I do not believe you have met Aric's father, Lord Burkhart. Lord Burkhart, may I introduce Lady Rosamunde, your new daughter-in-law."

Smiling reassuringly into Rosamunde's horrified face, the older man stepped forward, taking her hand from Robert's. "It is a pleasure to welcome you to the family, my dear. I hope Aric does not prove a difficult husband for you—"

Aric snorted at that and shook his head. "*Me* difficult? Excuse *me*, but does no one recall there is a *horse in my great hall?*" Another burst of escaping air from the animal in question made him stiffen, straighten, and correct himself. "There is a *farting* horse in my great hall."

"Husband!" There was no mistaking the reprimand in her voice, and it made Aric gape at her as she hurried over to soothe the animal lest it become offended. "You shall embarrass him. 'Tis not his fault that he has the flatulence. He is ill."

"Ah, 'tis a he," Lord Burkhart murmured with a nod. When Rosamunde peered at him curiously, he explained. "We were not sure. He is wearing both gowns and brais, you see."

Missing the teasing laughter in his eyes, Rosamunde frowned as she considered that fact. "You do not think it shall cause him embarrassment or confusion, do you?"

Robert and Gordon laughed gently and shook their heads. Aric was less amused. "Wife. Get this horse out of my keep."

"Nay."

His eyes widened incredulously at her rebellion. It was the first time she had said nay to him. "What?"

Biting her lip, Rosamunde briefly considered the fact that she was disobeying her husband—despite the vow she had made to obey, both to God during the wedding ceremony and then to her father afterward. But then she decided that since it wasn't for her own benefit, or out of some whim for her own pleasure, it was all right. After all, the matter affected the horse's life. Besides, quite simply, her husband was wrong! Surely she wasn't expected to obey when he was so obviously wrong?

Her conscience salved by this reasoning, she forced a smile and endeavored to explain the situation so that he would see the error of his decision and hopefully change it so that she need not continue to disobey. "He is ill, my lord. He has a cold, which he got from those damp and drafty old stables." The words came out a bit snappishly, since the building's state was wholly his fault for not listening to her. Regaining her temper, she continued, "He must be kept warm and dry. The only place to do that is here in the keep, by the fire. 'Sides," she added quickly as he opened his mouth to shout again. "'Tis not just any horse. 'Tis Black."

Aric's eyes shot to the clothing-covered beast with alarm, but it was his father who moved over and lifted the material from around his face. "Aye," Gordon said with surprise. "'Tis Black! I did not recognize him in disguise."

Robert gave a laugh at that, but Aric moved quickly to the horse, examining the beast's weeping eyes with dismay, then jumping back with a curse as Black suddenly drew his head up and sneezed squarely in his master's face.

"You must leave him covered," Rosamunde chided, hurrying forward to rearrange the clothing she had wrapped around his head. Aric wiped his face with disgust. The horse suffered her ministrations without fussing, and even leaned its head into her shoulder as if to thank her. This was not Black's typical behavior. Normally he liked no one but Aric. He tended merely to suffer anyone else's presence.

"How ill is he?" Aric asked, concerned now, but keeping his distance.

"He has a bad cold." Rosamunde gave the horse a soothing pat as he sniffled miserably from under his coverings, then bent again, urging his front leg up so that she might tug a stocking onto the hoof. "He will recover if handled gently. But if you put him back in those damp stables, he could worsen, get the lung complaint, and die."

"Die?" Aric asked worriedly, then frowned as he got a good look at what she was doing. "Are those my stockings? By God, they are!" he said incredulously, gaping at her where she knelt. "Madam, you are putting a stocking on a horse. My stockings on my horse, in fact."

"Aye, 'tis fitting, do you not think?" Rosamunde murmured with an absent-minded smile, straightening and moving to the next leg to repeat the action.

"Fitting? *Fitting?*"

Frowning over her shoulder at him, Rosamunde slowly stood. "There is no need to shout, my lord. I am standing right here. Besides, you shall disturb Black." As if on cue, the great black beast gave a sniffle, followed by a pitiful whinny. Rosamunde turned to run a soothing hand down his neck. "There, there. You shall feel better soon." Peering back at her husband, she smiled angelically, distracting him briefly until her words sank. Then he recalled he was upset. "You see? He does not feel well at all."

"Fine! He is ill. But that does not mean you needed to bring him in here, stand him by the fire, and dress him in my great cape," Aric protested, but some of the bite had gone out of his tone.

"I needed something to keep him warm," she explained patiently. "I can always wash your cape, my lord. But I cannot produce another fine horse like Black out of the air." Finished with the stockings, Rosamunde straightened and started toward the front of the horse, where Aric now stood glaring at the beast. She paused, however, to smile at a young servant girl who hurried out of the kitchens to hand her a pail.

"Thank you, Maggie," she murmured, accepting the bucket and pausing to dip a finger into its contents before turning with satisfaction to hold it up for the horse.

"What the devil is that mush you are feeding him?"

Rosamunde grimaced at his choice of words. "It is porridge, my lord. Blackie shouldn't eat anything hard while he is ailing. The soft food will be easier on his digestion, allowing his body to concentrate most of its effort on fighting the cold."

"That explains the stomach staggers," Robert murmured from where he stood some distance away, Lord Burkhart beside him.

Aric ignored the comment in favor of frowning at his wife. "His name is Black, not Blackie. And I want him out of here ere the sup," he said grimly. Then, turning on his heel, he strode toward the keep door.

"Where are you going?" Robert asked, hurrying after him.

"To set some men to build the new stables."

"That is probably for the best," his father murmured, beginning to follow.

"Aye," Aric agreed dryly, casting a pointed look over his shoulder at where Rosamunde stood feeding his horse. Then he added, "Then I am going down to the village, where I can enjoy an ale and some food without this stench."

Grinning, Robert glanced back toward the table. "Lord Spencer? Bishop Shrewsbury? Shall you join us?"

"Certainly, certainly. It will be a pleasure," the blind man murmured, rising and moving forward with the aid of Joseph. Shrewsbury, too, rose.

Rosamunde watched the men slip out of the keep, then glanced back at Black with a sigh. "Ah, well, never fear, Blackie. I will stay here with you." A gaseous emission from the horse in response made her wrinkle her nose. "But you *are* a stinker."

Sucking in some fresh air, Rosamunde smiled slightly, then sank onto the keep steps with a sigh. She had come outside to get a few moments away from the stink and heat in the keep. Between Black's flatulence and the heat pouring off of the inferno she had built in the fireplace to sweat out some of the chills the horse was suffering, it was a mite uncomfortable in there just now. She planned to allow the flames to die down and move Black an hour before the sup to allow the room to air out, but was still not yet sure to where she would move the horse. The kitchen would be nice and warm, but she did not think Cook would appreciate it—and he did seem the irascible sort. Mayhap she could persuade Black to mount the stairs and get him into one of the empty bed-chambers.

She was distracted from her thoughts by the sound of a child's sobbing. Frowning, Rosamunde allowed her eyes to focus on the bailey before her, concern tugging at her lips as she spied a small boy moving past the steps, stumbling under the weight of a dog he carried. The animal was unconscious, blood matting its normally brown fur. Standing abruptly, Rosamunde started down the stairs, hailing the boy as she went. "Boy? Boy! What has happened?"

Halting, the lad turned to stare at her, tears streaming down his face. He hitched his awkward burden higher in his arms and watched her approach.

Pausing before him, Rosamunde reached out to smooth some of the coarse fur away to get a better look at the animal. She had at first thought it a full-grown dog because of its size, but up close she could see that it was really just a rather large pup. Its paws and head were larger than the body deserved; the animal had not yet grown into them. The animal was hardly breathing.

"What happened?" she repeated, frowning over the injury to its throat and side.

"The bull," he answered dully. "Laddie got in the paddock with him. He was just playing. He's a pup and don't know better. I should have trained him better, kept a closer eye on him. Now he's dead." His voice broke on a heartfelt sob, and the boy gasped through his tears. "Da says I should bury him outside the gates."

Rosamunde took in the guilt and grief struggling on the child's face and felt her heart tighten. "What is your name, lad?"

"Jemmy," he got out somewhere between a hiccup and a sob.

"Well, Jemmy, you had best not be burying your friend there too quick. He is not dead."

"He isna?" The boy gaped as she took the pup from him. "But . . . he looks dead."

"Looking is not always being," Rosamunde assured

him, turning toward the keep steps with her burden. "Come along. Let us see what we can do."

An hour later, after laboring tirelessly over the small dog, Rosamunde was satisfied with her efforts. She had cleaned his wounds, bandaged him, wrapped him in a blanket to ward off the shock he was suffering, and the puppy was now awake and staring around in confusion. He was in a lot of pain, and it would take a while for the pup to recover, but recover he would.

Beaming with relief and pleasure, Jemmy threw his arms around her in a spontaneous show of gratitude, not even minding that she insisted his pup must stay in the keep so that she might keep an eye on his injuries. The boy then rushed out of the keep to tell his father that she had "brought my dog back from the dead."

Between Jemmy and Stablemaster Smithy chattering away to everyone about her work with Black, word spread quickly that the keep's new lady had a special way with ailing beasts. Before Rosamunde knew what was about, she found herself besieged by peasants. Pigs, goats, sheep, and dogs were paraded into the keep. Chickens, hawks, cats, and kittens were carried in. Even a mule and a couple of cows. The great hall filled up quickly, and Rosamunde found herself knee-deep in animals by late afternoon.

"With all the men you've assigned to this, it should not take more than a couple days to finish the new stables."

Aric glanced at his father as they crossed the bailey toward the keep. "Aye, and you can stop your fussing. I am no longer angry at my wife." A wry smile twisted his lips. "I should not have lost my temper in the first place. She was only trying to save Black. I was just a bit over-set. When I said Smithy could consult her, I did not expect her to take it to mean he should bring the horses into the keep."

"Aye, well." Robert laughed. "Once the stables are up, she will most likely leave the horses there. Although . . ."

Aric stiffened slightly, his eyes narrowing on his friend.

"Although it does seem to me that much of this could have been avoided. Had you just allowed her access to the stables, I suspect she may have just bundled Black up there and stayed nearby to keep an eye on him."

"And when you are married, you may decide how you deal with your wife! In the meantime, pray do not try to tell me how to handle mine," Aric interrupted, starting up the keep steps.

"As you wish, my lord," Robert said a touch dryly, then jogged lightly up the stairs. Reaching the keep doors, he pulled one open, made a snappy little bow, then held the door as a servant might do. Aric ascended the steps toward him.

He was nearly at the top when Shambley suddenly stiffened, cocking his head briefly as if trying to discern the source of some sound, then turned his head to glance sharply into the great hall. In the next moment, Robert slammed the door shut and threw himself before it.

"What is it?" Aric asked suspiciously as he paused before him, frowning.

"Nothing," he said quickly. But the fact that the word was squeaked out in an uncustomarily high voice, as if he were choking on it, made it hard for either Aric or his father to believe. Especially when Robert added in a desperately cheerful voice, "Say! Why do we not go have another ale in the village?"

Taking in Shambley's expression, Lord Burkhart frowned, then peered briefly toward the door the younger man was blocking. Suddenly he nodded. "Mayhap that is not such a bad idea. I could use—"

"Move." It was one word and said pleasantly enough, but the hard look in Aric's eye said more than the word could.

Heaving a sigh, Shambley stepped out of the way. "Just remember, you are the one who refused to allow her the stables."

Aric reached for the door, suddenly positive that Rosamunde had neglected to move Black, and that the farting horse was still ensconced by the fire. He prepared himself for just such a sight as he slowly opened the door, determined that he would remain calm. He would not lose his temper. He would simply tell her in a reasonable tone of voice to move the animal and she would—

His thoughts stopped dead at the sight that met his eyes as he stepped inside the great hall—or what used to be the great hall. This could *not* be Goodhall's great hall, he assured himself. This was the great hall of another castle. Somehow they had lost their way on their return from the village and left his land. This room, filled with twenty or so people and twice as many animals—all milling, clucking, squawking, or quacking about—was some other poor lord's great hall, and he really should turn around and make his way back to Goodhall now, he thought faintly. But then there was a shifting of the people and animals, and he saw the chair at the head of the trestle table. Yes, that definitely looked like his chair at the head trestle table in his great hall. In fact, he was suddenly quite positive that that was his chair, and that this was his great hall.

What made him so positive, despite the animals that he was certain he had not made welcome in his dining area?

Well, it would be the fact that there was presently a hawk perched on the back of that head chair at the trestle table in this great hall, and that that hawk was presently relieving itself on the chair. Yes. And there was only one person Aric could think of who might see it as acceptable to allow a hawk to relieve itself on her lord and husband's chair. The same person who thought it was quite alright to dress a horse in her lord and husband's clothes, cape, and cap and coddle him by her lord and husband's fire. And that person would be his—

"*Wife.*"

The roar had barely left his lips when Aric found himself grabbed from behind and dragged back out of the keep by both his father and Shambley. The outer doors slammed closed and Aric began to swear and shout in earnest as he was dragged backward down the stairs.

Bishop Shrewsbury, Lord Spencer, and Joseph all paused at the foot of the steps they had just reached—as usual, they had been slightly slower in their return—and gaped after him briefly as he was carted bodily across the bailey toward the stables. Then Lord Spencer murmured something. Shrewsbury shook his head, then hurried up the stairs to the keep doors. He opened one, stuck his head in, then pulled it back out, slamming the door again as he whirled back around. He hurried back down the stairs and past Lord Spencer and Joseph. Shouting something to the others that Aric couldn't hear, the bishop hurried across the bailey after them. Grabbing Joseph, Lord Spencer quickly began to follow as Shambley and Lord Burkhart dragged Aric into the ramshackle old stables.

Sure she had heard her husband's voice over the cacophony of animal sounds around her, Rosamunde straightened from the duck whose broken wing she had just finished binding and glanced around the hall anxiously. There was no sign of the man, but guilt suffused her as her eyes slid over the myriad animals surrounding her. Ducks flocked, geese squawked, and chickens clucked between and around the feet of the thirty or so peasants waiting their turn to see her. A goat was tethered to the table. Several sheep were sleeping nearby. A hawk was perched on the head chair, her husband's, where she saw with dismay that it had relieved itself several times. A couple of pigs were poking through the rushes, rooting for grub. There were several dogs here now, as well as cats, and even a cow. The great hall fairly echoed with various animal sounds, and it smelled like a stable. If that were not enough, Black still stood miserably by the fire, adding his own horrible perfume to the air every other moment.

How late was it? she wondered a bit uncomfortably. Her husband would not be pleased to return to this madness in his great hall, but the time had gotten away from her. Excusing herself briefly, she made her way past and around the animals and people so patiently waiting, and slipped into the kitchens to find out. To her dismay, Cook was nearly finished making the sup. It was nearly the dinner hour!

Biting her lip, Rosamunde hurried back out into the great hall, forcing a smile for the benefit of the bevy of servants, farmers, and children who owned the animals around her. "I am sorry, but I fear we shall have to stop now for the day. 'Tis almost the dinner hour and we must clear the great hall," she announced.

There was a general shifting of people as they began to gather their animals in preparation for leaving. No one complained, but Rosamunde still felt bad at having to turn them away—despite the fact that the only cases that remained were minor injuries or ailments. She had seen the serious cases directly as they had arrived. While no one had seemed to mind the preemptive treatment of these more critical cases, Rosamunde could not help but feel guilty about how long some of the people had been waiting for their animals to be seen.

"I shall make myself available again on the morrow to aid the rest of you," she assured them as the great hall began to empty. Then her gaze slid over the lord's chair, the trestle tables, the benches, and even the rushes as they were abandoned.

"Oh, damn. Damn, damn, double damn," she cursed. This was awful. Horrific. Just terrible. There was animal waste everywhere. Groaning aloud, she ran for the kitchens. Thrusting the door open, she peered frantically at the various servants rushing this way and that. "I need help! Now! Right now! Lots of it! Quickly!" she cried.

The cook took one look at her panicked expression and hurried over to peer past her into the great hall. She heard his gasp, then, "*Sacre bleu! Qu'est-ce que tu fait?*" Then he let the door close and peered at her with terror as he seemed to recall that she wanted help cleaning up that mess. Backing away, he began shaking his head. "Oh, *non. Non, non, non, non, non.*"

"Oh, *oui. Oui, oui, oui, oui, oui,*" Rosamunde cried, dismayed by his negativity. Were they not her servants? Shouldn't they *have* to help her if she asked for it? Cook seemed to come to that conclusion even as she did, for, cursing more in French, he turned on the others in the kitchen.

"*Allez! Allez! Vite vite, depechez-vous!*" he roared, and everyone began to move. Every last servant in the kitchen suddenly rushed past her and out into the great hall. Everyone but the cook—but Rosamunde wasn't about to push her luck. Besides, someone had to keep the supper from burning.

"*Merci.*" She beamed her thanks at the man as she backed out of the kitchen. "*Merci beaucoup, monsieur.*"

"Bah!" Making what she suspected was a rude Gallic gesture, the man turned away and hurried over to a pot bubbling upon the fire, leaving Rosamunde to join the servants now rushing about cleaning. But the door had barely closed behind her when a whinny and a fart drew her gaze toward the fire.

"Oh, Blackie!" She sighed, then hurried toward the horse. Her husband had ordered that he be out of the great hall by sup.

"Let me up!"

"Not until you regain your temper," Gordon Burkhart announced calmly, shifting to a slightly more stable position on his son's chest before glancing at Robert, who knelt at Aric's head in the straw, holding his hands down. They had dragged Aric here, and were now holding him down in the hopes of giving his temper a moment to cool before he encountered his young wife. "How are you doing, Robert? Can you hold him?"

"Aye, I am fine, I—"

"Regain my temper? *Regain my temper?*" Aric interrupted to roar. "That woman has turned my great hall into a stables!"

Lord Burkhart nodded solemnly. "Aye. It would seem so. 'Tis a good thing you have started on the new stables. Mayhap if you added a few more men it will be ready sooner."

"It matters little. It will not aid in this situation."

Eyes widening slightly, Burkhart glanced at Bishop Shrewsbury who was making his way along the stalls toward them. "Why will it not help?"

Shrewsbury shrugged idly. "He has refused her access to the stables."

"And so she has brought the stables into my keep?" Aric cried, stricken.

"Oh, do stop bellowing like a wounded bear," Gordon snapped irritably, then turned impatiently back to the bishop. "So he has denied her the stables. I have heard that several times now, but still do not understand why it is so important. What does it matter whether she is allowed in the stables or not? Surely, once the animals have some protection she will not feel the need to interfere?"

"'Tis not interference. This is what she does. The healing of animals is the gift God gave her. It was her task at the abbey. She was valued highly for it there," Bishop Shrewsbury explained quietly. The prelate turned to peer down at the younger Burkhart sadly. "Truly, my lord, you should return her to where the gifts God gave her are valued. I pray you, send her back to the abbey. There she may take the veil and lead the life she was meant to live. She would be so much happier there. She is miserable here."

Aric glared at the man for a moment, his face flushing with growing rage. The idea of Rosamunde being returned to the abbey upset him much more than the fact that she was turning his home into a shambles and allowing a hawk to relieve itself on his damn chair! For a moment, his mind was filled with the memory of her sweet smile, the soft smell of her, her singsong voice as she had tried to cheer his stupid horse, and her soft coos of passion and delight as he had pleasured her last night. The very idea that this sanctimonious ass standing over him was trying to talk him into giving her up, and claiming she would be happier if he did so, made him want to choke the breath from him. When the fury built to a point beyond containment, Aric roared, "*Get out!* Get out, get out! *Now, damn you!*"

Eyes wide as he took in his son's fury, Gordon Burkhart glanced over his shoulder at the cleric. "It may be better if you did . . . er . . . leave for a bit, Bishop," he suggested delicately. "Mayhap a nice ride would be a good idea."

"Come!" Lord Spencer said bracingly, stepping in to assist in the awkward moment of silence that followed. "We shall return to the village for our meal. These fellows will sort things out here, hmmm? Find Smithy, Joseph, and have him prepare the wagon."

Clearing his throat, Smithy stepped out of the stall he had stood frozen in since Aric had been forcibly dragged into the stables. He quickly set about his task as Joseph ushered Lord Spencer and Shrewsbury out of the building.

Aric, Robert, and Gordon remained still and silent until Smithy was finished. Once he had gone, Gordon turned back to his son with a sigh. "Are you feeling any more reasonable?"

"Reasonable?" Aric laughed bitterly. "There was a hawk relieving itself on my chair."

Gordon sagged slightly and sighed. "Aric, you are married now. There are certain adjustments you must make—"

"Adjustments!" Aric squawked. "There was a goat eating one of my banners."

"Rosamunde meant well," Robert tried, and Aric glared at him.

"There was a cow crapping in the corner."

When Shambley gave a bark of laughter at that, then quickly turned his head away, clearing his throat loudly, Gordon sighed and asked, "Why do you not simply allow her to work in the stables?"

Aric's mouth clamped shut at once.

Eyes narrowing, Gordon pointed out, "She did look happy amongst all her little charges."

Aric frowned, his memory drawing up an image of his wife as he had briefly seen her, tending to binding the broken wing of a duck held in a little girl's arms. She had been smiling widely and chattering away as she worked. Whether she had been chatting to the duck or the child was anyone's guess, but she did seem to have an affinity for animals. Still, to allow her to frequent the stables, where the animals could be brought to her . . . With all the men hanging around. He scowled at the idea.

Spotting his dark look, Lord Burkhart sighed. "I have only been here since midday, and you have been close-mouthed about your wife, but it seems to me that you are behaving like an idiot."

At Aric's startled look, he shrugged. "You gave Smithy the job as stablemaster. Why?"

Confusion clear on his face, Aric murmured, "Because he is good with animals."

Gordon nodded. "And how did you choose your first in command?"

Aric blinked. "He is a natural leader. He is organized and has a good head for battle."

"That's right. He does. And I taught you to utilize a person's skills, that if you do not, they will find somewhere else to use them, or grow bored and bitter and get into trouble. Did I not?"

"Aye."

"And yet here you are doing that very thing to your wife."

Aric jerked slightly beneath his father as if he had been hit. But the man wasn't finished. "With your fear of her being unfaithful and your efforts to prevent it, you will push her right into being so." He gave a short laugh at Aric's stunned expression. "What? Did you think I do not understand you, son? You have no problem with her being consulted on the matter of ailing animals, so long as 'tis done in the keep. You probably would not even have minded the animals being in the keep at the moment, except that they are relieving themselves all over everything. So if 'tis not the animals you wish to keep her away from, what else could it be?"

When Aric turned shamefacedly away, Gordon reached out to force his son to look at him. "Trust me on this, son. You do not want to make the same mistake with your wife that I did with your mother."

Aric stilled. "What?"

Releasing his chin, Gordon sighed and got off of his chest, then paced to the nearest stall and leaned against it, staring blindly at the horse inside.

"Your mother was a gifted healer when we married," he continued after a moment.

Aric gave a start. "I did not know that."

"Nay, well, that is my fault." Shaking his head, he clutched the top bar of the stall in both hands. "But she was. She had helped her own mother tend the ill while she was growing up, those in the castle, the men-at-arms, and even the sick or injured in the village. Then we married." His head lowered briefly before he continued. "She wanted to continue her healing work, but I refused to allow it. We already had a village hag who tended to such things—I saw no reason for my noble wife to do so. She was at me constantly, but I stood fast. . . . I was stubborn, is what I was," he muttered bitterly.

"I told her that her place was to have my babies and tend to my keep. After a while, she gave up and seemed to resign herself to that. And at first it kept her . . . well, I convinced myself she was content. But she wasn't. She thought I valued her only as a brood mare. And while she loved you and your brother and sisters, she began to resent me. Her love died."

Pausing, he sighed and shook his head wearily. "She was a beautiful woman. I should not have been surprised that others could see what I was blind to. But her unhappiness did not go unnoticed, and eventually another man convinced her that he knew her value where I did not and persuaded her to run away with him. I would have seen it coming if I had bothered to take time out from being the lord of the manor." He spoke the words with self-disgust, then paused a moment before turning back to where Aric had sat up. "Do not repeat my mistake, son. Value her skills. Use them. Give her a place here as something more than a brood mare."

"Damn," Aric said miserably as he took in what his father was telling him, then he cocked his head uncertainly. "But if that is what happened, why have you always been so bitter about her leaving? You have never even hinted that—"

"Of course I was bitter," Gordon snapped impatiently, then turned away again. "She was happy without me, while I was alone and lonely. I saw her again before she died. She was happy, tending the ill, being valued for more than the children she produced. Even though she could never marry the man she was with, she knew his love and how he valued her and was content. Even when she fell ill.

"Well, she died content, knowing she had done what she had been meant to do in this life. While I am left to regret my mistakes."

Getting to his feet, Aric moved to place a hand on his father's shoulder. "Thank you for telling me this, Father. I know how hard it must have been for you."

"Aye. 'Twas hard. But 'twill be worth it if you learn

from my mistake. Save yourself some heartache, boy," he murmured, staring staunchly ahead.

"I think I have," Aric assured him solemnly, then turned away. "I had best go talk with Rosamunde. I have been a fool and worse. I will tell her she may tend to her animals here in the stables—as she did at the abbey."

Robert was silent as Aric left the stables, uncomfortable with this new intelligence. He shifted slightly and murmured for lack of anything else to say, "So Aric's mother was a healer, too?" He had heard about his friend's mother, but he had never heard the whole story.

"Hmm?" Glancing around blankly, Lord Burkhart stared at his son's friend for a moment, then grimaced. "Aric's mother was a whore. She lay down so often and for so many of my friends and acquaintances, I'm surprised he ever saw her standing upright."

"But all that stuff about seeing her just before she died, about her being happy, and doing what she was meant to do," Robert said in disbelief.

Aric's father made a face. "She did not possess the knowledge or the desire to heal anyone. Even her own children. She died in a leper colony. She caught it from one of her lovers. Lord knows which one."

"But you said—"

"I lied, Robert," Burkhart said dryly. "Aric was traumatized by his mother's behavior. It scarred all of the children. And Delia's sluttish behavior has hardly helped the situation."

"And so you lied so that he would not mess things up with Rosamunde?" Shambley reasoned aloud.

Gordon shrugged. "I have not proven a good judge of women. Mayhap Rosamunde will betray him, too. I do not know. But I do not think so, and she deserves to be given the chance to prove herself. Women should be judged by their actions, not by their sex." His gaze sharpened suddenly. "But you will keep this last bit of information to yourself, will you not?"

"Aye, my lord," Robert assured him quickly, then hesitated. "Can I never tell him?"

Gordon smiled slightly. "Why?" he asked with amusement. "Wait, I know. You think Rosamunde will be true, and that Aric will someday realize he was being an ass. You're looking forward to rubbing his nose in it!" He shook his head. "Here is the deal. You may tell him when you are both old and gray and sitting over mulled wine and telling tall tales."

Robert grinned slightly. "I shall look forward to it."

"Good!" Lord Burkhart laughed, slapping the younger man on the shoulders and urging him toward the stable doors. "Sup should be ready by now, do you not think? I find coming up with lies gives me an appetite."

"You tell them well," Shambley complimented him.

Burkhart nodded proudly. "I was making it up as I went along. There were no holes in the tale, were there?"

"None that I noticed," Shambley assured him.

Chapter 11

THE main doors to the keep were both wide open when Aric reached them. Stepping inside, he gaped as he looked around the great hall, hardly able to believe the changes that had been wrought while he had been held down in the stables.

The doors had been left open to allow the room to air, no doubt, and the action had been successful, he realized with a sniff, then shook his head. If he had not seen it himself, he would not have believed it; there was not even a hint of the chaos that had reigned just minutes before. Every last animal that had crowded the room was now gone, but even more amazing was the absence of any sign that they had ever been there. There was not a cow pie, or a feather to be seen, and his chair, he saw with relief as he slowly crossed the room, had been cleaned and shined. Even Blackie—Black, he corrected himself irritably—was no longer flatulating by the fire.

He was standing, marveling over this wonder, when the sound of footsteps drew his gaze to the stairs. His wife came tripping lightly down them. Pausing when she saw him, she glanced around the room a tad nervously, then gave him a smile of mingled relief and welcome.

"You are back, my lord," she said, then continued down the steps to greet him. "How was your tour?"

"Very informative," he murmured. He had learned much in the last few minutes.

"Oh, good." She beamed at him. "Well, sup should be ready soon, and—" She started to walk past him as she spoke, but her words died on her lips as he suddenly caught her arm and whirled her around to face him.

"Rosamunde." He breathed her name, and she blinked at his husky tone.

"Aye, husband?"

"Say my name," he urged, drawing her into his arms. "I liked the way you said my name last night when I was holding you."

"Aric." It was barely a gasp on her lips as his hands slid over her hips, urging her against his lower body. He smiled at the breathy excitement in her voice and the way her eyes were suddenly heavy-lidded with desire.

"Would you really prefer to return to the abbey, as Shrewsbury says?" he asked.

Rosamunde blinked at the sudden change in topic, then stiffened and tried to pull back. He held her in place against him.

"Answer. Honestly."

Biting her lip, Rosamunde glanced away, then sighed. "I was upset when I spoke to Bishop Shrewsbury. I . . . We had not yet . . . and I thought . . . the bedding . . ." she trailed off in embarrassment. "And then I missed . . ." She paused again, and looked away uncertainly.

"You missed working in the stables," Aric finished for her.

She glanced up quickly to see if he was angry. Seeing his gentle expression, she nodded hesitantly.

He nodded back, then bent to press gentle kisses to

her lips, her cheek, and her ear. Then he whispered, "You may attend the stables in the future."

She froze. "My lord?"

Pulling back, he nodded solemnly. "Your skill is valuable. 'Twould be a shame to keep you locked here in the keep and waste it. The new stables will be done in a day or so. Until then, you will have to make do with the old one. I—" His words halted on a grunt of surprise as she suddenly threw her arms around him with a squeal of delight.

"Oh, husband! You are wonderful. The best husband a woman could have. Truly, my father was wise to pick you!"

Aric felt himself go all soft inside at her praise and he closed his arms around her, holding her tightly as she babbled on in happy gratitude. Smiling slightly, he buried his nose in her hair, inhaling the scent of her. She smelled so good, so sweet and natural. His hand slid up and down her back, then farther down, curving over her bottom through her gown as he began to nuzzle her ear.

"My lord," Rosamunde said softly, and drew back slightly.

Aric lowered his lips at once to cover hers, giving her a quick kiss. She sighed as he drew his lips away, and upon hearing it, he kissed her once more, slower. Again she gave a broken little sigh when he stopped, and he couldn't resist recovering her lips with his own. This time he kissed her thoroughly, rejoicing in her little mewls and sighs of pleasure before forcing himself to stop.

"We shall continue this after sup," he murmured, nipping at her ear.

"Oh, Aye. Please," Rosamunde said softly, her eyes glittering with desire.

Smiling, Aric took her hand and led her to the head

of the table as the first of the dinner crowd began to filter into the hall.

"Well." Covering his mouth, Aric feigned a long loud yawn that drew everyone's curious gaze. "It has been a rather long, eventful day. Do you not think?"

"Oh, aye, my lord husband," his wife murmured, her solemn expression belying the laughter sparkling in her eyes. "Most long. And tiring, too."

"Aye, exhausting," Aric agreed, his own expression so solemn it was almost mournful. "Mayhap we should—"

"Rosamunde tired?" Robert interrupted with a laugh before Aric could finish his suggestion that he and his wife retire early. "Impossible!" Leaning forward, Robert peered past Rosamunde and Aric to address Lord Burkhart on his son's other side. "She was always the last to sleep and the first to awaken on our journey from Godstow. She inherited her father's fortitude, I think."

"Nay. I did not," Rosamunde denied quickly. "I was j-just excited by the experience of my first journey."

"Nay." Robert shook his head. "You rose ere the birds . . . every morning!" He leaned forward again, telling Lord Burkhart, "Why, one morning she had risen, bathed, caught a rabbit, skinned it, cleaned it, skewered it, and built a fire to cook it over, and was done cooking ere we even awoke."

"She was just excited by the journey—as she said," Aric snapped, irritably. "She is tired now."

"I do not believe this!" Robert crowed. "She cannot be tired. 'Tis early yet and—" He paused, swallowing the rest of his words in surprise. Rosamunde had kicked sideways underneath the table, hitting him in the ankle. "What did you do that for?" He gave her a hurt look.

Rosamunde rolled her eyes at his expression. "I am sorry, my lord. You see, I am so tired I am losing control of my limbs." Standing abruptly, she turned to Aric, brushing a hand gently across his cheek though he continued to sit glaring at his friend. "I think I shall retire early."

Giving a start at her touch, Aric glanced up, his expression softening as he read the promise in her eyes. "Aye. That is a good idea," he said in a growl, the anger in his eyes replaced by a different fire. Standing, he took her arm. Muttering a good night in the general direction of the table, he escorted Rosamunde across the hall and up the stairs.

They had nearly reached the top before Rosamunde gave in to the giggle at the back of her throat, but once she had started, she couldn't seem to stop. And when her husband paused on the final step to peer down at her, she collapsed against him, muffling her amusement in his chest. She finally raised her head to say with a gasp, "I thought sure you were going to hit him. You looked so angry."

Aric's lips slowly curled upward in amusement as well. He admitted, "I was thinking about it. 'I do not believe it. 'Tis early yet,'" he mimicked his friend with annoyance, then sobered as he peered down into her laughing eyes. "But he is right. 'Tis early yet." Moving closer, he caressed her cheek with the back of his hand.

"Aye," Rosamunde said softly, turning her face to his caress. "And we have all night."

With a groan, Aric tugged her into his arms for a long, deep kiss right there at the top of the stairs, his lips and tongue bringing her to tingling life even as his hands began to rove over her body. Rosamunde withstood it for several moments, then tugged away, caught his hand, and rushed down the hallway. He allowed her to pull him along until they reached the door to their bedchamber. There he drew her up short. Twirling her around, he tugged her into his arms again, his mouth capturing hers.

Moaning against his lips, Rosamunde slid her arms around his neck. Delving her hands into his hair, she tangled her fingers there, arching into him as his hands skimmed down her back, molding her to him. She felt his hardened desire press against her; then he slid his hands between them and up over her body until they covered her breasts.

Jerking in his arms, Rosamunde kissed him hungrily, excitement burning through her as he pressed her against the door, one of his knees riding up between her legs and pressing against her. Then he grazed his hands down her outer thighs, caught her skirts, and slowly pulled them up until he was able to slip his hands beneath and around behind. He caught her by the backs of her thighs. Lifting her upward, he urged her legs around his waist, then lifted her into his arms before feeling behind her to unlatch and open the door. He stumbled inside with her riding his hips, pushed the door closed, and staggered to the bed still kissing her.

Laughing breathlessly when he released her lips, Rosamunde tipped her head back and closed her eyes as his mouth nibbled and bit her neck on a path downward. When his knees bumped against the bed, he tumbled forward with her, dropping her to its soft surface. He followed, but caught his own weight with his hands so that he didn't crush her.

Rosamunde immediately began tugging at his clothes. Pulling his tunic upward, she pushed it over his chest, pressing kisses to that wide expanse as he grabbed the material and drew it over his head. Eyes narrowing in appreciation, Rosamunde ran her hands over the heavily muscled flesh, then leaned up to catch one pebblelike nipple between her teeth. She smiled in satisfaction when Aric closed his eyes and lifted his head with a groan of pleasure. In the next moment, he had caught her face between his hands and brought her lips back to his. His tongue thrust aggressively into her mouth as he impatiently tugged at the lacings of her gown.

Phfffphhphphttt.

Aric stiffened, his mouth stilling on Rosamunde's briefly before he slowly lifted his head.

"What is it?" Rosamunde asked in confusion.

"I thought I heard something," he muttered, frowning.

"I did not hear *anything*," she said impatiently, tugging his face back down to hers. Covering his lips with her own as he had repeatedly done to her, she slid her tongue boldly out to explore his mouth. Her hands made their way over his chest.

Aric remained still for a moment, then took over the kiss, his hands pulling the bodice of her gown open and tugging it down her shoulders and arms until her breasts popped free. Tugging his mouth away from hers then, he curled a hand around one breast and lowered his mouth to suckle at it eagerly.

Phfffphhphphttt-phft-phft-phffphhphhphpht!

"Now I *know* I heard that," Aric said, lifting his head to peer at his wife. Suspicion filled him when he saw that her eyes were now squeezed closed, and not with passion. Realization and dread were warring on her features. Then the smell hit—just at about the same moment that Black whinnied. Jerking his head to the side, Aric simply stared at the horse by the fire. It let out another horrible emission.

"Sweet Jesu," he said with horror. "You . . . you . . . He . . ." He closed his eyes briefly, but when he opened them, the horse was still there.

"*Well,*" Rosamunde drew out the word and winced. "You said to move him ere the sup."

"So you moved him to our chamber?" Aric cried with disbelief, then closed his eyes. He slowly counted to ten as his wife began to babble in explanation.

"I meant to put him in a spare chamber—but your father is in one, Lord Shambley in another, and then there are Bishop Shrewsbury and Lord Spencer and . . ." She paused and he could feel her shrug beneath him. "There no longer is a spare chamber."

"Wife," Aric began carefully, but Rosamunde did not wait to see what he would say. Pulling quickly from beneath him, she tugged the bodice of her gown back in place and hurried across the room toward the horse.

"I am sorry, my lord. Honestly, I forgot all about him."

Sighing, Aric flipped over onto his back, staring at the ceiling as he listened to her continued chattering.

"He is most likely just thirsty. Are you not, Blackie? Poor you. Here you are ill and feverish and I forgot to fetch you more water."

Turning his head, Aric watched morosely as his wife fussed over the horse and bent to retrieve an empty pail. Pushing himself to his feet, he grabbed his shirt and quickly tugged it on. "I shall send a servant up with fresh water," he announced grimly, taking the pail from her as she started for the door.

Pausing, Rosamunde eyed him with alarm as he pulled the door open. "But where are you going?"

"Below."

"Below? But what about . . ." Flushing, she glanced away and toward the bed unhappily.

Aric followed her gaze, then glanced back to Black. The horse emitted another loud, noxious emission. "I need a drink," was all he said. With that, he stepped into the hall and tugged the door closed with a snap.

Shoulders slumping, Rosamunde sighed unhappily. Her breasts still ached for his touch. And they weren't the only place she was aching.

Black whinnied and clip-clopped across the floor to nuzzle her shoulder.

Sighing again, Rosamunde raised a hand to pat his clothing-wrapped nose. " 'Tis all right, Blackie. Everything will be all right."

Other than a couple of raised eyebrows, no one had questioned what Aric was doing back at the table so soon after having left it. He'd ignored those few inquisitive looks, though, in favor of concentrating on some serious drinking. And by the time Shambley, the last man at the table besides himself, had decided to call it a night, Aric was seriously drunk.

Stumbling to his feet, he staggered up the stairs with his friend. Wishing Robert a good night, he weaved his way to his bedchamber door, which seemed to have a serious problem staying in one place. It now danced around in his vision like a firefly.

Zeroing in on it, he unlatched and pushed it open, then tottered into the room. Inside, his wife was sound asleep in the center of the bed. She certainly did seem to like to take the whole bed, he thought somewhat peevishly as he closed the door. Turning then, he made a face and wagged one finger at Black. He didn't say anything, just wagged his finger, and even he would have been hard-pressed at that point to figure out what he was forbidding the horse to do.

He continued on to the bed, tugging and fretting at his clothes as he went, so that he had only to remove his brais by the time he reached it. Swaying on his feet, he pushed them down over his hips, then tried to step out of them—raising his knees high and stumbling around in the effort, until he lost his balance and dropped onto the side of the bed.

"Hmmm. That's better," he decided, realizing that the room tended to move less sitting down. He also decided that he didn't really need to take his brais all the way off. Leaving them tangled around his feet, he collapsed back upon the bed, then rolled toward its middle until he bumped up against his wife's warm body. Cuddling close, he threw his arm across her, his hand automatically squeezing the breast it landed on as he promptly passed out.

He was having those erotic dreams about his wife again.

Aric was riding through the woods at a trot. Black was healthy and strong beneath him—and also no longer had a flatulence problem. The day was warm and sultry, and Aric had started to sweat in his tunic and brais when he came upon Rosamunde. She was wearing the white gown she had worn the day of their wedding. Standing with her back to him, she gazed upon Goodhall where it was nestled in the valley below, but turned suddenly upon hearing his approach. Smiling seductively when she recognized him, she opened her arms in welcome.

"You are the most wonderful of husbands."

Aric straightened in the saddle at her soft words, then slid from his mount. He strode forward to take her masterfully into his arms—and as soon as they had closed around her, his wife's white gown disappeared. A growl slipping from his throat, Aric ran his hands over her naked flesh, then caught them up in her deep red tresses. He tugged her head back to press a kiss onto her lips.

Cool air moving across his own flesh made him pull back slightly to see that he, too, was now naked. Thrilling at the sensation of her soft skin against his rougher body, he kissed her again, his tongue delving into her mouth. She was all soft coos and mewls as she arched against him, rubbing against his excitement, her hands clutching at his shoulders, then dropping over his back and down to his buttocks to knead the flesh there and urge him closer still.

The breeze seemed to suddenly pick up then, chilling his vulnerable flesh and Aric frowned and nestled closer into the warmth of his wife's body. He pulled his lips from hers and kissed a path over her chin and down her neck to the delicate hollow at the base of her throat. He would have continued on down to find her breasts, but just then it started to rain, great drops of the warm liquid splashing against his cheek. Grimacing, Aric muttered under his breath, the sound of his own voice awakening him from his dream to find that it hadn't all been a dream. Rosamunde was naked and warm in his arms, sleepy gasps and moans still slipping from her lips. His lower body was nestled against hers.

And it *was* chill. An early-morning breeze was blowing into the room and the bed linens were missing, leaving them uncovered. No doubt the sheets had slipped to the floor, he thought fuzzily, then grimaced again as another drop of warm liquid splashed upon his cheek. Rolling onto his back, Aric found himself staring into a hideous, elongated, clothes-covered animal face. If that wasn't startling enough, there was a long, slimy gob of liquid hanging precariously from the apparition's nose, ready to drop onto him. That explained the rain in his dream, some part of his mind realized. He gave a startled shout of alarm and tried to avoid his horse's dripping nose. He jerked instinctively to the side, banging his head into Rosamunde's.

"What? Huh?" Rosamunde gasped, awake at once and grabbing at her head in pain as she sat up. "What is about? What is wrong?"

"Get that damned horse out of here!"

Blinking the last of her sleep away, Rosamunde turned to see her husband doing his best to scramble out of the way of a drooling and runny-nosed Blackie. The horse was standing at the side of the bed, its head hanging over where Aric had been lying a moment before.

"Oh, dear!" She gasped, leaping up and hurrying around to quickly urge the horse away from the bed. "Blackie, what are you doing? Poor thing, do you have a runny nose?" she cooed.

"Aye, and he dribbled it all over me," Aric snapped with disgust, wiping at the liquid on his cheek with a grimace.

"Oh, dear." Rosamunde said again and sighed. She bent quickly and picked up Aric's discarded tunic from the night before to swiftly wipe the mess away from the horse's mouth and nose.

Realizing what she was doing, Aric began squawking. He leaped from the bed to stop her. "What are you doing? Oh, God, that is my tunic!"

"Oh." Rosamunde peered down at the crumpled—and now quite revolting—tunic guiltily before asking, "Surely you have another one, my lord. A man of your stature must have more than one tunic."

"Aye, I do," he said grimly. "That green one there wrapped around Black's head, and the blue one on his tail."

Biting her lip, Rosamunde peered at the shirts Aric spoke of and briefly considered taking them off, then decided he probably wouldn't appreciate the gesture. Glancing back at him unhappily, she shook her head woefully. She had muffed up again. "I am sorry, my lord. I was not thinking when I wrapped all of our clothes around Blackie! I was just worried about how unhappy you would be if he should fall seriously ill."

Aric's anger left him as quickly as it had come. She had done all of this for him, trying to please him. He felt himself go all soft and warm inside, just as he had when she had proclaimed him the the most wonderful of husbands. Aric could not remember the last time a woman had acted out of consideration for him. Certainly Delia had never bothered to during their long betrothal. From childhood on, she had expected that he would do things for her, while she merely sat about looking pretty. But then, Rosamunde is not Delia, he reminded himself. He smiled wryly as the thought struck him that it had been silly to make that mistake. The two were nothing alike. Delia would not have cared about Black's illness no matter how upset Aric might have been. Besides, she had been dark-haired, short, and plump, while Rosamunde with her red hair was willowy and fair—and completely naked at the moment, he realized with interest. Of course, she also had the despondent air of a chastised puppy.

That simply would not do.

Stepping forward, he tugged Black's reins from her limp hand and headed for the door, dragging the reluctant horse behind him. He wasn't at all pleased that his mount suddenly seemed to prefer Rosamunde's company to his own, but he wasn't terribly surprised either. He himself was becoming inexplicably fond of her as well.

Opening the door, Aric ignored his own nakedness and half pushed and half tugged the horse out into the hall, nodding abruptly at his father as the older man passed by. He ignored the stare he received. Pushing the door closed, Aric moved slowly back across the room toward his miserable-looking wife.

"Get on the bed," he ordered, and her head snapped up in surprise.

"On the bed, my lord?" she asked with amazement.

Aric nodded. "On your hands and knees as you were the day we married."

Rosamunde hesitated, her gaze shifting to the bed and back before she asked uncertainly, "Are you going to punish me for dirtying your shirt, my lord?"

"Oh, aye," he assured her with a gleam in his eye she suddenly recognized. "But I promise you will like it. Get on the bed."

His voice was like warm honey, and it, along with his expression and his words, caused an immediate tingling in Rosamunde. Turning away at once, she moved to the bed and crawled atop it, positioning herself on her hands and knees there as she had the day of their wedding. Oddly, she felt ten times more vulnerable than she had then; she was completely naked this time. She felt the bed sink behind her. Glancing back, she saw Aric kneel behind her and move forward, urging her knees farther apart. He shifted between them until his abdomen gently bumped her behind.

Recalling the painful debacle of their wedding day, Rosamunde cleared her throat uncertainly. "Are you sure you would not rather do it the right way, my lord?"

"The right way?" he inquired, his hands gently clasping her hips. "Who says this is the wrong way? Surely God's creatures cannot be wrong, can they? Think of cats, and cows, and horses," he teased lightly.

"W-well," Rosamunde began uncertainly. "Aye, but that other time—"

"That other time we left out some good bits."

"Good bits?" she asked uncertainly.

"Aye. For instance, there is this." Sliding his hands forward past her waist, he urged her to straighten until she knelt before him upright, he drew her back until she rested against his chest. "And this," he whispered into her ear, one hand sliding up to catch and caress one suddenly aching and swollen breast. The other slid down over her tummy, then farther to cover her womanhood and press softly against it. "There are important bits, and you would not let me include them the first time."

"Oh, aye." Rosamunde gasped, then gave a breathless laugh. Her body unconsciously arched, which pressed her bottom snugly against him and thrust her breast forward into his hand. "I thought you were trying to milk me like a cow."

"I *am* trying to milk you," he whispered by her ear. "But not like a cow."

"Then how?" She moaned as he began to nibble and lave the ear he had been speaking near.

"I am trying to milk pleasure out of you."

"Ohhhh." The word came out on a shudder as he slid his fingers between her legs. "Oh, my lord."

"Say, my name," he instructed, fondling the nubbin he found at the apex of her thighs.

"Ooohhh, Aric," she said softly.

"Again."

"Aric." She gasped as he slid a finger into her, one hand lifting to touch his head.

"Again," Aric said, turning his head to kiss the palm of her hand, then stiffening slightly and gasping as her other hand slid back between them, feathered across his thigh, then found and clasped his manhood.

"*Aric,*" she said huskily, her tone low and throaty this time.

Groaning as her fingers tightened around his manhood, Aric thrust his finger into her again, more aggressively this time.

"My lord?" she gasped, shifting her legs farther apart of her own accord and curving into his touch.

"Aye?"

"I think . . ."

"You think?" He moaned as her hand began instinctively to stroke down his hardened arousal.

"I need . . ."

"You need?" He gasped, his hips beginning to move with her caresses.

"You." She groaned.

"I need you, too." The words came out pained and husky as he urged her back to her hands and knees. He caught her hips and thrust eagerly into her.

"I do believe you may be getting better, Black," Rosamunde murmured cheerfully as she rewrapped Aric's shirt around the horse's head. It had been over an hour since Aric had shown her that doing "it" the way animals did wasn't necessarily wrong—if one did it right. He had then fallen fast asleep, leaving Rosamunde to get up, attend her personal needs, dress, and move Blackie from the hall outside their bedchamber, back down to stand by the fire in the great hall. She had cleaned him up again, for his nose was running horribly, but she knew it was nothing to worry about, just the bad humors leaving his body. She also fed him before unwrapping the clothing from his head to check his temperature. Now tucking the tail end of the tunic under another strip of the cloth to keep it out of the way, she smiled at the animal.

"You are not nearly as hot as you were yesterday. And you are regaining your appetite. You should be your old self again in no time."

"Thank God for that."

Whirling in surprise, Rosamunde smiled shyly at Aric as he approached, then blinked at the brown shirt he wore. "You found a clean tunic."

"Nay. 'Tis mine," Robert announced, drawing her attention to the fact that he was a step behind her husband. "What could I do when he showed up at my door in nothing but brais, begging for—Ouch!"

Rosamunde bit her lip to keep from laughing and gave her husband a reprimanding look for cuffing his friend.

"There's gratitude for you," Robert grumbled, then winked at Rosamunde to let her know that such tomfoolery was common between the two.

"Hmmm. Well, 'twas most kind of you to clothe my husband, my lord," Rosamunde murmured, even as she decided she would have to find something else to wrap Black in. She would clean her husband's clothes this day. Lord Robert's mustard-brown shirt looked horrid on her husband. It really wasn't his color at all.

"So." Aric moved to her side. His hand ran absently up and down the flesh of her upper arm as he peered at his horse. "Can this beast be moved to the stables again—since he is so much better?"

"Not quite yet, my lord," Rosamunde said apologetically, shivering slightly under his light caress. "In another day or two perhaps, but he is still vulnerable, and what with the stables in such rough shape—Where are you going?" she asked in amazement as he suddenly whirled away and strode toward the doors to the bailey.

"To add more men to the building detail. The stables shall be done today if I have to raise them myself. That horse is not spending another night in our room."

"Wait for me, Aric," Robert called, hurrying after him. "There is something I must discuss with you."

"But the two of you have not even broken your fast," Rosamunde cried in dismay. But they merely waved at her and continued on their way, their heads now close together as they spoke.

"And how is Lord Aric's horse this morning?"

Rosamunde glanced away from the men disappearing through the keep doors to smile at Bishop Shrewsbury. He crossed the great hall toward her from the direction of the stairs. "Good morn, my lord Bishop. He is better today. Thank you for asking."

"Good, good." The older man beamed at both her and the horse in question. "I knew you would mend him. 'Tis a gift you have."

Blushing slightly at the praise, Rosamunde smiled slightly, then turned to collect the horse's reins. "I was just about to take Black outside for a moment. Why do you not sit down and break your fast? Lord Spencer should be along soon to eat with you."

"Ah, no. Not this morning, I fear," Bishop Shrewsbury said sadly. "Joseph was on his way down here to have a tray brought up to Lord Spencer when I left my room. He said Spencer's rheumatism is bothering him something fierce this morning and he will remain abed. He seems to think that means rain," he added, then shrugged. "I told Joseph I would see to it, so he need not leave Lord Spencer alone."

"Oh." Rosamunde hesitated, her gaze moving to the kitchen door, but Shrewsbury patted her arm reassuringly.

"You go ahead and take Black outside before he does anything unpleasant. I shall ensure that Lord Spencer's tray is sent up."

"Thank you, my lord Bishop," Rosamunde murmured gratefully, starting toward the keep doors. Black followed docilely behind her. "I should not be long. Then I will keep you company while you eat."

"Good, good. Then we can talk about how to approach your husband."

Pausing, Rosamunde turned back with surprise. "How to approach my husband? About what?" she asked uncertainly.

"Why, about returning you to the abbey, my dear. I am sure that if we just find the right approach, he will see the sense in it. Unfortunately, he does seem to have a temper. He was quite upset with me yesterday when I—"

"My lord Bishop," Rosamunde interrupted, leaving Blackie where he stood and moving slowly back. She had quite forgotten all about that day in the stables when she had sobbed that she did not belong here, that she could do nothing right, the day he had arrived with the news of her father's death. So much had happened since then. "My lord, I know that I was upset the day you arrived—"

"Of course you were, child. Hearing of King Henry's death on top of your own misery here as Burkhart's wife—"

"I do not wish to return to the abbey," Rosamunde said before he could make her feel any worse than she already did about not grieving longer over the loss of her father. The cleric would hardly understand, even if she explained that while she had loved and admired Henry, it had been from a distance—always from a distance. She had seen him only once a year, usually a quick visit on his way somewhere else. He had never once stayed the night at Godstow, and the meal she had been told he ate while she had prepared for her wedding had been only the second he had ever consumed at the abbey. In truth, she had spent more time with him on his last visit—and they had exchanged more words then—than they ever had before. Ere that, he had always been quiet and regal. He had always been her King more than her father, and though she had loved him and sought his approval, his title had always stood between them—something she now regretted.

The abbess and all the women at the abbey had been her true family. They had nurtured and loved her, watching and helping her grow, enjoying her victories and commiserating with her in failure. Her father . . . Well, she grieved his passing, and the loss of a good king, but he had been a very poor parent.

Still, she would have died before being ungrateful enough to admit that. And she could never, ever have said as much to the man who stood before her, a man who had spent the last thirty-odd years of his life at the king's side, the most faithful of servants.

"I do not understand," he said slowly at last. "You said you could do nothing right here. That you—"

"I was very upset at the time." Rosamunde sighed. "I had been torn from the abbey, refused to be allowed to work with animals." She shook her head helplessly.

The bishop nodded helpfully. "Aye. And if we return you to the abbey, you can take the veil, and continue to heal and nurture the animals—as God meant."

"I can do that here, too. Well, not take the veil, of course—but Aric has agreed to allow me in the stables. He even said it would be a waste of my gifts to deny them." Her face fairly beamed as she told him that, and Shrewsbury smiled slightly in return. Then he seemed to catch himself and shake his head.

"That *is* wonderful. But what of the marital bed? You said you found it painful and humiliating. Surely you do not wish—"

"Oh, well," Rosamunde interrupted, her face beginning to burn with embarrassment. "That was . . . I mean . . . Well, the first time is always painful, is it not?"

"Aye, I have heard as much," Bishop Shrewsbury murmured carefully, watching her face closely. His eyes suddenly widened in amazement. "Are you saying you do not find it unpleasant and humiliating anymore?"

Rosamunde was finding this conversation uncomfortable and decided it was time to bring it to an end. "My lord Bishop, I cannot . . . This is a most discomfiting discussion. I fear we shall just have to leave it at the fact that I am no longer unhappy here. I am content to stay."

"Just a moment," the bishop murmured anxiously as she started to turn back toward Black. When she paused, he sighed and made a face. "I know this is an uncomfortable conversation for you, child, but this is important. I must ask you—you do not *enjoy* the marital bed, do you?"

Rosamunde's face colored at the question, and she looked at him warily.

He sighed impatiently. "I do not mean to offend. I ask only because I am aware that the abbess—thinking that you would forever remain with the abbey—may not have taught you about such matters." When Rosamunde made no reply but looked uncertain, he said gently, " 'Tis a sin to enjoy the marital bed."

Chapter 12

HAVE you given any thought to what kind of trouble King Henry may have been worried about?" When Aric slowed to a stop at the bottom of the keep steps and turned a confused expression to his friend, Robert reminded him, "He was worried about Rosamunde's safety should anything happen to him. He said 'twas why he sneaked back to arrange the wedding."

Aric frowned slightly, then continued forward. They were nearly at the half-built stables before he admitted, "I have thought about little else, but I am still not sure what King Henry was concerned about."

"Do you think his concern was about Richard?"

"I do not know," Aric admitted with a scowl. That was his fear. That perhaps now that Richard was to be king, he might pose a threat to Rosamunde. But Aric did not know if the man was even aware of her existence. He wished, not for the first time, that Henry had been more specific in explaining his fears.

"I do not know either," Robert admitted on a sigh, drawing Aric's thoughts back to their conversation, then echoing them. "It would be helpful had King Henry been more forthcoming about what sort of difficulties he expected. And from what corner? Richard or John?"

"Aye." Aric considered the matter briefly, then murmured, "Well, now that Henry is dead, Richard will inherit the throne—so he is most likely the one King Henry feared might act against her."

Shambley nodded thoughtfully. "After all, Richard is most definitely his mother's son. Eleanor has great influence over him."

"Aye, but surely you do not think she could still be bitter over Henry's affair with my wife's mother?" he muttered with dismay.

"I do not know. That is why I brought it up. I wanted to hear your opinion on the matter," he said carefully. "King Henry's concern for her was my first thought when the messenger arrived at Shambley with news of his death. This sudden fear for Rosamunde, what could it mean?"

"Aye, that has been preying on my mind as well," Aric agreed.

"And the last thing you need is more concerns to trouble you," Robert muttered suddenly, amusement beginning to twinkle in his eyes. "Between acquainting yourself with your new responsibilities and Black's illness, you have quite enough in your trencher. Speaking of which, how are you enjoying him as a chambermate? Does he snore? Or do the stomach staggers keep him from sleeping?"

Aric glared at him coldly. "Enjoy it while you can, Shambley. No doubt the day will come when the tables are turned. I shall certainly enjoy my own good laugh then."

Robert merely laughed harder. "Truly, Aric, I do not know how you maintained your temper last night. It did not even occur to me to wonder where Rosamunde had moved the horse to. And to your room?" He shook his head. "Why, the great hall is huge, and the stench in there was staggering. Your chamber must have been suffocating!"

Aric exhaled in misery as he thought about it. But in truth, he had been so drunk when he returned to the chamber, he hadn't noticed any stench at all. In fact, his real irritation had been on awakening to find the animal's nose dripping all over his face. He kept that bit of news to himself, though. His friend had enough to tease him about.

"Back to our discussion of my wife and her possible danger," he said meaningfully instead.

"Ah. Aye, of course." Robert sobered quickly. "What will you do about the coronation? Tidings should come of that soon enough, and you will no doubt both be expected to attend. Do you expect trouble at the ceremony? Eleanor will be there, most like."

Aric considered the matter briefly, then shook his head. "Nay. I do not see that there should be any trouble. Rosamunde's mother's relationship with Henry was nearly twenty years ago. I cannot see any woman holding a grudge that long."

Robert raised an eyebrow.

"But just in case, I think I shall tell the men to be on the lookout for trouble."

"It cannot hurt to do so."

"Aye." Aric sighed. "I shall just have a word with my first in command ere I . . ." Frowning, he slowed, his hand raising instinctively to his cheek and coming away with dampness on his finger. His brow furrowing with displeasure, he held his hands out, palms to the skies. It was barely a moment before a fat drop of water plopped into one. It was followed quickly by a second. "Damn," he said in disbelief.

"Hmmm. It appears your work on the new stables shall have to wait," Robert managed to say, straight-faced. "I suppose this means you shall be sleeping with your horse again tonight. I do hope he's feeling better." He couldn't repress his laughter when Aric released a long growl of frustration.

"There you are, Blackie." Rosamunde set the bucket of water she had brought with her at the horse's feet. "That should do you for the night."

Straightening, she slid her fingers beneath the material covering his face, relieved to find him cooler. She considered removing the clothes wrapped around him, then decided against it. One more night wearing them would not harm him, and she was sure that if she removed the clothes, Aric would decide that Black was fine and could be returned to the stables. Which was not an option. Not when it had been raining all through the day and most of the evening.

Rosamunde sighed as she thought of the plight of the other horses in the stables tonight. Despite it being full summer, the days had been cool, the kind that seemed to seep right into one's bones. And on top of that, the horses were suffering from the damp, too. The old stables did not only have holes in their walls. The roof also leaked, as if it had been constructed of cheesecloth. Rosamunde had spent a good portion of the morning trying to move the horses around, doubling them up in the best stalls, emptying some to avoid the worst of the leaks. But by the end of the morning, she had given up the chore as useless; there simply hadn't been enough stalls that did not have leaks above them.

Rosamunde shook her head at the memory of that frustrating and wholly useless morning. It had not helped that Aric had trailed her around the whole time, grumbling and complaining about the rain and the way it was slowing—actually halting—his construction of the new stables. Had he been complaining about it out of concern for the horses, who had to stand in the mud getting a soaking, she would have grumbled along with him and not been so irritated, but there was no mistaking the fact that his main concern with the delay was that he would have to suffer another night with Black in the castle.

By the midday meal, Rosamunde had enjoyed quite enough of her husband's company, and she had hoped that he would remain behind in the keep during the afternoon. Alas, as soon as the meal was over and she rose to return to the stables, Aric was on his feet to accompany her. She had suggested then, gently, that he entertain his father and Robert in the afternoon rather than follow her around, but he had quickly put paid to that possibility. Nay, he'd said, he was happy to help her and keep her company.

All Rosamunde could do was sigh and shake her head. His statement would have been more believable had he not spit the words through gritted teeth as he trailed her through the pouring rain to the bull's paddock. *The* bull. The one who had stomped and gored poor Jemmy's pup. Its owner had approached her just ere the nooning meal to ask if she might not take a look at the animal. The beast seemed to be favoring one leg. Soaking wet and covered in mud to her knees, Rosamunde had arrived at the paddock, where the bull resided, in no mood for its cantankerous antics.

Aric had taken one look at the huge, angry beast and the way it glowered at them as they neared the wooden enclosure it was in, then drawn Rosamunde to a halt. He'd then turned to the bull's owner to begin discussing ropes or various other methods of subduing the animal so that she might safely enter the pen. Knowing it was useless to argue, Rosamunde had waited in the pouring rain until they moved off in search of such materials. As soon as the two men disappeared inside the ramshackle old shed that passed for the owner's barn, she had shaken her head, and moved to the fence. The bull had immediately turned to face her, lowering its head threateningly.

Rosamunde had tried a nice, soothing tone to calm the animal, but the bull had merely pawed the ground a time or two in response. She had deduced from that that it wasn't fear making him cranky. The bull was just miserable. *Wonderful.* Well, she hadn't felt her most charming at that moment either, and didn't appreciate the fact that she was getting cold and wet all for an ungrateful brute of a bull that stomped on poor, defenseless puppies.

Muttering under her breath, she had lifted her skirts slightly so that he could see her legs, then imitated his pawing motion—just to let him know she wasn't intimidated. Then she had climbed determinedly up on the fence. She had been about to swing one leg over the top bar, but froze when the bull had suddenly charged. The bull charged until it was a hairbreadth away from the fence, and then veered away.

She had known it would do that. The animal was feinting, warning her of what it would do should she not stay on her side of the fence. But Rosamunde hadn't been about to put up with such nonsense. As the bull started to turn away, she swung her sack of medicinals over the fence and clubbed the beast in the head with it.

Startled, the animal had sidestepped quickly and whirled to face her. Rosamunde could have sworn she saw an amazed and injured look in the bull's eyes. She suspected most people gave it a wide berth and did not challenge its posturing—except mayhap for puppies that didn't know better and were easy to trounce. But she had found that animals were a lot like people. And bullies were the same no matter the species.

Having gotten its attention, Rosamunde had smiled sweetly and slid her hand in her pocket. She dug about inside. Pulling out an apple, she waved it from side to side, then held it out. "Care for some?"

The bull had stayed put, but she'd been able to see the interest in its eyes. She had smiled slightly before tossing the fruit lightly onto the grass at its feet. Watching her warily, presumably lest she suddenly go mad and start thrashing him again with her bag, it lowered its head carefully and nudged the apple, then bit into it. Rosamunde waited patiently.

Angus, the bull at the abbey, had known a weakness for apples that Rosamunde had hoped that this bull would share. Much to her relief, this bull also proved susceptible. The succulent bribe quickly disappeared.

Reaching into her bag, Rosamunde had taken out another apple, waved it from side to side, then swung first one leg, then the other, over the fence so that she sat on it with both legs inside the paddock. Pausing, she'd leaned forward to hold it out.

The bull had stared at her, hesitating, then had taken one step forward. Then it stopped and simply stared at her. Rosamunde had hesitated, then tossed the apple to the ground halfway between them. The bull had eyed her warily, but closed the space. It quickly gobbled up the second offering. Rosamunde had promptly produced a third, and that had been the charm. All she had had to do was hold it out; this time the bull had moved cautiously forward and taken it carefully from where she held it out on her flat palm. While it ate that one, Rosamunde had eased off the fence and slowly circled it, murmuring soothing nonsense as she had raised a hand to caress its side.

By the time Aric and the farmer had returned with their ropes and other paraphernalia, Rosamunde was kneeling in the mud, fretting over a nasty gash on the bull's hind leg. It was a bite—the teeth marks had told her that much—and most likely from Jemmy's pup. It seemed the animal had defended himself. Ignoring Aric's dismayed orders for her to get out immediately, Rosamunde had quickly cleaned the wound and smoothed a soothing liniment over it. Straightening then, she had given the bull a reassuring pat. Then she had calmly left the paddock.

Aric had greeted her with a stern expression and escorted her silently back to the stables. There, the lineup of animals awaiting her attention continued. Her husband had remained silent and grim through her treatments, then escorted her back to the keep to sup. He had also sat silently through that. When she had finally left him, several minutes ago, he had appeared to be well into his cups.

Sighing, Rosamunde gave Black a pat, then moved to the bed and quickly removed her gown. She started to remove her shift, too, then paused and sighed. It was a sin to sleep nude. Bishop Shrewsbury had reminded her of the whole list of sins that morning, before Aric had been forced back to the keep by the rain that Lord Spencer's aggravated rheumatism had predicted. The very thought of her conversation with the clergyman made Rosamunde sigh wearily again.

That, of course, was the true source of her tiredness. She was weary of spirit, made miserable by the pleasure she had enjoyed with her husband—and by the fact that she was not supposed to enjoy it. It seemed sister Eustice had been correct about all the *do*s and *do-not*s she had listed on her wedding day. Rosamunde had rather been counting on her being wrong about everything. But the bishop had reiterated every single one of the rules Eustice had listed, and even introduced a couple the nun had neglected. The very thought of all the *do-not*s was enough to make Rosamunde wish to climb into bed and never come out.

Of course, she couldn't do that, but she could go to bed and turn her thoughts off for a little while, at least. And that was what she planned to do. Pulling the linens back, she slid into bed, then drew them back up to her neck. She lay watching the shadows that the fire was casting dance around the room until they lulled her to sleep.

The fire had burned low, and the room and the shadows in it were much darker when she awoke some time later. She had turned onto her side in her sleep, and now lay facing the window that looked out over the courtyard.

Wondering what had awakened her, she let her eyes drift closed again, then blinked them open at a sudden scream from Black. It wasn't a nicker or a whinny. It was a scream, or as close to one as she had ever heard from a horse. And the sound was followed by the sudden thunder of Black's hooves on the wooden floor of the chamber. It sounded as if a herd of horses were charging the bed. Sitting up in alarm, Rosamunde glanced a bit wildly around, her eyes widening as she saw that Aric had entered the room. And Black was attacking him! The horse had charged forward from his place by the fire and was now on his hind legs, pawing wildly at Aric's dark shape. He cried out and swerved to avoid those lethal hooves.

"Blackie!" Rosamunde shouted. She scrambled out of the bed and rushed around toward where the dark shapes of the man and animal danced in the dim light. "Blackie, stop that!"

Reaching the horse just as Aric stumbled and fell, she grabbed desperately at the horse's reins and pulled hard on them, dragging the animal away before he could trample her husband where he lay. Once she had him a safe distance away, she held the horse steady. She asked anxiously, "Are you all right, husband?"

Without answering her, he merely stumbled to the door, tugged it open, and hurried out.

Sighing, Rosamunde turned away from the open door to peer at Blackie. The horse was breathing hard and shaking slightly. His continuous fever over the past few days had weakened him, and this incident had apparently taken a great deal of his remaining strength. Which was another reason that his behavior bewildered her. Keeping his reins firmly in hand, she moved around him to grab another log from the basket and toss it onto the dying embers in the fireplace. A second log followed it; then she picked up the iron that lay beside the basket. She quickly poked and prodded the logs around in the fire. Replacing the iron, she turned back toward Black, but paused at the sound of heavy footsteps pounding through the hall.

"Rosamunde?"

"Aric?" she answered, confused by the fact that he sounded quite worried rather than furious. She had expected him to be angry at his horse's betrayal. Rosamunde took a couple of careful steps through the darkness toward the door, only to pause when two dark shapes suddenly appeared in the archway.

"Are you all right?" They both asked at once; then silence briefly filled the room. The first shadow made its way to the table, collected something from it, then moved to her side by the fire. Aric: His worry was illuminated for her as he bent to light a candle from the first of the weak flames beginning to lick at the logs she had added to the fire. Then he straightened and turned to peer at her, his gaze taking in the fact that she wore only her shift.

"What happened?"

Rosamunde blinked at the question. "I was about to ask you the same question. Why did Blackie attack you?"

"What is going on?"

Aric and Rosamunde glanced toward the door at that question, but it was not Robert who had spoken. He stepped quickly out of the way to reveal Aric's father in a nightshirt, a candle in his hand. Its light added to the growing illumination of the room.

When Aric scowled from his scantily clad wife to the men peering curiously into the room, then moved to retrieve her dress for her from the end of the bed, Robert took it upon himself to answer. Shrugging in bewilderment as Bishop Shrewsbury and the servant Joseph appeared behind Lord Burkhart, he murmured, "We were sitting downstairs and heard a scuffle up here. It sounded like thunder. Black was screaming, and Rosamunde screamed, and we hurried up here to see what was going on!"

They all turned to peer at Rosamunde. Aric dropped the gown over her. Quickly finding the hole for her head, Rosamunde pulled it down over herself and turned on her husband with alarm. "You were still at the table? You mean it was not you Blackie attacked?"

"Why would my own horse attack me?" Aric asked irritably, tugging and fretting at the material of her gown until it covered her to her ankles, hiding her luscious legs from view. Then he stiffened. The meaning behind her words sank in. "Are you saying there was someone else in here?"

"Aye." Rosamunde struggled to get her arms through the holes meant for them. Aric had simply pulled the gown down to cover her without allowing her the time to don it properly. "I was asleep. Something woke me. I heard Blackie charge across the room; then he started screeching and—" Getting one arm free and into its sleeve, she gestured toward the side of the bed nearest the door. "There was someone beside the bed and Blackie was attacking him. I thought it was you."

"Why did you think it was Aric? Did the fellow look like him?" Lord Burkhart asked curiously. Rosamunde paused in her efforts to find the other sleeve, and blinked in surprise.

"Well . . . I am not sure. It was quite dark. I—I just assumed." She shrugged helplessly, then returned to trying to free her arm from its trapped position inside the gown. "Who else would be in our chamber?"

"More to the point, *what* were they doing here?" Robert asked, giving Aric a meaningful look.

"Did you see anyone in the hall as you approached the room?" Bishop Shrewsbury asked, stepping past Lord Burkhart and glancing around the chamber curiously. Rosamunde finally freed her other arm to slip it through its sleeve. When the cleric's gaze widened slightly as it fell on Black, Rosamunde thought that it must be because he was surprised by the horse's presence in the room, but then the gentleman cleared his throat and gestured. "It appears your horse is relieving himself on the—"

The rest of the bishop's comment was drowned out by Aric's curse and Rosamunde's gasp. But her reaction wasn't to what he was doing, but because her gaze had landed on and stopped at the horse's chest. Blood was running from a wound there.

"He is hurt," she cried, hurrying over to the beast to examine him anxiously. "Aric, fetch me my bag, please. It is in the chest in the corner."

When he moved to her side instead, to examine the wound with as much interest as she did, she glanced around to see that Robert was moving to retrieve her medicinals.

"It is a knife wound," Aric announced grimly as his friend approached. Robert gave Rosamunde her bag.

"And there is the knife."

Glancing over her shoulder at Lord Burkhart's words, Rosamunde saw the bishop straighten beside the bed, a bloodstained knife in hand. Aric moved to join him as the older man picked off some of the rushes sticking to it. Once he had the worst of them off, Shrewsbury handed the knife over. Rosamunde scowled at the sight of the weapon, then turned her attention back to the horse. Let the men worry about that. She had to mend Blackie.

Aric met Shambley's gaze as the other man joined them by the bed. They all peered at the wickedly sharp dagger for a moment, then turned to peer at Rosamunde as she fussed over the horse.

"Black saved her life," Robert murmured quietly as Lord Burkhart and Joseph stepped nearer.

"Aye." Aric nodded solemnly.

"Oh, but surely you cannot think that someone came in here deliberately to hurt her?" Bishop Shrewsbury asked anxiously. "Who would wish to harm Lady Rosamunde?"

"The one Henry feared?" Lord Burkhart suggested grimly, drawing Aric's surprised glance.

"You know about that?" He hadn't had the chance to tell his father that yet.

"Robert explained it to me after the messenger arrived. 'Tis why he accompanied me here."

"Oh, aye." Aric frowned. "This *could* be the kind of

thing Henry was worried about. I do not know. I wish he had told me more about . . ." Pausing, he glanced at the bishop sharply. "You had his ear. Why was he worried about Rosamunde? Who did he hope I could protect her from if he died?"

The old man shook his head in confusion. "I do not know. He spoke of no peril that I recall."

Aric frowned slightly, his gaze moving back to his wife as she bandaged Black's wound. It wasn't deep. He had seen that much when he had looked, but that reassured him little. No doubt it would have been deeper—and most likely deadly—for Rosamunde. He did not doubt for a moment that the horse had saved her life. But from whom? And why?

"What are you going to do?" Shambley asked as Aric continued merely to stare unhappily at his wife.

Glancing around in surprise, as if he had momentarily forgotten the presence of the other men, Aric grimaced. "I shall have the soldiers at the gate doubled, restrict all comings and goings, and keep her guarded until we find out who was behind this—and what his intent was. It is all I can do for now. That and ask if any strangers were seen today or tonight." He frowned suddenly. "No one came down or went up the stairs after Rosamunde retired. From whence did her attacker come and go?"

"The only empty room up here would have been mine," Robert muttered, following his thoughts, then shook his head. "But the hallway is quite dim, pitch-black in some spots even. Perhaps he had been waiting in the hall for her to come above and retire, and hid there again after leaving."

"We may have rushed right by him," Aric realized with dismay, then clenched his hand on the knife handle. He started toward the door, only to be stopped by his father's touch on his arm.

"If he was there, he is long gone now," Lord Burkhart pointed out quietly. Aric's shoulders slumped slightly. "The best you can do for now is order extra torches placed in the hall and ensure that they are kept lit at all times."

"Aye, I shall do that now. I shall also send a servant to remove the rushes Black fouled." He said it with a grimace, and started to move away again, only to pause and glance uncertainly toward his wife.

"Shambley and I shall stay with her while you tend to that," Lord Burkhart assured him, reading his son's reluctance to leave her alone.

Muttering his thanks, Aric hurried out of the room.

"Well, I am sure Lady Rosamunde is safe with the two of you here to watch her, so I think I shall take my old bones back to bed," Shrewsbury announced with a sigh, then glanced at Joseph. "Will you walk with me? I am sure Lord Spencer is awaiting a report of this excitement."

"Yes, my lord." Joseph accompanied the old man from the room as Shambley and Lord Burkhart moved to join Rosamunde.

"How is he?"

Rosamunde glanced around with a start at Robert's voice, then sighed slightly. "The wound was not deep, but I worry about its effect when Black was so weakened by illness already."

"Hmmmmm," Lord Burkhart mused, reaching out to pat the horse affectionately. "Black is a strong one. I gave him to Aric when he earned his spurs. He has seen worse wounds than this and come through. He will recover quickly from this scratch."

"Aye, my lord," Rosamunde murmured, but she wasn't as confident. She continued to fuss over the beast even as a servant arrived to tend to the mess on the floor. She was still fussing over Black when Aric returned. Lord Burkhart and Robert said their good nights.

"Come to bed, Rosamunde," Aric ordered as the door closed behind his father and friend.

Patting Black one last time, Rosamunde moved reluctantly to the bed.

Satisfied that she was obeying him, Aric removed his belt and sword, then started to work on shedding his tunic, only to pause when Rosamunde reached the side of the bed. She began to undo and remove her gown. She caught the hem of her gown, lifting it slowly upward, and Aric's eyes drank in each inch of skin revealed, her delicate feet, her ankles, her calves, knees, thighs—but then her shift intruded. Still, his gaze slid over the thin material, following the curves of her hip, waist, breasts.

He nearly sighed as she lifted the gown over her head, her breasts lifting and pressing against the thin linen as she did. Then he caught himself and shook his head, tending to removing his own tunic as she lightly shook her gown out, then laid it carefully over the chest on her side of the bed. Dropping his shirt to the floor, he reached for the waist of his brais, then paused to frown at Rosamunde as she began to slide into bed. "Your shift."

"What of it, my lord?" She was busily tugging the linens up to cover herself, but he recognized her attitude for the nervousness it was. He felt himself stiffen slightly, knowing there was trouble afoot.

"Are you not going to take it off?"

"Well, I . . . er . . ." Giving up on the linens, she sighed miserably and met his gaze. "Bishop Shrewsbury said 'twas a sin to sleep or—anything else—unclothed, my lord."

"Oh, he did, did he?" Aric asked slowly, feeling his temper begin to rise at the old man's interference.

"Aye." She nodded unhappily.

Aric remained silent as he considered how to approach this problem. He knew the Church's stand on such matters. Nudity was a sin. People were even expected to wear their undertunics in the bath, lest they be espied naked. But he *liked* his wife naked. He liked to see her that way, and to touch her that way, and to press his naked body against hers, and. . . .

Feeling his manhood perk up at his wandering thoughts, Aric forced himself back to the matter at hand, getting his wife out of her clothes. He wasn't foolish enough to think it would be an easy task. After all, she had been raised in an abbey, and the Church's opinion on such matters no doubt meant a great deal to her.

Sighing, he pushed his brais down and stepped out of them. Leaving them on the floor, he got into bed beside Rosamunde, then turned to consider her. She was lying on her back, her eyes closed—no doubt in hopes that he would think her sleeping and let the matter lie, he supposed.

He couldn't do that. *Wouldn't* do that.

Smiling slightly to himself, he slid his hand under the linens and moved it to cover the soft mound of one of her breasts, through the cloth of her tunic. She stiffened, her breathing suddenly increasing in speed as he ran his thumb lightly over her already protruding nipple.

Rosamunde squeezed her eyes tightly closed for a moment, fighting the pleasure that flooded her at his simple touch, then swallowed and opened her mouth to tell her husband that Bishop Shrewsbury had told her that fondling was a sin, too. But the moment her mouth opened, her husband covered her lips with his own, his tongue taking advantage and slipping inside.

Oh, this was too wrong, she thought, panic sweeping through her. The bishop had also said lewd kissing was a sin, and she was pretty sure that he would consider this lewd. Worse yet, she realized with dismay, was the fact that she was enjoying it—and he had claimed that that was a sin, too. Oh, Lord, she would surely burn in hell if she did not stop him.

Bringing her hands up, she pressed them somewhat frantically to his shoulders, trying to push him away so that she might tell him, but he was large and heavy and seemed not even to notice the pressure on his shoulders. Then he tilted his head, his mouth shifting and moving, doing things with his tongue that were guaranteeing her pleasure and a place in hell.

Rosamunde groaned in combined agony and ecstasy as his hands skimmed over her body, fighting her enjoyment even as she wanted to clutch him close and arch into his caresses. When he pressed a hand to the spot between her legs, grinding the cloth against her, she whimpered pleadingly into his mouth, silently begging God to save her from her own carnal desire. But He was busy elsewhere, it seemed, for her mental plea went unanswered; she was left to handle the matter on her own. Aric dipped his hand between her legs, moving her shift with it, and seemingly oblivious to her efforts to squeeze her legs tightly closed to prevent his touch.

As Aric broke the kiss then, she took a breath and opened her mouth to warn him of his soul's peril. Instead, she gasped as his fingers burrowed into her, sliding the material of her gown against the sensitive bud of her pleasure. Rosamunde promptly bit down on her lower lip, trying to deny the sensations that shot through her then, clamping down hard enough to draw blood when his mouth suddenly dropped to one of her breasts, closing over her hardened nipple through her linen gown. His teeth, toying with the sensitive tip through the damp cloth of her shift, were such exquisite torture that it left her breathless and panting.

It wasn't until he drew his hand from the damp cloth now gathered between her thighs to tug her gown up her legs that she was able to speak. Rosamunde immediately tried to voice what she was compelled to say to save both their souls.

"My lord husband." She gasped. "Bishop Shrewsbury—"

Lifting his head from her breast, Aric covered her mouth with his free hand and shook his head. "Hush."

"But—" She gasped again against his hand, only to be silenced by the application of more pressure.

"Nay. I will not hear any more of Shrewsbury's nonsense."

"But—"

"Nay," he repeated firmly. "I know the Church's views on being unclothed. I also know their views on the marital bed. I need no instruction from either you or Shrewsbury on the matter."

Rosamunde stared at him wide-eyed, her mouth closing on any further argument. There was no sense to it; he had just admitted that he knew the Church's views. There was little use in telling him what he already knew. Now what was she to do? The bishop had made it quite clear that to enjoy the pleasures of the flesh would jeopardize her soul, yet her father had ordered her to obey a stubborn man who seemed to care little for his own soul or hers.

Her thoughts were distracted when he suddenly took her hand and pulled her upright until she was sitting. When he then instructed her to shift to her knees,

Rosamunde did so without argument, but couldn't keep herself from covering his hands with her own, trying to stop him when he started to pull her gown up over her hips. She didn't say anything, just peered at him, silently pleading with him.

Aric took in her expression and felt his impatience build, then firmly crushed it. He glanced away, his gaze moving around the room as he considered his options. Finally he relaxed, a small smile twisting his lips briefly before he forced it away to eye her solemnly.

"Rosamunde, do you recall your vows on our marriage day?"

She blinked in surprise at his question, her body relaxing somewhat. "Aye, of course I do."

"Of course." He nodded slowly. "And was a promise to obey not one of them?"

Her expression turned wary again. Though she did not look pleased to admit it, she nodded. "Aye."

"So if I were to order you to allow me to take your shift off—to fulfill your vow before God and man to obey me—you would have to allow it, would you not?"

She frowned slightly, considering, then nodded. "Yes my lord. Since I vowed before God and man to obey you, I suppose I would."

"Then I *order* you to do so."

Rosamunde hesitated the briefest moment, then removed her hands. She remained silent and still as he tugged the gown up past her hips, over her stomach then her breasts. When he paused there, she raised her arms for him to lift it over her head, but he suddenly seemed to lose interest in removing the gown. Instead he leaned forward, his mouth finding and fastening on the same nipple he had toyed with through the linen undertunic. The garment dropped suddenly to cover his head, draping across his shoulders as he snaked one arm around her waist, bending her back slightly as he suckled one breast, his free hand shifting to cup her other.

"Oh, God." Rosamunde breathed the words like a prayer, her fingers closing and her nails digging into the flesh of her palms. She tried to fight the sensations suddenly flooding through her. Then Aric shifted, slipping one of his legs between hers, pressing it against her womanhood, and she decided she could stop worrying about going to hell. How much worse could it be than to feel all the wonderful things you weren't allowed to and being too scared to enjoy them.

Squeezing her eyes closed, she began to pray again as Aric shifted his mouth from one breast to the other, then let his hand drop down over her stomach and between her legs. Her eyes popping open as he found the center of her pleasure, she dug her nails into her palms a little deeper and began to bite her lip viciously to avoid bucking and thrusting under his touch, but there was nothing she could do to stop the warm, damp heat that he stirred with his caress.

A moment later, Rosamunde released a breath of relief when he left off his touch, but then she realized it was only so that he could finish removing her undertunic. Dragging it over her head and off her arms, he tossed it to the floor. Then Aric dropped to his haunches with one leg still between both of hers and pulled her forward; fully upright on her knees as she was, his face was level with her breasts.

Rosamunde clamped her teeth down hard on her lower lip again, silently reciting the Lord's Prayer. It was a desperate battle to ignore the sweet joy he was giving her as he licked, nibbled, and kissed his way from breast to breast, then down over her stomach, and when he nudged and rubbed and shifted his leg between hers, he ignited a fire she feared would consume her.

Just when she thought she could stand it no more, he tugged her down to sit on his thigh, his fingers delving into her hair and holding her head still as he devoured her mouth with his own. Rosamunde remained quiescent in his arms, neither fending him off nor participating, only gasping in surprise. The small sound was caught in his mouth as he turned and lowered her to the bed, coming down on top of her and sliding himself into her with one smooth movement.

Tugging his mouth away, Aric remained still as he gazed at her face, taking in her swollen lower lip and the tense, almost pained expression on her face.

Frowning slightly, he withdrew himself from inside her, then slid slowly back in, noting the way she sucked her lip between her teeth again. She bit down almost viciously, he noted with confusion, and her gaze was focused on something over his left shoulder. When he repeated the movement, she remained stiff and silent, though her teeth seemed to bite harder. Her sighs, moans, and passion from before were gone. She was like a different woman entirely in his arms, and he did not understand why. And he bloody well didn't like it. "What are you doing?"

Rosamunde's eyes shot to her husband. "My lord husband?" she asked uncertainly.

"You are biting your lip, and you seem hardly even to be here! What is wrong?"

Rosamunde sighed unhappily, but turned her gaze away. She merely said quietly, "You ordered me not to talk about it."

"Shrewsbury," Aric guessed irritably, knowing he had spoken correctly by her apologetic expression. "What else did he tell you?"

"He said it was a sin to enjoy this," she admitted

quietly, and Aric felt himself relax somewhat. At least that explained her stillness and silence. He had begun to fear . . .

"What else?" he queried, now determined to get to the bottom of it all.

Rosamunde bit her lip and glanced away, then sighed and began to list all the prelate had told her. "Never during my woman's time, never while with child or nursing, never during Lent, Advent, Whitsuntide, or Easter week. Never on feast days, fast days, Sundays, Wednesdays, Fridays, or Satur—"

"Enough!" Aric bellowed, then pressed his face into the crook of her neck. He stayed like that for a moment, then took a deep breath and lifted his head again. "Listen to me carefully," he demanded quietly. "I order you to forget all of that and to enjoy my touch. Do you understand?"

"Aye, my lord," she said with relief, making Aric smile.

Just to be sure they understood each other, he added to that. "And my kiss, you must enjoy that, too."

"As you wish, my lord,"

"And anything else we choose to do together that feels good to you. Do you understand?"

"Oh, aye, my lord."

Rosamunde smiled, but tears were pooling in her eyes and Aric frowned. "What is it?"

She remained silent for a moment, struggling briefly with the feelings that were overwhelming her. He was giving her permission to enjoy the pleasure he gave her and taking upon himself the burden of her guilt, and she knew that this was something special. He could have simply continued to do as he had been doing, leaving her to suffer alone under her fear of being a sinner. Or he could have taken his pleasure and not concerned himself with hers. Instead he had found a way for them both to enjoy it—without her having to bear the burden of the guilt the church would attach to it.

"Wife?" Aric murmured uncertainly, caressing her cheek. Rosamunde's smile widened tremulously and she reached out to touch his face. "I am so very glad that my father chose you to husband me. You are truly a wonderful man. So clever and sweet and—" Her words halted as he covered her mouth with his own, but the feelings inside of her did not, and Rosamunde knew that eventually she would have to examine them. She very much feared she was falling in love with this grumpy, stubborn, bossy, jealous, wonderfully sweet man. It was something she hadn't expected to happen—and really didn't wish to suffer if he did not love her back.

Chapter 13

"WELL?"

Aric wiped a bead of sweat from his brow, and turned to glance at the man behind him. His father had come to see how the work went on the stables. And just in time, too. Aric had just finished hanging the doors with Shambley's help. Other than clearing away the bits of wood and stone left over, it was done. *Finally*.

He smiled silently at himself with the thought. It could have been done earlier had he pushed the men as he had originally intended. But the day of rain had delayed it, and then the attempted attack upon Rosamunde in their bedchamber three nights earlier had convinced him to move a little more slowly at the work—at least until he could find a replacement for Black to guard their bedchamber. And Aric had found that replacement just that morning.

With that worry out of the way, he had set to the stables with a vengeance, driving the men hard to complete the building. Tonight Black would rest in the new stables. No offense to the horse. Aric was as fond of the animal as any man was of his steed, but while the horse had been recovering nicely from his fevers and his wound, Rosamunde was still feeding him soft food. She claimed it taxed his body less and helped the healing process. Unfortunately, that meant that while Black made a great guard horse it was rather hard to tell if it was due to him or the stench that surrounded him.

Nay, this was better. He'd put Black back in the stables with the other horses, and place the dog he'd bought with Rosamunde. Also, the dog could trail her around during the day, whereas Black could not. The horse was left in the keep by the great hall fire during the day while she worked in the stables.

When she had refused a human guard, Aric had tried to convince her to take the horse around with her. But she had peered at him as if she thought he had lost his senses, then simply walked off. Rather than push the point, Aric had trailed her around again that first day after the attack. But that had not gone well at all.

Rosamunde had worn a blue-gray gown that accented her fair coloring and emphasized the shade of her eyes. But it had also obviously been a touch old, probably a gift from her father during one of his visits over the years, Aric had decided. While the gown was obviously expensive and well cared for, it was also a touch tight. Everywhere. Her breasts had pressed eagerly against the material, looking more fulsome than usual, thanks to being a bit squished, and while the gown had barely glided over her waist, it had pulled slightly around the hips, seeming to emphasize their curves and the way they swayed when she walked.

Recalling the king telling him to buy her some gowns, Aric had been annoyed with himself for neglecting to do so. He should have seen to that first thing! He should have seen her fitted out with at least a dozen gowns, all of them big and roomy, so that the material would not seem to threaten to burst its seams every time she stretched or reached for something. And nice, sedate colors like brown and black would be better, too, he had decided as he watched her flit around in her old gown. She had seemed a bright and colorful bird in the bailey, the stables, the keep, and everywhere else she had been that day.

Unfortunately, he had not outfitted her, and Aric had grown increasingly surly throughout the day as he stood by watching her. It seemed to him that there were an inordinate amount of men coming to her with their injured animals as opposed to women. Surely men should be too busy for such a task? They should have sent their wives or daughters in their place, he had thought with disgust, glaring and glowering at anyone who peered at her with anything like a smile or a look of appreciation. Never mind that it was likely gratitude for her abilities and charity. Nay. Aric had been positive that every look and glance was one of lust, and he had grown more and more short-tempered and irate throughout the day.

Rosamunde had put up with his behavior without a word, but he knew they had both been relieved when the dinner hour had rolled around and they had returned to the keep. At least, until they had approached the trestle tables and Lord Spencer had spoken.

"Ah, my lady Rosamunde," the blind man had murmured appreciatively. "It never fails to amaze me how you can spend the day working around the foulest of smells and yet still manage to smell so sweet yourself at the end of the day."

Aric hadn't even thought; he had merely snapped, "Keep your nose to yourself, old man."

As soon as the words had left his lips, though, he had wished he could bite his own tongue off. Good Lord, he had just been beyond rude to an old blind man! And out of jealousy, he realized with dismay and regret. But before he could apologize and make amends, Rosamunde had slammed the mug she had lifted back onto the table. She'd turned on him furiously.

"Well, that rips it, my lord. I have had quite enough of your nonsense today. You can just apologize to him right now, and mean it! As for me, I cannot stomach eating in such churlish company. I am to bed. *Alone*." Rising, she had stormed off upstairs, leaving Aric to squirm in the sudden silence filling the great hall as every single person present turned to stare at him in silent condemnation.

He had apologized profusely to the old man, but that had not seemed to ease their censure much, not that he could blame them. He had been rude and churlish to most of the people seated at the table at some point or other during the last few days. To every soldier who had dared to smile and wish Rosamunde a good day. To every farmer who had smiled in gratitude for her help with his animals. Even to some of the servants who had smiled shyly when she had thanked them for some small service or other.

Aric had sat miserably through the meal, drinking more than he ate and wondering just how angry his wife was. He had found out when he finally retired. She had been silent and unmoving in bed, though not sleeping, and the moment he had approached, she had turned her back to him and given him a definite cold shoulder. She had continued to treat him rather coolly all throughout yesterday. She had not thawed much this morning. Which he supposed he deserved.

"Rosamunde will be pleased."

Drawn back from his thoughts, Aric glanced at his father, then back at the new stables. "Do you think so?"

"Aye." Lord Burkhart smiled slightly. "Mayhap she will even start speaking to you again."

Glaring at his father for enjoying his suffering, Aric moved over to collect his shirt from the stack of wood where he had left it. He had been working since early morning. The summer days had finally turned hot, and Aric had shed the garment several hours ago. Now he pulled it back on, glancing toward Shambley as the other man came from inside the stables and moved to join them.

"The men are nearly finished removing the extra wood. When are you going to tell Rosamunde she may start moving the horses in?"

"Now," Aric decided, starting away. His father and Shambley immediately fell into step on either side of him, and they were still there when he entered the old stables a moment later. Glancing around the dim interior of the old building, Aric grimaced to himself. The place was really a mess.

He would have it torn down as soon as the horses had been moved, he decided, frowning when his wife wasn't immediately visible. Neither was Smithy. There was just a lad kneeling at the back of the stables, digging for something in the rushes.

"Oh, my lord." Smithy stepped out of one of the stalls near the back, and hurried forward. "Is there something you wanted?"

"Aye. My wife. Where is she?" Aric snapped. He had told the stablemaster to keep an eye on her. Actually, he had told him to watch her every minute and not let her out of sight, else he would twist the man's head off his shoulders like a stem from an apple. But that had been the morning after his surly behavior and he had still been a little cranky at the time. More cranky, mayhap, since not only had Rosamunde not talked to him, she had avoided his very touch.

Smithy looked confused for a minute, then turned to

gesture toward the lad at the back of the stalls. "Right there, m'lord."

Aric peered blankly at the brais-covered bottom at the back of the stables, only now recognizing it as his wife's curvaceous derriere. Slowly he began to flush with fury. When he opened his mouth to bellow, all that came out was a grunt of surprise, for he was suddenly grabbed by the arms and dragged backward out of the stables by his father and Shambley.

"Not again! Let me go, damn you!" Aric shouted, tugging at his arms and trying to make his way back into the stables once they had stopped a good distance from the building.

"Not until you calm down," Lord Burkhart announced.

"Calm down? Did you see my wife?"

"Of course I saw her. But she was not doing anything wrong. She—"

"Are you *blind?* Did you not see what she was wearing?"

"Ah. The brais." Lord Burkhart sighed. "You dislike her wearing them in the stables, I take it?"

"They are . . ."

"Practical," Shambley suggested when Aric paused in search of the word he wanted. He nodded when Aric's head snapped around at him. "They *are,* Aric. Far more practical for working in the stables than a skirt."

"I don't care if they are more practical; they *are* indecent. Unsuitable for a lady."

"Indecent?" Shambley gave a disbelieving laugh. "When did you become so stuffy?"

"When I saw my wife's behind encased in tight leather breeches and realized everyone else was getting the exact same view!"

"Jealous?" Robert taunted.

Aric's mouth snapped closed. It was one thing for him to recognize he was being overly jealous. It was another thing entirely for his best friend to be aware of it. How humiliating.

"Aye. That's it, all right," his father murmured, taking in his expression. "If I were you, son, I would walk softly. You cannot go storming in there and bawl her out as if she has committed some horrible sin."

Aric's gaze narrowed. "I cannot?"

"Nay, of course not," his father chided.

Seeing his agitation, Robert took over trying to reason with his friend. "Aric, think. You are reacting as if she deliberately dressed like that in an effort to attract male attention. Yet we both know that she dressed like that at the abbey, probably every day, and no one there thought it indecent."

"They were all nuns there," Aric protested.

"Aye," Lord Burkhart said, suddenly agreeable. "And that is what she is used to. It probably has not occurred to her that your men are a bunch of slavering dogs, all looking for the first likely bitch to mount."

"My men are not . . ." Aric began indignantly, only to pause as both men began to grin. He had stepped right into their trap. "Ah, I see," Aric said. Rosamunde was not deliberately dressing to entice. She did not even realize that it was enticing. And his men were all loyal—they were not likely to jump her or even approach her. And yet he was acting as if they were.

Sighing, he closed his eyes and forced himself to take several deep breaths. This was just his jealousy making him react again, of course. He was acting as though she were untrustworthy, another Delia. And it wasn't fair. She had done nothing to make him believe she would be unfaithful, yet he had been about to charge in there as if she had.

"I shall talk to her calmly," he said finally. "I shall tell her that I would *prefer* her to stick to more traditional garb in future to avoid any discomfort or embarrassment for her, me, or the men. After all, she would not wish to be caught so even by another lady. I shall be reasonable."

"Very good!" His father proudly patted him on the back.

"Aye, very good," Shambley agreed, not even bothering to hide his amusement. "You may be able to beat that green beast jealousy yet. With a little help."

"Shut up, Robert," Aric snapped, and stalked off into the stables. His friend burst out laughing behind him.

Aric's new calm lasted until he reentered the stables and got another gander at his wife. She was still on her hands and knees, still trying to retrieve something from under the rushes. And her leather-covered posterior was still poked invitingly into the air.

Every time he saw her in this position it reminded him of their wedding day and her thoughts on the marital bed, and then how he had taught her the truth.

Ah, hell, who was he trying to fool? Every time he looked at her he thought of getting under her skirts—or into her brais, as the case might be—and now was no different. In fact, seeing her in this position in the tight leggings made his desire a bit more urgent. They covered her like a second skin, emphasizing her curves. He could live with that, if it weren't for the fact that he was positive others must have similar thoughts as well. And at the moment, Smithy was standing several feet behind and to the side of Rosamunde, enjoying what Aric was sure was an eyeful.

Before he could recall that he was going to be reasonable, he had started barking like a rabid dog. "Wife! Get off your damned knees now and . . ." Pausing at a sudden throat-clearing behind him, Aric turned a scowl on his father that slowly faded as he took in the old man's arched eyebrows and meaningful expression. Swallowing his temper, he peered back at his wife to see that she was still on her knees, but had straightened and sat back on her haunches. She was now peering over her shoulder at him in amazement.

"Good day, wife," he said in a growl; instead of finishing his original thought. Then he frowned at his tone of voice, for in truth he sounded like an angry dog instead of a husband.

Rosamunde's eyes narrowed warily now. "Is there something amiss, my lord husband?"

"Aye!" The word snapped out like the crack of a whip. There were sudden nervous and loud throat-clearings and nudgings that came from his father and Shambley. Grimacing, he managed a pained smile. "I . . . You . . . Your—"

"I believe," Lord Burkhart interrupted as his son floundered, "that Aric is concerned by your dress, my dear."

"My dress?" Rosamunde glanced down at her clothes uncertainly. "I am not wearing a dress."

"Exactly!" Aric said triumphantly, only to pause and glare at Shambley when the other man stepped forward to elbow him very hard in the ribs. When Robert peered back at him innocently, Aric turned back to his wife, then sighed and tried for a softer tone. "Rosamunde, I want . . . You should . . . Your clothes . . ."

When he stumbled to a halt again, Rosamunde glanced down at the clothes she wore. "Is there a problem with my wearing brais, my lord?" she asked at last.

"Aye," he said thrilled that she grasped the problem without his actually having to say it.

"I am sorry, my lord. I was not sure if brais were

quite the thing now that I am a lady. But I do not have many gowns, and I feared ruining them here in these moldy old stables. Besides, I was sure it would not matter much, since Smithy is the only one likely to see me."

"Oh." Aric blinked, his anger deflating like an empty gown. She had already considered that it might not be appropriate, but had worn them to save her gowns. Not to attract men. Not to tempt them all, as Delia had done with her low-cut tight gowns. And Rosamunde hadn't expected anyone to see her dressed so here in the stables—except for Smithy, who was old, toothless, and balding. Surely she was not trying to lure him?

"I put out the news that I could not see any animals today unless 'twas an emergency. You said the new stables would be ready today, and I wished to oversee moving the horses."

"Of course you did," he said, then managed a smile. "And so you shall. They are ready now."

"What?" Her eyes widened. "Truly? Already?"

"Aye." His smile became slightly more natural at her obvious surprise and pleasure. "Come. You may inspect them."

Turning, he led the way out of the old stables and crossed the short distance to the new ones. He himself was a bit anxious now, worried at whether she would approve of them or not. She had seen them, of course, from the outside. Rosamunde had walked by the stables several times over the past four days, and while he had seen her peer at them curiously as she passed, she had not been inside them yet. He supposed she had been too irritated with him to show that much interest. Now he led her right up to the doors he had just finished hanging, threw them open, then waited for her to walk inside.

She entered slowly, her gaze moving over everything

with measuring eyes, inspecting it all as she walked slowly along the numerous stalls.

Aric waited by the door, watching her nervously. He had made the stables doubly as long as the old ones. There were twice as many stalls, and each of them was roomier than the old ones. He had had hooks and shelves made for storing things, and he had added a loft to store fresh hay. He watched her take it all in, and still she said nothing.

Disappointment was just starting to fill him when she turned slowly.

"Husband?"

"Aye?" he asked uncertainly.

" 'Tis magnificent."

Blinking, he smiled slightly. "They will do, then?"

"Do?" A peel of laughter slipping from her lips, she launched herself at him, kissing him exuberantly on the nose, cheeks, and lips before whirling away, her arms wide. "They are marvelous! Wonderful! Beautiful! The horses will love them. *I* love them. And Black and Marigold shall love them. Thank you, my lord." She whirled back to give him another exuberant hug, then whirled away and hurried for the exit. "I shall fetch them right now. And change into a gown while I am at it." Pausing at the door, she glanced back to flash a grin at him. "I need not bother with brais in here. 'Tis as clean as can be."

Aric watched her go with a sigh, his expression becoming more stern as he noticed his father and Shambley eyeing him with amusement. Scowling at them, he glanced back at his departing wife. "She wore the brais only to save her gowns. She is changing now," he explained, as if *they* were the ones who had been outraged by her attire.

The two men managed to maintain somber expressions,

and merely nodded solemnly. Aric was just beginning to feel uncomfortable when a man appeared at the door to the stables, blocking his view of his wife.

"I brought the dog, m'lord."

"Oh, good, Jensen." Moving forward, he peered down at the animal. Dark brown, huge, hairy, and drooling, the dog seemed to be grinning up at him, and it didn't look very bright. On the other hand, the size of the beast alone would intimidate most people. Hopefully, it would intimidate the fellow Black had attacked in their bedchamber the other day. Jensen had assured him that the beast was trained to guard whatever it was placed with, whether it was sheep, horses, or people. It would make Aric feel better to know Rosamunde was looked after during the day. He would not worry about her quite as much.

"What sort of dog is that?" Shambley asked curiously, moving to Aric's side. He stared at the beast.

"Well, now . . ." the animal's owner hesitated and scratched his head, uncertainty clear on his face. "He's a good dog. Does his job," he answered, then brightened slightly. "I know he's got some Irish wolfhound in him."

"That explains the size," Lord Burkhart murmured, bending to pet the animal's dirty, matted fur briefly before grimacing, straightening, and turning to arch an eyebrow at Aric. "But how do you intend to get Rosamunde to take him about with her?"

Aric frowned at the question. "I will tell her to," he announced firmly, then saw his father's expression and began to worry. "You think she would disobey me?"

"Rosamunde?" Lord Burkhart asked with surprise. "Nay, nay. Not her. After all, women are the most obedient of creatures, are they not?" He didn't bother trying to hide his amusement as he turned to walk away. "Good luck to you, son."

Aric glanced from his father's departing back to the mutt at his feet. Surely, if he ordered it, Rosamunde would take the dog about with her. Wouldn't she? She would have to see the sense in it. Someone had attacked her in their bedchamber. She should have protection. Of course, she had refused to believe that anyone had reason to harm her. She was positive that her midnight visitor had been some sort of mistake. Besides, he had wanted her to take Black around with her on her daily chores and she had flat-out refused to do that. Actually, she hadn't flat-out refused; she had merely looked at him as though he were quite mad and said that was not possible, that it could endanger the horse and bring about the return of his fever. Nay, he was better off where he was, she had announced, and he had not pushed the point. The animals' care was the one area where she did not always obey him.

"It is a shame he is not injured."

"Hmmm?" Aric glanced up from his thoughts. "What was that?"

"I said it is a shame he is not injured," Shambley repeated. "Were the dog injured, she would coddle and baby him. Then she would most like drag that beast all over the keep and bailey with her just to keep an eye on him." He gave a shrug. "She does seem to have a soft spot for ailing or injured animals."

"Aye, she does," Aric murmured thoughtfully, turning to look the animal over again. But he could see just by glancing at the beast that it was as healthy as could be. His gaze swept to the owner. "You do not happen to have a sick or injured dog as big as this one, do you?"

"Sick?" The man stared at him as if he were mad. "Ah . . . nay, my lord."

"I did not think so." Aric sighed with disappointment, then reached for his sword.

"Aric! What are you doing?" Robert grabbed his hand, pulling it away from his weapon.

"I was just going to cut him a little. You know, someplace not too painful so Rosamunde will keep him nearby. She'll wish to watch it for infection."

Robert stared at him in shock for a moment, then shook his head.

"Nay?" Aric asked uncertainly.

"Nay. Why do we not see if mayhap he already has a small cut somewhere."

Dropping to kneel beside the dog, Shambley began searching the animal, sifting through the dirty fur on each leg, then on its back and head. "Aha!"

Aric knelt beside him. "You have found something?"

"He has a scratch here on his ear."

Aric leaned forward to peer at the spot at which Shambley was pointing. When he saw the tiny wound, he scowled. "That is not even enough to make her get out her medicinals."

"It could infect," Robert argued. "And that is what you said you wanted; a cut she would fret over to keep the dog near. This is such a cut."

Aric frowned at it with displeasure, fondling the handle of his sword as he considered the situation. Finally he shook his head. "That is barely a mark at all, Robert. She will not fret over that. I should just—" He started to unsheathe his sword as he spoke, but the dog's owner yanked on the rope Aric had tied around the dog's neck, dragging the animal away from him and Shambley.

"Now see here. I said you could be borrowing the beast, not killing him," he snapped, eyeing Aric grimly.

"Leave go, Aric," Shambley urged. "You know you cannot just cut that dog up. Just claim you worry over his scratch becoming infected and would like her to keep a close eye on him. Tell her that as a child you had a dog that had a very similar wound that festered and killed the animal. That this dog reminds you of him and you would not wish the same thing to happen."

Sighing, Aric let his sword slide back into its sheath unhappily. "All right," he muttered, noting that the dog's owner had relaxed slightly, but was still eyeing him warily.

"Why such long faces, my lords? Surely this is a grand day, what with the stables finally being done and all."

Aric turned at that cheerful voice to find that Rosamunde had returned. She had changed into a green gown that looked quite lovely on her, and Black was trailing behind her as she entered the new stables.

"See, Blackie. I told you they were lovely. You shall be nice and warm and dry here."

She pressed her face to the horse's head, rubbing under his neck as she spoke, and Black, Aric saw with irritation, was acting like a lovestruck teenager, nickering and pressing his face against hers in a most affectionate manner. It was then that Aric realized, with some disgust and regret, that she had ruined his warhorse. This was not the wild animal who bit viciously at opponents' steeds and trampled fallen warriors beneath his powerful hooves. This beast would be good for naught but parades from now on. She had tamed him.

"Come along. You may have your choice of stalls," she told the beautiful animal, patting him on the back. "Which one would you like?"

Aric exchanged wry glances with Shambley at that, thinking the horse would hardly understand what she was saying, and probably cared less where he slept. But they were both proven wrong. The animal walked slowly among the stalls, glancing from side to side as if inspecting them, then stopped before the one farthest from the door. He walked sedately inside the open stall.

"A brilliant choice, Blackie," Rosamunde told the horse with a grin, moving up the aisle now herself to the stall he stood in. "You shall be far from the door. Less drafty in the winter and cooler in summer. And you shall have only the one neighbor, which shall be less troublesome, I should think. And I believe it shall be Marigold."

Aric shook his head in despair as she settled his mount in the stall, then waited impatiently until she stepped out and closed the stall door before calling her over.

"Wife."

"Aye, my lord?" Smiling, she hurried back to them, her gaze dropping curiously to the dog Jensen was urging forward. "Oh, hello, puppy."

Aric rolled his eyes as she bent to pet the dog. "He is hardly a puppy, wife. He weighs as much as you do."

"Mayhap, but he is still just a pup," she assured him, ruffling the matted fur with a frown. "Look at his feet. He has not grown into them yet. He cannot be quite a year old."

"She's right, my lord. He's just a year old this month. He still has a bit of growing to do," Jensen announced, drawing a frown from Aric that made him add quickly, "But he is well trained for all his youth."

"Hmmm," Aric muttered, then announced, "He is wounded."

"*What?*" Much to his satisfaction, Rosamunde showed concern at once, then frowned as she looked the dog over quickly. "Where?"

"Oh. The ear," Aric told her. Then, as she began to check, he continued, "'Tis a small wound, but these things can fester and . . ." Pausing when she appeared not to see the wound in question, Aric bent to point it out. "Right here."

"Why, 'tis barely a scratch and nearly healed," Rosamunde said with a laugh. "You had me worried there for a moment, my lord." Her gaze lifted to Jensen. "He will be fine. No need to worry."

Aric scowled at this announcement and turned to Shambley. His friend gave him a meaningful glance. Recalling the story Shambley had suggested he use, Aric sighed. "I had a dog as a child with a very similar wound that festered," he told her, then for good measure decided to add a few details of his own. "His ear rotted and fell right off."

Rosamunde's eyes widened. "Rotted and—"

"Fell right off." Aric gave a satisfied nod. "He was deaf, the poor, sad mutt." He gave a pitiful sigh, pleased to see he was affecting her. "We had to put him down." When her face colored at this news, he added quickly, "It was swift. We cut his head off."

"You killed a dog because he was deaf?" Rosamunde cried. Suddenly he realized that he had made an error.

"Well . . . nay. Not because he was deaf," he assured her quickly. "It was because the festering spread and he was dying slowly and painfully so we . . . Well, we cut off his rotting head." He shifted uncomfortably under her bemused stare, then frowned. "Anyway, I had a real affection for that dog—and this one reminds me of him, so I would not wish the same thing to happen. I would consider it a kindness to me on your behalf should you keep him close and watch over him so that something of a similar nature does not happen."

"Oh." Finally closing her mouth, Rosamunde peered down at the dog, then nodded slowly. "Well, surely, my lord. I shall tend to him for you."

"And keep him near you," Aric insisted. "So he does not fester and die while you are not looking."

"If you like. Certainly."

"Good. Well, then . . ." He nodded, glanced around, then sighed. "Well, then, I shall order some men to help you and Smithy start moving things over from the old stables."

Rosamunde watched him leave the barn, then shook her head and glanced at Shambley. "Cut off his rotting head?" she said quietly.

"Aye, well, he was most fond of that dog," Shambley assured her uncomfortably. "It was quite upsetting for him."

She looked skeptical. "Well . . ." Her gaze slid to Jensen, who was looking terribly amused. "What is his name?"

"His Lordship's?" the man asked with surprise, and Rosamunde rolled her eyes.

"Nay. The dog's name. What is it?"

"Oh." He shrugged. "I just call him Dog."

"Dog," Rosamunde muttered dryly. "I should have known."

Shambley glanced at her, curious. "You should have known?"

"Well, aye. Certainly. After all, Tomkins calls his bull Bull, and more often than not my husband calls me Wife. What else would Jensen call his dog but Dog?" Shaking her head, she took the rope the man had placed around the animal's neck and started to lead the animal away. "No imagination. That is what it is. Names seem to be beyond these people, are they not, Dog? Come along. I shall give you a bath and clean up your ear— just to be sure it does not fall off or anything silly like that. And once I have you clean and can see what you look like, mayhap we shall pick you a proper name like

Rufus or Champ. Unless you are a female. Are you a female?" she asked the mutt as he traipsed along happily
beside her. When he merely peered up at her, appearing
to grin with his tongue hanging out of his mouth, she
sighed.

"Well, I suppose I shall find out when I bathe you. It
seems I was a bit premature in changing into a gown.
Brais would definitely be more appropriate for bathing
the likes of you."

Chapter 14

"I WILL be only a moment, my lady. I just have to saddle Black for His Lordship; then I will accompany you down to check on Bull."

"Uh-huh," Rosamunde murmured, smiling sweetly until Smithy turned away to concentrate on Black again. As soon as his back was turned, she rolled her eyes and made a face at the horse. Lifting and lowering his head as if nodding in agreement, Black gave a soft whinny that made Rosamunde smile. It really did seem at times that the horse understood her thoughts, or at least her facial expressions. But then, he was a rather magnificent animal.

It had been nearly a week since the completion of the new stables. Black was recovered fully from his cold. His wound—really only a scratch—was almost completely healed as well, and the horse was starting to get restless from being stuck in his stall so long. Rosamunde had mentioned as much to Aric that morning, and he had apparently listened, for he had come down to the stables several moments ago and asked Smithy to saddle the horse for him. He had then glared at her slightly as he had noted Summer tied up outside the stable doors.

Summer was the name Rosamunde had settled on for

the dog that had turned out to be a female. She had also turned out to be quite lovely underneath all that dirt and muck matting her fur. And she had become Rosamunde's devoted companion, following her everywhere throughout these past several days, usually without the necessity of the rope that Jensen had looped around her neck. But Rosamunde still utilized the rope when she was at the stables, to keep the pup outside. Summer had come inside with her the first day, but she had shown something of a herding instinct, and had nipped at the heels of the horses as Smithy led them out. Which was dangerous with animals that were eight or nine times the dog's size and easily made nervous. Rosamunde had decided it was best to keep Summer tied up outside until the pup could be taught that horses were not sheep and should be respected.

Apparently Aric had not appreciated how far away from the door she had tied the pup, though, for he had moved the dog closer, affixing the rope near the open door of the stables, and leaving it loose so that Summer could enter if the necessity arose. He had explained rather gruffly while doing so that it was so that Rosamunde could keep an eye on its ear.

She didn't know who he thought he was fooling. Rosamunde knew Aric felt she needed a guard, though she had tried telling him that it was not necessary. She was positive the attack in their bedchamber had been some sort of mistake. The man Black had attacked must have thought the room empty and been looking to pilfer a jewel or two. After all, who would wish to harm her?

But Aric had not been convinced and had insisted she not be alone. First he had followed her about himself. Then he had set Smithy on her. The stablemaster had accompanied her everywhere in the few days before the stable had been finished. She had hoped that Aric would ease up on his protective behavior once she'd taken on Summer, but it seemed he was taking no chances, and Smithy was still under orders to keep track of her. The stablemaster acted as if he were attached to her at the hip, and frankly Rosamunde was sick to death of tripping over the man. Not that he wasn't nice and didn't try to be helpful, but really, Rosamunde simply wasn't used to having a shadow. Especially one who followed her to the privy and waited outside like an impatient nurse.

Which was why Rosamunde decided not to wait for Smithy this morning. Collecting the apples she had brought with her, she popped three of them into her pocket, kept the fourth one in hand, collected the sack containing her medicinals, and slipped silently out of the stables. Smithy would know where she had gone. He could catch up to her as he was able, she decided rebelliously.

Pausing outside, she bent to give Summer a pat and murmur a few words to her. She couldn't take the dog along this time. Summer's presence had made the bull nervous the last time she had gone down to check on his foot, and Bull had been even more cantankerous than usual. With that in mind, Rosamunde told the dog to stay, and headed out.

Tomkins was nowhere in sight when Rosamunde reached the paddock. She hesitated, considering going in search of the man, then decided against it. She didn't need his presence to tend the animal, and really this was just a checkup. The wound on the bull's leg had been nearly healed when last she saw him. This visit was just to be sure nothing had happened to reopen or infect it. She would look at Bull first. Then, she hoped, she would search out Tomkins to tell him all was well and she need not check on him again.

Walking to the fence, she smiled at Bull as he turned and eyed her with interest. His snout immediately lifted to sniff the air. No doubt he was aware of the scent of the apples she carried with her, she thought with amusement. The big brute really seemed quite taken with the succulent fruit. *Thank goodness.* Without them to bribe him, she did not know how she would have gotten the animal to allow her near him. Climbing onto the lowest slat of the wooden fence, she leaned slightly over the top, lifted the one apple she still held in her hand, and followed her usual routine. She waved the fruit from side to side, then held it out.

Bull took a step toward her across the paddock, then paused, lowering his head slightly. He gave her what she considered his mean look, and he blew air through his nose. Her eyes widening slightly, Rosamunde waved the apple again.

"What is the matter, Bull? Not interested in fruit anymore?" she asked gently, frowning when he actually pawed the ground and snorted. His head lowered still more until his horns were pointed in her general direction. Sighing in exasperation, Rosamunde climbed up to straddle the fence and swung her legs over, then paused to hold out the apple again. Far from appearing tempted, the beast seemed to grow more nervous and agitated. It wasn't unlike his behavior the other day, when Summer had accompanied her. Rosamunde had finally been forced to have Smithy take the dog around behind the small barn and out of sight before Bull would relax enough to approach her.

The snap of a twig behind her startled Rosamunde, and she nearly fell into the paddock. Catching herself, she started to turn to find the source of the sound.

"Where is Rosamunde?"

Smithy glanced up from the saddle he was cinching

to peer at Aric blankly. Frowning as his question sank in, the man peered about the stables as if expecting to spot her. "Well . . . I am not sure," he admitted reluctantly, his frown deepening.

"What do you mean, you are not sure? You were supposed to keep an eye on her, damn it!"

"Aye, my lord, but . . . she was here just a moment ago." Leaving Black in his stall, Smithy stepped out, peering up and down the new stables.

"My lady?" he called hopefully, as if she might suddenly appear. When silence was his only answer, he bit his lip and admitted, "She was wanting to go down to check on that bull. I told her I would accompany her once I finished saddling Black for you." He scratched his head unhappily, then suddenly brightened. "Mayhap she went up to the keep to fetch some apples for the beast."

Aric sighed, relaxing a bit. He had felt the vague beginnings of dread seep into him. Concern and something akin to fear had seemed to be squeezing at his insides. Now the feelings eased, however, and he turned to move toward the stable doors. "You finish saddling Black. I shall go check and see if she is at the keep."

"See if who is at the keep, my lord?" Bishop Shrewsbury asked, having just caught Aric's words as he entered the building.

"My wife," Aric answered shortly, continuing past him.

"Oh, she is not there. I thought she was here."

Aric paused at that announcement and whirled sharply to face the man. "You are sure?"

"That she is not at the keep?" Bishop Shrewsbury asked with surprise. "Aye. I just came from there."

"Mayhap you just missed her," Smithy suggested hopefully. "She may have gone to the kitchens in search of apples for—"

"I believe I saw her taking apples with her when she left the keep this morning," Shrewsbury interrupted. "And I am quite positive that she did not enter or leave by the main doors since the nooning hour."

They were all silent for a moment as that sank in; then Smithy glanced toward the hook where Rosamunde usually hung her bag of medicinals. His shoulders slumped unhappily. "Her bag is gone," he admitted reluctantly. "She must have gone down to the paddock alone. I told her I would only be a moment, but mayhap she . . ." His voice trailed off as Aric suddenly whirled and hurried from the stables with the bishop on his heels.

"Well, hell," he muttered to himself, then closed Black's stall door and hurried anxiously after them. His neck was surely in a noose right now. He hadn't kept an eye on her as he was supposed to. If anything happened to Lady Rosamunde . . . Well, he didn't even want to think about that, he decided. He'd never seen anything before of which his lord was so protective.

Something was dragging across her back. No, she realized with some confusion as she opened her eyes and saw the clouds move overhead. Something was dragging *her* across the ground on her back.

"Rosamunde!"

"Aric?" she mumbled, recognizing his shout though it sounded a good distance away. Turning her head as she was tugged a couple more inches through the dirt, she peered at the blurry fence several feet away, watching as it grew a little more distant. Her vision wasn't the best at that moment, but she thought that it must be her husband racing down the path from the keep toward the paddock.

A snorting sound and a nudge at her hip made her

turn her head slowly to the other side to see Bull nosing at her skirt. The beast pawed the edge of the garment a time or two, nudged at it with his nose until he found the shape of one of the apples she had brought for him, then closed his mouth carefully over it and her skirt. He pulled again. Backing up a step or two, he dragged her along the ground another several inches before stopping and shaking his head in what was obviously bovine disgust. He had failed to free the apple from her pocket so that he could eat it.

"Rosamunde!" Aric's voice sounded much nearer now. She drew her head back around to see that he had reached the fence and was even now climbing frantically over it. Unfortunately, it also drew Bull's attention—and while the animal apparently didn't mind Rosamunde's presence, her husband hadn't been bribing the beast with apples for the last week. Blowing air through his nose in a warning snort, the bull pawed the ground a time or two and prepared to charge. And he probably would run right over her in his excitement, Rosamunde realized with dismay. She raised a hand in warning.

"Nay! Stop! Stay there, husband," she shouted. Well, she had meant to shout, but it had come out as a gasp. She wasn't feeling too strong at the moment.

Much to her relief, Aric seemed to recognize the danger he was putting her in and stilled, his hands clenching the fence post. "Are you all right? Can you get up?"

"Aye," she assured him, but she stayed where she was for another moment, aware of her husband's mounting frustration, but unable to do anything about it. She felt quite sick and winded and really didn't feel like getting up at all. Finally she forced herself to sit up, grimacing as the world seemed to tilt slightly around her. Once it slowed to a stop, she glanced toward the fence again.

Aric's shouts had apparently been heard by others. Well, good Lord, he had been shouting as he ran—all the way down the small hill toward the paddock. They had probably even heard him in the keep, she thought as Smithy and Bishop Shrewsbury suddenly appeared, anxiety on both their faces.

"What happened?" the bishop asked in alarm.

"Is she all right?" Smithy gasped.

A snort from Bull drew Rosamunde's gaze back to the animal. He was glaring at the fence, looking ready to charge should anyone dare try to come over. Patting his nose, she murmured soothingly to him, then began to climb painfully to her feet. Her head was aching something fierce, throbbing behind her ear with a pain that radiated to her eyes and down her jaw. But that was not as bad as the way the world began to spin, everything moving this way and that as she regained her feet. She would have liked to sit back down for a moment, but knew that if she did not see herself out of there within the next few seconds, Aric would come in after her, Bull or no Bull. She really didn't feel up to patching him up just now, should the bull gore him, if he survived it.

"Rosamunde." His voice was tight as he ignored the questions of others who were arriving on the scene.

"Coming, my lord," she called out, grimacing at the stringy quality to her voice, then reached out for something to grab on to for balance. The world continued to dance around her. She ended up grabbing one of Bull's horns.

"Sorry," she muttered to the animal, but he seemed unfazed at her touch. Or perhaps he simply didn't care, since the fact that she was standing gave him better access to her pocket and the apple she had secreted there. He was now nosing and licking at her skirts, trying to get his too-large snout into her pocket to retrieve the juicy fruit. It wasn't working. Sighing, she nudged Bull's nose away, reached into her pocket, and retrieved the apple for him, then held it out on the flat of her palm for him to take. It was gone in one loud crunch.

"Rosamunde!"

Glancing toward the fence, Rosamunde swayed slightly and realized that they didn't know what she was doing. Her body was blocking their view. She considered explaining, then decided it would take too much energy and instead gave the wretched beast a pat.

"Rosamunde! Get out of there!"

"Please stop shouting, my lord. You are alarming Bull here," she said wearily. Never mind the fact that every one of his shouts seemed to pound through her brain, adding to her pain.

"*I* am alarming *him?*" Aric snapped. "*You* are taking years off my life just by being near that wild animal! Now get over here before I—" He had thrown one leg over the fence, but stopped when Bull turned sharply, eyeing him with baleful dislike. It was her experience that cows and bulls had excellent hearing. No doubt Aric's shouting was as grating to his ears as her own.

"It is not *me* he wishes to gore, my lord," Rosamunde pointed out.

"She does appear to be right, my lord," Bull's owner, Tomkins, muttered anxiously. "He appears comfortable with her. She seems safe enough—and she's coming out *now*, aren't ye, m'lady?" he called. No doubt he was hoping she would get the hell out of there before the bull did gore her. That would see the man in a potful of trouble!

"Aye, I am coming," she assured them, digging the last apple out of her pocket and holding it out. She had originally brought four. Bull must have managed to get one out while she was unconscious. Patting the brute's neck, she bent to touch his lower leg as he munched contentedly, and Bull cooperated by bending his leg for her to peer at his wound. A quick glance was all she needed to tell her that he appeared fully recovered.

"Wife!"

Apparently Aric was too impatient to bother with her name anymore, she thought with some amusement, straightening and giving Bull another pat before turning to make her way to the fence. It was a good six feet away. Though it was not far, it seemed quite a distance at that moment. Grasping the fence when she reached it, she paused, trying to find the energy to climb. Much to her relief, she didn't have to. As soon as she stopped, Aric leaped up the fence, leaned over, grasped her by the waist, and lifted her out of the paddock.

But he'd not set her down for more than a second before he swept her back up into his arms, this time with one arm under her legs, and one at her back. Holding her close to his chest, Aric then pushed his way through the crowd that had gathered and started back to the keep.

He did not say a word all the way home, and Rosamunde was content to leave it so. She didn't feel much like talking herself. In fact, she felt that if she opened her mouth, she might be ill all over him. Really, she was quite nauseated. Her head was still spinning and throbbing, and the world didn't seem to wish to stay steady around her. It was wavering and blurring and zooming near, then far away. Sighing, she squeezed her eyes closed against the increased throbbing in her brain as he jogged up the stairs with her.

"Aric? My God! What happened?"

Blinking her eyes open, Rosamunde turned her head to see Robert Shambley's image wavering in the open door of the keep. When Aric reached the top of the stairs without answering, Robert stepped out of the way, holding the door open.

Muttering his thanks, Aric crossed the hall toward the stairs, ignoring the alarmed questions from his father as the man stood up from his seat at the trestle table, where he had apparently been enjoying a discussion with Lord Spencer.

Rosamunde tightened her arms around his neck and clenched her teeth as he bounced her up this second set of steps, relieved when they reached the hall and the ride became smoother. He walked straight to their room and carried her inside and to the bed where he set her down. Then, before she could quite catch her breath, he began undressing her with quick, efficient motions. There was nothing sexual to his actions, however, and she felt rather like a child under his ministrations. It was something she had never felt like around her husband, especially in their bedchamber—while naked.

Once he had dropped the last item of her clothing to the floor, he stepped back, running his eyes quickly over her body. Seemingly satisfied, he turned her around and presumably made the same inspection from behind.

Clearing her throat, Rosamunde asked uncertainly, "Husband? What are you doing?"

The question had barely left her lips when she felt his hands slide under her hair at the base of her neck and begin to move gently up over her scalp. In the next moment, she was gasping and wincing as he found the knot on the back of her head.

Cursing under his breath, Aric caught her by the shoulders and turned her to face him. "What happened?"

Knowing she was about to get a lecture—and one she might even deserve, considering the outcome of her rebellious activities of the day—Rosamunde grimaced and sighed. "I went down to check on Bull—"

"Alone!" Aric said, glaring at her. "Sneaking off while Smithy's back was turned, like a child evading her nurse."

"Ah. Well, aye, I guess—" she began tentatively, only to have him interrupt.

"What happened?"

Clearing her throat again, she continued, "I got to the paddock and Tomkins was nowhere in sight. I considered searching him out, then decided that I would look for him after I checked Bull's foot." Seeing his mounting impatience, Rosamunde began to speak a little faster. "So I climbed up on the fence and tried to lure Bull with an apple, but he was acting odd."

Aric stiffened, seeming surprised at this bit of information. "Do you mean to say that Bull attacked you?"

"Oh, nay," she assured him quickly. "Bull did not attack me. He just would not come any closer. He just . . . well, at first he seemed interested, but then he started acting all cranky, snorting and pawing the ground. Then I thought I heard a sound behind me, started to turn and . . ." She shrugged helplessly before admitting unhappily, "The next thing I knew I was waking up in the paddock and you were shouting my name."

Crossing her arms over her naked chest, she peered down at her feet and shifted uncomfortably in the silence that followed. "How did you come to be there?"

Venturing a glance upward, she saw him glare at her. "I went to the stables to collect Black. Smithy was still saddling him, and you were nowhere to be seen. When I asked where you had gotten to, he said that he was supposed to go with you to check on the bull when he finished saddling Black. He'd thought mayhap you had gone to the keep to fetch some apples for the beast. But

Shrewsbury entered the stables then and said he had just come from the keep, and that you had not been there. When we saw that the bag you carry around when you tend to ill or injured animals was missing, we knew where you had gone."

"Oh." Shifting uncomfortably, she glanced around, then murmured, "Do you think I might get dressed again, my lord?"

Aric blinked as if just realizing that he had left her naked through this discussion, then sighed and leaned past her to pull the linens back on the bed. "Nay. You cannot get dressed again. You can get into bed and rest."

"Oh, but—"

"In bed," Aric snapped. "Do not try my patience, wife. I am already angry at you right now for going off on your own when you *know* I wish you to be accompanied at all times—"

"I am sorry, my lord," Rosamunde interrupted quickly, sitting on the edge of the bed to appease him. "But truly I did not think there was anything to fear. I felt sure that night was just a robbery gone awry. And nothing has happened this last week—"

"Nothing happened this last week because someone has been watching you every moment," Aric interrupted. Rosamunde looked stricken.

"Surely you do not think . . . I mean . . ." She shook her head in bewilderment. "But why would anyone wish to harm me? I have done nothing to anyone."

Seeing her dismay, Aric sighed and sank onto the bed beside her. Wrapping an arm around her shoulders, he drew her against his chest. "The night your father came to collect me and take me to marry you, he said he would worry for your safety should anything happen to him." He sighed unhappily. "I half suspect he knew death was stalking him. And he wanted you safe. He felt I could protect you."

"But from what?" Rosamunde asked in bewilderment, pulling back to peer at him.

"I do not know," he admitted, pulling her back against his chest. "He spoke of your mother."

"My mother?"

"Aye. He said he felt sure she was murdered."

Rosamunde tugged away from him again to stare at him in horror. "What? Nay! She died at the abbey. She—"

"He suspected poisoning."

Rosamunde had been pale since he had come upon her lying unconscious in the paddock, but she went white at this news. "Poisoned?"

Aric nodded.

"My mother?" she asked painfully. He felt his heart pinch at her horror.

"Aye."

She was silent for a moment, absorbing this; then she peered at him again. "And he thinks whoever did it may try to kill me, too?"

Aric scowled at the question. "I am not sure. He was not very specific, unfortunately. I just know he worried about your well-being should he die. And now, with these two attacks, I fear this is what he was afraid of."

"But my mother . . . Who did he think poisoned her?"

Aric grimaced. "Eleanor."

Rosamunde's eyes widened briefly; then she nodded slowly. "Aye, I suppose she would be the most likely suspect. She may have feared my father might annul their marriage to be with my mother."

Aric nodded thoughtfully.

"But I do not see why she would wish to harm *me*. I am no threat to her position."

"Nay," Aric agreed. "I do not understand it, either." They were both silent for a moment; then Aric shifted on the bed until he faced her and took her hands in his. "Rosamunde, you cannot run off on your own like that again. When I saw you lying in that paddock . . ." His hands tightened on hers briefly; then he glanced away. When he turned back, his grumpy expression had returned. "You vowed to obey me, and I am ordering you not to go anywhere alone. Now." Getting to his feet, he gestured to the bed. "Rest. I must go and see if anyone saw anything. Not that anyone probably did," he muttered irritably as he moved to the door.

Chapter 15

HUMMING under her breath, Rosamunde straightened from examining the pregnant mare in the stall across from Black's and patted the horse soothingly. "Everything seems all right, Charlotte. I'd say another day or so and you should drop your foal. You must be looking forward to that, hmmm?" she cooed walking to the front of the mare to caress her snout.

When her husband's horse shifted restlessly and let out a whinny from the next stall, Rosamunde glanced toward him reprovingly. "What is the matter, Blackie? Surely you are not jealous? You know I love you, too."

Black shifted again, this time shaking his head around angrily, and Rosamunde frowned slightly. She stepped out of Charlotte's stall. "What is the matter with you? You are not ailing again, are you?" she asked, moving toward his stall. She had taken only a step or two when the creak of lumber from the loft overhead drew her gaze upward. It took a moment for her mind to grasp what she saw: a bale of hay suspended in the air above her head! Nay. Not suspended. Falling. A bale of hay falling toward her!

Crying out, Rosamunde lunged out of the way. She slammed hard into Black's stall as the bale slammed to the floor beside her, sending straw and dust flying in all directions as its straps broke. The hay spilled out across the floor, making a small hill. Shaking slightly, Rosamunde gaped at the bale blankly for a moment, then peered upward again, staring at the loft above. Surely it could not have just fallen down by itself? Surely the men stacked the hay up there better than that?

Then again, if it had not just fallen off . . . Her mind refused to process any more than that. Swallowing, Rosamunde patted absently at Black's nose and drew comfort as he leaned his head over her shoulder. The horse was completely calm now, and she had to wonder if the source of his agitation had not come from his sensing of some danger. Mayhap he had noticed the bale hanging over the edge or—

"Well, now you are really getting a bit silly," she told herself dryly. Black was a pretty smart animal, but her proposition was a bit of a stretch. Sighing, she patted Black one more time, then moved away from the stall, glancing up warily as she did. The bale had to have simply fallen, of course. It was a straightforward enough explanation. Accidents happened, and this had been one. And any thought that this might be anything else was just Rosamunde letting her imagination run away with her.

"Then you should really go up there and be sure the rest of the bales are more safely stacked," she told herself, reassured by the sound of her own voice. Straightening her shoulders slightly, she moved to the ladder and glanced up, pausing as Blackie became agitated again and kicked the door of his stall. "Stop that," she ordered him shortly. "You are as bad as your master. There is nothing up there."

Still, she hesitated. Not because she feared that the bale had not simply fallen and that someone up there had pushed it off, she assured herself, but because . . . well, she was wearing a gown. She had been wearing more proper attire ever since Aric had complained, and while they were not as convenient as brais, her gowns had not gotten in her way too much.

Still, they did restrict certain things, like climbing up into the loft. Should anyone enter and come to the ladder, no doubt they would have a lovely view up her skirt. Rosamunde grimaced at that. Were Smithy not busy outside, she would have left the checking of the loft up to him. But he was presently hitching Lord Spencer's wagon to a horse out front. That left Rosamunde alone to climb up into the loft and look around. And there was really no sense in stalling any longer, she told herself firmly.

She needed to prove to herself that her husband's fears were all for naught; otherwise she would spend her life looking over her shoulder. And she wasn't going to do that. She started to climb.

"My lord."

Pausing beside the wagon Smithy was working on, Aric nodded at the other man. "Is my wife—"

"Inside, my lord," the stablemaster told him, nodding toward the door at his back. "Giving Charlotte the once-over."

Aric's eyebrows arched. "Charlotte?"

"A mare, my lord. She used to be named White, but—"

"But my wife insists on giving every animal a 'proper' name," Aric interrupted.

The man grinned ruefully and nodded. "That's so, my lord."

Shaking his head, Aric turned away and entered the stables, his eyes moving from side to side searching for his wife. He started up the aisle. When he reached Black's stall—the last there was—and still had found no sign of his wife, Aric scowled and turned back. "Smithy?" he called.

"Oh, hello, husband."

Whirling back, Aric glanced around, then up, his angry expression easing somewhat as he spotted his wife perched halfway up the ladder to the hay loft. Moving to its base, he glanced up, his eyes widening when he found himself staring straight up her skirts. "What the devil are you doing? Get down from there this instant!"

"My lord?" Smithy's voice echoed down the stalls. The man had come running at the shout of his name.

"I—Nothing. Get out of here," Aric ordered. "And close the damn door. Let no one in until I say so. I want a word with my wife."

"Aye, my lord." The doors closed quietly, leaving the stables dim and cool.

"Is there something amiss, my lord?" Rosamunde peered down at him anxiously.

His gaze slid from her face to the view he had up her skirt, then back. Aric frowned slightly. "I can see right up your skirt." He had meant to order her to get down off that ladder again, but his comment had the same effect. Flushing bright red, she immediately began backing down the ladder. Her downward steps faltered, however, when she felt his hands slide under her skirts up the back of her calves.

Her fingers clenching around the ladder rails, Rosamunde glanced down sharply—blinking and flushing even redder as she saw that as she had descended, her skirt had lowered over her husband's head. Or had he stuck his head underneath? Whichever the case, he now stood beneath her; his face was somewhere around the backs of her ankles, she would guess from the feel of his breath there, and—Oh, yes, her guess was correct, she realized as he suddenly licked the inside of one of her ankles. She gasped, fingers tightening even further around the ladder rails, Rosamunde leaned her forehead against the rung before her face. She closed her eyes briefly as he began to lave the inside of her other ankle. Her body's reaction was startling, to say the least. He was licking her ankles, for gosh sakes! And yet she was getting tingles shooting up her legs, making them so weak she wasn't sure they would continue to hold her up.

"H-husband?" she murmured.

"I said, get down here," Aric reminded her huskily, his voice muffled by her skirts.

Taking a deep breath, Rosamunde forced herself to open her eyes and step down another hesitant step, her stomach jumping and her flesh singing as his hands and lips slid slowly up her legs. When she stopped again, his mouth was nibbling at the back of one knee, his fingers trailing over the backs of her thighs, nearly at her buttocks. They slid back down along the inside of her thighs, and ran lightly over the tender flesh there, and Rosamunde grasped the ladder tightly and closed her eyes again. Her legs were shaking violently now. Surely he must see that. "Husband?"

She felt cool air hit the back of her legs as he lifted her skirt to free his head, then the garment fell back into place and he raised her up and set her down upon her feet. She was facing away from him. "You are not to climb that ladder again."

Rosamunde nodded in understanding, but he did not release her and step away, as she had expected. Instead his hands moved to clasp the ladder before her, encompassing her in the cocoon of his body as he leaned forward. Nuzzling the side of her head, he found her ear with his lips. "Do you understand?"

"A-aye," Rosamunde murmured breathlessly as he began to nibble at the lobe of her ear, his body pressing against her from behind. "I am not to climb the ladder again."

"You smell so sweet," he whispered, and Rosamunde tipped her head to the side, her hands closing over his on the ladder as he kissed and nibbled her neck. "You taste sweet, too," he whispered, licking her neck teasingly, his hands slipping out from beneath hers. They moved to catch her upper arms, pulling her back against him, then slid around the front of her to capture her breasts, to hold and palm and caress them through her clothing. "Turn your head more. Give me your lips."

Doing as he said, Rosamunde turned and tilted her head, her mouth opening eagerly under his. He found and devoured her lips and tongue hungrily, catching her groan as he pinched her hardened nipples through the cloth of her gown. She was desolate when his hands left her breasts.

She gasped into his mouth, her kiss becoming more frantic as his hand brushed down over her stomach until it found and grazed the apex of her thighs. He urged her backward with that touch until her bottom nudged his front, and Rosamunde was so distracted, she did not notice how he worked at her lacing with his other hand, until she felt his rough fingers suddenly catch and caress one naked breast.

Stiffening, she pulled her lips free and glanced down at herself, shocked to see her bodice gaping open and her breasts spilling out, one naked in the dim light of the stables and the other covered only by his hand. His other hand had slid from between her legs and was drawing her skirt up, baring her calves.

"Husband?" She grabbed at the hand tugging her gown upward in a feeble attempt to stop its actions.

"Husband, stop!" she cried with dismay. "We are in the stables. Someone could enter at any—" She choked on the last word, stiffening against him as he finally got her skirt high enough to snake his hand beneath it. Nudging a knee between hers from behind, he urged her legs apart to allow his fingers to slide up her inner thigh to the center of her.

"No one is going to enter. Smithy will not allow anyone in here until I say so," he assured her quietly.

"Aye, but 'tis full daylight," she pointed out weakly, arching into his touch despite her protests.

"So?" He laughed breathlessly into her ear, pressing himself against her bottom even as she arched back into him.

Rosamunde hesitated, then blurted, "Bishop Shrewsbury said 'twas a sin in the Church's eyes to conduct marital relations in full day—"

A muttered curse from Aric, and the way he stopped all caresses and seemed to freeze behind her, made her pause and bite her lip unhappily. Then she heard him release a pent-up breath against her neck.

"Wife."

"Aye?" she asked uncertainly.

"We have already been through all of this," he reminded her gently, the hand at her breast beginning to caress her again.

"We have?" she asked uncertainly, closing her eyes as he pressed a kiss to the crook of her neck.

"Aye. During the wedding ceremony you vowed to obey me. A vow you made before God, your father, and witnesses. Did you not?"

Eyes closing as her nipple tightened beneath his touch, Rosamunde nodded silently.

"Well." Releasing her abruptly, he caught her up in his arms. Carrying her to the small mound of hay in front of Black's stall, he laid her upon it, then straightened to peer down at her as he quickly removed his sword belt and set it on the ground. "I say that we are going to make love in full daylight in the stables, and I order . . ." Dropping to his knees in the straw, he urged her legs apart and eased between them, then lowered himself to cover her lower body with his. His stomach resting on her pelvis, he peered down at her breasts where they lay at face level, and collected them in his hands before bending his mouth to kiss one rosy peak.

"And I order you to enjoy it," he finished against her flesh before sucking it into his mouth to swirl with his tongue. He watched her face as he did this, taking in the way her mouth opened and her eyes closed, then he withdrew his mouth and waited for her eyes to slowly open. "What say you to that, wife?"

Swallowing the smile that wanted to curve her lips at his pleased grin, Rosamunde nodded with credible solemnity and murmured, "As you wish, my lord."

Chuckling, Aric climbed farther up her body until he reached her lips, then kissed her with a passion that curled her toes inside her sandals. Slipping her arms around his neck, she kissed him back just as passionately. At last, he pulled his lips away with a gasp and rested his forehead on hers. Eyes closed, he tried to catch his breath, then shook his head and opened his eyes.

"I need you."

Rosamunde's eyes widened slightly at the words. He said it apologetically and so seriously. Slipping a hand between them, she found the top of his brais and slid her hand inside. His desire was big and hard against her fingers.

"Aye, you do," she murmured solemnly and he gave a short laugh, his eyes squeezing shut as her fingers closed around him and squeezed. He caught her hand, then tugged it out of the way and quickly pulled his brais down in the front. Tugging her skirt out of the way then, he slid a hand up her thighs, relieved to find her warm and wet for him.

"I am sorry. I cannot wait," he said with a gasp, guiding himself into her.

Rosamunde made no protest, shifting and arching slightly to accept him, then wrapping her legs around his hips and pulling him closer, driving him deeper inside. Finally he was all the way in. Then she reached up to caress his cheek, drawing his gaze and his attention to her.

"Tell me what to do to pleasure you," she whispered.

Except for their first time together, he had always kissed and caressed her to the point of such feverish desire that by the time he entered her, she simply arched and thrust blindly beneath him. She had reacted and responded to his body and touch. This time there was more. Now she wanted to pleasure him, to feed his hunger.

Aric stilled at her expression, his heart fluttering. She wished to please him. She was interested in sharing this experience, both taking and giving. Delia would never have done so. Oh, aye, Delia had enjoyed sex—he'd known that long ere he had caught her in bed with another. But she had been a demanding and shrewish lover—and despite his attention to her pleasure, she had never once seemed to consider his.

"Husband?"

Aric drew his mind away from his thoughts to peer at his wife. She awaited his instructions, her face soft and questioning. Delia had always stripped away her clothes slowly, teasing him with the slow revelation of her body, then posed herself in bed seductively—but that had been the end of her effort.

And after, she would lie still, her eyes closed, her

expression as flat and unchanging as a portrait, her body as limp and cold as an empty gown. She would never have shared with him the true passion Rosamunde often did. She never would have asked how she should proceed to pleasure him. Rosamunde, with her untaught passions and genuine enthusiasm, was much more than he ever could have dreamed of.

Dear God, he had made a narrow escape, he realized suddenly. He had nearly been tied to Delia for a lifetime. Night after night of her cynical little smiles and selfish little moues, her warm, willing body in his bed but her uncaring eyes staring through him. Suddenly the day he had walked in on her and Glanville in the stables—what before had seemed the worst day of his life at the time— seemed like the luckiest.

"Aric?" Rosamunde asked uncertainly, her eyes widening in surprise as he let loose a full, robust laugh of pure pleasure.

"Rosamunde."

"Aye," she prompted, meeting his shining eyes uncertainly.

"Just being yourself pleasures me immeasurably," he told her softly, then bent to press a gentle kiss to her surprised lips, her nose, her eyes. His passion still alive, but no longer desperate, he began to kiss and caress her, his teeth grazing her breasts, his tongue tasting them, his lips suckling them.

Rosamunde clasped his head in her hands, watching him cherish her body with a confusion that slowly turned to sultry desire. Her body began to move beneath his, pulling him into her. She felt herself squeezing around his manhood, and her breathing grew shallow as her heartbeat sped up.

He suddenly rolled onto his back, she automatically went with him, pressing her hands into his shoulders to lever herself upward until she was astride him. Then she shifted her gaping gown out of the way and covered his hands with her own. He reached up to run his hands across her chest, and she suddenly felt deliciously wanton with her hair wild around her face, her eyes sleepy with desire, her lips swollen from his kisses.

"Show me how to please you," she whispered, shifting against him impatiently.

Smiling, he lifted his hands to her hips to direct her movements, his eyes darkening when her hands replaced his and she cupped her own breasts. Her eyes closing and her tongue darting out to wet her lips, she followed his guidance and moved against him, taking him in, then sliding apart from him. Keeping one hand on her hips to encourage her, he slid the other between them, found her womanhood and caressed it.

She groaned then, her head tipping back, her hands covering her breasts completely and squeezing them as she urgently moved against him. Excited by her enjoyment, Aric released her hip and cupped the back of her head, drawing her face down until he could kiss her. His tongue pressed through her lips and thrust into her mouth even as he bent his pelvis, thrusting into her. Then he tumbled her onto her back again.

Catching her knees and pulling them up slightly, he used them to brace himself, and began to thrust into her in earnest. He watched her face as she began to twist her head back and forth in the straw in that way he liked, a high, crooning wail slipping from her lips as she arched and shuddered and bucked beneath him, meeting him thrust for thrust.

"Open your eyes. Look at me," Aric gasped and her eyes blinked open with confusion, focusing on him fuzzily. He could see her question, but simply held her gaze as he drove into her; he could not explain that he wanted to see that she was here with him, and that she knew who it was who pleasured her.

"You were right, my lord."

Aric blinked his eyes open slowly and peered down at Rosamunde. He was on his back in the straw trying to recover from their lovemaking. She lay cuddled next to him, her head resting on his shoulder as she ran her fingers lightly over his tunic, caressing him through the cloth. She didn't appear to need to recuperate, he noted.

"Of course I was right," he agreed, then after a hesitation asked, "What about?"

Chuckling, Rosamunde tipped her head to grin at him. "Why, everything, of course," she teased. "But I was referring to wearing a gown in the stables."

"Hmmm." Aric frowned slightly as she returned to absently caressing him. "You do not find it inconvenient?"

"Well." She drew the word out, her fingers gliding teasingly down his shirt toward his brais. "Mayhap for some things like climbing the ladder and such. But for things like pleasuring my husband, a gown is definitely more convenient." She gave him a wicked grin. "Do you not think?"

Aric started to smile in response, then frowned instead as the truth behind her words sank in. Her gown had made this brief tryst incredibly easy. And fast. Whereas her brais . . . He was distracted from his thoughts by Rosamunde standing and brushing out her gown. His gaze slid unhappily from her to the ladder, and he frowned.

"What were you doing climbing up that ladder?" He had asked earlier, of course, but he had also distracted her from answering him. Now he was curious to know what had been so all-fired important that she had gone traipsing up the ladder in a gown, rather than waiting for Smithy to finish with the wagon and come inside to do it for her.

"Oh." She frowned up at the loft overhead. "Well, that bale." She gestured to the mound of hay he was now lying in. "It fell out of the loft and I was climbing up to be sure that the others were secure."

Sitting up, Aric peered blankly down at the straw around him. "This is all from a bale that fell out of the loft?"

"Aye."

She was suddenly very intent upon her lacings, and Aric found his eyes narrowing on her suspiciously. "Where were you when it fell?"

Rosamunde grimaced. "Under it at first, but I managed to get out of the way in time."

"Damn!" Surging to his feet, he pulled his brais up. "Why did you not tell me this right away?"

"Well, I did try," she muttered, a bit exasperated as he moved to the ladder.

"Well, you should have tried harder."

Rosamunde rolled her eyes, but remained silent as he drew his sword, climbed quickly into the loft, and disappeared. She heard him curse a moment later, and moved closer. "Are you all right, husband?"

There was silence for a moment, long enough for Rosamunde to start up the ladder; then Aric's head poked over the side to glare down at her. "What are you doing? Get down."

"Well, pray forgive me for being concerned about you," she snapped shortly, returning to the ground.

"Someone was up here," Aric told her irritably, starting down the ladder.

"Oh?" Rosamunde's irritation slid away, replaced with surprise.

"Aye. There is a nest where they were lying—and it is

still warm," he told her grimly, turning to glance around the stables. He frowned as he saw that the stable doors were open a crack. Smithy had closed the doors all the way. He was positive of that.

"Surely you are mistaken, husband? Why, there is nowhere for anyone to go from up there but down here. And we would have seen him."

"We were a bit distracted at one point, as I recall," he said, almost sorry he had said the words when she flushed with embarrassment, then paled with shame.

"You think that someone was up there, but climbed down the ladder and slid out while we were . . . But then they saw—"

"My lord!" Smithy's voice came from outside.

"What now?" Aric muttered impatiently and strode down the aisle to the door, tugging it open with irritation to scowl at the stablemaster. "What is it?"

"A messenger has arrived," the man murmured, intimidated by Aric's expression. "Bishop Shrewsbury here"—he gestured toward the man beside him, obviously eager to direct Aric's attention and anger elsewhere—"says—"

"One of Richard's messengers has arrived," the cleric announced. Rosamunde moved to join her husband in the doorway.

Sighing, Aric glanced toward his wife, then took her arm and started forward, obviously not willing to leave her behind in the stables now that he suspected someone had been there. But he had barely taken a step when he paused to whirl back upon Smithy. "Did you see anyone leave the stables after I entered?"

Smithy's eyebrows rose slightly. "Nay, my lord. But then, I wasn't really watching for anyone to leave. I was . . ." His voice died as Aric waved his explanations away and turned back toward the keep.

Rosamunde allowed him to tug her behind him distractedly, her mind fretting over the fact that someone had been up in the loft. It was all terribly upsetting. First, that meant someone might actually have thrown that bale down at her on purpose—though why anyone should do that was beyond her. It would have knocked her down most assuredly, but probably wouldn't have given her but a bruise or two. Unless she had hit her head. But even that would be unlikely to hurt her seriously. And then she most assuredly would have checked the loft, or had Smithy do so. Then whoever it was would have been caught.

Nay, it must have been an accident. The someone up in the loft must have accidentally knocked the bale out.

Of course, that left the question of who would have been up there and why, but there were any number of logical answers. Someone shirking their chores and seeking out somewhere quiet to do so. Or a child playing hide-and-seek.

Rosamunde sighed to herself. None of that really mattered to her as much as the fact that there had been someone there, and that meant that they had seen her and Aric. How dreadfully embarrassing.

Aric paused suddenly in his headlong rush to the keep, and Rosamunde glanced about to see that they were at the foot of the steps. Aric had paused to address his friend Robert.

"Aric. I was just about to come looking for you. A messenger has arrived—"

"From Richard," Aric finished, leaving Robert blinking at him in surprise. "Aye, I know. Is my father inside with him?"

"Aye. We were both here when he arrived."

Nodding, Aric started up the stairs, dragging Rosamunde behind him and leaving Robert to follow.

"Ah, here he is now," Lord Burkhart announced as Aric entered the keep, headed for the trestle tables with Rosamunde still in tow. "Son, this is Lord Whittier. He comes from Richard."

"Lord Whittier," Aric greeted the man. "Nay, stay seated," he said as the man set his ale down and made as if to rise. "You must have had a long journey. I understand you have a message for me?"

"I have many messages for many lords." The man sighed, taking his drink in hand again and swallowing some. "I am one of many men Richard has dispatched in the last few days. We have been sent to inform his barons all over the land that the coronation shall be September third at Westminster Abbey. Each lord is required to present himself and pledge his fealty to his new king."

Chapter 16

ROSAMUNDE stepped out of the tent and peered around at the slumbering soldiers with relief. Like his men, Aric was still asleep, too, but she had certain personal needs that needed attending right away. She had considered waking him, but he was really such a grouchy-bones in the morning, the idea had not appealed to her.

Of course, had one of his men been awake and seen her, she would have had to wake her husband. Every single one of the men had been warned that she was not to go anywhere unattended, and if someone had to accompany her on her quick trip to find a handy bush, it would be Aric. There were just some things that only a husband, or another woman, need know about.

Fortunately, since no one was awake and the guard was nowhere in sight, she didn't really have to worry about it. She just had to hurry before someone else awoke and spotted her. Avoiding traipsing through the men, lest she accidentally wake one, Rosamunde decided that the forest behind the tent would do well enough. She slipped around into the bushes.

Aric rolled onto his side, feeling around automatically for his wife, and waking slowly when she wasn't there.

Blinking his eyes open, he stared at the blank spot beside him in the pile of furs and frowned. She had beaten him awake again, he realized with a sigh, and had to wonder if the day would ever come when he would awaken before her.

Most likely not, he admitted with a grimace, dragging himself from the comfort and warmth of the soft furs to find his clothes. It was a shame, really, for he had yet to teach her the pleasures of marital relations first thing in the morning. Thinking upon it now, he was really rather eager to do so. Which was part of the reason he found himself stomping around grouching at everyone like a bear with a burr in its paw these past few mornings. He usually awoke from erotic dreams with a hankering for making them come true, but it never failed that he awoke to a cold and empty bed, his wife already up and puttering about.

Sighing, he tugged his brais and tunic on. Reaching for his sword belt, he began to strap it on as he moved to the tent flap. Stepping out into the early-morning chill, he peered around at the rest of his party, scowling at the fact that every last one of them save the sentry was still enjoying their slumber. He scanned the silent clearing they had chosen to camp in—this had been the first night of their travels to London—and the realization that his wife was nowhere in sight was slow to dawn on him. When it finally sank in, Aric felt as if he had been punched in the stomach.

"Rosamunde!" he shouted, starting forward. He paused to glance around the people stirring around the dead fire before rushing to Shambley. His friend was just starting to sit up.

"What is it?" the other man asked sleepily, rubbing at his eyes.

"Rosamunde is gone."

"Gone?" Robert was awake at once.

"She has probably just wandered off to tend to personal needs," Aric said, trying to reassure himself and ease the fear growing in the pit of his stomach. "Wake the men and start . . ." He waved vaguely toward the horses. "I am going to go look for her."

Nodding, Robert got to his feet as Aric hurried off into the woods in search of his wife.

"Oh, grand," Rosamunde muttered under her breath as her husband's shout reached her. Sighing, she quickly finished her business, muttering under her breath. She put her clothes back in order and began to make her way back toward the campsite, but didn't rush. *Why bother?* She was already in trouble. Aric would not be pleased with her. Why hurry back to be lectured and yelled at like a recalcitrant child?

"Rosamunde!" Robert rushed to her side the moment she came around the tent. "Where were you? Aric woke up and saw you gone and—"

"Where is he?" Rosamunde interrupted with a sigh. Shambley grimaced.

"He went in search of you. Toward the river, I think."

Nodding, Rosamunde started across the clearing, weaving her way around the men who were stumbling sleepily about as they now set to their morning chores.

"Wait, I shall accompany you." Shambley hurried after her.

"Aye, aye, I know. I am not to leave the clearing without accompaniment," she snapped. "A body cannot even enjoy a moment's peace with you men fretting over her. You really need not follow me this time, however. I am sure Aric will protect me well enough once I find him."

"Actually, I thought to protect you from his temper," Robert responded, drawing a smile from her as she stepped onto the path leading to the river. It wasn't very far from the clearing, just a five-minute walk. Which was why Aric had chosen the clearing for their campsite.

The two were silent as they walked, which turned out to be for the best. Had they been talking, they most likely would have missed the broken shout from ahead.

"Aric?" Rosamunde called, pausing on the path. Silence was her answer. Even the morning sounds that she hadn't really been paying attention to were suddenly absent. There were no birds chirping or bugs buzzing, and the ever-present rustle of undergrowth being disturbed by small animals had come to a halt as well. It was too quiet, as if the forest itself were suddenly holding its breath. The hair prickling the back of her neck, Rosamunde broke into a run. "Aric!"

Aware that Shambley was right behind her, she crashed through the woods, stumbling to a halt when she reached a much smaller clearing at the water's edge. Her gaze shot frantically around in search of her husband. When she didn't see him right away, she started to turn back, thinking he must be in the woods somewhere. Perhaps they had charged right past him. But then she glimpsed something in the water and froze, her head turned, her eyes narrowing on the object, then widening in horror as she realized that it was a body floating facedown in the water. *Aric.*

Crying out, she rushed forward, charging into the water up to her waist before she was able to reach his foot. Grabbing it, she gave it a tug, drawing him backward until she could grasp his shoulder. She had just managed to turn him in the water, crying out at the pale gray tinge to his skin, when Robert caught up. Her alarmed gaze flying to her husband's friend, Rosamunde saw him pale slightly; then his expression firmed. Robert slid his arms under Aric.

"Come on. We have to get him out of the water," he said shortly. Hefting his friend in his arms, Robert turned back toward shore. Rosamunde followed him as quickly as she could, her wet skirts hampering her, her heart tight and painful with fear and worry. When she reached shore, Shambley had already set the other man down and was slapping his face.

"Water." Rosamunde gasped, struggling to his side. Robert peered up at her with confusion. "He will be full of water," she explained, recalling a tale Eustice had told her once about a friend of hers who had nearly drowned. "We must get it out."

"How?"

Rosamunde peered at him helplessly. Eustice had said that the girl's father had picked the child up by her feet and shaken her. They could hardly do that to Aric . . . or could they? Her mouth firming, she straightened determinedly. "Grab his feet."

"His feet?" Robert asked with bewilderment.

"Just do it, damn it!"

His eyes widening at the first curse he had ever heard her use, Shambley shifted to Aric's feet and peered at her questioningly.

"You have to pick him up by his feet and hang him upside down."

"What?" He was gaping at her as if he thought her mad, and Rosamunde glared at him furiously.

"Do as I say. We have to get the water out."

Shaking his head, Robert hesitated, then grabbed Aric's feet. He lifted them into the air, then knelt to grab him around the knees.

"Wait," Rosamunde cried as he started to lift him. "The other way."

"What other way?"

"From the front," she said impatiently. "I must pound his back while you hold him up."

Muttering a curse—a much more foul one—himself, he straightened. Then, and still holding Aric's legs, Robert moved around until he straddled his waist. Dropping to his haunches again, he grasped Aric around the thighs and straightened, lifting him until the man hung with his head just brushing the ground.

"Good." Rosamunde sighed, moving forward to start patting his back.

"It does not appear to be working," Robert muttered after a moment.

Rosamunde peered down at Aric's head worriedly, biting her lip before suggesting, "Mayhap if you jostled him a bit . . . ?"

"Jostle him?" he asked doubtfully.

"Aye. Shake him up and down."

"I do not think—"

"Do you know a better way?" Rosamunde snapped. She continued to pat Aric's back.

"Fine. I shall jostle him," Robert agreed between his teeth, but seemed for a moment to be at a loss as to how to do that. Just when Rosamunde was about to snap at the man again, he suddenly began to bounce Aric up and down and from side to side.

The first thing Aric became aware of was pain.

It was coming from two separate sources. Or it seemed to him to be, at least. One source was his back, where a burning pain was spreading from where someone repeatedly punched him. The second source was his head. Someone seemed to be bashing him repeatedly there. And there were tight bands around his thighs. He felt a roiling sensation in his stomach, moving its way inexorably up his throat, and out his open mouth. When water immediately splattered all over his face and up his nose, Aric sputtered and tried to open his eyes, only to find that the world had turned upside down.

Nay. *He* was upside down, he realized, peering blankly at the feet on either side of his head. And he was being shaken and dipped about, his head smashing into the ground repeatedly. Grabbing weakly at the feet in front of him, he tried to speak, and found another wave of watery goo splashing out of his mouth and across his face, forcing his eyes closed.

"It is working! He spit up the water! Oh, I think he is awake! Set him down."

Aric sighed at the sound of that voice. Who else could it be but his wife behind this madness and agony? This thought flitted through his mind just before his head hit the ground a final time. His neck nearly snapped as his body followed.

"Aric? Husband!" She was slapping his face now, anxiety clear in her voice.

"Are you trying to kill me?" He had meant to bellow those words, but instead they came out in a faint whisper. He blinked his eyes open. Still, it had the desired effect, he supposed. His wife sat back slightly, giving him room to breathe. She peered at him with wounded puppy-dog eyes.

"Kill you?" she said in horrified amazement. "Why, we saved you, husband! You nearly drowned and we saved you." She looked toward the man standing beside her as if for confirmation, and Aric followed her gaze to see Shambley. His friend made an odd face and hunkered down to peer at him.

"Which part was supposed to save me, pray tell?" Aric asked, lifting his head slightly to glare at the two of them. "Beating my back, or the slamming my head into the dirt?"

"Both," Rosamunde snapped, lifting the edge of her gown to begin wiping at his face. "You were full of water and we had to get it out."

"And the pounding of my head was for. . . ."

"Oh, do stop fussing." Rosamunde sighed irritably, cleaning his face as if he were a child. "It worked, did it not? You spit up the water and are breathing again. It is not our fault you are so big. We did the best we could under the circumstances. Mayhap we should have left you drowned. You were a bit quieter, and much more pleasant that way."

"She is right, Aric. You were drowned. I did not think we would revive you even with the shaking and pounding, but it worked."

Mouth twisting, Aric sighed and stopped grumbling. It was hard to argue with any efficacy when the proof of her words was up his nose and all over his face. Sighing, he let his head drop back to the ground, his eyes closing wearily.

"What happened? How did you end up in the water?"

Aric's eyes popped open again at that question, a frown tugging at his mouth. "Someone hit me from behind," he remembered slowly, then glared at his wife. "I was looking for you and came down here to see if this was not where you had run off to and . . . someone hit me from behind. It is the last thing I remember. They must have thrown me in the water."

"Did you see who it was?" Shambley asked with concern. Aric scowled at him.

"Did I not just say that he hit me from behind? How am I supposed to have seen who it was? I do not have eyes back there, you know."

"Oh, aye, of course." Shambley exchanged a glance

with Rosamunde that made Aric even more irritable. It was as if they were sharing a thought. He didn't want them sharing a thought. He did not want them sharing anything.

"Did *you* see anyone?" he snapped.

"Nay," they answered in unison, and he grimaced, then shifted in an effort to raise himself to a sitting position. He failed miserably as Rosamunde put a hand lightly to his shoulder, keeping him down.

"Just rest there for a moment, husband. You should not try to get up too quickly."

Making a face meant to express that he was lying back only to appease her and not because he felt weak as a baby, Aric reclined in the grass again with a sigh. "Where are the men?"

"Back at the campsite, preparing to leave, no doubt," Shambley answered, concern obvious in his eyes as he looked his friend over. "Mayhap I should tell them we will not be leaving for a while."

"Why? I am fine. Just give me a moment to regain my breath and we can go," he announced, hoping that it was so, and was irritated all over again when the two shared another glance.

"Surely you are fine, husband," Rosamunde murmured. "But doubtless you will wish to clean up after your trauma and refresh yourself. Then, too, we must discuss this latest occurrence and what it means."

Aric's gaze narrowed on her suspiciously. "What mean you by that?"

"Well . . ." She looked vaguely surprised. "It would seem to me that this makes it doubtful that I need watching. 'Tis you someone is after."

"What?" This time he did manage to get a little volume behind his words, and Rosamunde winced slightly, then sighed.

"Aye. Well, we must think on this reasonably, my lord. The man in the bedchamber, for instance—"

"He was coming after you," Aric interrupted. "You were the only one in the room."

"Aye," she agreed soothingly. "But 'twas *our* bedchamber, and mayhap he did not realize that you were not there."

Aric blinked at those words, seeing that it was at least possible. But then he shook his head. "Nay. What about the incident with Bull?"

"Hmmm." Grimacing slightly, she scratched the back of her head. "That is all still rather fuzzy in my head, my lord. I mean, I may have simply miscalculated and tumbled off the fence. I remember hearing a sound behind me, but . . ." She shrugged. "I do not recall getting hit or pushed. . . . I may simply have fallen, and you all merely jumped to conclusions because of the previous incident."

While his eyes widened incredulously at that possibility, Robert joined the conversation. "But what about the stables?"

Rosamunde turned a frown on the man. "How do you know about that?"

"Aric told me."

"How much did he tell you?" Rosamunde asked with a scowl that did nothing to hide the flush flowering over her cheeks as she recalled that someone had most likely seen her and her husband at a most intimate moment. Several moments of intimacy, actually.

"He said someone had thrown a bale of hay out of the loft at you," Robert murmured, his gaze moving curiously between the two of them.

"Oh . . ." Clearing her throat, Rosamunde tried to forget the rest of their time in the stables and brushed her hair self-consciously behind her ear. "I do not think it was thrown at me. I mean, what end would that achieve? It would have knocked me down, but really . . ." She rolled her eyes. "What would that have done except make me cry out and bring Smithy running? Whoever it was would have been discovered right away. Nay." She shook her head. "I suspect someone had just chosen the loft as a nice, comfy place to shirk their chores, then accidentally knocked one of the bales over. They slipped from the loft while Aric and I were . . . umm . . . deep in discussion."

"Discussion, eh?" Aric said, grinning at her obvious discomfort. "I had a discussion I wished to have with you when I woke up this morning, but as usual you had awakened early and sneaked off." His grin dissipated, replaced by displeasure as he recalled the purpose behind his being at the river's edge in the first place.

He was about to begin reprimanding her when Shambley suddenly murmured, "She may be right."

"Right?" Scowling, Aric turned to his friend. "Right about what?"

"Mayhap it *is* you who is in danger."

"What?" Aric peered at him in disbelief.

"Well, that hayloft incident *could* have been an accident. The bale would hardly have killed her, or even done her much damage. All it would have done was draw Smithy into the stables. And if no one pushed her off that fence, throwing her in with Bull—"

"Who would not have hurt me anyway," Rosamunde added. She refused to acknowledge that even she was not sure if, had she not had apples hidden in her pocket, he might have trampled her beneath his powerful hooves without a second thought.

"Aye. So that just leaves the incident in the bedchamber and this incident here as true attacks. And the former *is* where both of you sleep; the attacker *could* have thought you were in the room and really have been after you. But this morning's little incident . . ." He shook his head. "There is no way anyone could have mistaken you for Rosamunde. This was an out-and-out attack on you."

They were all silent for a moment as his words sank in, then Rosamunde reached out to pat Aric's stunned cheek. "Never fear, husband. We shall keep you safe. We shall not leave you alone for a moment. You shall have a guard at all times."

"Oh, this is stuff and nonsense," Aric snapped, struggling to a sitting position. He managed to climb to his feet, where he swayed slightly. Reaching out for something to hold on to, he found only Rosamunde hitching herself beneath his arm to help keep him upright.

"Why do you not go back and tend the men?" she suggested now to Shambley. "Inform them that, in the future, my husband must not be left on his own. I shall help him bathe, then accompany him back to camp."

"What about a guard?"

"Oh, I shall attend to that," she assured Robert breezily. "I have his sword if I need it, and will keep him safe."

Too busy trying to keep his stomach's contents where they belonged, all Aric could do was roll his eyes. Shambley nodded and turned to leave.

"Mayhap you could bring some fresh clothes back when you have a moment, my lord?" Rosamunde called after him.

"For both of you," Robert agreed just before disappearing into the woods.

"Well," Rosamunde said cheerfully as soon as he was gone. "Shall we get you out of these clothes so you may bathe?"

"I do not wish to bathe," Aric muttered grumpily as she turned him toward the water.

"Well, I fear there is not much choice in the matter, my lord," she announced with a combination of forced cheer and determination. She propelled him forward. "You have spit up all over yourself."

Glancing down at his chest to see that what she said was true, Aric grimaced, but kept any further protest to himself, allowing her to ease him onto a good-size boulder on the bank.

"Just think how nice it shall be to get rid of all that nasty old . . ." She wrinkled her nose in lieu of giving a name to the stuff presently dribbling from his chin, and bent to remove his sword belt. Unsheathing the weapon, she leaned it against the rock beside him, easily available should it be needed, then began to work on his tunic. "You shall feel much better once you are cleaned up."

"You are speaking to me in the exact same tones—and using nearly the exact same words—as you did with that dog when you tried to convince him that a bath was for the best," he pointed out irritably.

"Am I?" she asked distractedly as she lifted his tunic off over his head. "Well, I trust you shall not make as much fuss as *Summer* did when I gave *her* her bath." She stressed the dog's name and sex, since he seemed to have already forgotten her telling him both. Tossing the tunic on the ground, she then reached for his brais, but Aric caught her hands and held them with a sigh.

"I can do that myself, if you would just give me the room to stand."

"As you wish, my lord." Stepping back, she gave him the room he requested, holding her tongue and merely watching anxiously as he got to his feet. He swayed like a branch in a breeze as he began to push the brais down over his hips. He managed to get them a third of the way down, but when he had to bend over to push them further, he swayed dangerously and nearly toppled over.

Catching his shoulders, Rosamunde urged him back to a standing position, then knelt to remove the brais herself, doing her best to keep from peering at his manhood as she did. It was a difficult task, since it was right in her face, and even now growing in size. It seemed he had not been injured terribly after all, she decided with amusement. She helped him step out of the damp pants, then tossed them onto his tunic.

"There we are, then," she said happily and, straightening, stepped to the side. "In you go. A nice soaking and you shall feel much better."

"Do you have to be so damn cheerful?" he grumbled, taking a slow, careful step past her.

"Nay, my lord. But 'tis better than being so darned grumpy that someone would wish me dead," she muttered.

His head swiveling, he glared at her furiously. "What did you say?"

"Me?" she asked innocently. "I believe I said that that bump you took must have given you a sore head."

He glared at her suspiciously for a moment, then turned to continue making his way into the water, ignoring her until he was neck-deep. At that point he turned toward her, saying, "I—What the devil are you doing?"

Glancing up from the sword she had been inspecting—his sword—she raised her eyebrows slightly, but answered, "Guarding you, my lord."

"Put that damn thing down before you cut yourself. I do not need guarding."

"That bump on your head would seem to indicate

differently, husband," Rosamunde murmured, ignoring his order to set the sword aside.

"Which one? The one the unknown culprit gave me, or the dozen or so you and Shambley added while 'rescuing' me?"

Rosamunde peered at him silently for a moment, then slowly began to nod her head.

"What are you thinking?" he asked suspiciously.

"Just that it is most definitely you that our enemy must be after."

His gaze narrowed. "Why?"

"Well." She shrugged simply. "I am nice and polite to all I meet."

Aric blinked at that. "*What?* And I am not?"

Her expression spoke volumes, and Aric found himself somewhat hurt by her poor opinion of him. "I have a sore head," he reminded her by way of excuse. She nodded solemnly.

"You must have one every morning, then."

"Aye. Though not the same head," Aric muttered, splashing irritably at the water surrounding him.

"What was that?" Rosamunde called from shore.

"Nothing," he snapped, then sighed and concentrated on cleaning himself.

They were both silent for a while; then Rosamunde asked, "Do you suppose we shall come across your father on our way to London?"

"Nay," Aric answered. His father had returned home to Burkhart the day after the messenger's arrival. He, too, was expected to be present for Richard's coronation, and had headed home to make the necessary preparations. He also had to collect his eldest son and daughters for the journey.

"We shall meet up with them in London though, will we not?"

"No doubt."

"What are your sisters like?"

Aric shrugged at the question. "They are sisters."

Rosamunde smiled wryly at his answer, then announced, "If they are anything like your father, I will like them."

"You like my father, do you?"

"Oh, aye, he reminds me of the abbess. She was very like him: soft-spoken and gentle, with a streak of craftiness about her, but, Lord, beware her temper. Does your father have a temper?"

"Aye," he said, then peered at her a bit curiously. How had she picked up so much about his father during a visit when the two had hardly seemed to speak more than exchanging pleasantries? "So he reminds you of the abbess," he murmured, thinking he could not wait to tell his father that. He suspected the man wouldn't take kindly to being compared to a woman, no matter her position. "Does Shambley remind you of anyone?"

"Aye." She nodded slowly. "Sister Constance. She was one of the younger nuns, and she had the same sort of devilish sense of humor Lord Shambley does."

"Sister Constance." Aric grinned. "And what of the others?"

"The others, my lord?"

"Aye. Like Smithy, for instance."

"Oh, well, Smithy is easy. He is very like Sister Eustice. Not as knowledgeable as her, perhaps, but he has the same gentleness and way with animals."

"And what about me?" he asked, starting slowly toward shore.

Rosamunde blinked at him uncertainly. "You?"

"Aye. Do I remind you of one of the nuns from the abbey?"

"Oh, nay, my lord."

"Nay?" His eyebrows rose slightly at the emphatic way she said it, and he paused in the water. "No one?"

Making a face, she shook her head. "Well, how could you? You are my husband."

"So?"

"So you are a man."

Aric gave a bewildered laugh at that. "So are my father and Smithy."

"Oh, aye. Well, I suppose they are," she said doubtfully as he started forward again. She rushed on. "But I do not think of them as such. I mean, I know that they *are* men, of course, but I do not really think of them as men. They are just . . . well . . . *people*," she said helplessly.

Aric stared at her with sudden fascination, positive he needed to hear this. "You lump the abbess, my father, Smithy, Shambley, and the other men and women you know in one big category: people? Yet you think of me as a man," he clarified slowly.

"Not just any man, but my husband. *The* man."

"*The* man," he echoed.

Flushing, she nodded.

"And what separates me from being one of the 'people'?" he asked curiously. His eyebrows rose when her gaze dropped abruptly to what was revealed now that he stood only knee-deep in the water.

"Well, all men have that," he snapped irritably.

Her nose immediately lifted in the air as she hopped off the boulder. "Not as far as I am concerned, my lord. For all I know, half the nuns in the abbey may have had one, but yours is the only one I am concerned with. Because it is mine."

Aric gave a start at that. "Yours?"

"Well, of course it is," she told him impatiently. "I don't know why it should surprise you. You gave yourself to me in marriage and I to you. Everything of yours is mine and vice versa—and that includes *that*. And let me tell you, my lord," she added with a hard look, her eyes narrowed. "I am not so naive that I have not heard of adultery. And while I am very forbearing in a lot of things, should I ever get wind that you are sharing my '*that*' with anyone else, I shall surely cut it off and mount it on the mantel."

"Here we are!" Shambley breezed cheerfully into the clearing. "Fresh clothes for both of you."

"I shall change in my tent," Rosamunde snapped, snatching the gown he held out and stomping past him. "I trust you will keep an eye on my husband and be sure he is safe."

"Of course," Robert agreed, staring after her rather blankly. She marched off back toward camp. "Well, did I interrupt at a bad moment?"

"Hmmm?" Aric glanced toward his friend, distracted, then began to grin like an idiot. He stepped out of the water. "Nay, nay. She thinks of you as a 'people.'"

"Oh." His friend blinked. "Well, that is good. I guess."

"Aye. And she thinks of me as *the* man."

"And so you are a man," Shambley murmured, wondering what the hell his friend was jabbering on about.

"And she wants to mount my manhood on the mantel," Aric announced happily, taking the brais Robert held and tugging them quickly on.

That made Shambley pause and blink several times before asking cautiously, "And this is a good thing?"

"Aye. It means she cares about me."

"I see." Shambley nodded slowly. "If you say so. Er . . . I do not suppose Rosamunde thought to check that head wound of yours . . . to see what damage may have been done?"

"What?" Aric frowned at him, then scowled as he snatched his tunic from his friend. He began to don it. "There is nothing wrong with my head."

"Of course not," Robert agreed. He followed then, shaking his head as Aric snatched up his sword belt and started back through the trees toward camp.

Chapter 17

SIGHING, Rosamunde paced the length of the room she and Aric had been given, and glanced impatiently toward the door.

They had arrived at court the day before, and Rosamunde had been grateful for that at the time. Unfortunately, despite the fact that she had not left his side for a moment after Shambley and Aric had returned to their campsite the day he had nearly drowned, there had been another attack. Not on his person, though. That had not been possible now that they were on the alert. However, the last morning of their journey, their attacker had apparently become desperate and placed a sharp pin under Black's saddle.

The plan had been very clever. So long as there was no weight on the saddle, Black had been fine, but the moment Aric had mounted, the thick pin had stuck the horse, making him buck wildly.

Her husband had been thrown from the saddle. Luckily he had landed on Bishop Shrewsbury, else he might have been killed. Of course, no one had seen anyone strange near the horses, and once again they were unable to determine the culprit.

It had been a great relief to reach court, especially for

the bishop. He had knocked his head pretty hard when Aric had landed on him. The poor man hadn't even seen the trouble Aric was in, so had been unprepared for the warrior's weight upon him. The cleric had been quite testy the rest of the journey. Rosamunde suspected his head had been aching. He had retired to his own room as soon as they had arrived, not even leaving it to join them all at the sup.

The memory of the meal last night, her first at court, made Rosamunde again sigh unhappily. What a debacle that had been. Aric had been hailed by someone down the table just as they were being seated. Excusing himself, her husband had moved to speak to the man, leaving Rosamunde alone. She had still been alone a few moments later when a pale-skinned, dark-haired beauty with an apparently permanent expression of disdain on her face had been seated at her side.

Feeling a certain kinship with the other girl, since the two of them had been momentarily abandoned, Rosamunde had foolishly attempted to strike up a conversation with the newcomer. She had quickly regretted it. The woman had taken great delight in looking down her nose at everything about Rosamunde, from her pretty but plain blue gown to her undressed hair. When she had suggested that Rosamunde was in need of a better lady's maid, Rosamunde had blurted that she did not have one. The woman had immediately become even ruder. Rosamunde had been quite relieved when she had finally felt a slight pressure on her shoulder and heard Aric's voice just above her head.

"As you can see, Delia, my wife is beautiful enough that she does not need the artifices some women feel naked without. I hardly think that a maid could improve the beauty God has given her."

Feeling her heart warm and her stomach unclench

slightly at her husband's sweet words, Rosamunde had smiled up at him, then turned back to her tormentor. It was only when she saw the way the woman's face had paled, her mouth suddenly as straight and tight as a bowstring, that Rosamunde had recognized the name: *Delia*. This was the fiancée who had broken his heart, she had realized, watching silently as the other woman rose with a sneer and hurried away.

"I apologize," Aric had murmured, settling himself beside her. Rosamunde had glanced at him in surprise.

"For what, my lord? That was not your fault."

"Aye, it was," he had assured her quietly. "At least in part. I should have bought you new gowns as you deserve—as, indeed, your father instructed me to. And I should have thought of a lady's maid." He had shaken his head in self-disgust. "I have two sisters. I do not know how your lack slipped my attention."

"I do not want a lady's maid," Rosamunde had assured him quietly. "I have never had one and have no wish for one now. And had you bought those gowns, I am sure she would have simply criticized them as well. She seems a very bitter and unpleasant person. I think she takes pleasure in hurting people."

"Aye." He had smiled at that. "And you saw that after only a matter of moments. . . . I have known her all my life, and yet did not see it until I learned to love you."

When Rosamunde had smiled at him then, squeezing his hand gently, a dissatisfied frown started to tug at his lips. "I just said I love you, wife. Are you not the least surprised? Have you nothing to say to that?"

Rosamunde's eyebrows had risen slightly at his irritation. "But I already knew you loved me, my lord. Why would I be surprised?"

"You knew?" He had scowled, a muscle beginning to

twitch in his cheek. "How could you have known? *I* did not even know until I said it."

"Why, I knew the moment you stopped acting so jealous all the time, after the incident by the river. You no longer grumble at anyone who smiles at me, or—"

"You knew I loved you because I *stopped* being jealous?" He'd gaped at her reasoning, but Rosamunde nodded, for she'd realized it was true.

"Of course. It meant that you had come to trust me, my lord. And trusting me was the last hurdle you needed to overcome. You already liked me, desired me, valued my abilities, and wanted me near you. Trust was the last item needed."

When he'd began to shake his head in a sort of bewildered uncertainty, she had pressed a hand to his cheek in a soft caress. "And I recognized that because I had come to love you, too."

Relaxing then, he had covered her hand with his own and smiled. "Your father was a very wise man."

"Aye," she had agreed, tears pooling in her eyes. "He gave me a wonderful gift in you."

"Nay, . . ." Pausing as he was jostled by someone seating himself nearby, Aric had glanced around with irritation. "Are you really very hungry?"

"Only for my husband," she had whispered huskily.

Squeezing her hand, Aric had smiled widely, then stood, taking her with him as they departed the table. Once in their room, there had been no more need for words. They had proven with their bodies what had already been said in words, giving of themselves and sharing with a joy that still made her smile. Or would have, were she not so worried.

Sighing, she glanced toward the door again. She had awakened early this morning as was her habit, but whereas she normally would have gone below and puttered about, this morning she had remained abed, watching her husband sleep. She had no intention of leaving him alone and venturing out in this strange castle. So she had watched over him, until looking was just not enough anymore, and she had been unable to stop herself from gently caressing him: his cheek, his throat, his chest. Aric had awakened by the time her hand had dropped lower; then he had shown her the many benefits of awaiting his awakening.

One added benefit, oddly enough, was that he seemed to be much less grumpy. That morning, as they had dragged themselves from the bed and moved below to break their fasts, Aric had been the most pleasant of husbands.

But her husband's good cheer had lasted only until after they had eaten. As they were rising to leave the table, Shambley had approached with the news that Richard had granted Aric the audience he had requested and would see him right away. Aric had ordered Rosamunde back to their room.

Rosamunde had left reluctantly, positive that her husband had asked to see Richard in the hope that he might divine whether the prince was involved in the attacks that had occurred first at Goodhall, then on the journey here. Fear had been plaguing her ever since he had left. Now that she was alone, and with nothing to occupy her thoughts, her anxiety had grown. It was not that she feared he would not be careful in broaching the subject, but . . . she had a superstitious sense that things had been going too well, that she was too happy, and that payment for that happiness was coming due.

Her patience snapping, Rosamunde whirled and headed for the door. She could stand it no longer. She had to find her husband. She would wait outside the audience hall if need be, but orders or no orders, she could not wait alone in their chamber another moment.

"Oh, my lord. There you are."

Aric paused in the hallway outside the royal audience chamber, his eyebrows rising as he watched Bishop Shrewsbury hurry forward. He had just wasted an hour talking to Richard, telling him about the trouble he had had of late, the attacks on Rosamunde and himself, feeling the man out to see if he might be involved somehow. But other than a mild concern, the man had given nothing away.

Now all Aric wanted was to return to his chamber and his wife. He could not wait for this trip to be over so that they could return home. There were too many strangers here. Too much intrigue. He would take Rosamunde home as soon as the coronation was over. There he would look into different ways of ensuring their safety; he would replace every single person at the castle, if need be. Now that he had found happiness with Rosamunde, he had no intention of losing it.

"Thank goodness I got to you in time." The bishop spoke the words barely above a whisper. "I rushed here the moment Shambley told me that you had been granted an audience. You must not see Richard, at least not until I warn you—"

"I just came from seeing him," Aric interrupted brusquely. Bishop Shrewsbury's face was immediately filled with dismay.

"Oh, no," he gasped, wide-eyed. "What did you say? I wish you had waited until I could tell you . . ." Sighing, he shook his head. Aric frowned.

"Until you could tell me what?"

"I know who is behind the attempts on your life."

Aric stiffened. "Who?" he asked harshly.

Shrewsbury opened his mouth, then snapped it closed again as his gaze landed on the guards on either side of the door. He shook his head. "Not here. Come with me."

Turning, he hurried off down the hall, leaving Aric to follow him. After a brief hesitation, Aric did, trailing him down one hall, then another, until they reached and crossed the noisy great hall. There they came to the doors leading out into the garden.

Loitering. That was what she was doing, Rosamunde thought unhappily. She avoided looking at the guards outside Richard's door as she tried to pretend she was not there. She might be loitering for no good reason, either, for it was impossible to tell if Aric was still inside. She supposed she would know when the door opened.

She hoped that would happen soon. She had reached this hall only a moment ago and yet already felt terribly conspicuous. Aric would be furious, of course, when he realized she had disobeyed him and left their chamber, where he had ordered her to remain. But it could not be helped. She was too fretful simply to sit and wait. She would be glad when this business of the coronation was over and they could return home.

The door to the hall opened suddenly, and Rosamunde turned sharply, her eyes widening when she saw the man exiting the room. He was breathtakingly handsome. Over six feet tall with red-gold hair and blue eyes, he sported a short beard on his perfect features that gave him a slightly rakish look. There was no mistaking who this was. The *Coeur de Lion*. Richard the Lionhearted was famous for his beauty. This was her brother—half brother, she amended. This was the man who had caused her father no end of misery.

Remembering herself, Rosamunde dropped into a

deep curtsy, her eyes firmly on the ground at her feet until the heir apparent and his guards had passed. Slowly regaining her feet, she turned to watch them walk away down the hall before glancing uncertainly back toward the king's rooms.

Richard had been alone. Aric and Robert had not been with him. Surely she could not have missed them? Biting her lip, she took an uncertain step toward the chamber door, her mind running over possibilities. If Richard was the one behind the attacks, or if Aric had unintentionally allowed his suspicions to show and somehow angered Richard . . . Surely the new king would not have done anything to him? She took another step, glancing up the hall to be sure no one was around, then scurried the last few steps to the door. She would just take a peek inside and be sure. . . . Her imagination was running wild with thoughts of blood splattered on the floor, and Aric's broken body.

Pushing the door open, she started to poke her head inside, then glanced around guiltily at the sound of approaching voices. No one was in sight, but the voices were drawing nearer. In a panic, Rosamunde slid into the room, closing the door until it was only open a crack. Peering through that opening, she was just in time to see two men pass by the end of the corridor; then they were gone.

Releasing the breath she had been holding, Rosamunde eased the door closed and turned to glance around. Her eyes widened. The king's audience chamber was a huge room. Deep crimson canvases hung from the walls, the brilliant colors of the royal arms standing out upon them. Other than the rushes on the floor, the only item in the room was a lone chair at the far end. Scarlet cloth covered the seat, and the arms were ivory, with boars' heads carved into them.

Rosamunde stared at that chair for a moment, knowing it was the king's. Her father had sat upon it, and soon her half brother would. She tore her gaze away to glance over the rushes, relieved to see that while the walls were splashed liberally with bloodred canvas, the rushes did not show any similar color. She had just ascertained that and turned back to the door—intending to slip back out with no one ever being the wiser about her presence there—when someone spoke.

"Have you seen enough, then?"

Turning guiltily toward the voice, she saw a woman move away from the wall and toward the center of the room. Because the woman was dressed in a gown only a shade or so different from the crimson on the walls, Rosamunde had not noticed her. Now she stared at the lined face of the woman moving to stand by the king's chair, and she knew with a sinking heart that she had been caught by no less than Queen Eleanor herself.

"I am sorry, Your Majesty," she murmured, dropping into a curtsy. "I was searching for my husband. He had an audience with Richard and did not return to our chamber. I—"

"Decided to hunt him down," Eleanor finished her sentence with vague amusement. "Rise, child, and come closer. Who is your husband?"

"Aric Burkhart, Lord Goodhall." Rosamunde rose and moved reluctantly forward, not missing the startled expression on the queen's face as she peered at her.

"You look familiar to me. Have we met?"

"Nay, Your Majesty."

"Hmmmm." The older woman frowned slightly, her hands coming together to twist the ring on her left hand. She stared at Rosamunde consideringly. Abruptly she said, "Your husband has already been and gone. Yet my son was regaling me with the troubles that have plagued you. . . ."

"Oh." Rosamunde hesitated briefly, then bobbed in a quick curtsy. She began to back away toward the door. "Thank you, Your Majesty."

"I did not give you leave to depart," Eleanor snapped, and Rosamunde froze. Satisfied, Eleanor was silent for a moment. "Richard said that there have been attempts on your life. And your husband's, too."

"Aye." Rosamunde nodded. Then, shocking even herself with her brazen words, she blurted, "I have heard it suggested that you may be behind them."

There seemed no way the older woman could have feigned the genuine amazement that covered her face. "Me? Why would I trouble myself to harm *you?* I do not even know you."

"You knew my mother."

The older woman stilled at that, her gaze narrowing suspiciously. "And who was your mother?"

"Her name was Rosamunde."

Eleanor's hand fluttered to her throat, and she sank slowly to sit on the king's chair. "My God. The fair Rosamunde," she said softly, then shook her head. "I should have seen it at once. You look very like her. Except for your hair and eyes," she added with a grimace. "Those are definitely Henry's."

"My mother—"

Eleanor waved her to be silent. "Your mother was a beautiful but foolish young woman. She followed her heart. I learned long ago that the heart is fickle, and one is wiser to follow one's head." She paused. "However, I did not dislike your mother."

Catching Rosamunde's doubtful expression, Eleanor smiled wearily. "I did not say I liked her, either."

"I was told—" Rosamunde began uncertainly, but Eleanor waved her to silence again.

"Yes. I know about the rumors claiming I was behind her death. But I was not." She paused, seemingly lost in thought. "I might have been, had things turned out differently, but as it was, someone beat me to it."

Standing, she moved around to the side of the chair and stared at the wall behind it. Eleanor ran a hand back and forth over one of the chair's ivory arms, then murmured, "I always suspected Bishop Shrewsbury, myself."

Rosamunde gave a start at that. "Shrewsbury?"

"Yes. He studied the healing arts while growing up in the monastery and had a great knowledge of poisons. And he was quite distressed by the whole affair between your mother and my husband." She glanced back, a disturbed expression on her face. "His relationship with my husband was most odd. I could have sworn he hated him."

"*Hated* him?" Rosamunde asked with amazement.

"Yes. It was in his eyes sometimes—when he looked at Henry and thought no one else was watching." She was silent for a moment, then shook away the thought that held her attention and glanced at Rosamunde. "And yet he was as faithful as a dog to Henry. Perhaps I am mistaken. Perhaps he was just jealous."

"Jealous?"

"I think the poor bishop was madly in love with your mother. From what I gather, he thought her a saint. I happen to know that he was forever hanging around, watching her—spying on her, really. On them." She gave a shudder. "It was a mad sort of love."

"But if he loved her as you say, why would he kill her?"

"Because she did not love him back, foolish girl," she

suggested with annoyance. Then amusement tugged at her lips and she said uninterestedly, "Or mayhap because she allowed Henry to corrupt her. She fell from her pedestal rather hard, did she not? A saint could hardly live in sin with the spawn of the devil."

Rosamunde was frowning over her words when Eleanor suddenly suggested, "You look very like her—except for the hair and eyes. Did these attempts on your life start after he arrived at Goodhall?"

Rosamunde blinked at her in surprise. "How did you know he was at Goodhall?"

Eleanor gave her a patronizing look. "We have known he was at Goodhall for some time. I just did not realize who the new lord and lady of Goodhall were."

"Oh." Rosamunde accepted that at face value, then considered the original question. She frowned. "The attempts started shortly after his arrival," she admitted unhappily.

Eleanor did not look surprised. "I would keep an eye on him. He always gave me the shudders. He is a zealot, and while they are useful, they are also dangerous. Not that Henry would ever listen to me when I tried to tell him that." Her mouth twisted bitterly; then she shifted impatiently. "I tire of this conversation. You are dismissed."

Nodding slowly, Rosamunde curtsied and backed out of the room, but paused in closing the door to murmur sincerely, "Thank you. For all that you have told me."

Surprise crossed the old queen's face; then her expression softened slightly. "You are welcome."

Rosamunde closed the door. Whirling then, she hurried down the hall, her mind in a spin. Could it be Bishop Shrewsbury behind the attacks? She believed Eleanor's words, that the queen was not involved. Twenty years was a long time to carry a grudge.

Besides, Aric had relayed the conversation he had had with her father the night Henry had arrived at Shambley to ask him to marry her. And her father had said that he believed Eleanor had killed her mother not out of jealousy or love, but because she hadn't wanted to lose her title as queen and the power that went with it. Rosamunde was hardly a threat to that.

But then, there was nothing for Bishop Shrewsbury to gain either, she reminded herself. Her footsteps slowed. She had difficulty seeing the pious old man as a vile murderer.

"Surely this is far enough, Bishop?" Aric called out irritably as he followed the old man through the gardens, but if the fellow heard him, he neither slowed down nor stopped. He continued on at the same swift pace he had set, moving out of the castle and leading him deep into the gardens. Losing his patience, Aric finally snapped, "I am stopping here. This is safe enough for us to talk."

This time the prelate seemed to hear him. Pausing, he frowned back at Aric. "Just a little farther, my lord. There is a clearing ahead where I know we shall be both comfortable and safe from curious ears."

Grumbling under his breath, Aric started to walk again, but muttered, "A little farther, then, but that is all."

Nodding, Shrewsbury turned and continued forward.

"Rosamunde! Where is Aric?"

Rosamunde turned slowly to frown at Robert. Shambley hurried up the hall toward her. She had just arrived back at the room she and Aric had been given, and thrown the door open, only to pause in the doorway as she realized that the room was empty. "I thought you were with him."

"I was, but Bishop Shrewsbury said my parents had arrived and wished to speak with me. I—"

"Was it true?" Rosamunde interrupted urgently.

"Aye. My mother and father had just arrived." His eyes narrowed at the relief that covered her face at that; then he added, "But I do not know where he got the idea that they wished to speak to me. They knew nothing of that."

"Oh, no." Rosamunde sagged weakly against the door frame as her fears crowded in.

"What is it?"

"The queen . . ." She shook her head hopelessly. "Queen Eleanor said that she did not kill my mother."

"You *asked* her?" he asked in horror, but Rosamunde ignored the question.

"She suspected that if my mother was poisoned, it was Bishop Shrewsbury."

"What? Nay!"

"She said that he loved my mother. That he spied on my parents. That she suspected he hated my father."

"That is hard to believe," he said, then frowned. "And yet, he did lure me away from the king's chamber with that tale about my parents, and now Aric is missing." Her husband's friend shifted, then patted her arm reassuringly. "I shall take a look around and see if I cannot locate them. You wait here in case he returns."

Had he given her the chance, Rosamunde might very well have protested at being ordered to wait behind again. She was rather tired of such treatment. But he did not give her the chance, turning sharply on his heel and hurrying off down the hall. She was left glowering after him. He had barely disappeared around the corner when another voice hailed her.

"Rosamunde, my dear."

As she turned to peer down the hall in the opposite direction, her eyebrows rose, a smile briefly erasing the worry from her brow. She moved forward. "Lord Burkhart! You are arrived."

"Aye." Smiling, Aric's father took the hands she held out and squeezed them gently. He leaned forward to kiss her cheek. "We arrived about half an hour ago, but took the time to settle into our rooms ere coming in search of you and Aric."

"We?" Rosamunde smiled at him quizzically, then glanced curiously at the two young women standing shyly behind him.

"Yes. May I introduce my daughters? Aric's sisters, Margaret and Elizabeth."

The two women, as blond as Aric, and as pretty as he was handsome, curtsied; one offered a shy smile, and the other grinned mischievously, and Rosamunde bobbed a curtsy in greeting. "I fear you have missed Aric," she said. "He—"

"Aye. I know," Lord Burkhart interrupted wryly. "We saw him as we crossed the great hall."

"You *saw* him?" Rosamunde asked with amazement.

"Aye. But he was too distant and did not hear me hail him. I thought that if we found you, he would eventually find us, so I asked where your room was and—"

"I am sorry, my lord," Rosamunde interrupted. "Were you able to tell where he was going?"

Lord Burkhart's eyebrows rose slightly. "Well, it looked as if he were following Bishop Shrewsbury out to the gardens."

"Shrewsbury," she muttered faintly.

"Aye. Is there something wrong? You have gone quite pale of a sudden, Rosamunde."

"Oh . . . I . . ." Shaking her head, Rosamunde

began backing up. "I have to find him. I am sorry, my lord. I . . ." Shaking her head again, she turned and hurried away.

As Aric had expected, the clearing was more than "a little farther" ahead. They walked for another ten minutes before suddenly breaking out into a small clearing before a cozy cottage. Pausing at the edge of the trees, Aric scowled at Shrewsbury's back. "This is far enough. Tell me what you know. Who is behind the attacks on my wife and myself?"

Hesitating, Shrewsbury frowned between Aric and the cottage, then moved back reluctantly. "What I have to tell you would be easier seen than said," he murmured slowly.

"Seen?" Aric frowned. "What is there to see?"

The bishop peered at him consideringly, then glanced back toward the building. "If we could just go inside . . ."

His eyes hard, Aric arched an eyebrow. "And what is it I am supposed to see in there? You said you knew who was behind—"

"Your wife," Shrewsbury said abruptly. Aric blinked at him.

"*What?*"

"She is who you will find in the cottage, and she is behind the attacks on you." The older man sighed unhappily.

Aric stared at him blankly for a moment, then gave a short laugh and shook his head. "This is a poor jest, my lord Bishop."

"I wish it were a jest, my lord," Shrewsbury said quietly. "But 'tis true."

Aric shook his head. "Shrewsbury, I do not know where you got this idea, but you are wrong. She could not be behind the attacks on me. She was with

Shambley the morning I was knocked unconscious and thrown in the river. They found and dragged me from—"

"*They* knocked you out and threw you in the river. They only dragged you out when they thought you had drowned. They—"

"Shambley?" Aric was getting angry now. "Shambley has been my friend for over twenty years. We were children when we first met."

"Friendship means nothing when it comes to a woman," Shrewsbury said sadly. "He fell in love with her the moment he saw her. Everyone does. She is an angel of loveliness. Almost too perfect for this sinful world."

Aric shook his head, anger and disgust warring on his face. "I have heard enough. This is drivel, and I do not believe a word of it," he snapped, and much to his amazement it was true. He did not believe that Rosamunde had been unfaithful to him with Shambley. He did not believe she had been unfaithful with anyone. She had told him that she loved him, and while words were easy to say, she had shown that love in many ways: the way she had fussed over him after the near-drowning, then after the fall from the bucking Black. Her determination to guard him like a mother hen once she had become convinced he was the one in danger. Her overwhelming desire to pleasure him while making love, and her ability to. Above those things, she was caring and concerned and would never willingly hurt a living thing—or probably a dead one even, for that matter. The idea of her attempting to murder him was ludicrous.

Nay, he did not believe it. He had learned to trust his wife. Shaking his head, he started to turn away, determined to return to the castle and his love. His search for the real culprit was being delayed.

Shrewsbury caught his arm. "Wait. It is true, my lord. I swear it." When Aric began to shake his head again, the bishop's mouth firmed. "And I shall prove it. Wait here." Turning away, the old man suddenly rushed across the clearing to the cottage, threw open the door with a dramatic crash, and stepped inside. His shout echoed out. "Aha! Whore of Babylon! Strumpet! You are caught out! Your husband is—" A shriek ended the priest's words.

Stiffening, Aric stared at the empty cottage door for a moment, hesitating in the sudden silence, then started uncertainly forward, drawing his sword. He didn't believe Rosamunde was in there. Most like the silly old fool had walked in on another woman and her lover. Probably a large one, too, who wouldn't care for his woman being called the "whore of Babylon."

"Silly old fool," Aric muttered as he approached the door. He called out, then, "Bishop? Are you all right?"

Stepping through the doorway, he blinked in the suddenly dim light. His eyes were still struggling to adjust to the shadows when a shuffling sound made him turn. He was halfway around when something heavy slammed into his head.

Rosamunde paused and peered anxiously about once she reached the gardens. A sense of urgency had taken possession of her, and she knew it would not ease until she found her husband and Shrewsbury. But where were they? The gardens were huge and full of little hidey-holes. Why had the bishop led him out here? And more important, where had they gone? If Shrewsbury was behind the attacks. . . .

She grimaced at the thought. It made no sense really. If it was him, and it was all based around some mad love he held for her mother, why kill Aric?

Her thoughts were distracted by a titter of laughter as two women appeared ahead on the path, walking toward her. Pausing, she smiled at them as they drew abreast. "Excuse me, you did not happen to see two men while on your walk? One older, one younger?"

"Do you mean Bishop Shrewsbury?" the older woman asked. They appeared to be mother and daughter to Rosamunde. Both were similar in looks, blond and pale.

"Aye," she said quickly.

"We passed them. They were heading straight that way," the younger one told her, waving toward the path and through the trees. "Though I do not know why. They kept going even when the path ended, but there is nothing there, I do not think."

"Aye, there is," the older one announced. "Rosamunde's cottage."

"Rosamunde's cottage?" Rosamunde asked with a start.

"Aye. She was a mistress of Henry's some years back. She lived in a cottage through there until Henry took her into the castle proper. He never let anyone else live there. I'm surprised Eleanor never had it torn down." The girl giggled. "Especially if she hated that mistress as much as people claim."

Feeling the hair on the back of her neck stand on end, Rosamunde grabbed her skirts and rushed in the direction the woman had pointed.

Chapter 18

"$\mathcal{A}$H, you are awake."

Was he? Aric wondered a bit fuzzily, forcing his eyes open. It seemed to him he was asleep and caught in some maudlin nightmare. His head was throbbing, much as it had been doing the day he had been knocked into the river. He was presently lying on his back on a creaky old bed. A musty, tattered, and filthy old bed, he realized, his gaze sliding over the ratty material of the bed drapes. His eyes fixed with disgust on the myriad cobwebs that covered the top of them.

Aric hated spiders. Detested them actually. Always had. That being the case, his first instinct was to get the hell off the bed and away from them, but when he shifted to do so, something held him back. Glancing upward with a frown, he gaped at the rope that bound him to the posts at the top of the bed. A glance down at his feet showed that they, too, were tied to the bedposts. He was staked out like a sacrificial lamb.

"I considered just setting the cottage on fire and leaving you to burn alive—without your ever knowing who did it or why, but that seemed terribly unfair." Bishop Shrewsbury made the announcement conversationally, drawing Aric's gaze to where the man was presently coaxing a fire to life in the fireplace. "Besides, I *do* think that for me to enjoy the situation, you really need to be awake."

Having gotten the fire started, the older man now straightened and moved toward the bed, a happy little smile curving his lips.

Waking up fully, Aric eyed the other man warily as he approached, taking in his cold gaze, his flat expression, and the wicked-looking blade he was toying with. None of which eased the concern mounting within him.

"What? Did I waste my time?" Shrewsbury asked now, pausing at the side of the bed and tilting his head slightly. "Have you nothing to say? No questions you would have answered? Shall I get right to the killing, then?"

Flinching inwardly at the man's amused words, Aric cleared his throat, searching his mind for a question he could ask—any question that might delay whatever the bishop had planned long enough for Aric to come up with a way out of this. "I take it, then, that you were the one behind the attacks? First in the bedchamber, then—?"

"That was a mistake," Shrewsbury interrupted almost absently, peering down at the knife he was holding and running one finger along the edge of the blade.

"A mistake? What mean you by that?" Aric arched an eyebrow questioningly as he ever so slowly began to pull at the ropes binding his wrists. If he could loosen them without alerting the other man—

"Just what I said; 'twas a mistake."

"Do you mean you mistakenly thought I was in the bedchamber the night you entered and Black attacked you?" he asked, remembering Rosamunde's suggestion to that effect.

"No." The bishop smiled wryly. "I knew you were still below. I meant to attack Rosamunde and kill her in your bed."

"But why?" he asked with real confusion. "I thought you were fond of her."

"Oh, I am. And that is why I thought it best to kill her."

"You thought it best to kill her because you are fond of her?" Aric asked in disbelief.

"Exactly." Shrewsbury nodded with satisfaction. "I thought to save her."

Aric stared at him incredulously. "By killing her?" When the other man nodded, Aric shook his head. "What did you think to save her from?"

"Why, from you, of course. Just as I saved her mother from Henry. I could do nothing less than save the daughter from you." Sighing, he moved down to the end of the bed. He abruptly changed the subject. "This was her cottage. The fair Rosamunde's. Charming, is it not? I thought it a fitting place to end this."

Shrewsbury began moving slowly around the room, dragging his knife lightly over tabletops and chairs, any surface available, scraping it along the wood and kicking up small dust clouds as he went. "Rosamunde loved it here. She really had no wish or desire to live in the castle. She used to say that it was full of wolves and vultures, that there was not a moment of peace or privacy there. She preferred it here."

Pausing beside the bed once more, Shrewsbury stared down at Aric for a moment, his gaze becoming clouded. "This is where they fornicated. Henry and my fair Rosamunde. I can still see them in my mind's eye. Henry was younger then. Strong, tall, and lean. And

Rosamunde . . . ah. Rosamunde was a beauty. So much loveliness, it nearly hurt to look upon her. She was perfection."

His mouth twisting with disgust, he said with a sneer, "And Henry had to sully that, of course. Had to lay his grimy hands on her pure skin. Cover her with his sweaty, panting body. Fill her with his tainted seed."

Aric watched warily as the bishop clenched his hand around the hilt of the dagger he held, his teeth grinding together in impotent rage. A pulse was throbbing in his forehead, and his face was flushed with fury. Suddenly he burst out in a voice filled with outrage, "And she *let* him! Worse yet, she *liked* it!"

Aric stiffened as Shrewsbury furiously stabbed the dagger into the bed's surface mere inches from his hip, as if he were stabbing at the woman in his memory. "She would mewl, and cry, and *writhe* on this bed! Her body covered with nothing but firelight and his flesh, she would *beg* him for more as he pounded into her."

Straightening abruptly, he shrugged matter-of-factly, his rage gone as quickly as it had come. "They were both no better than animals."

Aric blinked, unable to keep up with the sudden shift from rabid rage to nonchalance. It was madness. Insanity. The bishop was deranged. He had figured that out a bit earlier, of course, when the man had been claiming he had tried to kill Rosamunde to save her, but he had not realized the depth of the madness then. Now he did, and he knew he was in trouble. He began to work harder at his bindings, a little less concerned with whether Shrewsbury realized he was doing so or not.

"It is amazing that your wife turned out as well as she did, considering she is the daughter of the fair Rosamunde and Henry. They called him 'spawn of the Devil,' you know. Actually, he liked to call himself that, too. He would say it rather proudly."

"Is that why you wanted to kill her? Because she was their daughter?" Aric asked, straining against the ropes and sawing his wrists back and forth within them, ignoring the burning pain it caused.

"Nay, of course not." Bishop Shrewsbury frowned at him. "I already told you that I was trying to save her. The bad blood she inherited from Henry had nothing to do with it. In fact, I had high hopes for Rosamunde all along. I was very proud of her when the message arrived announcing that she was going to take the veil. She will make a lovely nun."

"She will not be a nun," Aric said grimly. Sweat was beginning to bead on his forehead, and he could feel blood trickling down his wrist where the skin had been rubbed raw, but the bindings seemed looser. "She did not take the veil. She married me."

"Aye. More's the pity." He scowled. "I did all I could to prevent that. I kept the abbess's message from the king. I used every excuse possible to delay his getting to the abbey in time. But then he learned that you had broken your betrothal and were at Shambley—he decided on you rather than Rosshuen for the girl's husband. It shaved a whole day off the journey. He got there in time. He forced her to marry you. And you, in turn, forced her to enjoy your touch."

Aric stilled at that in surprise and the other man nodded.

"Yes. I know all about that. The disgusting things you did to her. The things you made her do to you. That was not bad enough, however." Anger and outrage flared in his eyes again. "Aside from subjecting her to such base behavior, you had to *order* her to enjoy it. I heard and saw it all in the stables. Thank

God," he added grimly, with a pious glance upward as he crossed himself. Then, shaking his head, he sighed and stared at Aric again. "Up until then I had thought that to save her, I had to put her at peace as I had her mother. But of course, that was not what God wanted at all."

He frowned, slightly distracted again. "I should have realized that sooner, I fear. He gave me several hints. First Black was in your room that night; then that stupid bull refused to trounce her. Your horse could have been happenstance, but with that vicious bull not attacking her, what else could it be but God intervening?"

What else? It could be Rosamunde, Aric thought with a sad smile. She seemed able to tame the wildest beast with a mere touch and kind word . . . or an apple. She had tamed him, after all. But he didn't dare say as much to Shrewsbury. He was not at all certain he could get himself out of this fix, and if he did not, he would rather die thinking that Rosamunde, at least, would be safe from this madman's murderous attentions.

"Then, in the stables," the bishop went on. "I knocked the bale down, intending to climb down and finish her, then place her in one of the horses' stalls to make it appear that the beast had gone mad. But, she got out of the way. Still, she started to climb the ladder then, and I thought it would work out after all . . . but then you arrived, preventing my finishing her off. Ruining everything again, I thought. But I was mistaken.

"I realized it after that animalistic display you gave me. I saw it *all*," he repeated with disgust. "God wanted me to see it. He wanted me to hear you order her to enjoy it. He wanted me to know that it was not her fault at all, but that it was yours."

"What was my fault?" Aric muttered distractedly,

glancing toward his wrists to see that the rope was indeed loosening. Not enough for him to slip free yet, but it *was* loosening.

"Her enjoying the bedding!" Shrewsbury snapped, then explained, "When she admitted to me that she enjoyed your touch in bed, that she no longer desired to return to the abbey, I thought it was because she was like her mother: a fallen angel, a whore, a sinner. But then I heard you order her to enjoy it, and I saw you take her there in the stables like an animal. I understood that she did not *really* enjoy it, but that you ordered her to."

The bishop sighed, shaking his head sadly. "My God, the humiliation she must suffer every time you touch her. But she has to claim to enjoy it. She vowed to obey you, and you had given her an order. Well, that is when I realized. I was not meant to kill her, but you."

"Of course," Aric said without much enthusiasm.

"Aye. Once you are dead, she will return to the abbey and the life she was meant for," he said firmly, then paused to tap the tip of the dagger against his chin thoughtfully. "I wonder now if I should not have killed Henry rather than her mother. I fear I may have erred there, as well." He looked briefly worried over that, then shook his head. "Ah, well, He will forgive me my mistakes."

"He will forgive yours, but no one else's, then? Is that how it is?" Aric and Shrewsbury both peered sharply toward the door at those harsh words, to gape at the woman standing there.

Rosamunde filled the entrance to the small cottage like an avenging angel. Sunlight was pouring through the door behind her, surrounding her in a golden glow and setting her hair afire. She was magnificent . . . and Aric could have throttled her. She was supposed to be waiting safely in their chamber, but was she? Nay. Here she was, gallivanting about court and setting herself in harm's way.

Rosamunde took in the situation at a glance. She had arrived at the clearing around the cottage a few moments ago. Old and neglected, the building had not looked inhabited, but she had decided to check it anyway.

She had heard Bishop Shrewsbury's calm voice announcing his intentions to burn Aric alive as she had reached the door. Her heart pounding violently in her chest, Rosamunde had stood just out of sight, beside the door, and listened to the conversation inside as she had considered her options. Running back to the castle for help had been out of the question. She had feared her husband would be dead ere she could return with assistance.

That had meant she was his only hope. Her. An unarmed female, against an armed madman. The odds had not looked favorable. Straightening her shoulders, she had silently berated herself for the fatalistic thinking. This was one time when she could not afford to fail. This time she had to do it right. Turning away from the door, she had peered about the overgrown clearing for a weapon. She had her dagger, but it was small and dull with use; it would be of little use in this situation. She needed a real weapon. But nothing had looked very useful to her as she had peered around the clearing. A small rock. A stick. Lots of brush . . .

Then her eyes had fallen on a tree stump several feet away from the door of the cottage and the small ax embedded in the top of it. It was a rusty old ax, probably as dull as a mallet, but even that would be better than nothing. Leaving the door, she had hurried to the stump and managed to remove the ax with some effort. Then she had quickly hurried back to her position beside the doorway to listen to Shrewsbury talk while she examined her weapon.

It was old, rusty, and—as she had expected—terribly dull. But it was also solid and heavy and, despite its dullness, would do some definite damage if swung at someone. Rosamunde intended on doing just that. Lowering her hand, she had held the weapon against her side, then leaned forward to peer around the door frame to get an idea of the layout of the cottage. Relief had flowed through her as she had spied Aric on the bed. Despite being tied down, he was unharmed . . . so far. She had drunk in the sight of him for longer than she should have, then had scanned the rest of the interior. The cabin held an old and rather small table, large enough only for two, a chair, the remains of a second chair, a fireplace, and Shrewsbury. Other than that it was just dirt and debris.

Rosamunde had considered creeping up on their foe and smashing him over the head as he raved, but the dirt and debris on the floor had scotched that idea. Shrewsbury's own movements were accompanied by the rustle of leaves and various other items that littered the cottage. It would be impossible for Rosamunde to approach in her skirts without making some sound and drawing his attention. That took away the possibility of a sneak attack—but not of a surprise attack, if she could keep the ax close to her side and hidden by her skirts.

And so she had chosen her moment and entered, her weapon concealed at her side. Now both men gaped at her. She glimpsed the shock, anger, and fear for her on Aric's face, but ignored it to focus on Shrewsbury.

"I heard it all, my lord," she said now accusingly. "How could you?"

"I did it for you. I was trying to save you." Shrewsbury gasped, stumbling across the room toward her. "I gave you the potion to show you the error of your way."

"Potion?" Rosamunde frowned at him and shifted away from him as he approached. "Error of my ways?"

"Aye. The potion is what made you ill. I was trying to show you that you are not meant for Henry! You are too good for him, my dear. Far too good to allow him to taint you."

Rosamunde continued to sidestep, staying out of his grasp and moving slowly closer to where Aric lay tugging frantically at his bindings. Her mind was racing as she moved. Shrewsbury was not just mad; he was confusing her with her mother. She began to consider how she could use that as he continued to stalk her around the cottage.

"You were meant to be a bride of God. Only He is worthy of you. And I tried to show you that. The potion is slow-acting, and I thought that if I gave it to you every time you were here, with Henry, and you became ill every time you were with him, you would realize that he was no good for you. And it seemed to work after a while. You reconsidered your life, went to Godstow, had your child, and even decided to take the veil."

He paused, a frown scourging his face again. "But then Henry . . . always Henry! He came to you and talked of marriage and raising the child together. I saw that you were wavering," he said with bitter disgust. "You wanted him even then. Despite your pledge to God. You still loved and wanted *him*. You would have returned. I saw it all, so I had to . . ." Confusion replaced his rage and bitterness suddenly as he stared at Rosamunde and whispered in bewilderment, "I killed you."

"Aye. You killed me," Rosamunde agreed slowly. "But God sent me back to tell you that you were wrong. And to prevent you from repeating your mistake." She eased another step closer to the bed and Aric, digging out her dirk with her free hand as she went. If she could slip that to Aric without Shrewsbury realizing it, it might help him to free himself.

"Wrong?" Shrewsbury didn't look pleased at that thought.

"Aye," Rosamunde assured him firmly. "You are not supposed to kill Aric. That is why the drowning in the river and the pin in Black's saddle failed. Aric and Rosamunde are supposed to remain married."

"Aric?" He looked confused for a moment, then peered blankly at the man he had tied to the bed and muttered, "Oh, aye." Then his eyes widened and he gasped in horror. "Oh, nay. Nay! That cannot be. They will bear fruit and spread their devil-spawn across the land. Nay." Straightening abruptly, he shook his head. "Nay. That was not God intervening again, 'twas Satan."

Wonderful! Rosamunde thought impatiently. God stopping his attacks on her he could believe, but God stopping his attacks on Aric he could not? That *had* to be Satan's work. She was so put out by his reasoning that she almost missed the fact that she had moved close enough to the bed to slip Aric her dirk. She quickly did so now.

"Aye, it was Satan interfering. And he probably sent you here to tempt me again," Shrewsbury charged bitterly, drawing her attention back to him. "Always to tempt me. To tempt me to give up my own vows as you did yours. To tempt me to be a sinner like you. To tempt me to—"

"Oh, stuff it, Bishop," Rosamunde snapped, her

patience with the drivel he was spouting breaking now that she had gotten the dirk to Aric.

Rosamunde had inherited her father's temper along with his hair color. And after the stress and strain of the last couple of months—leaving the abbey, the only home she had ever known, adjusting to married life, her husband's jealous outbursts, her father's death, and the attacks on herself and then on Aric—she was understandably frazzled. Or had been. Today's events had, unfortunately, pushed her past frazzled to furious. Rosamunde felt as if she had aged ten years in just this one morning. Between the fear and anxiety she had suffered while Aric was missing, and her outrage and pain as she had waited outside the cottage listening to Shrewsbury not only confess to murdering her mother, but call her everything from sinner to whore on top of that. Frankly, she had had enough, and the temper her father had been infamous for was rearing its ugly red head.

Shrewsbury blinked at her briefly, then drew himself up. "I—"

"I do not want to hear it!" Rosamunde interrupted sharply. "I am sick unto death of listening to you go on about what a sinner my mother was and how she tempted you! She was not the sinner. You are!" She grimaced with distaste. "Standing about outside the cottage and gawking in here, watching them in their intimate moments like some depraved satyr! It probably excited you, spying on them like that. But that was not my mother's fault!"

"She—" Shrewsbury began, flushing bright red, but Rosamunde interrupted him again.

"She loved my father. She was not some whore who bedded everyone; she loved only my father. And you killed her. Murdered her. And even *I*, daughter of

'Rosamunde the whore' and Henry the 'spawn of the devil,' know that *that* is a sin. You are the one who is Satan's agent!"

Sick of even looking at the man now, Rosamunde whirled on her husband impatiently. "Have you not gotten yourself untied yet?"

Aric blinked as he gazed up at her. Her face was flushed, her eyes spitting fire, her chest heaving with her anger. In short, she was magnificent. And while he had managed to cut through the bonds of one wrist by holding the knife awkwardly between it and his flesh, it was slow going.

"Almost," he told her, holding his free hand up for her to see.

"Well, hurry—" Rosamunde began, her words ending in a gasp of surprise as Aric suddenly used his free hand to thrust her aside. Distracted though she was by trying to keep her feet, Rosamunde did catch a glimpse of the problem as she stumbled toward the end of the bed. Aric had been pushing her out of the way of a lunging Shrewsbury. Catching herself on the bottom bedpost, she glanced back in time to see Aric roll toward his still-bound hand and out of the way of the bishop's dagger. It slashed harmlessly into the bed, but his thrust had been meant for her, she realized. Her hand tightened on the ax still hidden in her skirts as she watched Shrewsbury straighten and whirl toward her.

He looked pretty mad. The angry kind, not just the crazy kind, Rosamunde thought, some of her anger slipping away, replaced by momentary fear.

"Go," Aric shouted at her, sawing furiously at his still-bound hand with the dirk she had given him. "Get out of here, Rosamunde! Run!"

Rosamunde's fear fled as quickly as it had come at her husband's bellow. He did like to bellow a lot, she thought irritably. And he enjoyed ordering her about far too much. And just exactly what sort of woman did he take her for if he thought she should flee, leaving him here tied up and helpless? Well, half-tied, anyway, she corrected herself as his second hand came free and he sat up, reaching to start working on the ropes around his ankles. He was her husband. They were a team, in this together, she thought with satisfaction, raising the ax she had been shielding with her skirts and grimly facing Shrewsbury.

The bishop froze as he saw the weapon, his gaze shooting to the dagger he held. Apparently he didn't like the odds, for he stumbled to the side suddenly, and Rosamunde was just feeling triumph rise within her, thinking he was fleeing, when he stopped at the fireplace and grabbed a log. Picking it up by an end that was not yet ablaze, he held it up, smiling at the torch he now held.

"Wonderful," Rosamunde muttered as he started toward her.

"Jesu!" she heard Aric say as he paused in his sawing to glance around. "Rosamunde! My sword!"

"Well, at least he has stopped trying to get me to leave," she muttered under her breath, eyeing Shrewsbury as he approached.

"My sword, Rosamunde! Grab my sword!"

"I am a bit busy at the moment, husband," she snapped tartly, then dove to the side as Shrewsbury swung his torch at her head. The fiery club slammed into the bed post, its flames catching at the bed drapes. Old, withered, and shredded with time, the cloth went up with a whoosh. Flames quickly shot upward, encompassing all of the drapes above the bed even as it started a slow, but still dangerous descent toward the bed and Aric, who had freed one leg but was still working on his other.

Distracted by her worry for her husband, Rosamunde was too slow to get out of the way of Shrewsbury's next blow. It was only her instincts that saved her. Raising the ax, she used it to block the blow, wincing as the torch and the ax met in the air in front of her face and sparks flew in all directions. They bit at her hands and face, and burned holes into her gown. Ignoring the stinging pain, Rosamunde concentrated on the matter at hand as Shrewsbury pulled the torch away and swung again. This time he brought it down toward her head.

Crying out, Rosamunde shifted her hands on the ax as she raised it, holding each end in one hand as she again blocked the blow. Again there were sparks, but this time they showered down over her like rain. Painful rain. Closing her eyes, she turned her face away, then forced herself just as quickly to look at him again as she felt the weight of the torch lift from her ax. He was swinging back for another blow, she saw, and grimly prepared to meet it. But it never came. Just as he started to bring it forward, his chest seemed to shudder, his eyes widened incredulously, and his burning cudgel then slid from his fingers to the ground. In the next moment, he had collapsed to the ground atop it, and Rosamunde was left staring at Aric.

Lifting his gaze from the dead man, he met her eyes as he lowered his bloodied sword. Stepping forward, he caught her close and pressed his face into her neck. "Oh, God, Rosamunde, if he had killed you—" Pulling back slightly, he cut his own words off by covering her mouth with his and kissing her desperately.

It was beginning to get a tad hot in the cottage by the time he broke the kiss. They both glanced around to see that the bed was completely in flames, the fire spreading quickly across the floor. Added to that, Bishop

Shrewsbury had landed upon the log he had used as a weapon, and the lit end and his dry robes had made him a human torch.

"Come. Let us get out of here." Holding her close to his side, he guided her quickly from the cottage and out into the fresh air.

"Aric!"

Moving a safe distance away from the burning building, Aric and Rosamunde watched Robert Shambley and Lord Burkhart hurry from the trees and rush forward to meet them.

"Thank God you are all right!" Lord Burkhart said, pausing before them and looking them both over quickly before turning to frown at the inferno the cottage had become. "What happened?"

Aric shrugged the question away. "I shall explain later. How did you find us?"

His father turned back with a grimace. "Well, when I told Rosamunde that I had seen you heading out into the gardens with the bishop, that news seemed to upset her. She rushed off before I could ask why, but I had a bad feeling, so I deposited your sisters back in their rooms and sought out Shambley."

"We had no clue where to look at first," Shambley continued. "We were checking every path until we saw the smoke rising over the trees. We knew instinctively then that if we found the source of the fire, we would find the two of you. Trouble does appear to follow you lately," he pointed out wryly as Aric arched an eyebrow in question.

"Aye, it has seemed to," he agreed with a sigh, then glanced down at Rosamunde. He hugged her a little closer before adding, "But no more."

Shambley's eyes widened at the way the couple smiled at each other, then frowned as he noticed his friend's raw wrists. "What happened?" he asked; then his eyes widened. "Where is Bishop Shrewsbury?"

Aric glanced toward the inferno that used to be the cottage. "In there."

"In there?" Robert followed his gaze, shook his head slowly, then glanced sharply back toward Aric. "Surely he was not truly behind all the trouble?"

"Aye. He was. The man was quite mad." Aric shook his head and opened his mouth to say more, but paused when his gaze landed on Rosamunde and he noticed the small burn holes in her gown and the small blisters freckling her hands and face. "I shall explain it all later," he decided. "For now, I think I should get Rosamunde back to our chamber. She has had quite enough excitement today."

He started to usher her back toward the castle then, but they had just reached the edge of the trees when Aric's father called out. Glancing back to see the older man hurrying after them, they paused to wait for him.

"Son," the older man began as he reached them, then grimaced. "I need to talk to you about something. Something that has been bothering me."

"Can it not wait?" Aric asked with a frown.

"Aye, but I am afraid you will hear the truth before I can explain," he said unhappily. Rosamunde placed a hand gently on Aric's arm, drawing his gaze.

"It is all right," she murmured. "I am fine."

Nodding, Aric glanced back to Lord Burkhart. "What is it, Father?"

"Well . . ." Shifting uncomfortably, he sighed. "It is about all I told you about your mother."

Aric arched his eyebrows. "Aye?"

"Aye." Lord Burkhart grimaced again, then confessed, "Well, I thought at the time that what I said was for the best, but it has occurred to me since that you may hear the truth elsewhere." Sighing, he shook his head. "About your mother—"

"Father," Aric interrupted quietly. "It does not matter."

"Nay?" Lord Burkhart looked uncertain.

"Nay. Whatever she did, she is dead now. Rosamunde is not my mother. Nor is she Delia. Confusing her with other women was my mistake. Rosamunde is *Rosamunde*. A gift to me from God and our king. And I shall treasure her until the end of my days."

"Oh," Rosamunde said softly, tears sparkling in her eyes.

"I see." Lord Burkhart cleared his throat and turned away to blink rapidly against a suspicious moisture in his eyes. He watched Shambley walk toward them, then murmured, "Well, I am glad to hear it, son. Rosamunde is a jewel, and I am proud of you for not allowing the past to affect your future."

"Who are you talking to?" Robert asked curiously as he reached his side.

Burkhart scowled at the younger man, then turned to gesture toward Aric and his young wife. The couple was gone. They had left while his back was turned.

"Never mind," he muttered, starting toward the trees now himself. "Come, we should inform someone of the bishop's death—and get someone to put out that fire."

"I do not think your father was quite finished," Rosamunde murmured as Aric rushed her back through the gardens.

"Aye, well, he can finish later." Pausing as they reached the castle, he opened the door, then urged her inside and toward their room. Both of them remained silent until they had reached their chamber. Aric ushered her inside, then turned to close the door. When he turned around, it was to find Rosamunde digging around in her bags.

"Sit you on the bed," she instructed as she straightened with a small bag in hand.

Aric hesitated briefly by the door, then shrugged and moved to do as she said, settling himself and waiting patiently as she poured water from a pitcher into a bowl, then dipped a cloth in it and moved toward him.

"Now hold out your arms," she ordered, setting the bowl on the floor at his feet and taking one of the hands he held out to begin cleaning his wounds.

Aric watched her work, noting her frown with interest. "What are you thinking?"

Her mouth tightened slightly. "I am thinking it is a good thing that the bishop is dead, else I would surely rake him over the coals for this," she muttered as she finished cleaning the wrist and began to wrap it. "Does it hurt very much?"

"Not much at all," he assured her with gentle amusement as she turned her attention to the other wrist. "What of you?"

Her eyes slid to his in surprise. "Me? What do you mean?"

Using his free hand he gently brushed her cheek, running a finger over the small sprinkling of red spots and blisters there from the sparks from Shrewsbury's torch. "Do they hurt?"

"Nay." She shook her head, concentrating again on his wrist. "They shall heal quickly."

"As will my wrists," he murmured, grabbing her hands as she finished bandaging him and would have moved away.

Still clutching the now bloodstained cloth she had used to clean the wounds on his wrists, Rosamunde peered at him questioningly.

"You disobeyed me . . . again," he said quietly, and Rosamunde's eyes widened at the solemn pronouncement, then narrowed warily as he went on. "I distinctly recall telling you to wait here in the room for my return. But you did not do that, did you?"

"Oh, well, . . ." Rosamunde's gaze began dancing around the room behind where he sat, but jerked back to him when he drew her between his legs until her knees bumped against the bed.

"Nay," he interrupted firmly. "You did not do what I asked."

Reaching up, he began to undo the ties of her gown. "Instead you left the room and came in search of me, even managing to save my life in the process. And for that . . ." He finished with her stays and slid one hand behind her neck to draw her head down toward him.

"For that I am eternally grateful," he whispered against her lips, then covered her mouth with his own, kissing her at first with gentle tenderness, then with a passion that built quickly to consume them both. Rosamunde was vaguely aware of his hands skimming down over her breasts, across her stomach, then lower over her hips and down the outside of her legs. It wasn't until his hands slid their way back up, his callused fingers caressing her bare flesh, that she realized that he had been removing her gown and undertunic.

Shuddering under his touch, she moaned into his mouth, her own hands moving to his shoulders to brace her weight. His hand caught and cupped one breast as his tongue delved into her mouth. Pulling his lips away, he kissed a wet trail down her neck, then dropped suddenly to lave the nipple of the breast he cupped. Then he breathed the words, "Thank you for saving my life."

His words were spoken against her wet skin, his breath warming the damp flesh and making her shudder. Opening her eyes, she watched him continue to lave her breast, then caught her fingers in his hair and urged his head away. When his eyes opened and he peered up at her, she said softly, "Thank you for saving my life, too."

Smiling, he stood and pulled her into his arms, pressing his body against hers as he again covered her mouth with his own, his lips strong and searching, until they were both panting and breathless. His hand suddenly dipped between her legs and found her warm, wet heat. She gasped.

"I need you," he said gruffly against her mouth, then moved his lips to her ear and nibbled there briefly. "Until you arrived in the cottage, I thought I was a dead man. That I would never hold you again, never touch you, taste you—"

"Hush," Rosamunde murmured gently, hugging him tightly and closing her eyes as his fingers began to move, stimulating a rather urgent sensation inside her. "Husband, I—" she began a bit breathlessly, then moaned as he slid a finger inside her, stretching her gently.

"Aye?"

Rosamunde curled her fingers into his tunic, her head turning into the nibbling kisses he was applying to her ear, even as she shifted into his caressing hand. "You have too many clothes on," she muttered in frustration, tugging at the tunic.

"It is a sin to fornicate unclothed, wife," he teased, then groaned when her hand found him through the cloth of his brais. She squeezed gently at first, then with a stronger grip. "Do that again and I shall—" He bit his words off when she did so again.

"You shall what?" she taunted, aware of her effect.

He grew firm and bulged against the cloth of his brais.

Growling, Aric bit her ear gently, then used his free hand to push at his brais until his swollen flesh sprang free. Her hand closed around him at once, sliding along its length like a sheath.

"I feared I had lost you, too," Rosamunde admitted suddenly, her grasp tightening. "I thought—"

"Shhh," Aric murmured, ensuring her silence by covering her mouth again. He caught her around the waist and lifted her slightly, taking her down onto the bed with him. Nudging her legs apart again, he brushed her hand away and took himself in hand as he shifted between her legs. He brushed himself against her, making her groan.

"I need you inside me," she said in a moan, wrapping her legs around his hips and attempting to pull him nearer. "Now."

Aric gave a husky, breathless laugh. "You are a demanding wench, wife." He rubbed himself against her again, then slid into her, covering her joyful cry with his mouth as he did. He kissed her passionately as he withdrew and thrust into her once more, driving himself into her again and again until at last they cried out and found their release.

Several moments later, Aric opened his eyes and peered at the woman in his arms, then down at himself. She was as naked as the day she had been born.

"I am still dressed," he murmured with wry amusement.

"Hmmm," Rosamunde murmured, beginning to pluck at the cloth of his tunic absently. "We should attend to that."

Smiling, Aric pulled his arm from beneath her and sat up to remove his tunic.

Shifting to lie watching him, Rosamunde murmured, "Husband?"

"Aye?" he asked, tossing the shirt to the floor before slipping his legs off the bed and setting to work at removing his brais. They had barely made it off his hips.

"You are not angry that I disobeyed you about leaving the room, are you." It wasn't really a question—it was more a statement of fact—but Aric glanced at her and answered anyway.

"Nay, of course not. You saved my life."

"Hmmm." Rosamunde was silent as he stepped out of his brais, then asked hopefully, "Does that mean that I am released from my vow to always obey you, my lord?"

Snorting, Aric straightened, brais in hand, and pointed out with amusement, "You haven't *always* been obeying me anyway."

"Aye," she agreed wryly. "But I *have* felt guilty every time I disobeyed."

Laughing, Aric tossed his brais on the floor with his shirt and crawled back into bed. Settling on his back, he pulled her into his arms again. "You have, have you?" he asked with amusement. When she nodded her head and peered up at him unhappily, he managed a solemn expression. "Well, we cannot have that, can we?"

Rosamunde shook her head.

"Well, then, I release you from that vow, so long as you keep the other."

She stilled at that, and he could see the frown plucking at her brow even before she asked uncertainly, "What other vow?"

"To love me," Aric said softly, and she melted against him, her gaze softening on his face.

"Oh, aye, my lord husband," she whispered, meeting

his gaze clearly. "I vow to keep that one. I shall love you. Always."

"And I shall love you always, too," Aric swore. A smile was tugging at his lips even before he pulled her face up for a kiss; then he began to make love to her again.

Keep reading for a sneak peek at
Lynsay Sands' new Argeneau novel,
ABOUT A VAMPIRE
Available now from Avon Books

CRAP," Holly muttered, staring down at the sheaf of papers she'd just stepped on. The small disc stapled to the top corner told her that it was the paperwork for one of their clients. It included the burial permit, the coroner's certificate, the application for cremation and the coversheet with the client's name and info . . . and it should have been given to John Byron when he arrived to start his shift at 4:30 that afternoon. Obviously, it hadn't. This bundle must have fallen off her desk at some point that day.

Holly continued to stand there for several seconds, simply staring at the bundle. She didn't even remove her foot, because once she did, she'd have to do something about it . . . like take it to the crematorium . . . and she really didn't want to go down there. Not at this hour. Making the trek during the day was one thing, but it was just past midnight now. She'd have to make her way through the graveyard to get to the building that housed the chapel; the columbarium, where the urns rested; and the crematorium, where the bodies were stored and waiting for their turn at the retort.

Retorts is what the owner of Sunnyside Cemetery, Max, had called them when he'd given her the tour the day she'd started. He could call them what he liked, but *retort* was just a fancy word for the oven where they burned the bodies.

Shuddering at the thought of the coffins shelved in the cooler, Holly closed her eyes briefly. A popular game here seemed to be to freak out the new worker with tales of the "ovens." Jerry, the day technician, and John, who took the evening shift, as well as her boss, Max, and even Sheila, the receptionist, had all told her one horrific tale or another. But the most memorable was John telling her how the coffins burned away first and the corpses sometimes sat up inside the oven, muscles contracting in the heat and mouths agape as if screaming in horror at their doom. That image had stuck with her, convincing Holly she really didn't want to be cremated. In fact, she'd decided dying was to be avoided at all costs if possible.

Sighing, she opened her eyes and peered at the papers, wishing she could pretend she hadn't seen them. After all, in the normal course of events, she wouldn't have found them until morning. She shouldn't be here now except she'd got home after work, made dinner and looked for her purse to get her blood tester to check her sugar levels, but hadn't been able to find it. Thinking she'd probably left her purse in the car and not wanting dinner to get cold, she'd decided the blood test could wait. Of course, by the time dinner was finished, she'd forgotten all about it . . . until she was brushing her teeth before bed. She'd been halfway done when she'd remembered.

Pulling on her trench coat over her pajamas, Holly had hustled out to the car in her slippers to retrieve her purse . . . only it hadn't been there either. That had stymied her briefly, and she'd stood in the cold garage for several moments, trying to think where it might be.

She'd had it at work when she'd paid Sheila for lunch, Holly recalled. She then tried to bring up a memory of slinging it over her shoulder as she left work, but instead remembered that her hands had been full of tax forms and receipts . . . no purse. Holly hadn't noticed at the time because her car keys had been in her coat pocket.

After wasting another few minutes debating whether she could just skip testing that night, she'd slouched with resignation and got in the car to drive back to work. Missing one test once in a while wasn't that bad, but skipping two in a row wasn't good. Besides, the cemetery was only a ten-minute drive from her home. It simply wasn't worth risking a diabetic coma.

Of course, Holly thought now, if she'd realized that coming back would mean having to make a trek through the graveyard—in her pajamas no less—she might have risked the coma.

Grimacing, she bent and snatched up the papers. There was nothing for it, she would have to drop them off before heading home. Otherwise, the cremation wouldn't happen until tomorrow or the next day, which could be a problem depending on when his service was scheduled to take place.

Clasping the papers firmly in one hand, Holly slung her purse over her shoulder with the other. But as she headed out of the office, she couldn't help thinking that life would be a lot easier if she were a little less conscientious. Being a responsible-type person was really a pain in the ass at times, she thought as she stepped outside and dug her keys out of her pocket.

The funeral-home key was easy to find despite the dark night; it was on its own ring. It was also shiny and new, though that was hard to tell in this light. She'd only received it last Friday. It was now Monday. Why did a brand-new and temporary employee have a key to the company? The answer to that was simple enough: because her coworkers weren't as conscientious and responsible as she was. During her first week there, Max hadn't shown up much before noon even once, and Sheila, the receptionist who also happened to be Max's daughter, had been late three times. The apple really hadn't fallen far from the tree with those two.

On Friday, after twiddling her thumbs in the funeral-home parking lot for over an hour and a half for the third morning that week, Holly had let some of her irritation show when Sheila finally arrived. She'd also suggested that perhaps she should start later in the day rather than waste her time and their money sitting in the parking lot waiting. Sheila had what she considered to be a better solution—she'd gone out and had a key made for her. Now Holly could get in on time.

She'd like to believe that it was her conscientiousness and responsible nature that had led Sheila to give her the key, but knew the truth was it was pure laziness and convenience. So long as Holly had a key and could open the office on time, Sheila could be as late as she liked. The other woman had proven that today, when she hadn't shown up until lunchtime, and then it was with lunch for them both that Holly hadn't wanted but had paid her back for her half anyway.

Holly locked the door and turned to glance toward the crematorium, only to pause and frown when she couldn't see the building. It was the fog. It had made driving here something of a pain, but she'd forgotten about it while in the building. Now, she found herself staring into the misty darkness surrounding her and felt a little shiver of anxiety shimmy its way up her spine.

She was in a graveyard on a dark and foggy moonless night. This was way too much like a scene from a horror movie. Any minute decomposing corpses would begin to claw their way out of the ground and drag themselves toward her, lured by the scent of fresh flesh.

"Get a grip," Holly muttered to herself.

The sound of her own voice in the night was a bit bracing, but not enough to make her move in the direction of the crematorium.

Holly shuffled her slippered feet briefly, and then sighed and turned to unlock the door again. Perhaps there was an umbrella or something in the office that she could carry with her. Having a weapon, even a mostly useless one, might help boost her courage for the trek ahead.

When a quick search of the offices didn't turn up an umbrella, a cane, or a flame thrower to fend off those imagined zombie corpses, Holly resorted to grabbing a large pair of scissors she spotted sticking out of the pencil holder on the reception desk. She hefted them briefly, considered their size and then decided they would do. She probably wouldn't need anything anyway. She was just being a ninny, but felt better clutching the scissors as she headed back outside.

Sadly, there had been no helpful gust of wind to sweep away the fog during the few minutes she'd been inside. If anything, it seemed to her that the fog had thickened, but that might have simply been her own anxiety making it seem that way. It had probably been just as thick earlier as it was now, she reassured herself and wished she had a flashlight.

The thought made her glance toward the parking lot. She kept a flashlight in the glove compartment for emergencies. Holly hurried to her car, unlocked it and settled in the passenger seat to open the glove compartment and make a quick search. Not finding it, she sat back with a sigh, then grabbed the papers and the scissors and got out. She left her purse inside. It would eliminate the possibility of accidentally leaving it behind in the crematorium, she thought as she locked the door.

Trying not to think of movies like *The Fog* or *Night of the Living Dead*, Holly headed determinedly in the direction of the crematorium. She moved as quickly as she dared along the paved path, her ears straining for any sound that might indicate she wasn't alone. Now that she was resigned to the task, getting it over with and getting back home was all she cared about. It was always better to get unpleasant tasks done quickly.

Unfortunately, it did seem that the unpleasant tasks often took the most time. She knew it was probably just her fear and anxiety, but the walk to the crematorium seemed to be taking much longer than it should. Holly actually began to worry that she'd headed in the wrong direction in the fog and lost her way, that she could be wandering the graveyard in her pajamas until the sun rose to burn away the fog, so was relieved when she spotted the weak glow of a light ahead. Knowing it must be the wall sconce over the building entrance, Holly headed for it at a faster clip, relieved when she was able to see the door beneath it.

Holly released a little pent-up breath of relief once she slipped inside. She'd made it, alive and well and un-molested by rotting corpses.

"Awesome," she said, and grimaced at how weak her voice sounded in the dimly lit entryway. Giving herself a little shake, Holly started forward, moving quickly past the doors to both chapels and through the columbarium with its niche banks full of urns. Some were visible be-hind glass, some were hidden by brass plates with names and dates on them, and a lot had flowers and whatnot stuck in special holders on or beside them. Her gaze skated to the floral tributes and then determinedly away as she passed. Holly used to love flowers, but two weeks of working here had changed that. She now associated flowers with death.

She should have been more relaxed now that she was inside. After all, the urns held only the ashes of the dead, which couldn't spontaneously form into bodies to clamber after her in search of brains, but Holly found herself still anxious and jumpy. It didn't take much thought to figure out why. She was about to head into the crematorium itself, where coffins holding the newly departed waited to be burned.

During that tour on her first day working here, the process of cremation had been explained to her in fine detail. Definitely more than she'd wanted to know, but apparently, the fact that she was a temp in the office to work on the taxes and wasn't a sales associate didn't remove the possibility of her having to explain things to customers. Holly hoped to God that never happened, because she would not want to explain those details to the loved ones of the newly deceased. It had all seemed gruesome to her.

Holly had never really thought much about cremation, but if she had, she would have assumed that the coffin was rolled into the retort, flames shot out and poof, a nice urn of ashes came out the other end. Not so. First of all, it took much longer than she'd imagined. Despite reaching temperatures of 1600 or 1700 degrees, the actual cremation could take two to three hours. And no neat little urn of ashes came out at the end. The ashes, which weren't all ashes, remained in the retort to cool, and then a magnet was used to remove anything metal such as fillings and pins. Once cooled, the ashes were swept out onto a tray using a corn broom as if the remains were so much debris on the floor. They were then allowed to cool further before being placed into a cremulator, which looked much like a garbage disposal unit to Holly when she'd peered inside. There the remains, including some bone that didn't break down completely, were pulverized to make it all smooth and ash-like before it was placed in the urn if one was supplied. Otherwise it was bagged and boxed for the family to take away.

Gruesome, Holly thought as she pushed through another door into a short hall.

Here the dim lighting gave way to glaringly bright fluorescents overhead, and cinder-block walls painted a pale cream. It was almost sterile in its lack of color, and Holly paused and blinked, the buzz of the fluorescents loud in her ears as her attention shifted to the door ahead.

John Byron worked the 4:30-to-12:30 shift and should still be on duty, she thought, glancing at her wristwatch. She'd met him several times and while he was a bit of a cynic, with a sarcastic, self-deprecating sense of humor, he seemed a nice enough guy. She didn't think he'd give her too hard a time, although she'd no doubt have to explain why she was at the offices this late. Holly hoped he was alone though and Rick Mexler hadn't yet arrived. Rick was the man who took over the crematorium from 12:30 to 8:30. She didn't start work until 9:00 so hadn't yet met him, but had heard he was a grumpy S.O.B. who didn't like people. That really wasn't something she wanted to have to deal with, so she was a bit alarmed when she stepped through the door into the crematorium and heard two men's voices.

The crematorium was a large long rectangle, but the cooler took up a ten-by-ten space along the left on entering. The rest of the room was a large L shape, with the retorts against the wall that was around the corner of the cooler, out of sight. That was where the voices were coming from, so she didn't at first see the men. But Holly assumed it was John and Rick.

Her gaze slid to the front of the cooler as she started forward. The door was a metal roll-up almost as wide as a garage door. It was open at the moment, leaving the contents on view—a set of tall wide shelves with various coffins on it. Two were cardboard boxes, two were the less-expensive blue coffins, and three were actual oak coffins. She noted that the mini forklift was positioned in front of the open door as if John had been about to retrieve a casket when he'd been interrupted by Rick's arrival.

Holly turned her gaze away from the cooler, trying not to think of the loved ones resting in the coffins . . . or their intended future. She'd nearly reached the corner when she realized that neither voice sounded like John Byron. Had he left already? And if so, who was Rick Mexler talking to? She slowed and then paused just out of sight around the corner to listen to the men's conversation.

HIGHLAND ROMANCE FROM
NEW YORK TIMES BESTSELLING AUTHOR

LYNSAY SANDS

Devil of the Highlands

978-0-06-134477-0

Cullen, Laird of Donnachaidh, must find a wife to
bear his sons to ensure the future of the clan. Evelinde
has agreed to marry him despite his reputation, for the
Devil of the Highlands inspires a heat within her
unlike anything she has ever known.

Taming the Highland Bride

978-0-06-134478-7

Alexander d'Aumesbery is desperate to convince the
beautiful and brazen Merry Stewart that he's a well-
mannered gentleman who's nothing like the members
of her roguish clan. But beneath it all beats a heart as
intense and uncontrollable as hers.

The Hellion and the Highlander

978-0-06-134479-4

When the flame-haired Lady Averill Mortagne braves
an unexpected danger at Highland warrior Kade
Stewart's side, she proves that her heart is as fiery
as her hair. And he realizes that submitting to their
scorching passion would be heaven indeed.